"Sensuality, passion, excitement, and drama . . . are Ms. Miller's hallmarks."
—*Romantic Times*

PRAISE FOR THE WARM, WONDERFUL NOVELS OF *NEW YORK TIMES* BESTSELLING AUTHOR

LINDA LAEL MILLER

SHOTGUN BRIDE

"The second McKettrick western romance is an exciting, action-packed tale starring two delightful lead protagonists. . . . The coda of *Shotgun Bride* is a wonderful set-up for the youngest brother's story that will keep the audience breathless in anticipation."

—Harriet Klausner, thebestreviews.com

"Pure delight. . . . I laughed out loud in some places and had a warm heart in others. . . . The McKettrick Cowboys is a great series—not to be missed."

—*Old Book Barn Gazette*

HIGH COUNTRY BRIDE

"Linda Lael Miller is one of the finest American writers in the genre. She beautifully crafts stories that bring small-town America to life and peoples them with characters you really care about."

—*Romantic Times*

"Miller ably portrays the hardscrabble life of the American west . . . [in a] winsome romance full of likable characters."

—*Publishers Weekly*

"Just the beginning of a fantastic new dynasty. . . . Join the gang at the Triple M Ranch and share in the love and laughter with some of the most wonderful characters to come your way in a long time."

—nettrends.com

THE LAST CHANCE CAFÉ

"The Last Chance Café delivers powerful romance flavored with deep emotional resonance."

—*Romantic Times*

"This novel is dead-on target . . . [with] suspense, down home comfort, and sizzling tension. . . . Ms. Miller has a timeless writing style, and her characters are always vivacious and appealing."

—*Heartstrings*

"[An] enriching tale. . . . Linda Lael Miller brings to life the modern-day descendants of her popular Primrose Creek settlers with the vivid clarity and rough-hewn beauty of Nevada's rugged terrain bathed in sunglow."

—*Romance BookPage*

"An entertaining story."

—*Booklist*

SPRINGWATER WEDDING

"Fans will be thrilled to join the action, suspense, and romance. . . ."

—*Romantic Times*

"Pure delight from the beginning to the satisfying ending . . . Miller is a master craftswoman at creating unusual story lines [and] charming characters."

—*Rendezvous*

Also by Linda Lael Miller

Linda Lael Miller

Daniel's Bride

POCKET STAR BOOKS
New York   London   Toronto   Sydney

In loving memory of that other Daniel,
Jacob Daniel Lael,
who left a legacy of true grit and pure stubbornness.
(Thanks for the grit, Grandpa,
but I could have done without the stubbornness!)

An *Original* Publication of POCKET BOOKS

 A Pocket Star Book published by
POCKET BOOKS, a division of Simon & Schuster Inc.
1230 Avenue of the Americas, New York, NY 10020

ISBN 978-1-4516-1127-4

First Pocket Books printing September 1992

20   19

POCKET STAR BOOKS and colophon are registered trademarks of
Simon & Schuster Inc.

Cover illustration © Matthew Frey: Wood Ronsaville Harlin, Inc.

Manufactured in the United States of America

For information regarding special discounts for bulk purchases,
please contact Simon & Schuster Special Sales at 1-800-456-6798
or business@simonandschuster.com.

1

The noose lay heavy around Jolie McKibben's neck, smelling of sweat and horseflesh and hemp. Frantic protests of innocence had long since rendered her throat too raw to speak, and she felt nothing except a certain defiant numbness as she stared back at those who had gathered to see her hanged. Her blue-green eyes were dry and hot, but a tiny stream of perspiration trickled between her breasts, like a tear gone astray.

She stood in the bed of Hobb Jackson's hay wagon, her fair hair sticking to her scalp under the dusty bowler hat she wore, her wrists bound tightly behind her back, her chin at the most obstinate angle possible. She could hear the team of horses behind her, neighing and blowing impatiently in the slow heat of a summer morning. In another few moments, the marshal would give the signal, the horses would pull the rig from beneath her feet, and she would be left to dangle and choke at the end of that dirty rope.

All because she'd had the bad judgment to fall in with Blake Kingston. It didn't seem just that she had to die for what he'd done, but then, Jolie had never known life to be fair. For her, it had been a struggle, right from the very first.

The undertaker, a heavy man sweating in a dark suit, dried his brow with a handkerchief and raised his round face to look into Jolie's eyes. "Let's get this over with," he said. "Miss McKibben's been duly tried and sentenced and there's no sense in dragging things out."

Jolie felt her knees go weak and tried to put the starch back into them by sheer force of will. "I didn't rob the bank," she croaked out, needing to say the words one last time even though they'd been falling on deaf ears for a month. "And I didn't shoot anybody, either."

"Just hang her," someone called from the crowd.

It was then that a big man came out of the mercantile, a flour sack over one thick shoulder, his face hidden by the brim of a large, stained hat. He wore plain brown trousers, a rough-spun shirt the color of buttery cream, and an old buckskin vest. He silenced the yammering spectators just by sweeping them up in a single scathing glance, then set the bag on the wooden sidewalk with an unhurried motion and came down the steps. He crossed a street paved in mud, manure, and sawdust and stood at the rear of the wagon.

"Now, Dan'l," fretted the wizened old marshal, "don't you go interferin' in this here hangin'. We done tried this woman right and proper, and we found her guilty."

Daniel. Jolie's heart gave a surging thump, but she couldn't afford to hope for rescue. The disappoint-

2

ment would be another burden, and the load she carried was already crushing.

The farmer swept off his hat, revealing a head of wheat gold hair, and gazed up at her with eyes the same shade of blue as a summer sky in the early morning. He was not handsome, this man, and yet something wrenched painfully inside Jolie as she regarded him.

"This the lady bank robber?" he asked, his low voice revealing none of the agitation that raised an invisible charge from the small mob gathered to view the proceedings.

Jolie ran the tip of her tongue over dry, cracked lips. For reasons she couldn't begin to sort through, it was crucial that this particular man not walk away believing she was guilty of robbery and murder. She took a step forward, and the rope chafed the delicate skin of her throat.

"Doesn't look like the type to me," Daniel reflected, raising one brawny hand to rub a clean-shaven chin. Desperate to find something to focus on other than the grim realities, Jolie took note of the fact that he was the only male present who didn't sport a mustache, a beard, or both.

The corpulent undertaker—his wagon stood waiting nearby, with the name Philias Pribbenow stenciled on the side—waddled forward, mopping his nape with the kerchief. "If you were interested in the proceedings, Daniel," he said, "you should have shown it before now. The time for arguments and consideration is past."

Judge Chilver, a man with red-rimmed eyes and skin that seemed too loose for his face, stepped forward, a little smirk curving his lips. "'Course, there is the weddin' ordinance," he said, pushing back his coat to tuck his thumbs into the pockets of a food-spotted brocade vest. He scanned the impatient lookers-on before fixing another unctuous smile on Daniel and cocking a thumb toward Jolie. "You marry the lady and we'll call off the hangin'. Have no choice but to string her up if she breaks the law again, o' course."

Another man, this one young and darkly handsome, wearing black trousers, a matching vest, and a gambler's ruffled white shirt, called a suggestion from the porch of the Lone Wolf Saloon. "I think Beckham should cover what Jolie McKibben stole from the bank, too, if she's going to be his wife."

There was a general murmur of agreement at this, and Jolie didn't dare breathe as she watched Daniel's jaw tighten. He muttered a curse and slapped his dusty hat against a solid thigh. "It wouldn't be right," he said, narrowing his eyes as he gave the prisoner a swift inspection, "hanging a woman. You'd better send her on up to Spokane and let the territorial court handle the trial."

Until moments before, Jolie would have sworn she'd cried out all her tears. Now, moisture was pooling in her lower lashes, and her vision was blurred. She was only twenty years old and she'd never known a man or held a baby of her own, and she didn't want to die.

Chilver got out his pocket watch and flicked open the case with a brisk movement of his thumb. His eyebrows arched as he checked the hour. "Time's a wastin', Dan'l," he said.

"I'll marry her," Daniel said, and it was as though the words were dragged out of him. He plopped the hat back onto his head, vaulted into the rear of the wagon with surprising agility for someone of his size, and lifted the rope from around Jolie's neck. She came near to sagging against him in relief but caught herself at the last moment.

He undid the rawhide ties that were cutting into her wrists, hooked his hands under her arms, and lowered her easily to the ground. Then he was towering beside her, as hard and substantial as a tamarack tree.

Jolie swayed slightly, and he caught her briefly against his side. She was tall for a woman, nearly five feet nine inches, but her chin reached only as high as Daniel's shirt pocket. She heard the murmurs and mutterings of the townspeople as if through a wall of water, and saw Hobb Jackson scramble into the wagon bed and pull down the rope he'd slung over the tree branch earlier.

The judge was peering into her face, his breath ripe with whiskey and a general lack of hygiene. "How about you, little lady? You want to marry Dan Beckham?"

Jolie swallowed. She'd never seen Mr. Beckham before and, for all she knew, he was a Republican, a drunkard, and a woman-beater, but it seemed to her that her choices were severely limited—at least, for the moment. "I'll marry him," she rasped. Now that she was fairly certain she wouldn't swoon, bile was stinging the back of her throat and her stomach was jumping.

"You sure about this, Dan'l?" the old politician inquired, rocking back on his heels, cocky as a bantam rooster.

The muscle in Daniel's jaw flexed again. "I'm sure," he said, avoiding Jolie's gaze this time. "Let's get on with the marrying. I'll draw up a draft for the money later."

Jolie's surroundings undulated around her as she

struggled to absorb the shock of unexpected salvation. All the while, she was praying she wouldn't throw up on the farmer's boots and convince him to withdraw his offer. The throng moved in closer, as curious to see a wedding as they had been to witness a hanging, and Jolie made herself meet one pair of eyes, then another and another.

I'm alive, she challenged them silently, *and damn you to hell for wanting to watch me die.*

"I've got a license on my desk," Mr. Chilver said brightly. "It's just a matter of saying the words."

The irony of being married by the same judge who had sentenced her to hang by the neck until dead was not lost on Jolie, but she was still too shaken to grasp all the nuances of the situation. She was going to live to see another sun blaze over the ripening wheat and the timbered foothills, and that was all that mattered.

Judge Chilver provided the necessary paper, and Daniel and Jolie stood under the oak tree that would have been her gallows. The townspeople pressed close, paying avid attention, elbowing each other and snickering.

Jolie made the responses that were required of her, unaware of the tears that were making pale tracks in the mask of dust that covered her face. When it was over, she and Daniel both signed the ornately decorated document, then her new husband took her elbow and ushered her toward a battered wagon waiting in the alleyway between the mercantile and the feed and grain. Only when she saw the man's signature on the appropriate line did she realize that her name was no longer McKibben, but Beckham.

Mr. Beckham handed her into the box in an offhandedly solicitous way, then went back to pick up the burgeoning sack he'd set down when he came out of the feed store. After loading this into the back of the wagon, he climbed up into the seat beside Jolie, who sat ramrod straight with her hands folded in her lap, reached for the reins, and released the brake lever with one boot heel.

He favored the population of Prosperity with a cool nod and set the team of two sturdy brown mules in motion with a flick of one wrist.

Jolie's thumbs twiddled, and she bit her lip, her eyes narrowed under the brim of her hat as she watched the weathered facades of the town's main street fall behind. "Why did you do it?" she finally asked, when the wagon wheels were jostling over two hard-packed ruts and spring wheat waved on either side of them. "Why did you marry a woman you don't even know?"

Daniel waited so long to speak that Jolie was beginning to think he didn't plan on responding, but then he looked squarely into her filthy face and said, "They were going to hang you."

It was the obvious reply. Jolie realized she had been hoping for something quite different, though she didn't know exactly what that something was. "Suppose I really am a criminal?" she ventured cautiously. After all, it wouldn't do if she got Daniel Beckham to thinking he'd made a mistake and ought to take her back to hang from the single oak tree in the center of town.

"Are you?" he countered, gazing thoughtfully on the rumps and sweaty backs of the long-eared mules pulling the wagon.

Jolie felt her cheeks burn beneath the coating of dirt. "No," she replied, a little indignantly. "I was just *with* Blake and Rowdy, that's all. I didn't know they were going to rob the bank." Even though she'd been over the fact a thousand times, it still stung Jolie that

Blake and Rowdy had not only done that horrendous thing, but had abandoned her to face the consequences alone.

Daniel—she couldn't quite bring herself to think of him as her husband—shifted his hat slightly forward to scratch the back of his head. "That raises another question. What were you doing with the likes of Blake Kingston in the first place?"

Again, Jolie flushed. It made for a long, complicated story, the way she'd hooked up with Blake. She didn't delude herself that anyone, least of all Daniel, would believe the truth—that she had never been intimate with either Blake or Rowdy, even though she'd traveled with them for nearly two weeks. "I worked as a maid, back in Seattle, in the same house with Blake's mother. She was the cook."

The team and wagon topped a knoll, and Jolie's attention was diverted to a large, white frame house flanked with tidy-looking outbuildings. There was a well house with a shingled roof, and as they drew up in front of the barn, she saw a moat of bright blue cornflowers blooming around a black iron pump a few yards from the kitchen door. A board spanned the mud puddle beneath, supporting a bucket to catch drips.

A row of poplar trees stood guarding the place from wind, and all around the wheat flowed and rippled like a golden sea. The stalwart blue of the sky was poignantly beautiful to Jolie, since she'd come so near to closing her eyes to it forever.

Daniel set the brake, wound the reins around the lever, and got down, raising his big, calloused hands for Jolie.

She took solace in his strength as he lifted her to the ground.

"Get yourself cleaned up, then see what you can rustle up for dinner," he said.

Since Jolie had never really known kindness from a male, Daniel's order didn't strike her as particularly abrupt. Besides, she was too grateful to quibble over a little thing like how a man framed his words. She nodded, and when he turned to walk away, she reached out impulsively and caught hold of his shirtsleeve with two fingers.

He looked back at her over one shoulder, his expression unreadable because his features were hidden by the brim of his hat.

Jolie let go of his shirt and spoke shyly, her eyes lowered. "Thank you, Mr. Beckham."

Daniel did not acknowledge the offering, neither was there an unspoken "you're welcome" in his tone. "There's food in the pantry," he said instead. "Deuter and I will be hungry, so make sure you put plenty on the table."

With that, her unlikely knight turned and walked away, toward the barn. Jolie watched him go, wondering who Deuter was even as she decided it would be inappropriate to ask, then set out for the house.

The back threshold was at least a foot off the ground, so Jolie hoisted her riding skirt and goose-stepped into the kitchen. It was a surprisingly clean place, with whitewashed walls and solid wood floors and a big iron and chrome cookstove that gleamed in the fierce light pouring in through spotless windows.

Jolie took off the derby hat that had given her some protection from the sun and hung it carefully on one of the pegs next to the door. There was a shaving mirror on the wall opposite the stove, and she frowned as she looked into it. Her blond hair was straggling down from its pins and clinging wetly to her

9

gritty neck, and there was a mask of dirt covering her face.

She found a basin in the pantry, along with shelf after shelf of preserved fruits, meat, and vegetables and enormous supplies of sugar and lard and beans. Yearning for a bath and clean clothes, Jolie contented herself with a splash to her face and hands, helping herself to tepid water from the reservoir on the side of the stove.

When she felt presentable, Daniel Beckham's new bride set two places at the table and brought a jar marked "sausage" from the pantry. She built up the fire with wood from the box beside the stove and dipped water into a saucepan, setting the preserves inside so the heat would melt the lard that encased the meat. She found cold milk, butter, and cheese out in the well house, and fresh-baked bread in a metal-lined storage bin in the kitchen.

The aroma of just-brewed coffee was pungent in the air when the back door opened and Daniel appeared, immediately followed by a young, husky boy with dark red hair, huge brown eyes, and shoulders that could have been measured with a wagon axle.

"This is Deuter," Daniel said, hanging up his hat. "Deuter, Mrs. Beckham."

Jolie was pleased to be referred to so formally; it made her feel a little less like some stray found on the side of the road. Despite the pass her life had come to, she had some pride. "Hello, Deuter," she said, with a polite nod. By then, the lard surrounding the sausage had melted, and Jolie drained the fat into a tin can and dropped the meat into a cast-iron skillet.

"Pretty enough to kiss all over," Deuter remarked, drawing Jolie's harried attention back to him with a start. Out of the corner of one eye, she saw Daniel turn away to hide a grin.

Jolie's cheeks were hot. "I'll thank you to keep such comments to yourself, Mr. Deuter," she said stiffly.

"Just Deuter," replied the farmhand, showing resignation but no sign of remorse. "And I pretty much have to say whatever comes into my head. Don't exactly know why."

"Let's get washed up," Daniel told him, ladling hot water from the stove reservoir into a basin. This he carried outside, along with a bar of yellow soap, and Deuter followed.

Jolie heard splashing, then Deuter returned to fill the basin with fresh water for himself. Daniel, looking scrubbed, sat down at the table, frowning as he regarded the two place settings.

"Aren't you eating?"

Averting her eyes, Jolie shook her head. "No, Mr. Beckham—not now. My stomach isn't feeling right."

Daniel sighed and reached for the platter of reheated sausage when Jolie put it on the table. "Guess that's no great wonder," he commented, and dropped the matter at that.

Deuter came in, hung the blue enamel basin on its nail next to the stove, and joined Daniel. The boy looked strangely ingenuous, with his slicked down hair and clean hands and face, like a first grade student eager to please his teacher.

"I'd—I'd like to look around the place a little, if you don't mind," Jolie dared, sinking her teeth into her lower lip while she awaited Daniel's answer.

"You could sure use a good scrubbing," Deuter remarked, cutting off a chunk of the ground sausage with the side of his fork and scraping it onto his plate.

11

Again, Jolie saw just the hint of a smile touch the corner of Daniel's mouth, though he made no comment.

"And you could use a lesson in manners," Jolie responded.

Deuter wasn't in the least chagrined. "No good. My ma and all my teachers tried everything. Didn't work."

"Look around all you want," Daniel said with diplomatic formality, although his amusement had now risen to his eyes.

Relieved at the opportunity to escape, Jolie dashed through the dining room and found herself in a genuine ladies' parlor, complete with frilled pillows, china figurines, potted palm trees, and photographs in ornate silver frames. There was an organ in front of the bay window, and delicate ecru lace curtains of the finest quality billowed in a stray breeze around the polished instrument.

Jolie went to the fireplace, which was fronted with white and gray fieldstones, and squinted at the daguerreotype displayed prominently on the pinewood mantel. It was obviously a wedding picture, and the groom was Daniel. Behind his chair, with one graceful hand resting on his shoulder, stood a bride resplendent in lace and silk. She was small, delicate as a cameo, with rich dark hair and large, expressive eyes.

Jolie felt diminished, just looking into that guileless face, and she was consumed by a need to know the woman's name and what had happened to her. And because she was in no position to ask, she propelled herself out of the parlor and inspected the small, simply furnished study on the other side of the entryway. Here, Daniel kept ledgers and books of all sizes and sorts.

Reading was a trial for Jolie, though she could make out what she needed to know if she tried hard enough, and she felt a pang as she backed out of the study. She wondered what Daniel would think when he realized he'd married a woman who was practically ignorant.

Mr. Beckham probably wouldn't be at all surprised to learn she could barely manage the written word, she reflected with a long sigh. After all, their entire courtship had taken place within five minutes, under the shadow of a hangman's noose.

Her face throbbed with heat as she climbed the stairs, clutching her dusty skirts in her hands to keep from tripping on the hem. It wouldn't do to get romantic ideas; she was lucky just to be alive.

Upstairs, Jolie found three spacious bedrooms, two of which were furnished. Jolie felt the first flash of alarm she'd had since the rope had been draped around her neck that morning. She was Daniel Beckham's legal wife, never mind that they were complete strangers, and there was little doubt in her mind what he would expect after the sun went down.

If he waited that long.

Her knees sagged, weakened by the prospect of lying down for a man for the first time. If it hadn't been for that, Jolie wouldn't have sat on the edge of Daniel's sturdy four-poster bed the way she did.

The creak of hinges startled her, and her eyes went wide when she realized Daniel was standing in the bedroom doorway. There was a look of quiet hilarity in his gaze, but there was also wanting; even in her relative innocence, Jolie would have recognized that anywhere.

"Why do they call that boy 'Deuter'?" she asked in a shaky voice, hoping to distract Daniel from the inevitable, at least for a little while.

Holding his hat in one hand, he rested one shoulder against the doorjamb, and everything in his manner said he'd seen through Jolie's ploy. "It's short for Deuteronomy. The lad did his damnedest to learn to spell it, but he could never get any further than Deuter, so he finally just stopped there."

Under other circumstances, Jolie might have been amused. As it was, she was too terrified to appreciate levity. "He should have kept trying," she threw out, desperate to keep the exchange going, puny as it was.

Daniel shrugged and straightened. "There's where you and I don't see eye to eye," he replied easily. "If he hadn't been the most determined kid in three territories, he probably would have stopped at 'Deut.'"

Jolie swallowed hard. "I suppose you have lots of work to do out in the barn and the—the fields."

To her wild relief, he set the hat back on his head. "Yes, ma'am," he said. "I do. I'll see you around supper time."

The relief left Jolie dizzy, and she couldn't help closing her eyes for a moment as it swept through her system like warm brandy mixed with sugar and cream. "Aren't you afraid I'll take off or something?" she asked, after a short interval of catching her inner balance.

Daniel was just about to turn away when she looked at him again. "It would be my guess that you don't have much of anywhere to go," he said. And then he was gone, his boot heels making a rhythmic sound on the naked wooden stairs.

Jolie thrust herself off Daniel Beckham's mattress. When she heard a door slam in the distance, she went to the big, plain oak wardrobe opposite the bed and opened it. Shirts hung neatly within, along with trousers, but there was nothing for Jolie to wear.

She moved on to the second bedroom, which was smaller and boasted only a washstand, a trunk, and a narrow iron bed. Daniel had been only too accurate in surmising that she had no place to flee to, and the fact nettled Jolie almost as much as the disheveled state of her person.

She found a blue calico print dress in the trunk and, although the garment would definitely be too short for her, she figured she could squeeze into it and thus have something to wear while she washed out her own clothes.

Jolie hurried downstairs and, after a visit to the outhouse, which was all but covered in fading purple lilacs, she returned to the well house for the washtub she'd spotted there earlier. As she left the cool darkness for the bright afternoon, with its buzzing bees and pungent aromas, the toe of her shoe caught against the edge of a loose board, and she tripped. The washtub went thumping and clanging onto the hard-packed dirt path outside and Jolie gripped the sides of the door frame to keep from falling, a splinter stabbing into her palm.

She flinched, then turned to stomp the offending board back into place with a vengeance. Outside in the sunshine, she plucked the piece of wood from her skin and pressed the small wound against her mouth, exasperated.

First, she'd come as near to hanging as any sensible person would care to, then she'd been married to a man she'd never laid eyes on before in her life. Now, she'd practically been crucified.

This was turning out to be one hell of a day.

* * *

As Daniel chopped and stacked the firewood he and Deuter had brought down from the hills the day before, he recalled the time he'd seen Hobb Jackson drop a bulging burlap sack into Caldron Creek. Daniel had been hunting that morning, and he was on foot, carrying a brace of grouse in one hand and his rifle in the other.

The moment he'd seen the bag drop from Hobb's hand, he'd known it contained another batch of kittens. Seized by a rage that made him want to bellow even as it strangled all sound from his throat, Daniel had flung down the rifle and his game and run to the creek.

Hobb was long gone by the time he got there, and Daniel splashed into the icy, thigh-deep water and wrenched the sodden bag from the rocky creek bottom. By the time he got back to the bank and carefully cut the burlap open with his hunting knife, four of the small, furry bodies inside were still, but one, a sputtering tom, gave a watery yowl and promptly bit Daniel's finger.

He smiled as he swung the ax. Even though she wasn't of the same gender, his new bride had more in common with that ornery little feline than the luck to survive. She'd had the same expression of terrified rebellion in her eyes, standing there in the back of that wagon, waiting to be hanged, and Daniel figured the biting would come next.

He stopped, mopped his sweating forehead with one sleeve, and set another chunk of wood on the block. Deuter was moving in and out of the shed, stacking the split pine and fir to season for a few months.

Just then, Daniel saw Jolie chase the washtub out of the well house, the palm of one hand pressed to her mouth. A moment later, she was heading purposely toward the kitchen door, carrying the tub by its handle.

The deduction Daniel made was both simple and ordinary. Jolie was about to take a bath—something most people did at least once a week—but now the knowledge made his blood burn in his veins like kerosene. He felt his groin tighten painfully as he imagined her stripping away those seedy old clothes of hers and stepping naked into clean, hot water.

By that point, Daniel's concentration was so strained that the ax head bounced off a knot in a piece of wood and came within an inch of opening a crevice in his shin. With a mighty swing, he set the blade deep into the chopping block and then swept off his hat.

"Guess you could go watch her wash if you wanted to," Deuter commented, from the doorway of the woodshed. "She's your wife now."

There were times when the boy's peculiarities got on Daniel's nerves, and this was one of them. Although he had no fond feelings for Jolie, he didn't like the idea of another man—even one as young and backward as his hired hand—speculating about such private matters. "I want that wood stacked by sundown," he said evenly. "You'd best get back to work."

After that, Daniel gathered his forces and forced himself to take up the ax again. And the image of Jolie bathing didn't cross his mind more than four or five hundred times in the next half hour.

2

Jolie lugged one last bucket of hot water to the pantry and poured it into the washtub, then carefully pulled the door closed. A single kerosene lantern on the shelf beside jars of green beans provided light, since there was no window.

Hastily, holding her breath for long intervals, Jolie peeled off her clothes, rolled the garments into a wad, and set them on top of the potato bin. Then, furtively, fearing she would be interrupted at any moment, she stepped into the first bath she'd had in weeks.

Jolie dropped slowly to her knees and then bent forward to wet her hair, and it was bliss. But there was a painful lump burgeoning in her throat; she hadn't forgotten that she'd nearly died that morning. The experience had left her with a tangle of ungovernable emotions.

Reaching for the bar of hard yellow soap she'd brought into the pantry with her, Jolie began to lather herself. She scrubbed from her scalp to her toenails, all the while struggling to contain the wild contradictory feelings that howled and thundered in her spirit like a storm.

When she was clean, she rose trembling from the water and dried her glistening pink and alabaster flesh with a rough linen towel swiped from Daniel's washstand upstairs. She donned the blue calico dress over a similarly appropriated muslin camisole and drawers and was sitting by the stove, combing the tangles from her hair, when the stranger who was her husband once again entered the house.

His fine cheekbones were a ruddy tan from constant exposure to the elements, and she thought she saw his sunburn intensify slightly as he ran his gaze over her. "We'll see about getting you some proper clothes tomorrow," he said, and his voice was gruff, as though he needed to clear his throat.

Jolie lowered the tortoiseshell comb to her lap and regarded Daniel with solemn eyes, resisting the temptation to bolt to her feet like a soldier coming to attention. "I don't need much."

He took a blue metal mug from a shelf and came to the stove to fill it with coffee left over from the midday meal, taking obvious care not to brush against Jolie or meet her gaze. He still sounded hoarse when he spoke again. "Deuter's gone fishing. There'll probably be trout for supper."

Jolie had never been so conscious of a man's presence as she was of Daniel's in those moments. He seemed to fill the kitchen with his huge shoulders and masculine scent, the hardness of his muscular body, the intangible substance of his character.

Thinking of that woman in the picture on the parlor mantel, Jolie wanted to ask, *What was her name? Did you love her?* But she didn't quite dare. This man had saved her from certain death, and he owed her exactly nothing in the way of explanations.

Still carefully avoiding her eyes, Daniel got the basin down and lifted the lid on the stove reservoir. Jolie had forgotten to refill it after her bath, and she quailed inwardly, expecting wrath. So great was her haste to correct the omission that she was out of her chair and on her way to the door in almost the same motion.

She collided hard with Daniel, and he dropped both the basin and the lid to the reservoir to grasp Jolie's shoulders and steady her.

"It's *all right,"* he said slowly, pressing her back into her chair. "I can pump my own water, Jolie."

She flushed hotly and looked away, embarrassed now because she'd been so eager to please him. Unable to think of anything sensible to say, she bit her lower lip and waited for her blood to cool.

Jolie could feel Daniel's eyes on her, but he didn't speak again. She heard the water buckets clank together as he took them from their place beneath the iron sink, caught the scents of fading lilac and the barnyard as he opened the door to go out.

She'd tied back her hair with twine when he returned, and fed the stove chunks of dry, pitchy wood from the box nearby. When Daniel returned and poured fresh water into the reservoir, Jolie made sure she was busy on the other side of the room, opening a jar of pickled carrots at the sink.

"There must have been a woman here, not so very long ago," she said, because the house was in such good order, and the moment the words had left her mouth she would have given anything to be able to call them back. Her cheeks throbbed painfully and tears of frustration blurred her vision as she stared down at the jar in her hands in utter mortification.

"The neighbor woman, Mrs. Dailey, comes in to clean now and again," Daniel replied, somewhat shortly. And then he was gone once more, retreating into that broader world that was peculiarly his own.

Through the kitchen window, Jolie watched as he worked the pump handle and filled both buckets. Deuter came around the corner of the barn with a fishing pole in one hand and a twig lined with shimmering trout in the other. The boy waited while Daniel stepped into the kitchen and then followed.

"I already cut their guts out," Deuter said proudly, holding out the fish to Jolie.

Jolie was unperturbed, since she'd cleaned fish so many times herself. She accepted the trout with a nod and laid them in the sink, then she set a skillet on the stove to heat, adding a dollop of lard. In the process, she bumped into Daniel again, since he had just finished pouring water into the reservoir.

"Deuter and I will wash up outside at the pump," he said, in a tone that told Jolie nothing about his frame of mind.

While her husband and the boy were attending to their ablutions, Jolie made another quick trip to the pantry. Deuter's fish were frying up nicely and the scent of baking biscuits was in the air when the men returned.

Deuter sniffed appreciatively and gave Daniel a playful elbow to the ribs. "Mrs. Beckham cleaned up right pretty, didn't she, Dan'l?" he crowed, as though he'd had some part in the enterprise himself.

Jolie bustled past the table as the men sat down, reaching for a pot holder and expertly removing the biscuits from the oven. After scooping those onto a platter, she dished up the carrots and the crisply browned fish, served everything and then sat at the place she'd set for herself. Her appetite had returned after her bath, voracious as a flash flood.

She ate as slowly and politely as she could, keeping her eyes lowered and adding nothing to the conversation, which concerned the prospective purchase of a new manure spreader. Although she still didn't know quite what to make of him, Jolie was grateful Deuter was there to occupy Daniel's attention.

After supper, she cleared the table and washed the dishes, while the men went out to the barn. They hadn't returned when Jolie finished her chores, and now that her stomach was full, she was possessed of a sudden and overwhelming weariness.

She climbed the stairs, forced herself over the threshold of the master bedroom, and sat down on the edge of the mattress to take off her shoes. Moments later, she was stretched out full-length on top of the covers, with a breeze rippling over her from an open window.

Jolie thought she heard the wheat whispering a rustly lullaby as she closed her eyes against the last gaudy rays of a brazen August sun.

She was lying on his bed.

Daniel stopped in the doorway for a few moments, just watching the way her honey gold hair curled as it dried in the warm twilight air. Then he crept into the room, pulled the extra quilt from the shelf in the top of the wardrobe, and spread it gently over her.

Standing there, looking into Jolie's scrubbed, sleeping face, Daniel couldn't help wondering what kind of people she came from and how she'd ended up standing in the back of Hobb Jackson's wagon, about to be hanged.

She stirred slightly but didn't awaken, and Daniel pulled the rocking chair closer to the bed and sank into it. It creaked slightly under his weight, like always.

Daniel sighed and shook his head as he reflected on the unexpected twist his life had taken. When he'd gotten out of that bed in the small hours of the morning, the sky had still been dark and littered with stars, and the big house had seemed especially lonely. Now there was a pretty woman curled up on the mattress, her scent as subtle and appealing as that of fresh strawberries floating in sweet cream. He reached out to touch a gossamer tendril of hair as the draft set it dancing against her cheek.

She looked so innocent, lying there, trusting as a child. It was hard to believe she could have willingly participated in a robbery and been a party to a killing.

Daniel drew back his hand, and his brow furrowed as he frowned, recalling the hearsay that had kept Prosperity buzzing for the past month, as well as the trial accounts he'd read in the weekly newspaper. According to those sources, Jolie McKibben had ridden into town with Blake Kingston, an outlaw of some prominence in the territory, and a friend of his called Rowdy Fleet. She'd held the horses while Kingston and Fleet were inside the Fidelity Bank that day in early July, and when old Hamish Frazer, the president and founder, had run outside shouting for the marshal, one of the three had shot him down.

Witnesses had been unable to agree on exactly who had pulled the trigger, but the judge and jury had finally decided Jolie was guilty, since she'd had a six-gun just like the others, and they'd decided to string her up. Daniel figured she'd gotten the blame mostly because she was the only one caught—her friends had fled without so much as a backward glance.

Jolie moved on the bed, and Daniel felt the now-familiar grinding ache in his groin. She was his wife, he reminded himself. He had a right, before God and man, to the pleasures her warm, soft body could afford him.

Still sleeping, Jolie sighed and lifted her hands to rest on the pillow, palms up, fingers slightly curled. Since the quilt reached only to her waist now, Daniel could see her plump breasts pushing against the too-tight fabric of the blue calico dress. The first breath of evening came in through the window, hardening her nipples and causing them to jut beneath the cloth.

Daniel shifted uncomfortably in his chair, then thrust himself to his feet. He stood looking down at Jolie for several agonizing moments, wanting her as he had never wanted Ilse, his beautiful child-bride, or even Michi, a Japanese woman he'd known in San Francisco a long time before. It had been Michi who had taught him to pleasure a woman.

He rubbed a beard-stubbled chin with one brawny, calloused hand, then turned and strode from the room, leaving the door to gape open behind him. Jolie had been through enough for one day, what with nearly being hanged and then getting herself hitched to a total stranger. But Daniel couldn't help thinking about her as he stood in the kitchen sipping leftover coffee and watching through the window while Deuter chased the cow in from the pasture.

Daniel knew he would never love Jolie; he'd given

everything he had to Ilse and she'd taken the best part of him to the grave with her. But his new wife was tall and sturdy, with none of Ilse's flowerlike delicacy. Jolie was built to bear strong, healthy children, and to stand up under the hard work inherent in living on a farm. She was even a fairly good cook, though her portions tended to be a little on the skimpy side.

Daniel set his cup in the sink and snatched his hat from the peg beside the door. And as he went out to see to the last of the day's chores, he reminded himself that, for all of it, Jolie was also a bank robber. Maybe even a murderess.

When Jolie awakened, the room was dark. Immediately, panic seized her, like a hand grasping her throat, and she bolted upright. She could barely breathe, and her heart was thumping a drumbeat in her ears. Tentatively, she explored the opposite side of the bed with one hand.

She was alone, and the knowledge calmed her slightly. When her eyes had adjusted, she reached out and lifted the glass chimney off the lamp on her nightstand. Then she struck a wooden match and lit the wick, half expecting to find her husband lurking in the shadows, waiting to pounce.

There was no sign of him, and while that was undeniably a relief, it also puzzled Jolie, and a sensation that might have been loneliness brushed softly against the inner wall of her heart. Perhaps she wasn't attractive to Daniel, or he thought she was dangerous. Maybe he'd even locked her in for the night, like a prisoner in a cell!

Terrified again, she hurled herself off the bed and raced to the door, clutching the knob with both hands. It turned easily, and Jolie ventured into the hallway and stood there awhile, just because she had the freedom to do it. And then she made her way slowly down the stairs, thinking a cup of warm milk might calm her so she could get back to sleep.

To her surprise, for a clock somewhere on the first floor had just chimed three times, Jolie found a lamp burning in the kitchen. "Daniel?" she said, freezing on the threshold and pulling the collar of her dress close around her throat.

There was no answer, so Jolie went to the stove, stoked up the banked fire with a piece of wood, and, guided by cloud-thinned moonlight, made a hasty trip to the privy. The bower of lilacs did little to mask the smell, and Jolie's nose was wrinkled as she approached the pump to give her hands a quick washing.

She was headed toward the well house, where she'd seen a five-gallon can of milk cooling earlier in the day, when her gaze was drawn to a lone maple tree standing well away from the house. The moon was unveiled in those moments, and its silvery glow revealed the frame of a man standing with his head bent. She knew instantly that it was Daniel.

Although Jolie sincerely believed that discretion was the better part of valor, it was a tenet she'd never been able to practice with any real constancy. She crept closer, gasping and slapping one hand to her heart when a cat suddenly dashed across her path. The summer grass felt warm and soft under her feet, sending up its sweet fragrance as she passed.

When she came within a hundred yards of the single tree, she realized that it sheltered a small, fenced area surrounding two carefully tended graves. Daniel was just standing there, staring at the stones, his hat in his hands, and he didn't so much as glance in Jolie's direction.

She swallowed and pressed both hands to her stomach. The quiet rawness of Daniel's grief speared her middle like a well-aimed pitchfork, though she couldn't think why it should trouble her. She was a stranger to this man, just as he was to her, and he'd married her out of charity, strictly to save her skin.

Whatever happened, she had to keep that fact in perspective. Daniel could decide to wash his hands of her at any time—heaven knew, enough other people had done just that—and when he did, he'd probably turn her right over to the law. A chill seeped through Jolie's borrowed dress, and she wrapped her arms around her middle, turned, and fled back toward the house.

Now she felt even less like sleeping than before. After getting a mug from the kitchen, she went to the well house for fresh milk. When she returned to pour the creamy beverage into a saucepan waiting on the stove, Daniel was in the room, standing behind his chair at the table.

"Tell me why you were with those men," he said, and though the words were quietly offered, Jolie knew Daniel was not making a request. This was an order.

Jolie pushed back a lock of hair that had strayed from the twine tie at her nape and busied herself with the milk. "Blake Kingston was a friend of mine," she said. "Or at least I thought he was."

She heard the chair scrape against the wooden floor, and when she dared to look back over one shoulder, she saw that Daniel had taken a seat at the table. He sat astraddle, his powerful arms resting across the chair back. His pale blue eyes held her gaze without apparent effort.

"What about your folks? Do you have any?"

Jolie sucked in her breath—after all this time, the

27

reminder was still painful—and shook her head. "No," she said, averting her eyes. She couldn't remember her mother at all, though she did recall the funeral, and her aunt Nissa and uncle Franklin, God rest them, had died during a cholera epidemic back in Nebraska several years before. Her father was dead, too, though he hadn't been "folks" even when he was alive, and Jolie certainly didn't think of her stepmother, Garnet, as family. "Have you?"

"Five brothers and two sisters, back in North Carolina," Daniel replied, with a brisk nod. "But we're not talking about me. I guess I'm asking how you fell in with such bad companions, Mrs. Beckham. And I won't be put off, so you'd better just go ahead and tell me."

Jolie's embarrassment was so keen that it was actually painful. Her hands trembled slightly as she poured the simmering milk from the pan into her mug.

Because bravado was virtually the only weapon she had to protect herself with, she squared her shoulders and lifted her chin. "Blake and I met because his mother and I were working together. I told you that."

Daniel didn't respond verbally, he just rested his chin on his forearm and arched his eyebrows.

After taking a steadying sip of the hot milk, Jolie forced herself to sit at the table. She entwined clammy fingers around the mug, and took small comfort from the warmth. "Some things were stolen, at the house where I worked . . ." She paused, her cheeks flaring with color at the memory. "Some of Mrs. Bonfield's jewelry. Her nephew, Gerard, claimed he'd seen me trying to sell a diamond broach and a strand of pearls to one of the shopkeepers on the waterfront. The Bonfields dismissed me, and I tried to find another job, but word had gotten around and nobody wanted to hire a suspected thief. Blake said he knew a family in Spokane that needed somebody to look after their children, so I left Seattle with him."

Daniel shoved a hand through his hair. "What about the jewelry? Did you steal it?"

Indignation boiled up inside Jolie with such force that the effort to contain it made her shake, but she succeeded. "No. Gerard took the things himself, to pay a gambling debt. The police found that out before I left, and of course they told the Bonfields."

"Didn't they offer to take you back?"

Jolie took another drink of her milk and set the cup down with an irate thump. "Of course they did, but how could I have gone on working for them, just as if nothing had happened? Besides, Gerard was still there."

"You could have found a position somewhere else, since your name had been cleared."

"I'm afraid it wasn't quite that simple," Jolie swallowed. "People tend to go right on thinking you're guilty, once you've been accused of something. And it doesn't seem to change things much when they find out they were wrong."

"Did Kingston take you to Spokane, like he promised?"

Jolie lowered her eyes for a moment and shook her head. "I realize now that he never intended to." She drew a deep breath and made herself meet Daniel's gaze squarely. "He wanted folks to think I was his woman. Maybe he even wanted to think that himself."

Daniel cleared his throat and looked away for a moment, and Jolie knew for certain that he didn't believe her. "You're saying you were never . . . close with him?"

She put down her cup and clasped her hands tightly together in her lap. "That's what I'm saying," she replied firmly, though inwardly she was quavering.

"There's no call to lie," Daniel said reasonably.

Jolie was tired of being blamed for things she hadn't done. Practically all her life, it seemed, someone had been pointing an accusing finger in her direction. "I'm not lying, Dan—Mr. Beckham," she said.

He shrugged one shoulder and pushed back his chair to rise. "We'd best be getting to sleep. It'll be dawn soon enough."

Jolie's palms tightened against the sides of the mug. She was nettled, knowing Daniel still thought she was lying, and she was afraid he meant they'd be sharing a bed after all. "It's my woman time," she said, and that *was* a lie, because she'd finished bleeding a few weeks before.

Daniel frowned and gestured toward the inner door, and Jolie preceded him, after setting her cup in the sink.

"You're up pretty late," she said, in a voice gleaming with false brightness, desperate to make conversation. She picked up the lamp that had been burning in the center of the table and started toward the front hall and the staircase.

"So are you," Daniel countered evenly.

Jolie bit her lower lip as she mounted the steps, feeling a sort of exhilarated terror. She was afraid of Daniel's size and strength and power, and yet some part of her wanted to take shelter in those very things.

She moved hesitantly into the room where she'd been before and set the lamp down on the bureau with shaky hands. "I guess you probably want to lie down with me," she said, in a jittery whisper.

She thought she saw Daniel smile, though she

couldn't be sure in the dim and flickering light. Gripping the back of the rocking chair with one hand, he kicked off his boots, then removed his vest and began unbuttoning his shirt.

Jolie turned away, mortified, and pressed one hand to her throat. "I-I'd be glad to sleep in the spare room," she offered valiantly.

This time, she was sure she heard a chuckle. "That's real generous of you, Mrs. Beckham, but I'd rather you'd stay right here."

Jolie's heart leapfrogged into her throat. She was afraid to look at Daniel, so she kept her eyes averted even after he'd blown out the lamp. When she climbed back into bed, she was still wearing her dress, and she lay on the very edge of the mattress, a hair's breadth from toppling onto the rag rug below.

Daniel's weight made the bed sag slightly, tilting her toward him, and she clung to the side with one hand, as though she were on the brink of a high cliff. And for all her efforts, every pore of her skin pulsed with the awareness of Daniel's heat and substance. When his big hand came to rest lightly on her hip, a sweet shudder went through Jolie, and she squeezed her eyes shut, needing all her wits to battle the riot of feelings the simple gesture had unchained within her.

"Your wife," she whispered, when she dared to speak. "What was her name?"

Daniel withdrew his hand, and Jolie was both relieved and sorry. "Ilse," he said, after a very long time.

"She was very pretty," Jolie offered, sensing his lingering pain and wanting somehow to lend comfort. She owed this man every sunrise she would ever see, though she had no real idea how to pay up. "I saw her picture in the parlor."

31

There was another silence, and then Daniel said, "I'll be wanting children."

Jolie felt tears squeeze past her lashes, and she couldn't help smiling a little. More than anything, she longed for a baby of her own. She forgot her fear and rolled over to look at Daniel, but she couldn't see his face in the darkness. "By me?" she whispered, amazed.

"You *are* my wife," he reminded her, and she heard amusement in the low tone of his voice.

"But I'm—they were going to hang me."

He fitted her close to him, and she drank in the warm solidity of his body even though she was afraid. Her cheek rested against his hairy chest, but she didn't dare let her mind reach any lower than that. "You didn't kill anybody," he said, with a certainty that was balm to Jolie's bruised spirit. And then, remarkably, he drifted off to sleep.

Jolie lay nestled against this husband she hadn't known before today, burning with a strange invisible fire while she listened to his deep, even breathing. And oddly enough, for the first time since before her pa had dragged her away from Aunt Nissa and Uncle Franklin's farm, when she was fourteen and he'd just married Garnet, Jolie felt safe.

It seemed only a short time later that Daniel nudged her lightly and rolled out of bed. Somewhere beyond the dark glass at the window, a rooster was crowing.

Remembering where she was, Jolie came awake instantly and pulled the covers up over her head so she wouldn't see Daniel getting dressed.

"We'll be going into town later in the day," he said, moments later, pulling the quilt down far enough to look into her face. She couldn't be absolutely sure, but she thought his eyes were dancing with some pleasure

32

he wanted to keep to himself. "Have breakfast on the table in half an hour."

With that, he turned and left the room. Jolie bolted out of bed, hastily donned her shoes, and rushed downstairs to get the fire in the cookstove going. She was outside at the pump when the sun burst over the timbered foothills in the east, pouring pools of copper and crimson over the wheat, and the beauty of it made her throat catch.

Thank You, God, she thought, only too aware that she could easily have spent the night in a coffin instead of Daniel Beckham's bed. It was only by pure grace that she was breathing fresh morning air, with cornflowers swaying at her feet, pumping icy well water into a bucket and watching a new day begin.

Deuter came out of the little shed next to the barn and waved his hat in good-natured greeting. At his heels trotted the ugliest cat Jolie had ever seen, an enormous speckled tom, with a chunk of one ear and big patches of fur missing. His right eye was nothing more than a jagged slit in his face, and his left was like an amber marble, glistening and hard.

"Well," she said, feeling charitable, as she carried the water bucket toward the house, "who's this?"

"This here's Leviticus," Deuter replied, pleased at her interest. "Dan'l named him that because he knew me and this cat was gonna be friends." Jolie hoisted the water bucket over the threshold and was about to climb up after it when Deuter stopped her. "Here, Mrs. Beckham," he said, producing an apple crate from the tall grass and setting it down in front of the door. "Dan'l and me, we'd smash this if either of us was to step on it, but you're a lady and you can't be hauling your skirts up like that."

"Thank you, Deuter," Jolie said, touched by the

gesture and pleased because he'd addressed her as "Mrs. Beckham," just as if she were a real wife. The apple crate did indeed make it easier to enter the kitchen and, while Deuter and Leviticus went off to the barn to help with the chores, Jolie put a pot of coffee on to brew and then quickly attended to a few simple ablutions.

The wheat was ablaze with sunshine and the sky was the same festive blue as Aunt Nissa's favorite sugar bowl when she went out to the henhouse. She hummed as she filled her apron with brown eggs and hurried on to the well house for a slab of pork.

In the house, she sliced bread and put it into the oven to toast while she fried up the eggs and bacon. When Daniel and Deuter came in, skin glowing from washing up in the cold water from the pump, she set their plates in front of them with a proud flourish.

Daniel glowered at the single egg, two slices of bacon, and thick wedge of toasted bread she'd given him.

"This wouldn't keep Verena Dailey's lapdog alive," he grumbled, and all of Jolie's pleasure evaporated in an instant.

3

Jolie's motions were brisk and angry as she silently fetched more pork and eggs from the larder and put them on the stove to cook. Maybe Daniel had saved her life, but that didn't give him the right to treat her like a slave. After all, she hadn't *asked* him for so much as the time of day.

"That dress looks like you slept in it," Deuter commented cheerfully, when she refilled the platter and set it back on the table with a resounding thump. "Not only that, it's too small for you. Maybe you're getting fat, like Mrs. Anstruther over at the land office. You could hide a loaded hay wagon behind that woman."

"Deuter," Daniel interrupted gruffly, scraping more food onto his plate. "Just eat your breakfast and get on with your work."

Deuter certainly wasn't a judicious conversationalist, but he was obedient. He lowered his eyes and tucked into the eggs and bacon.

Jolie escaped to the side yard, where she'd hung her

own clothes out to dry the night before, after washing them, and promptly forgotten their existence. Now, the garments were stiff and wrinkled and still damp with the morning dew, but they were clean.

Not wanting to pass Daniel again until she had to, Jolie changed in the well house, and when she came out, her husband was striding purposefully toward the barn. Deuter was nowhere in sight.

Jolie shoved the apple crate into place and hastened into the kitchen, where she quickly cleared the table. She was dipping hot water from the reservoir into the dishpan when Daniel came in.

Since she'd already seen the team and wagon waiting in the barnyard, all hitched up and ready to go, she knew it was time to leave for town.

"Leave that for later," Daniel said.

Jolie bristled. Even though she would always be grateful to this man for what he'd done, she also resented his indisputable power over her. "It might serve you better to address me more politely in the future, Mr. Beckham," she said.

"It might serve you," Daniel replied, unruffled, "to do as you're told and keep your mouth shut."

Fiery humiliation swept through Jolie's soul, and her cheeks felt as though they'd been doused in kerosene and set ablaze. With her chin high and her shoulders square, she dried her hands on a blue and white striped dish towel, set her hat on her head, and started toward the yawning door.

Daniel stepped down to the ground first and reached for her, and Jolie shut her eyes tightly as his big hands closed on her waist. There was that strange feeling again, starting in her most private places and bouncing wildly into every part of her, like a herd of tiny wire springs just released from narrow confines.

The moment she was standing before him, slightly breathless because of the odd effect the contact had had upon her, Daniel reached out and removed her derby. Passing the garden, which was neatly tended like the rest of the Beckham property, he set the hat on the scarecrow's nodding cloth head and smiled slightly to himself.

Once again, Jolie was roundly insulted, but she refrained from comment. She didn't know much about Daniel Beckham, but there was one thing she'd learned: once he'd made up his mind about something, there was just no sense in crossing him.

She climbed up into the wagon without waiting for help and settled herself primly on the hard seat, smoothing her frayed brown riding skirt the way a lady would do with rich velvet. All Jolie had left was her dignity, and she didn't mean to give that up lightly.

"That was a perfectly good hat," she said, without so much as looking at Daniel when he hoisted his muscular frame into the seat beside her. "It kept the sun off my face."

"It'll do to scare away crows," he replied, and Jolie felt the motion of his arm as he gave the reins a flick. "You'll be needing some proper bonnets and a Sunday hat."

Jolie stiffened at the word *Sunday* and narrowed her eyes as she turned to study Daniel's profile. "I'm not a churchgoing woman," she said plainly.

Daniel was navigating the driveway that led down to the main gate and the road beyond, and even though this was clearly an easy task, he appeared to be concentrating hard on it. "Maybe you haven't been, but you are now."

Thinking of all the three-hour sermons she'd been

forced to sit through—sending Jolie to church had apparently assuaged her father's guilt over his *own* sins—she groaned. "You might just as well have left me to hang."

Her husband's laugh startled her, even though she should have been prepared, should have expected it to be big and daunting, like he was. "The Reverend Blackborrow will appreciate your enthusiasm, I'm sure."

Jolie sighed. "I reckon he's long-winded, like most preachers," she lamented, with resignation. There was no point in pretending she didn't have to obey Daniel; she knew she had no alternatives at the moment.

Daniel chuckled again and resettled his battered old hat on his head, but he didn't meet Jolie's gaze and he didn't offer a comment on her remark.

On either side of the wagon, the wheat stood still in the heavy August air, and the team snuffled and nickered as they trotted along. Jolie's thigh touched Daniel's rock-hard one and she flinched as if he'd jabbed her with a pin. Perspiration beaded in the tender crevice between her breasts, on her nape, and along her upper lip.

"Sure is hot," she said, finding the relative silence untenable.

"It's August," Daniel allowed.

In the distance, Jolie could just glimpse the raggly-straggly beginnings of the town of Prosperity. She focused her attention on that. "You don't say much, do you, Mr. Beckham?" she ventured.

"Not much, no," he conceded, taking off his hat long enough to drag one sleeve across his brow.

Had Jolie known the man better, she would have elbowed him hard in the ribs for being so blamed *quiet*. There were times when a woman just plain

38

needed to hear talk, and plenty of it, and this was one of them. "Why do you suppose that is?" she proceeded. When the image of Daniel standing beside his first wife's grave burst unexpectedly into her mind, she pushed it aside. "That you don't care much for conversation, I mean?"

Daniel made a sound meant to hasten the horses a little and pondered the question in silence for a few moments. "Doesn't matter," he finally answered. "It's clear enough that you'll be doing enough jawing for the both of us."

The words stung a little, but it wasn't the first time Jolie had been accused of talking too much, and besides, she had plenty of other things on her mind. Like where she would go when she left the farm, and how she would support herself.

They reached Prosperity and Daniel drew the wagon to a stop in front of the bank. "I've got to write out that draft," he said, and Jolie made sure she got herself down before he had a chance to help her. "You head on over to the mercantile and pick out a ready-made dress and some yard goods." His blue eyes drifted critically over her tattered riding skirt and shirt, both hand-me-downs from her former employer. "Get a comb and brush, too, and some bonnets."

Jolie gnawed at her lower lip to keep from answering him back—even though most folks would have said Daniel Beckham was being generous, there was something in his manner that made her temper jump like a lid over a pot of boiling water.

"And mind you stay out of trouble," he added, as an afterthought, waggling a finger at her.

She turned on her heel and trooped across the dusty street, taking care not to put her feet down in the wrong places, and mounted the rough wooden steps

leading up to the sidewalk. The inside of the mercan·
tile smelled of tobacco and tea leaves, vanilla and
sawdust, coffee beans and aging cheese.

Jolie walked along beside the long counter toward
the back of the store without looking either to her left
or to her right. Although she didn't let on, she was
painfully aware of the hush that had fallen over the
other people in the mercantile when she'd entered.

She passed the black iron wheel of the coffee
grinder, the glass jars filled with grainy peppermint
sticks, the pickle barrel. The yard goods were displayed on a long table at the back of the room, behind
the potbellied stove with its circle of rocking chairs.
There were bonnets and bridles pegged to the walls,
and spools of gaily colored ribbon and delicate lace
trim lined a metal rod attached to the table.

"You'll be needing something?" That was Mrs.
Craybrook asking; Jolie remembered the small, gray-
haired woman from the trial. And the hanging.

"Mr. Beckham wants me to have a dress and some
bonnets and yardage," Jolie said, forcing herself to
meet Mrs. Craybrook's marble-bright brown eyes.
There was no telling how long she'd have to stay
around this town, and she couldn't go kowtowing to
every old heifer who looked at her crossways.

The proprietress inspected Jolie thoroughly. "Do
you sew?" she trilled. It would have been impossible
to challenge the woman gracefully, but her tone
indicated the most scathing censure.

After coming so close to dangling by the neck from
the sturdiest branch of a maple tree, it took more than
one little bantam hen with her feathers ruffed up to
scare Jolie McKibben Beckham. "If you'd prefer not
to take my husband's money, Mrs. Craybrook, we can
send away to the catalog company for what we need."

For a long moment the two women just stood there, staring each other down like two gunfighters in a dusty street. It was Mrs. Craybrook who finally retreated. "Nonsense. You can never be sure those people will send what you ordered, or *when* they'll send it, for that matter. Besides, you're so tall that anything you buy ready-made is going to need altering to keep your ankles hidden." She paused to purse her lips, after whispering the last few words, and flushed, momentarily undone, evidently, at being forced to speak of so specific an extremity aloud. "How many dresses did Daniel have in mind?"

"None at all," Jolie couldn't resist saying, a smile teasing at the corners of her generous mouth. "I don't believe he's at all given to wearing them. I, on the other hand, expect to need at least three."

Two red patches glowed beneath the pale rice powder covering Mrs. Craybrook's cheeks, and her lips went very thin across her teeth. But before she could render a reply, the little bell over the shop door jingled and Daniel walked in. He took off his hat and hung it from one of the pegs next to the door before ambling back to run his eyes critically over the array of poplins and calicos and ginghams offered for sale.

"See that you buy at least one ready-made dress, and make sure you get some stuff for nightgowns, too," he said, and Jolie was amazed at how simply he could mortify her. He didn't seem to put any effort into it at all. "Can't have you sleeping in your clothes for the rest of your life."

Mrs. Craybrook cleared her throat and pretended to straighten the spools of ribbon that glowed in the dim light like a rainbow.

Jolie's face was flaming, and she turned her head to hide it. Swallowing, she reached out to lay one hand on a bolt of crisp yellow and white gingham, imagining herself in a pretty summer dress with ruffles. "I'd like this, please," she said awkwardly. After that, she chose plain butter-colored muslin for drawers and petticoats and camisoles, and several links of finely woven white cotton for nightdresses. She would have stopped at that, being overwhelmed at such wealth as it was, but Daniel insisted that she select enough cloth for six other dresses, with bonnets to match. He also bought her shoes and black ribbed stockings and perfumed soap and a stick of green and white peppermint from one of the glass jars on the counter.

Soon, Mrs. Craybrook's skinny, gap-toothed son was hefting an enormous brown paper parcel into the back of Daniel's wagon, and the old woman herself was chattering away about the upcoming harvest. It seemed that virtually everyone in that part of the territory depended upon Daniel and his special machinery to bring in their crops.

When he deemed it time to leave, he splayed the fingers of one hand over the small of Jolie's back and steered her toward the door. He said good-bye to Mrs. Craybrook by putting his hat back on and touching the brim, but Jolie was hardly aware of that. All she could think about was the weight of his palm against her skin and the way his fingertips seemed to shoot fire into the depths of her muscles.

Outside, the smells and noises of a small western farming town assailed her senses, but still Jolie barely noticed the wagons, horses, and people. She imagined how it would be if Daniel were to touch her bare flesh, and prayed he hadn't felt the quiver that resulted.

He lifted her easily into the wagon, then climbed up after her.

"Thank you," Jolie said, when he released the brake

lever and slapped the reins down onto the sweaty, flyspeckled backs of the two horses.

Daniel only shrugged and sent the team and wagon into a wide U-turn, sending dogs, squawking chickens, and small boys scattering.

Jolie looked up at a bright satin sky, remembered that she was supposed to be dead, and laughed out loud for the sheer merriment of being alive. "Oh, *thank you,"* she told Daniel, resting her head against his shoulder for a moment.

He smelled of soap and sweat and road dust, and Jolie found the combination pleasant. He looked down at her, and she felt his frame tighten beside her as she ran her tongue slowly along the length of the peppermint stick he'd given her. His gaze shifted quickly back to the road, and although Jolie couldn't have sworn to it, it seemed to her that he pulled away from her slightly.

"Is something wrong?" Jolie didn't really want an answer to that question, but she wasn't able to keep herself from asking it.

"No," he answered, and she knew he was lying, but there wasn't much she could do about it. She concentrated on getting the most possible enjoyment from her candy and kept her opinions to herself. Several times, out of the corner of one eye, she caught Daniel stealing a look at her.

When they reached the farm, they found Leviticus chasing his tail on the roof of the privy, while Deuter labored near the kitchen door. The bare white skin of his back and shoulders glistened in the hot sunlight as he braced a long wooden plank with one hand and worked a saw with the other.

He looked up with a delighted grin as Daniel lifted Jolie down from the wagon, but the smile faded almost instantly. Jolie followed the reaction back to its obvious source and saw that Daniel was glowering at the boy.

"Put on your shirt," he said, striding around to jerk the parcel out of the wagon with one hand.

Deuter reached for the garment, which had been resting nearby on the woodpile, and shrugged into it. Ignoring her husband who, to Jolie's way of thinking, had spoken too harshly, she smiled as she walked toward the young farmhand.

When she realized that Deuter had been building steps to make it easier to go in and out of the house, she was so touched that her throat constricted a little. "How thoughtful!" she said, smiling.

But Deuter only nodded and averted his eyes, and Jolie tossed an impatient glance back at Daniel. Then she went around to the front of the house and let herself in that way.

Reaching the kitchen, she found Daniel standing beside the table, where he'd set the parcel. He was frowning at the thick string tied around the package as though it caused him some deep puzzlement. Outside, Deuter had given up sawing for hammering, and Jolie silently blessed him for his enterprise, even though the noise was starting to give her a headache.

Seeing a fresh chicken lying in the sink, all plucked and cleaned, Jolie pushed up her sleeves and took the basin down from the wall. When she'd finished ladling hot water into it to wash with, she was surprised to turn around and find that Daniel hadn't moved.

Although there had been a lot of silence in Jolie's life, she'd never learned to like it. Something inside always made her want to fill the void with chatter. "I guess we know what Deuter wants for his dinner," she chimed, nodding toward the poultry as she carried the basin to the counter, set it down, and began washing her hands with harsh yellow soap.

Daniel looked at her thoughtfully for a long moment, then folded his arms. "Have a decent dress ready for church on Sunday," he ordered bluntly. "Use that shiny brown cloth."

Jolie silently reminded herself that beggars couldn't be choosers, dried her hands, and reached for the chicken, which needed cutting into parts. "The sateen," she said, with a sigh. She hadn't liked the dowdy fabric, but Daniel had insisted on buying a length. "It'll make me look plain as a mud hen."

"Ilse always wore a proper dress to church," Daniel pointed out. "Cook some potatoes and gravy to go along with that bird, and boil up some green beans with bacon and onion."

"Have a decent dress ready," Jolie mimicked in a low voice, once he'd gone outside to mind his own business. "Get in the wagon, get out of the wagon, see that you do this, make sure you do that, and fry me up a buffalo for breakfast . . ."

It took an hour to prepare the meal, including peeling the potatoes, raiding the garden for green beans and washing them, flouring the chicken, and mixing up a batch of biscuits for good measure. By the time she was through, the kitchen was muggy and hot and Jolie had no appetite at all, so she served up the food and went outside for a breath of weighted air.

She had already reached the little picket fence surrounding the two graves before she even realized she'd been headed that way. Pushing damp tendrils of hair back from her face and grateful for the shade of the maple tree, Jolie opened the gate with one hand and stepped through.

Ilse's gravestone was made of good black-and-white

marble, and a small brass plate had been cast with her name and the dates of her birth and death. Jolie hugged herself, even though it was so warm that her clothes were sticking to her body, as she read that the first Mrs. Beckham had died only sixteen months before.

Jolie fought down a sense of overwhelming sadness and turned to the small grave next to Ilse's. A statue of an angel blowing a trumpet guarded this other plot, and sudden tears welled in Jolie's eyes even as a cool breeze caressed her shoulder blades through her damp shirt. The marker bore only two words . . . *Our Baby.*

Jolie sniffled and tilted her head back to draw a deep breath and bring herself under control. Children died every day, it was a grim reality of life, and if she stopped to grieve each time she encountered a tiny grave, she would get nothing else done for drying her eyes.

"Dan'l and me might eat all the chicken if you don't come back inside," a voice said, and Jolie jumped, startled. She hadn't heard Deuter approaching.

Hoping her tears had left no traces on her face, Jolie faced her friend. "How did Daniel and Ilse's baby die?" she asked.

Deuter held the gate open for her, neatly closed and latched it when she'd passed through. "Came down with the whooping cough a few days after Christmas," he said, his voice quiet and somber. "Mrs. Beckham never got over it. She just walked all around the farm, cryin' and wringin' her hands. Didn't seem to make no difference that she had another baby growin' inside her. She was a little thing herself, and she got so big with that young 'un—well, she just looked like she was going to topple over from the weight of it."

Sensing Deuter's innate kindness, Jolie slipped her arm through his. "And?" she prompted gently.

"Something went wrong when Mrs. Beckham started to have that baby." Deuter paused for a moment, gazing off at a heat mirage shimmering over the wheat, his jawline set tight. "She died, and the doc couldn't get to the little 'un in time. Dan'l buried a son and a wife in the same grave."

"Tell me about the first child," Jolie urged, after recovering her own emotions. She and Deuter were nearing the house now, but there was no sign of Daniel.

Deuter sighed. "Her name was Eugenia, and she was two when she fell sick."

Jolie had known enough tragedy in her own life to appreciate the degree of Daniel's suffering. She felt a rush of sadness, only too aware now of why he'd been willing to marry a woman the world regarded as an outlaw. He'd chosen someone he wouldn't have to care about, someone who couldn't hurt him.

Deuter and Jolie parted in the side yard, Jolie heading around to the front of the house while Deuter went back to building the steps. She walked through the house to the kitchen, where she consumed the one piece of fried chicken that remained, then cleared the table and washed the dishes.

After those chores were done, Jolie added a leaf to the big oak table in the dining room and spread a length of white cotton for cutting. When supper time rolled around, she was sitting in the rocking chair on the front porch, putting a tidy hem in a sleeveless nightgown. She rose with a contented sigh and went into the house.

It was a surprise to find Daniel in the kitchen,

47

making sandwiches with bacon and big, juicy tomatoes from the garden.

"I would have done that," Jolie said, instantly chagrined.

Daniel shrugged. "You were busy."

Jolie glanced toward the open door and the newly built steps beyond. "Where's Deuter?"

"He's gone to town to spend the night at his sister's place." Daniel assembled the last sandwich and carried the platter to the table. "Sit down and eat," he said.

Just the suggestion made Jolie's stomach rumble. She took a seat at the table and helped herself to one of the thick sandwiches. "Does she have a Bible name, too?" she asked, just to make conversation. "Deuter's sister, I mean."

Daniel smiled slightly as he sat down and shook his head.

The food was delicious, and Jolie chewed the combination of toasted bread, sun-sweetened tomatoes, bacon, and fresh lettuce with pleasure. "Tell me about your family."

Daniel's gaze sliced to her face, and Jolie felt a sudden chill even though the breeze coming in through the open door was a warm one. "They're no concern of yours," he said.

Jolie lowered her sandwich back to her plate, all appetite gone. "Well, *that* was certainly a gracious remark," she snapped.

"I told you before; Ilse is dead."

"I wasn't asking about Ilse. I wanted to know about your mother and father and your brothers and sisters."

Daniel continued to eat. "They raise tobacco," he said, looking a little sheepish.

"Why didn't you stay in North Carolina and raise tobacco with them?"

"I wanted a place that was all my own, so I came west and homesteaded."

He'd obviously built up a large and productive farm, and Jolie had great respect for the accomplishment, but she couldn't understand why someone with a home and a family would want to go traipsing off to the other side of the country. "Don't you get lonesome for them?" she asked. "All those other Beckhams, I mean?"

"They write now and again," Daniel answered, taking another sandwich.

Jolie was determined. "Which one do you miss most?"

Daniel washed down a bite of food with a swallow of milk. "I guess that would be Enoch, my youngest brother. He and I have written back and forth about him coming out here to help me work this place, but he's got a wife and two little ones to feed, so he'll probably stay right where he is."

Feeling hungry again, Jolie went back to eating. Daniel refilled her milk glass from a yellow crockery pitcher.

Presently, he pushed back his chair and hooked his thumbs through his belt loops. "I'll be going up to Spokane to hire a harvest crew the first of the week," he announced. "And I'm taking Deuter along."

Jolie gathered the crumbs from her sandwich on the tip of one finger and ate them with a flick of her tongue. "Aren't you afraid I'll run away?" she asked, raising one eyebrow.

A moment before, Daniel's manner had been almost indolent. Now, he was leaning toward her, his eyes narrowed. "Like I said before, I don't figure you have anyplace to go. But if you try, I'll track yo down, take my five hundred dollars out of your hid and turn you over to the authorities in Spokane."

"Five hundred dollars?" Jolie practically choked o the words, so enormous was the sum. "Blake an Rowdy took *five hundred dollars?"*

Daniel nodded, rose, and took his plate to the sink "I would have thought you'd know that. It must hav been mentioned during the trial."

Jolie's eyes remained wide. "I suppose it was, but t tell you the truth, I wasn't paying much attention t details. I just wanted to put this place behind me while I could still touch the ground with both feet."

After filling a basin with hot water and adding soap flakes, Daniel washed the few dishes they'd used brushing Jolie aside when she offered to help. Anothei troubling silence fell.

"I guess you won't be able to afford the new manure spreader now," she said, standing in the tiny porch Deuter had built and watching as the sun dipped behind the barn, making a fiery splash.

She was aware that Daniel was standing directly behind her. When his hands came to rest gently on her shoulders, she closed her eyes, letting the fearsome pleasure wash over her.

He made no mention of the manure spreader when he turned her in his arms, cupped one hand under her chin, and tilted her head back for his kiss.

Jolie's toes curled inside her shoes as she tried in vain to get some kind of grip on the earth. And when Daniel touched his mouth to hers and parted her lips with his tongue, she seemed to float up to meet him. Sweet fire blazed up around her, consuming her, and yet Jolie was not a martyr but a queen. Even though her heart was pounding with joyous terror and she was so dizzy she feared she'd swoon, it came as a shock when Daniel gently set her away from him.

"I think I'll go into town for a few hours," he said gruffly.

Jolie held her dignity close, like a woolen coat on a bitter January day. Her life had certainly not been a sheltered one; she knew what kind of company Daniel would seek out when he reached Prosperity, and she was frightened by the furious jealousy she felt.

"Good night to you, then, Mr. Beckham," she said evenly. And only when she'd washed and brushed her hair and changed into her brand-new nightgown did Jolie stretch out on Daniel's bed to weep.

4

Pilar watched Daniel's reflection in the mirror over her vanity table, her dark eyes luminous. With nimble fingers, she worked her glistening black hair into a single plait over her shoulder, and she'd exchanged her colorful dancing dress for a wrapper of threadbare white velvet. "Why did you do it, Daniel?" she asked, in her careful, accented English. "Why did you marry that woman?"

Daniel sighed and slapped his hat against one thigh. He'd come to the Ivory Rose intending to swill a little whiskey downstairs and then ease the natural stresses of his body with Pilar. From the moment he'd stepped through the swinging doors, however, he'd been able to think of nothing and no one but Jolie. Even Ilse's features were indistinct in his mind, and that fact troubled him more than anything. "You know why I married her," he finally answered. "Chilver and January and the rest of that bunch meant to string her up just because she was handy."

Pilar secured her braid with a faded pink ribbon and turned to look directly into Daniel's face. "Do you love her?" she asked, keeping back any opinion she might have had concerning Jolie's guilt or innocence.

Daniel felt his blood rise. "Damn it, what kind of question is that? I've known her for less than two days!"

"And yet you no longer want me," Pilar pointed out, with a little pout.

He shoved splayed fingers through his hair and sighed again. "It wouldn't be right," he said quietly, at great length, "my being a married man and all."

"Most of the men who come in here have wives," Pilar responded evenly. "Besides, this isn't the same. Not if you don't love her."

Daniel was certain he didn't have tender feelings for Jolie, but he sure as hell wanted her, and he couldn't begin to deny the fact, even to himself. So he decided not to discuss it at all. "I'd better be getting home," he said. Then he turned and left the room where he'd taken his pleasure so many times, with nothing asked in return except money. He'd never been expected to open his heart, to care.

On the stairs, Daniel encountered Ira January, the slick young gambler who'd started up his own timber business, cutting trees in the foothills and planing lumber in a new mill. Folks said he'd won the necessary capital in a poker game down in San Francisco. Daniel didn't like him much, and he'd never taken the trouble to work out why that was—he just avoided the man whenever he could.

Now, January stopped him by laying one beringed hand on his arm. "It would seem," he said, "that the

honeymoon is over. Has Mrs. Beckham proved to be
an unsatisfactory wife, as well as a robber and a
murderess?"

Daniel wanted to knock January backward through
the banister, but he didn't because he would have had
to pay damages and he didn't have the money to
spare, thanks to Jolie's bail and the things she'd
needed just to look decent. He let his contempt show
plainly, though, glaring until the gambler retreated
down the staircase a few steps.

Although he looked nervous, January laughed,
showing white teeth that overlapped slightly in front,
and shrugged. "Pilar is a tasty little confection. I don't
blame you for not wanting to give her up."

Daniel's right hand bunched into a fist, but he
relaxed the muscles by force of will and walked
around January and on down the stairs. He'd learned
to restrain his temper long ago, rarely allowing himself to forget that one blow could knock out a man's
teeth or even kill him.

When he reached the street, Daniel looked up to see
legions of stars crowding the dark sky, and he thought
there must be other beings out there somewhere,
struggling with concerns of their own, and dreaming
dreams.

He untied his gelding, a giant gray draft horse with a
streak of mule in him, and swung wearily up into the
saddle. For himself, Daniel had long since decided it
was safer not to dream at all.

Reaching the farm about twenty minutes later, he
noticed first thing that there was a bright yellow
square of light glowing in the upper part of the
house—his room. Scowling, Daniel dismounted and
led his horse into the barn, where a single lamp

burned, blending with moonbeams to cast a shimmer over the hay.

Deuter sat on an overturned nail keg, rubbing oil into a worn leather harness. He greeted Daniel with a companionable nod and nothing more, and Daniel was grateful. He put the horse away for the night and wandered reluctantly toward the house.

Daniel had worked from sunrise until long after twilight had fallen, and strong as he was, his big body ached with fatigue. He needed to stretch out on his own bed—the only one in the house that would accommodate his frame—but there was a problem.

Jolie.

Lying beside her all the night before, feeling the warm, soft promise of her shape pressed against him, had been a kind of ecstatic agony. His forbearance had only seemed to heighten the pleasure. But this evening things would be different, and Daniel knew it. His need had risen to such a shrill pitch that his entire being seemed to vibrate with it, and he couldn't trust himself to so much as step over the threshold of that familiar room upstairs.

Jolie heard the kitchen door open and close and bounded out of bed, dashing tears from her cheeks with the back of one hand and sniffling once. Whatever Daniel had done, wherever he had been, she mustn't allow him to know he'd caused her to weep. She smoothed her new cotton nightgown and her just-brushed hair and went to the top of the stairway to wait.

Daniel appeared below, a kerosene lantern in one hand, and she saw his throat work as he looked up at her.

"I was just . . . reading," Jolie lied, and every word resounded with a light note. "Did you have a nice evening?"

Her husband frowned and started up the steps. "You'll sleep in the spare room tonight, Mrs. Beckham. I need my rest and I won't have it with you tossing and turning in my bed."

Although Jolie was relieved that Daniel didn't expect anything—well, *conjugal*—she was also indignant. He clearly didn't find her attractive. She bit her lip to keep from asking where he'd been and stepped back to let him pass.

Without another word, Daniel handed her the lantern, disappeared into his room, and summarily closed the door behind him.

For a long moment, Jolie just stood there in the center of the hallway, feeling as though she'd been slapped. Then it occurred to her that Daniel didn't want her as a woman because he thought she really was a criminal, and that realization stung even more than the idea that he didn't think she was pretty. It also made rage swell inside her like bread dough on a sunny windowsill.

She set her shoulders, marched into the spare room, and slammed the door hard just to let Daniel Beckham know that saving her life hadn't given him the right to treat her like a mangy stray. But her ire kept her awake most of the night, and when Jolie rose, there were pale shadows under her eyes.

Barefoot, she crept into Daniel's room to get some of her things. There was no sign of her reluctant husband, except for a mound of tangled sheets in the center of the bed and soapy water in the basin.

Jolie fetched what she needed and went back to the spare room, hastily washing with the perfumed soap

56

and then donning her new ready-made dress, a cheerful pink and blue calico. Once her waist-length hair had been thoroughly brushed, she braided it into two plaits and pinned these to the crown of her head in a coronet.

There was no time to primp, since Daniel and Deuter would be in from milking soon, expecting to find a meal on the table, but Jolie did pause long enough to smile at herself in the mirror over the bureau. She'd make Daniel want her if it was the last thing she ever did, and when she accomplished that end, she would take delight in telling him to keep his hands off.

Downstairs, Jolie found that the stove had been stoked and coffee had been put on to brew, and a large smoked ham was waiting beside the sink. She hurried down the steps Deuter had so thoughtfully built and along the path to the privy. After leaving there, she paused at the pump to wash her hands and splash icy cold water against her face.

The sun was just peeking over the horizon of whispering wheat, pushing back the shivery chill of the night with the promise of warmth.

Back inside, Jolie quickly washed and sliced half a dozen potatoes and set them on to fry, followed by eggs and thick slices of ham. She put bread in the oven to toast, leaving the door slightly ajar, and then raced to lay the table. By the time Daniel and Deuter came in, the skin on their hands and faces reddened from washing in cold well water, the meal was ready.

Jolie spoke not a single word to Daniel as she poured the coffee and served up platters of steaming, savory food, but she could not have been more solicitous of Deuter.

"I can't tell you how grateful I am that you put up

those steps outside the kitchen door," she said, beaming as she set a jar of strawberry preserves down in front of the hired hand.

Out of the corner of her eye, Jolie saw Daniel scowl. She suspected he hadn't slept any more than she had, and the knowledge lifted her heart.

"Maybe I should get myself a wife," Deuter said, looking over Jolie's new dress and tidy hairstyle with unabashed appreciation. "What do you think, Dan'l?"

"I think you'd better finish eating and get those mules hitched up," Daniel replied shortly, over the rim of his coffee mug. "These crops have to be in before it rains, and the teams have had all summer to forget what it's like being in harness."

Deuter was apparently incapable of real chagrin, so he didn't color up or look sheepish or anything, but he did eat a little faster. "A body'd think you'd be in a better frame of mind," he commented, chewing. "You did go into town to see Pilar last night, didn't you?"

Daniel gave the boy a look that would have cured pork. Then he shoved his chair back, shot to his feet, and strode out the back door, barely pausing to collect his hat as he passed the pegs.

Jolie was too furious herself, however, to take much notice of Daniel's reactions. She went to the stove, picked up the cast-iron skillet and slammed it down hard, just to let some of her steam escape.

"Who," she asked of Deuter, who was still blithely consuming his breakfast, when she could trust herself to speak, "is Pilar?"

Deuter chewed a piece of ham and washed it down with roughly a quart of milk. "She's a whore," he answered, with no more qualms than he would have had telling Jolie the woman was a schoolmarm or a housemaid or the leader of the church choir.

Although Jolie told herself over and over again that she'd *known* Daniel had gone to town to seek his comfort with a woman, having her suspicions confirmed was brutally painful. She kept her back to Deuter while she put the kitchen to rights, her cheeks flaming with humiliation, and she made a lot of noise washing up the dishes.

Once he'd gone, Jolie swept the floor, then went upstairs to make her bed and Daniel's. After that, she gathered eggs and weeded the garden. She'd washed her hands and was in the dining room spreading the length of brown sateen for cutting when she saw a smart little buggy whisk past the window.

She put down the scissors and hurried through the kitchen, her heart pounding at the prospect of company. Jolie longed for a friend, but she was braced for rejection, knowing the womenfolk of Prosperity would find her sorely wanting of any redeeming quality.

A woman dressed all in black climbed down from the buggy and approached, smiling. Her iron gray hair was partially covered by a small, delicately crocheted cap, and the scent of rose water came from the rustling folds of her crisp skirts.

"You must be Daniel's new bride," she said and, to Jolie's everlasting astonishment, the woman actually put one ringless, age-spotted hand out in greeting.

Jolie racked her brain, but she couldn't recall seeing this woman at her trial or in the crowd of eager vultures waiting to see her hanged. Her own hand trembled a little as she offered it, and resisting the urge to pull it back to her side took all her determination.

"Well," trilled the woman, *"are you?"*

Am I what? Jolie almost countered, but then she realized what the visitor wanted to know and decided it was a reasonable inquiry. "Yes," she said. "I'm Mrs. Beckham."

Her hand was squeezed tightly in a gloved one. "I'm Verena Dailey—I live down the road a piece. Up until you came along, I did most of the cleaning around here."

Jolie didn't quite know how to respond. Perhaps Mrs. Dailey was angry because she'd lost the wages Daniel had paid her for keeping house.

"I won't miss it at all, either," Verena went on, in a gleeful whisper, patting Jolie's cheek a couple of times for emphasis. "Lord knows, Dan Beckham is a friend of mine, but he's about as cussed a man as you'd find if you went over three counties with a mustache comb."

A smile broke across Jolie's face, feeling as warm as the sunlight when it spilled out over the wheat in the mornings. "Won't you come in and have some coffee, Mrs. Dailey?" she asked eagerly, stepping back out of the doorway.

"Verena," the older woman corrected. "I've never had any patience with such formalities as that—takes up too much time." She fanned herself with one hand as she entered. "Mercy me, but it's hot in here, child. You'd best leave the door open and let in some air."

Jolie tossed a nervous glance toward the kitchen clock. She'd been caught up in making the brown sateen dress Daniel had insisted upon, even though she thoroughly expected to hate the thing, and time had gotten away from her.

"Dear heaven," she muttered, dashing for the pantry door.

When she came out, carrying the ham one of the men had brought in from the smokehouse that morning, Verena was already slicing bread for sandwiches. "What shall I call you?" she asked chattily.

"Jolie," her hostess answered breathlessly, checking the coffeepot and giving a little moan when she found it all but empty.

"That short for anything?"

"No," Jolie answered, hurrying to the door and flinging the dregs of the breakfast coffee into the yard. The hens pecking near the steps squawked in disgruntled outrage and scattered, their red-brown wings flapping. "Just Jolie."

When she returned from rinsing and filling the coffeepot at the pump outside, Verena had already set the table, and she was constructing sandwiches of ham and butter and spicy mustard. She waved away a fly that had bumbled in through the open doorway and frowned. "Not Josephine?"

Jolie squinted at the clock again and imagined the look of glowering disapproval that would come over Daniel's face if he arrived before the midday meal was ready. "Just Jolie," she repeated, somewhat impatiently.

To her abject surprise, Verena caught her by the shoulders and pressed her into a chair. "Sit down and catch your breath, child. You train that man to expect you to jump every time he snaps his fingers and you'll regret it 'til Gabriel sounds the trumpet."

It was all Jolie could do not to bolt back to her feet, but she remained sitting and she listened. Even if her past was a bit on the questionable side, she had already decided she didn't want Daniel ordering her around like a coolie. She'd just forgotten for a moment, that was all. "You weren't at the trial, or the hanging," she said.

Verena put sandwiches and preserved pears on the table, then checked the coffee, which was perking along nicely. The kitchen was sweltering, though, and both women were glistening with perspiration. "I'm like Dan—I don't put much stock in such doings. Standing around gawking, well, that's for busybodies. I stayed home and put up my fruit and vegetables, just like always, and tried to keep this place reasonably tidy."

Daniel's garden was overburdened with vegetables, but they would soon be turning, and Jolie was determined to get as many of them in jars as she could. But canning was not a priority at the moment. "I'm surprised that you're being so friendly," she said.

"You've given me no cause not to be," Verena replied, as the sounds of horses and jingling harnesses and shouting men rolled in from outside. "Besides, Daniel needs a wife. He's been alone too long, grieving for that sweet Ilse of his and those lost babies."

Jolie lowered her eyes for a moment and bit her lower lip. Soon, Daniel would come through the doorway, covered in dirt and stinking of sweat, and for all of that she wondered how she'd face him without letting her great need of him show. "He must have loved her a lot," she said, unnecessarily, for she had not forgotten for a moment the way Daniel had looked standing beside those graves out by the maple tree.

"Too much," Verena said, quickly removing her apron and then filling cups with fresh coffee for herself and Jolie. "Let's go out onto the veranda and see if we can catch a breath," she whispered.

Jolie was glad of any excuse not to have to confront Daniel, and she led the way eagerly.

"I see you've been sewing," Verena said, when she and Jolie were outside, sitting in the rocking chairs that faced the front yard, with its picket fence and bushes brimming with pink tea roses.

Guessing that Verena must have glanced into the dining room as they passed, Jolie smiled and then wrinkled her nose. *"Brown sateen,"* she confided, with distaste. In the next instant, her face pulsed with color because she realized her neighbor was wearing the same fabric, only in black.

Verena chuckled and gracefully allowed the gaffe to pass. "If you trim that dress with a little ecru lace and maybe some ribbon, it could be quite pretty."

"I don't think Daniel *wants* me to look pretty," she said miserably, gazing out at the endless ocean of wheat that surrounded the house. "Last night he made me sleep in the spare room, and this morning Deuter told me he'd visited a—a bad woman."

When Jolie could bring herself to look in Verena's direction, she saw that the woman was watching her with an unreadable expression in her eyes. "You're a very discerning young woman, if you've fallen in love with Dan Beckham. God never made another man quite like him, and probably won't again."

"He's bone-stubborn!" Jolie pointed out, balancing her cup on one knee and hugging herself with her free arm.

"He's loyal," Verena argued good-naturedly.

"He hates me!"

"I don't think he would have married you if that were the case, my dear. I know Dan as well as if he were my own son, and I'm aware that he isn't the kind to stand back and let a woman be hanged on the whim of some small-town yay-hoo, but he didn't have to *marry* you to save your hide. He could have halted those proceedings anyway, and taken you straight to Spokane, to let the federal marshal deal with you."

Something wild and sweet spun through Jolie's heart, like a tiny hurricane, but it was gone in an instant. There was still Pilar. "He has a woman. He doesn't need me."

"He does," Verena argued smoothly, "though I'll grant you that he might not have realized it just yet. But don't misjudge him because he's so big, Jolie— that's a mistake a lot of people make. Daniel is sharp as the edge of a brand-new razor, and somewhere inside he knows you can give him what he wants so much."

Jolie took a steadying sip of her coffee. "Which is?"

"Babies," Verena said with a smile. "Plenty of sons to carry on after him, and daughters to fuss over and buy geegaws for."

It was clear to Jolie that Verena had a completely different picture of Daniel than she did. And if Jolie were to predict anything, it was that Daniel would wait until she'd worked off the five hundred dollars he'd paid for her freedom, then take her to Spokane and quietly divorce her. What an irony it was that that would be even more damning in the eyes of society than a conviction for robbery and murder.

Verena set her coffee cup on the railing of the porch and touched Jolie's arm lightly. "Give him time," she said. "Daniel is a farmer, and he understands things that grow slowly, from tiny seeds." With that, she rose and announced that she'd stayed long enough, and would say her farewells to Daniel and be off. She took her cup and went inside.

Jolie sat biting her lip for a long time, then poured what remained of her coffee into a bed of pink petunias and returned to her sewing. When she was sure Daniel had gone back to his work, she tidied up the kitchen and put what remained of the ham on the stove to boil, along with a panful of white beans. She'd figured out that her husband liked his biggest meal in the morning, and every subsequent repast noticeably lighter.

By the time the men finished for the day, Jolie was in the spare room, doing the finishing work on the dress. She'd found both lace and ribbon in a trunk, and the trim had saved the garment from total austerity, just as Verena had said it would.

She held her breath when she heard footsteps on the stairs—Deuter had a room in the barn and no reason to come up to the second floor, so that meant it was Daniel.

The knob turned and the door opened. Sure enough, Jolie's husband stood in the chasm, covered with road dust from his head to his feet. Efforts to wash his hands and face had only turned the stuff to streaky mud.

"Aren't you going to eat?" he asked, somewhat impatiently.

Jolie raised one hand to her mouth to stifle a giggle, then decided to give Daniel some of his own and assumed a stern look. "You are filthy, Mr. Beckham. I'll thank you not to trail through this house in such a state."

Amazingly, Daniel retreated without another word, and Jolie was exultant at the knowledge that, for once, she'd known just how to handle him.

She was not so certain of that an hour later, however, when she wandered into the kitchen, intend-

65

ing to have a bowl of bean soup and wash up whatever dishes Daniel and Deuter might have left. There was Daniel, right in the middle of the kitchen floor, taking a bath in a big metal tub.

Jolie froze, unable to turn around and flee, or even to look away. She'd seen bare masculine chests before, of course, having traveled west with her father on a wagon train and worked as a housemaid in a house containing two men, but the sight had never affected her quite the way it did that night. She felt as though someone had jerked the floor out from beneath her feet and left her tripping in empty space.

Daniel, on the other hand, seemed completely unruffled. He settled against the back of the big tub and sighed. "Mind you don't slip," he said, closing his eyes. "There's a little water on the floor."

The announcement gave Jolie the impetus she so desperately needed. She wrenched her eyes from the whorls of wet hair curling on Daniel's massive chest and marched into the pantry to get the mop.

"You might have warned me that you were planning to take a bath," she said, blushing and being very careful not to look at Daniel again as she mopped around the tub.

"It's Saturday," Daniel replied, as though that explained everything. "How about bringing some more hot water from the stove?"

Jolie sighed fretfully and set the mop in the corner, then lugged a brimming kettle across the room and dumped its contents straight into the water, never once looking at her target.

Daniel gave a shout of angry protest and shot upright in a roaring splash. "Damn it, woman," he bellowed, "I didn't ask you to pour it on my middle and *scald* me like a hen in need of plucking!"

Dropping the kettle, Jolie fled through the back door and into the night. Whenever her pa had yelled like that, he'd always ended up hitting her until she had bruises. She hid in the well house, never realizing that she was crying until she caught her skirt on that infernal board that was always sticking up. Her shoulders were quivering with silent sobs by the time she managed to work the calico free without tearing it.

After a while, she heard Daniel calling her. Her fear had ebbed away to stubbornness, and she didn't answer. She just sat in the corner of the well house, on top of a crock filled with water glass and eggs, and thought of how she'd like her life to be different.

She imagined herself married to a rich, handsome, *gentle* man who loved her, who doted on her every wish. She pictured silk dresses, glowing jewelry, fine coaches, and houses with pillars in front, like the drawings of Greek buildings she'd seen in books. She would have a dozen children, and all of them would wear velvet and speak to her only in French . . .

"Jolie!" Daniel was nearby, and it was plain that he was running out of patience.

She gasped when he wrenched open the well house door, letting in a flood of moonlight that seemed to swirl up around her like silvery water. "Don't," she choked, trying in vain to cover both her head and her upper body with her hands. "Please . . . don't strike me."

Daniel made a sound low in his throat, and his big hands closed on her waist, but he only pulled Jolie close against him and held her there, his chin resting on the crown of her head. "Nobody's going to lay a hand on you, Jolie," he vowed gruffly. "Not ever again."

Jolie sagged against him, this maddening, confusing

man, her fingers clenching the fabric at the back of his shirt. She could no longer keep up the front of proud defiance she'd been struggling to maintain, and pressed her forehead into Daniel's chest and gave a wail of mingled grief and despair.

He lifted her easily into his arms and carried her out of her hiding place and along the path leading to the house.

"I didn't kill anybody," Jolie sobbed wretchedly, desperate for one person, in all the vast scheme of things, to believe her. "Oh, Daniel, I swear I didn't sh-shoot that poor old man, and I didn't know Rowdy and Blake were going to rob the bank!"

"Hush, now," Daniel said, as they mounted the steps and crossed the threshold into the kitchen. There, he blew out the flame in the lamp on the table and found his way deftly in the dark, still holding Jolie in his arms.

Her cries turned to sniffles when she realized he was taking her into his own room, instead of the one he'd consigned her to so brusquely the night before. He laid her gently on the bed, in a pool of moon glow, and stood looking down at her for what seemed like an eternity.

Then, slowly, with surprisingly agile fingers for a man so large, he began unbuttoning her dress.

5

For Jolie, the experience of being undressed by Daniel was achingly sensuous. It was not in her nature to submit, and yet she could find no shred of resistance within herself. Slowly, with unbelievably light fingers, he took away her shoes, unrolled the long stockings that reached up under her drawers to midthigh.

Jolie gave a little whimper and rested the knuckle of her index finger against her mouth.

The calico dress came off next, and Jolie saw a muscle tighten and then relax in Daniel's jaw as he gazed upon her. And she felt rapturously beautiful, for once in her life, instead of too tall and too awkward and too poor. Later, perhaps, she would think of these moments and be afraid, but at the time she could only marvel at the unexpected sweetness of just being a woman.

She tilted her head back as Daniel untied the ribbons that held her camisole closed and laid the thin cloth aside. He drew in his breath at the sight of her bare breasts, their points going hard and reaching, and Jolie felt as though her blood had turned to warm oil. She wanted to melt with the heat, and yet there was a driving urgency inside her too, a need she only partially understood.

"Daniel," she whispered, wanting him to explain, to tutor her, not with his voice, but with his body.

He knelt on the floor beside the bed, taking one of Jolie's breasts into his hand as though it were a creation of wonder, chafing the ready nipple with his calloused thumb. When he bent and touched the straining morsel with his tongue, such a jolt of passion arched through Jolie that she cried out and raised herself high on her shoulders and heels.

Daniel both soothed and inflamed her, continuing to suck, making large, slow circles on her belly with his palm. When he moved to attend the other breast, Jolie began to toss her head from side to side on the pillow in the utter joy of surrender. Never, in her wildest imaginings, had she ever dreamed that the things a man did to a woman could feel so good.

Her husband's hand ranged farther, not just over her belly now, but touching the breast he'd enjoyed so thoroughly, teasing the nipple, sloping around to flatten against the small of her back and then sliding down inside her drawers to grasp her buttocks.

Presently, he began stroking the insides of her thighs, letting her legs know that he would have them parted. Jolie's hips lunged upward in some inexplicable eagerness, but Daniel simply cupped his hand over the moist, silken mound of her femininity, still shrouded in muslin, and pressed her back to the mattress.

"Not yet," he whispered, sounding as breathless as

if he'd just come up from deep water. "God in heaven, not yet."

He touched her quivering stomach, first tentatively, with his lips, then with the tip of his tongue. Jolie grabbed frantically at his shirt, in a hopeless effort to drag him on top of her, but he only caught her hands together at the wrists and imprisoned them high above her head.

By then, Jolie was wild to have him, even though she didn't know exactly what he would do to her. Her flesh was damp with perspiration, and tendrils of hair clung to her cheeks and forehead and neck. And Daniel hooked his thumb under the waistband of her drawers, dragging them down and away.

Still holding her hands above her head, he began to caress Jolie, eliciting a series of small, despairing whimpers from her throat. She was a creature caught, she would not escape, and it had never occurred to her that being conquered could be so glorious.

Daniel nuzzled through the musky down guarding her most vulnerable place, and Jolie was unprepared for the sweet, tremulous shock of that. When he took her boldly, brazenly into his mouth, she gave a strangled shout of pleasure and writhed on the bed, brazen as a wild mare with her stallion.

"I thought so," she heard Daniel say, through a daze of sensation and need, and there was no rancor in his voice, only resignation and a touch of sadness.

Clasping the underside of her right knee in one hand, he raised her leg high so that his access was complete. Jolie dragged a pillow over her face to muffle the keening cries of ecstasy Daniel was driving from her with his lips and his tongue.

The terrible urgency inside her kept building and

building. The muscles in her stomach and bottom were sore from clenching and unclenching in response to the flood of sensations that were washing over her, drowning her.

And then something spun hard and hot in the core of her womanhood, like a new moon breaking free of the sun, and she gave repeated gasps of incredulous exaltation as the sparks reached into every part of her body and soul.

When Daniel was through with Jolie, he lowered her, trembling, back to the hard sanctity of the mattress, comforting her with long, gentle strokes to her thighs and belly. Gradually bringing her back inside herself.

When her breathing had slowed almost to its normal pace, he rose, pulled his shirt free of his trousers, unbuttoned it, hung it over the bedpost. His belt buckle made a quiet clinking sound as he unfastened it, and Jolie closed her eyes, afraid that if she looked too closely, she would lose her courage.

The warmth and heat and granitelike hardness of his frame made her smile, though, as he stretched out above her, careful not to let his weight crush her. She had had her pleasures, and now Daniel would have his. She resolved to bear the pain in silence, if for no other reason than to repay him for the wonderful responses he'd coaxed, then demanded, from her.

His voice was a low, hoarse rumble. "You've done this before, so you know . . ."

Jolie tilted her head far back, pretending Daniel hadn't said that, offering no answer but the supple eagerness of her young body. He trailed kisses along the length of her throat, and she felt his immense masculinity against her thigh.

Fear fluttered in the pit of her stomach, but she

didn't give in to it. After seeing a man die on the sidewalk outside the bank in Prosperity and being arrested, tried, and almost hanged for that same man's murder, it took more than the prospect of losing her virginity to scare Jolie.

Daniel muttered something Jolie could make no sense of and then, in one blindingly powerful thrust, he entered her.

The pain was beyond comprehension, and yet there was pleasure mingled in with it. Even as a sob of shock and fear escaped Jolie, she clutched at Daniel's bare back with both hands lest he leave her.

"My God," he whispered brokenly. "I thought . . ."

She entangled her fingers in his hair, which was just the color of the wheat at midday, and pressed his mouth to hers to silence him. His tongue swept her depths, as fiery an invader as his manhood, and Jolie was stunned to find her exhausted body beginning to buckle in a new, even wilder release than the one she'd had before. Daniel held her tightly while she caught fire in his arms, then he began slowly gliding in and out of her.

The fever of it simmered under her skin and wrung ragged cries from her throat as she strived to wrest from Daniel that intangible thing she'd never guessed she needed. He continued to take her in long, even strokes, murmuring gentle words as he nibbled at her throat and collarbone.

A red-hot shiver went through Jolie, and then, suddenly, with the fierce cry of a warrior's woman, she convulsed wildly in Daniel's arms . . . once, twice, three times. Finally, she was still.

Through the haze of satisfaction that surrounded her, however, Jolie began to realize that Daniel was working toward some violent surcease of his own.

Instinctively, she laid her hands on his muscle-corded, sweat-dampened back and urged him on with soft, meaningless words.

He finally lunged deep and stiffened, and with a low groan, gave up what Jolie's body had wrought from his. When he was finished, he fell to the mattress beside her, and the bedsprings creaked in protest. The fingers of his right hand delved deeply, gently into her hair, and his thumb traced the underside of her jawbone.

After a long, long time, his breathing slowed almost to a normal meter. "You didn't tell me you'd never been with a man," he said, in hoarse accusation.

Jolie's head was resting on Daniel's shoulder, and she sighed, still floating. "Yes, I did, Mr. Beckham," she argued, smiling. "You just didn't believe me."

Daniel was silent for several long, blissful minutes, but then he had to stir up the water again. Even without looking, Jolie knew he was frowning. "The way you carried on—nobody would have guessed you didn't know what you were doing."

Insulted, Jolie tried to sit up, but Daniel held her close against him, one arm curved around her hips. And though she'd never have admitted it, she loved the feeling of that.

"Most women don't have much use for lovemaking, Jolie," he said patiently. "It's something they do to get children, and because their men demand it of them."

Jolie blushed in the darkness. Trust her to get even *that* wrong, she thought miserably. "I'm sorry," she said.

"Don't be," Daniel replied, kissing her forehead.

Too sated and exhausted to try to follow the new twist the conversation had taken, Jolie settled herself against Daniel and went to sleep.

She awakened before dawn, when he stirred and then rose from the bed, but she pretended to be asleep, listening as her husband moved easily around the darkened room. After he'd dressed, the bedsprings protested as he sat down to pull on his boots, and Jolie bit her lip, thinking what a ruckus the two of them must have made the night before.

Hopefully, Deuter hadn't heard the commotion from the barn; if he had, he would be certain to comment, and Jolie didn't think she could bear that.

Daniel reached out and touched her blanket-covered thigh very lightly, and then he left the room. Only when he'd gone did Jolie realize it was Sunday. Today, she would have to wear the brown dress and sit through a sermon.

With a deep sigh, Jolie climbed out of bed and put on the white nightgown she'd made. Before church, there was breakfast to cook, and before that, she needed to wash.

Light was streaming into the kitchen by the time Jolie reached it, and she blew out the lamp Daniel had left burning in the middle of the table. After building up the fire and taking tepid water from the stove reservoir, Jolie hurried upstairs to groom herself and don yesterday's calico dress.

When she returned to the kitchen, Daniel was standing at the stove pouring coffee he'd evidently put on to brew himself, soon after he got up. There was no sign of Deuter.

Jolie was instantly possessed with shyness, even though she knew she would never have a more intimate experience with any human being than she'd had with this man.

"Good morning, Mr. Beckham," she said.

Daniel didn't look at her but instead went to stand

before the sink, gazing grimly out the window. Jolie knew he was staring at Ilse's grave, and she had a pretty good idea what he was thinking. His regret was apparent in the set of his broad, powerful shoulders. "Good morning," he replied, at length and somewhat grudgingly.

"I'll have breakfast ready in a few minutes," she said, snatching an apron—it had probably been Ilse's first, like the man—and tied it around her waist.

"Keep it simple," Daniel instructed, without turning around. "It's Sunday."

Jolie rolled her eyes. This would surely prove to be a long, tedious day. "I imagine the cows will still have to be milked and fed and the eggs will need gathering," she pointed out crisply.

"Deuter and I will leave for Spokane first thing in the morning," Daniel said, in neutral tones, when Jolie came in minutes later from the well house.

She set the slab of bacon and jar of cream down on the worktable near the stove. The thought of Daniel being away for any length of time filled her with gloom but, of course, she wasn't fool enough to let him know that. Nor would she allow him to see how disappointed she was that their lovemaking hadn't changed things between them.

"I'll expect you to look after the place while I'm gone," Daniel announced, when Jolie offered no response to his statement.

Jolie slammed a skillet down hard on the stove top, spooned in some lard, and cracked three eggs into it. "It isn't as if I'm planning to burn off the wheat fields or pour poison down the well, Mr. Beckham," she said haughtily. "I'm quite capable of looking after this farm for a few days." This last was pure speculation, but Jolie had survived so many crises in her life that she was undaunted by the challenge.

"If you have any trouble, ride over to the next place—it's about two miles to the west—and fetch Joe Culley."

At last, Jolie turned to meet her husband's gaze. He was sitting at the table, his hands curved around his coffee cup, and a heated tremor went through her as she remembered the exquisite pleasure those fingers had given her. "Verena Dailey is much closer," she reasoned, hiking her chin up a degree in hopes that Daniel wouldn't guess what she was feeling.

"Verena is a woman," Daniel reasoned, with a frown. In four words, he had dispensed with a generous ally who considered herself his friend.

Jolie turned the bacon, which was sizzling in a heavy black pan, and then grudgingly carried the coffeepot to the table and refilled Daniel's cup. "Are we just going to pretend that you didn't make love to me last night?" she demanded.

His neck glowed a dull red. "That's no subject for the kitchen, woman," he said sternly. "It's talk for the bedroom."

Jolie was so amazed that she forgot to pour coffee for herself, even though she was yearning for a cup. "I know I owe you my life," she marveled, setting the pot back on the stove and resting her hands on her hips, "and you're my legal husband, which gives you certain rights. But I'll be damned, Dan Beckham, *damned,* if I'll let you decide what I can say and where I can say it!"

Daniel's gaze did not waver, nor did the arrogance in his manner. "The bacon is burning," he said.

With a soft, strangled sound of rage and frustration,

Jolie whirled to remove the food from the heat and serve it up.

Her husband ate in silence, then ran his eyes over the calico dress. "I trust you've got something suitable to wear to church?"

Jolie waited until Daniel had turned his back and then made a face. When he went upstairs to change into Sunday clothes, she cleaned the kitchen, fed and watered the chickens, gathered the eggs. All during that time, she planned small rebellions, but when Daniel brought the team and wagon to the door, she was wearing the brown sateen dress, and her hair had been twisted into a sedate knot at her nape.

Daniel looked surprisingly dapper in his black suit and starched white shirt with its stiff celluloid collar. Instead of his normal sweat-stained leather hat, he wore a dark one of more modish lines.

Church was every bit the ordeal Jolie expected it to be, though for different reasons. Mr. Pribbenow, the undertaker, and Judge Chilver were in attendance, as was just about everyone else who had come to see Jolie's near-hanging. Somehow, that fact didn't mesh with the pretty words flowing from the pulpit.

It was some comfort that the preacher didn't run on endlessly, however, and Verena was there, too, greeting Jolie with a smile and some cheery words when the sermon was over and the congregation had gathered in the churchyard.

"I'll be frying my Southern chicken for Sunday dinner," Verena told Daniel, making sure her voice carried. "And I'd be pleased if you and Mrs. Beckham would come and share the meal, Dan. I'll be setting it out at one-thirty."

Daniel smiled, probably at the prospect of Verena's

chicken, and touched the brim of his hat. "Thank you kindly," he responded. "We'll be there." Having made that pronouncement, he handed Jolie up into the wagon box and climbed in to take the reins.

Jolie smoothed her skirts, painfully aware of the women in their severe Sunday clothes, looking pious, some with a hand raised to whisper behind. The future seemed bleak indeed when she thought of having to face these sanctimonious crows every week for the rest of her life, not to mention encountering them in shops and on the street.

Her shoulders sagged slightly as she and Daniel drove away from the church, under a bright August sun.

"I'll never be anything but an outlaw to them," she murmured, more to herself than to Daniel. If her husband heard her over the clomping of the horses' hooves, the jingle of the harness fittings, and the incessant whine of the wagon's springs, he kept any comment he might have made to himself.

No sooner had they reached the house when Daniel climbed down from the wagon and strode off toward Ilse's grave, his hat held respectfully in one hand. Jolie felt a twinge of jealous despair, but she quickly repressed that and went into the kitchen.

There was still plenty of coffee left from breakfast and, because it was so strong, Jolie added cream and a generous spoonful of sugar to her cup before drinking. It was all she could do, the whole time, not to go to the window and find Daniel with her eyes.

His grief was a private thing, and she wouldn't intrude.

Promptly at one-thirty, Daniel and Jolie arrived at Verena's small white farmhouse, which was the next place down the road. Here, lilacs and tea roses rioted in the yard, and lace curtains fluttered merrily at open windows.

Verena came smiling onto the porch. Even from the gate, Jolie could smell the tantalizing aroma of fried chicken, and her empty stomach gave an unladylike rumble.

They ate in Verena's dining room, with its pleasant clutter of potted plants, figurines, framed daguerreotypes, and books. A large conch shell stood on the crowded mantelpiece, giving silent testimony to the fact that Verena had been to the sea.

It was an experience Jolie envied.

"Things have changed between you and Daniel," Verena announced, her eyes sparkling, when Mr. Beckham had gone out to the barn for a look at her milk cow's lame foot.

Color washed beneath the skin of Jolie's face, and she lowered her head before nodding. "It was—I wouldn't have expected such—well, it wasn't like you'd look for it to be, with a man like Daniel."

Verena laughed. "I warned you once before not to let his size fool you. Daniel has been on his own since he was seventeen, and he's worked on ships and ranches, not just that wheat farm." She fluttered one hand briefly in the direction of Daniel's land. "And he's read his share of books, too. Yes, indeed, there's more to Dan Beckham than meets the eye, and I think you'll be finding that out in the months to come."

Jolie swallowed hard. "He wasn't pleased with me," she confided miserably. "He said I—I carried on."

Verena's eyes were still twinkling. "I imagine he was a mite surprised at that. Give him time, Jolie—he'll come to like having that kind of response."

The two women washed the dishes together, and

Verena smiled as she saw Daniel approaching the house from the barn. "He'll be wanting to go straight home now, I reckon," she said, with a note of mischievous mystery in her voice.

Sure enough, when Daniel came in, he spared a few words to say there was nothing wrong with Verena's cow that he could see, then suggested that he and Jolie had best be getting back to their own place. Excitement brushed Jolie's spirit like a passing wraith, though she brushed the feeling off immediately.

"What happened to Verena's husband?" she asked, when she and Daniel were rattling along the dry, dusty road toward home.

Daniel took so long in answering that Jolie was beginning to wonder if she'd have to repeat the question. "He died out in the field one day. It was probably his heart."

Jolie was filled with sympathy for the friendly, good-humored woman who was, so far, her only female friend in the whole community. "How does she manage?"

"I till and plant and harvest for her," Daniel answered, gazing straight ahead at the road.

A peculiar constriction tightened Jolie's throat momentarily. "That's kind of you."

Daniel gave the reins a seemingly unnecessary snap. "Out here, we stick together."

Jolie thought of the women of Prosperity, who hated her without having the first idea what kind of person she really was, but she offered no argument. "Verena says you've worked on ships," she ventured. "Have you been to China?"

He regarded her somberly for a long moment, then surprised her by laughing. It did something to her, way down deep, to see Daniel's face light up like that, even though she was stung that he'd found her question so amusing. "No," he said. "Just around the Horn from Charleston, and up to San Francisco and Seattle."

This was a Daniel Jolie didn't know, couldn't begin to comprehend. "What an adventure that must have been!"

The laughter had softened the Sabbath sternness of his face, and he smiled at Jolie with something that resembled fondness. "I never went a day without being seasick, or a night without praying to the good Lord for the sight of land. But I earned my pay and kept my misgivings to myself."

It was as though a wonderful stranger had suddenly materialized in Daniel's place, and Jolie felt something elemental stretch between herself and this man and make a connection. "You must have met some very interesting people," she said, hoping to maintain the ease between them.

"A few," he allowed. His voice was a little gruff, and his sky blue eyes took in the breeze-tossed tendrils of golden hair around her face, moving on to her lips and then to the base of her throat.

A pulse was hammering there. Jolie knotted her hands together in her lap and turned on the seat, so that she was looking straight down the road. To save her soul, she couldn't think of a single sensible thing to say.

"I'd like you to wait for me in our room," Daniel said, after he brought the wagon to a stop in front of the barn and was lifting her down. "Put on that white gown you were wearing last night."

Jolie's cheeks flared with heat, but she nodded her head and started toward the house.

Fifteen minutes later, when Daniel joined her in the master bedroom, she'd hung the brown sateen in the wardrobe and put on the cotton gown. She was brushing her hair in front of the mirror, powerfully glad she'd finally been able to set it free from its circumspect knot. A very light breeze lifted the curtains, making them resemble snowy lace ghosts.

In the looking glass, she saw Daniel's reflection. He was watching her as though he'd never seen a woman groom herself before, his hands poised to undo the black string tie at his throat. Jolie saw him swallow and suppressed a smile.

Daniel wanted her, no matter what opinion he might secretly hold of her, and to Jolie it was worth even the pain to feel the delights of his lovemaking again.

Finally, he managed to break the spell that had possessed him and began removing his tie. After that, he took off his coat and vest, and he was unclasping his cuff links when Jolie went to sit on the side of the bed, her hands calmly folded in her lap.

"I suppose I'll probably carry on again," she said ruefully and again that blinding grin broke over Daniel's face. He pulled her back to her feet and took her into his arms, and when he touched his lips to hers, Jolie felt as though she'd just tossed back a quart of homemade whiskey.

When he'd kissed her so thoroughly that Jolie was no longer sure just where the floor and ceiling were, he laid his hands over her cotton-covered breasts, making the nipples press urgently into his palms. It was a relief when he lowered her to the bed, because Jolie was too weak to stand.

She watched from beneath lowered lashes as Daniel stripped away the rest of his clothes, thinking how magnificent he was. There was a quiet grace about him, unspoiled by the muscular bulk of his body.

I love you, she thought, but she wasn't so far gone as to actually say the incredible words out loud. At least, not then.

Where before Daniel had taken infinite time with Jolie, this time there was an urgency about his movements. He pulled her nightgown off over her head, tossed it aside, and lay between her legs, letting her feel his power.

Jolie's hands rushed from Daniel's shoulders to his back and then to his chest. She splayed her fingers, feeling his masculine nipples harden under her palms. A summer wind, scented with road dust and sunshine and wheat, came through the open window to caress them both.

Daniel moaned, as though the breeze had broken some restraint inside him, and bent his head to lay light kisses along the length of Jolie's collarbone. Then he found her portal with the shaft of his manhood and thrust inside her, deeply and suddenly.

Jolie had expected more pain, but there was only a momentary soreness, followed by a thrill so keen that it made her eyes roll back in her head. Her breathing became shallow and quick.

"I haven't even started to move yet," Daniel reminded her, but Jolie could barely hear him for the hum of her body and soul as they sought that magical harmony her husband had taught her to want. She went wild beneath Daniel, thrashing and flinging herself at him, a primitive sound like the night cry of a she-wolf coming from the very depths of her.

Slowly, steadily, Daniel began to move upon Jolie, and each time he retreated, she begged for his conquering. She was still grappling with the explosive releases racking her body when Daniel gasped and emptied himself into her.

After the lovemaking, Daniel and Jolie slept, and it was after sundown when they awakened. Jolie made a soft crooning sound when Daniel immediately spread her legs and mounted her, and soon the sweet battle had resumed. Not until they were both slick with perspiration and their throats were raspy from crying out was a truce reached.

A long time later, Jolie got up, washed with water Daniel had brought from downstairs, and put on her calico dress. She was putting together a light supper of sandwiches and fruit when her husband joined her, wearing regular clothes and looking as cool and distant as ever.

A casual observer would never have guessed he'd been saying and doing such intimate things only a little while before.

Jolie shrugged to herself as she turned back to preparing the meal. Maybe her luck was finally turning after all. Maybe she was going to have all she had ever really wanted: a home, a husband, and a baby.

6

Jolie's hopes for a child were dashed in the morning when she woke to find blood on her nightgown and the sheets of Daniel's bed. She was instantly mortified, even though good sense told her the process was a natural one, and hurried to strip the mattress and roll the stained gown into the bundle of laundry. She'd put a supply of clean rags away in the spare room, and she went there to wash and put on her riding skirt and the old shirt she'd been wearing the day she married Daniel.

By the time she reached the kitchen, the coffee was already simmering on the back of the stove and her abdomen was tight with cramps. She took another jar of canned sausage from the pantry and cooked that up, along with eggs and potatoes and toast. When Daniel and Deuter came in from doing the morning chores, Daniel looked at her with a thoughtful frown.

"You feeling poorly?" he asked, when Deuter had finished eating and gone out to hitch up the wagon for the trip to Spokane. Jolie hadn't been able to swallow anything except for coffee, though she normally ate a large breakfast.

She averted her eyes, wondering why it was so hard to talk about such a natural woman-thing with a man who had explored her body in the most intimate ways. "I'll be all right tomorrow," she said, clearing the table. "How long will you be in Spokane?"

"Two, three days, probably," Daniel answered, still pondering her. "Ilse used to take a dose of laudanum sometimes, when the curse came." He went into the pantry and brought out a brown bottle.

So he'd guessed, or he'd seen the stain on the sheets when he arose that morning. Jolie was painfully embarrassed, and she knew she could take no relief from the medicine. Laudanum always put her straight to sleep, and she had dresses to sew and a week's wash to do. "I'll be fine," she insisted, a little shortly.

Daniel did not kiss her good-bye, nor did he take her into his arms. He simply said, "Don't forget to send for Joe Culley if something goes wrong. He'll be over to do the milking and take care of the livestock."

Jolie nodded, hoping Daniel couldn't see that she was already missing him, already feeling the old, aching loneliness of the days before she'd become Mrs. Daniel Beckham. "You take care," she said, making her tone as indifferent as possible.

Her husband hesitated for a moment, then turned and strode off to the wagon, where Deuter was waiting.

It was Deuter who smiled and waved a farewell. "I'd be beholden to you if you'd give old Leviticus a saucer of cream now and again," he called.

Again, Jolie nodded. She stood on the back steps,

watching as the team and wagon made a wide turn in the barnyard and then headed toward the front gate. Daniel didn't once look back.

Determinedly, she went inside the house and put the kitchen to rights. Then she laid a fire in the dooryard with dry wood garnered from the shed and lugged the laundry tub outside. While the blaze was gaining momentum, she worked the pump to fill the wash kettle and added soap. She filled another, smaller tub with cold water for rinsing, then went upstairs to fetch the soiled sheets and nightgown.

Only when those had been scrubbed clean and hung on the clothesline to dry did Jolie begin washing the pile of stockings and trousers and shirts that had accumulated behind the changing screen in Daniel's room. Despite the pain in her lower belly, the relentless glare of a summer sun, and the fact that the work was brutally hard, Jolie took a certain satisfaction in doing this wifely task.

When every garment was clean and there wasn't an inch of space left on the clothesline, Jolie went inside and sat down at the table, forcing herself to eat a slice of cheese and some buttered bread. The laudanum was still sitting on the cupboard, silently beckoning, but Jolie ignored it. God knew, she hated pain as much as anybody did, but she didn't subscribe to the theory that every discomfort should be immediately alleviated. Some types of suffering were just a part of being human, and there was a certain integrity in enduring them.

Over the course of that day, Jolie managed to cut out another dress from the fabric Daniel had bought for her, and when the cooling twilight finally came, she went outside to take the wash down and bring it in. In the morning, before it got too hot, she would press everything, and when her husband returned from his travels, he'd find his bureau drawers and his wardrobe full of clean clothes.

She was bringing in the last of the laundry when a buckboard jostled into the yard, carrying a man and a woman. The woman wore a bonnet, so Jolie couldn't tell if she was old or young or in-between. The man was about Daniel's age, but slender and wiry, with straight brown hair and a sun-weathered face.

This, Jolie thought, would be Joe Culley, come to do the chores. She braced herself inwardly, even as she forced a welcoming smile to her face, expecting nothing but censure from the wife of a God-fearing farmer. At least, she *supposed* the Culleys were God-fearing—she hadn't seen them at church. And she didn't remember them from the trial or the hanging.

"I'm Nan Culley," the woman announced eagerly, and Jolie was struck by her bright smile even before she made out the eager brown eyes and white, heavily freckled skin.

Joe went off toward the barn, sparing just a nod for Jolie.

In the next instant, she remembered her manners. "Won't you come in?"

"I'd dearly love to take off this bonnet," Nan replied, following Jolie into the house and sitting down at the table with a lack of hesitation that said she'd often been a guest here. With a sigh, she untied her bonnet strings and pulled it off, revealing a magnificent head of cinnamon-colored hair.

Jolie had no refreshment to offer but cold water, because it was still too hot for coffee. She filled two glasses from the bucket beside the sink and joined her visitor, wincing a little as she sat because of her cramps.

"You know who I am, don't you?" she asked, after gnawing at her lower lip for a moment. She was used to having people look down their noses at her, but she hadn't learned to like it.

"Certainly," chimed Nan, after relishing a sip of water from the glass Jolie had brought her. "You're Mrs. Daniel Beckham—the most interesting person to set foot in this county in five years. Did they really mean to hang you?"

Jolie swallowed, though she hadn't yet touched her water. "Yes," she said, at length. "I do believe they would have."

"Isn't it romantic that Daniel came along when he did and rescued you? Why, it reminds me of Robin Hood and Maid Marion . . ."

Doubting that anyone who had ever felt the weight of a rope around their neck would find the experience romantic, Jolie allowed the remark to pass. "I expected you to be, well, like the women in town."

"Mercy," Nan huffed, waving her bonnet in front of her face for a fan. "It's hot today." Her eyes smiled at Jolie. "Verena told me you were in need of a few friends, and I'm here to volunteer."

"But what about—aren't you worried that I might be a—a bad element?"

Nan dismissed the thought with another flick of her bonnet. "Dan would never have married you if you weren't a nice person."

Jolie closed her eyes for a moment, feeling her throat tighten, fearing she might cry. When she'd recovered her composure, she gave Nan a faltering smile. "Did you know Ilse?"

"My yes," her neighbor answered, and a touch of sadness showed in her vibrant eyes. "A dear thing she was, tiny and pretty as one of those porcelain dolls they send over from France. Everybody liked her, and when she died, Joe and I thought Daniel would pass on too, from the grief of it." She reached out to pat Jolie's hand. "It's good that you're here. Daniel needs you."

But he'd *loved* Ilse. Jolie felt an overwhelming frustration with her tall, sturdy body and her even but otherwise unremarkable features. In those moments, she would have given ten years of whatever life span had been allotted to her just to be small and delicate and pretty.

Needing to change the subject, Jolie showed Nan her sewing and the yard goods waiting to be stitched up into everyday dresses. Nan promised the loan of a new pattern book, and Joe, having finished the chores, came to the door to collect his wife.

Jolie thanked him and watched with regret as the Culley wagon disappeared around the house. By that time, the sun was almost down, and it was time to light lamps and think about supper.

She made herself a sandwich, using a plump tomato from the garden, and then built up the fire and pumped enough hot water to fill the stove reservoir and several large kettles. She'd put in a productive day, and a soothing bath would be her reward.

By the time Jolie brought in the larger tub from the barn—the one Daniel used for his baths—she was exhausted. And when she sank into the hot water, there in the middle of the kitchen, she immediately closed her eyes. She'd just rest for a moment, before scrubbing herself and going upstairs to bed . . .

Something cold was dripping onto her stomach and when Jolie opened her eyes, a scream swelled in her throat. Blake Kingston was standing over her, wringing out a wet bandanna and grinning as though he'd done something clever.

"Hello, Jolie-girl," he drawled, dragging a chair over so he could sit astraddle of it, his arms resting across the high, carved back.

Jolie's shock subsided in a backwash of cold fury. "What are you doing here?" she gasped, snatching up a nearby towel and using it to cover herself as best she could.

Blake raised one thin shoulder in a shrug. Some women considered him handsome, with his boyish face and wavy brown hair—Jolie had, once. But now she saw him more clearly: He was a murdering thief who would use innocent bystanders to accomplish his purposes and then leave them to die for his crimes. "Me and Rowdy, we figure to bide awhile. Nobody'll think to look for us this close to Prosperity."

"I want you out of here!" Jolie spat, rising out of the water, careful to keep the towel in place.

Blake arched an eyebrow and cocked his thumbs in the pockets of his dusty gray vest. In his cheap trousers and ruffled shirt, he looked like a gambler down on his luck. "This is Blake you're talking to," he said. "Not some dumb, hulking farmer. Tell me—how long will the big man be away?"

Jolie wet her lips with a quick, nervous motion of her tongue. "He's not away. He's just over at the neighbor woman's, seeing to her sick cow, and he'll be home any minute."

The desperate prevarication brought only contemptuous laughter from Blake. He shook his finger. "That's a lie, little girl. Rowdy and me, we saw him

92

headed north, bright and early this morning, toward Spokane."

Some of Jolie's anger was displaced by fear. She took a step backward, and Blake made a sudden move, without leaving his chair, and laughed when she flinched. In another few moments, that sly-eyed Rowdy—she'd never liked him—was bound to join his friend in the house. And Jolie knew the man didn't have the same disinterest in women that Blake did.

She lifted her chin, holding the skimpy towel with dignity. "They nearly hanged me because of you," she said coldly. "I'd be dead now, if Daniel Beckham hadn't seen fit to marry me."

Blake spread his hands in a magnanimous gesture. "He's obviously a smart man, for a sodbuster. After all, he's built up this place, just about single-handed from what Rowdy and me have been able to find out, and then he up and took you for a wife. Shows he knows good breeding stock when he sees it."

If the circumstances had been different, Jolie would have stormed across the room and slapped Blake back on his heels. As it was, she stayed near the door leading to the downstairs hallway. What hurt her even more deeply than Blake's remark was the distinct possibility that it was true. Daniel had lost one wife in childbirth, and he wanted sons and daughters. When he'd looked Jolie over that day when she was standing in the back of that wagon with a noose around her neck, he'd probably been thinking she looked big enough and healthy enough to deliver babies with ease. Like a trusty brood mare.

Blood rushed into Jolie's face. "Get out," she said. "Damn you, get out and don't ever come back here!"

Blake's look of chagrin was sheer, smug mockery, and he made no move to obey Jolie's command.

"You've gone and fallen in love with the farmer, haven't you? That's real interesting—and convenient, too."

"What do you mean, it's convenient?" Jolie asked, failing to see the trap that yawned before her until it was too late. By not denying her love for Daniel, she'd just admitted that she cared.

Her unwanted visitor looked around the dimly lighted kitchen with appreciation. "I mean, this is a pretty nice nest you've tumbled into. And since you're Beckham's wife, well, if anything happened to him, this whole outfit would probably be yours." He paused to smile fondly at Jolie, then drawled, "Did I mention, darlin', that you're the only woman I ever wanted to marry?"

Chips of ice flowed in Jolie's bloodstream, and she trembled. "Nothing's going to happen to Daniel!" she spat, and though she knew the words revealed her fears, she hadn't been able to hold them back.

Now, at last, Blake stood, pushing the chair aside. Jolie felt the door frame digging into her spine, so anxious was she to escape.

"I reckon that's what the banker's wife thought, too, when she sent him off to count money that morning a month or so back." He smiled again and then turned and opened the outside door. "Good night, darlin'. I'll be looking forward to a nice breakfast in the morning."

The moment he was outside, Jolie rushed across the room and braced a chair under the knob, though even while she was taking this measure she knew nothing so simple would protect her from the two outlaws.

She blew out the lamp, still holding tightly to her towel, and crept to the window. She could see the shadows of two men and two horses, out by the barn, and hear Blake and Rowdy laughing together. From there, Jolie ran to Daniel's small study and pulled the hunting rifle down from its pegs above the mantelpiece.

A hasty search of the desk drawers produced bullets, and Jolie shoved them into the chamber. She couldn't thank her pa for much, but he had taught her to shoot straight and true.

She carried the rifle upstairs with her, crawled into bed, and slept fitfully, awakening at every creak and thump. Her sleeping gown clung to her skin, the night air was so hot, but she didn't dare open a window for fear Rowdy or Blake might climb the trellis outside and catch her unprepared.

The sun was up when Jolie woke, and she sat bolt upright, her heart throbbing in her throat, when she heard the sound of an arriving team and wagon. Joe, she thought, flinging herself to the window and grasping the sill with shaking hands. He was approaching the barn, where the outlaws had most likely spent the night.

Jolie was struggling with the window latch, meaning to scream out a warning, when the neighbor disappeared into the large weathered structure where the hay was stored. She waited, her breath turned hot and solid in her lungs, but no shot rang out. All she heard, in fact, was the glass-thinned sound of a man whistling while he worked.

Hastily, Jolie washed, dressed herself in her own clothes and rushed downstairs. She stopped cold in the kitchen, staring at the table. Although she'd left it clear the night before, it was now littered with egg-stained plates, scraps of ham fat, and spilled coffee.

The chair was still propped beneath the doorknob, mute testimony that Jolie's efforts to protect herself had been vain ones.

Remembering that she'd left the rifle upstairs, Jolie whirled to run back, only to collide with the dirty frame of Rowdy Fleet. He was a small man, not nearly as tall as Jolie, and his skin, like many people's, was horribly pockmarked from a bout with the smallpox. He had little mean eyes the clear color of water, and greasy black hair that hung down around the collar of his long canvas coat.

He smiled and pressed the point of a pistol into the tender skin under Jolie's chin. "The horses is hid," he said, showing stained teeth that stood well apart from each other. "Me and Kingston, we figure on letting that ole boy ride right on outta here, with no holes in his hide, if you don't scream or anything stupid like that."

For a moment, Jolie thought she'd faint, but she managed to tighten the muscles in her knees and hold herself upright. She thought of Nan Culley, home waiting for her husband to return from doing a favor for a friend. "I won't scream," she said.

"Good," Rowdy replied, taking her roughly by the elbow and hurling her back into the kitchen. He might have been small, but he was tough as boiled owl and meaner than the devil's maiden aunt, and Jolie didn't even consider pushing him beyond his limits. "Tidy up this place. I can't abide a mess."

Numbly, Jolie began clearing the table, ladling hot water for dish washing. She dragged the big bathtub to outside the door and dumped its contents into the yard.

That was when Joe came out of the barn, carrying a bucket of fresh milk and smiling. Clearly, he expected to chat a while, and perhaps deliver some message from Nan.

Of course, Jolie didn't dare let him in the house—Rowdy wouldn't hesitate to shoot him. She stepped quickly onto Deuter's sturdy porch and pulled the door closed behind her. Even through the heavy wood panel, she thought she heard Rowdy's strange, labored way of breathing and the click of his forty-five as he cocked it.

"Thank you," she said to Joe, as cheerfully as she could, holding out one hand for the milk.

Joe looked baffled for a moment, then he shrugged one shoulder and handed over the bucket. "Nan allows as how she might come calling this afternoon," he said.

More company was the last thing Jolie wanted, but she was afraid of rousing Joe's suspicion. He surely knew that she and Nan were friendly. "You tell her not to forget to bring that pattern book," she said, praying Mrs. Culley would decide it was too hot a day to travel over roads choked with dust.

He nodded, gave her one questioning look, then got into his buckboard and drove off. As soon as he was gone, Blake came out from behind the barn, leading a pair of horses, and Rowdy pushed past Jolie, nearly overturning the bucket of milk at her feet.

"Will you look at this?" he whined, whipping his hat off and flailing it in the air with one hand. "Here it is, daylight, with the sun shining as bright as Gabriel's trumpet! I told you we should have headed for the hills while it was still dark!"

Jolie just stood on the porch, watching Blake approach. She'd thought she'd known him so well, before the bank robbery and the murder. Once, she'd seen him as a gallant rescuer, even fancied him as a husband, and it shook her to realize just how wrong she could really be about a person.

"We could always spend the day here," Blake suggested smoothly, grinning at Jolie.

"You'd better not," she said. "If Daniel finds you on his land, he'll kill you." That was, please God, if they didn't kill *him* first.

Rowdy swung deftly up into his saddle. "This place gives me the willies," he said, pushing back one side of his mud-encrusted coat so he could reach his holster without hindrance. "I say we get the hell out of here."

Blake smiled at Jolie and gave his hat brim a dapper touch, then mounted his own horse. "We'll be back, sweet Jolie-girl," he said. "You be watching for us."

Jolie was rigid, her hands clenching the sides of her old skirt. "I'll be watching, all right. And if I see you riding in, Blake Kingston, I'll pick you off like a buzzard sitting on a scarecrow's shoulder!"

The two men seemed to find the warning uproariously funny, even though they both knew that Jolie was a fair hand with any kind of firearm. They laughed and whooped and waved their hats in the air before riding off straight through Daniel's wheat, their horses' hooves crushing precious stalks into the dry earth.

Jolie opened all the doors and windows after they were gone, wanting to dissipate the stink of them. She scrubbed the table and all the plates they'd used, then she scoured the floor, too.

By then the day was burning hot, and Jolie had cramps for the second day in a row. Nonetheless, she heated up the flatirons and began pressing yesterday's wash. If she laid herself down or even stopped to think about Rowdy and Blake meeting up with Daniel, she'd probably start crying and screaming.

So she worked. And Nan didn't come to call.

The first stars of evening were popping out when Jolie remembered her promise to Deuter. Having just done the separating, she took a generous portion of cream out and set it near the base of the steps. Then, wearily, she sat down to enjoy the first cool breeze she'd caught since early morning.

Leviticus trotted out of the garden, from between two rows of cabbage, carrying a dead mouse in his teeth. He dropped the ill-fated creature a safe distance from Jolie, lest she try to steal it, no doubt, and cautiously approached the bowl of cream.

"You're a mighty ugly cat," Jolie sighed, as she cupped her chin in one hand and watched the battle-scarred beast lap up its dinner. "I imagine all you had to do was look at him and that poor mouse just keeled over stiff as a coffin nail."

The animal raised his head, wiped the cream from his whiskers with a practiced tongue, and gave a conversational *meow*. Jolie smiled, but she didn't quite dare pet the creature.

She stayed right there on the porch until the mosquitoes were biting and she couldn't keep her eyes open any longer. Then Jolie went inside and set chairs under both the back and front doors, for all the good it had done before.

The rifle was in easy reach when she lay down to sleep, but no one came to bother her.

The next day was a busy one—Jolie spent it putting up tomatoes and carrots from the garden—and she was almost able to convince herself that Rowdy and Blake's appearance had been nothing more than a bad dream. Whether or not she should tell Daniel what had happened was a question so thorny that she wasn't ready to tackle it.

Nan came to visit that afternoon, and she and Jolie sat on the front porch, chatting while Jolie hemmed another of her new dresses.

"What do you want most in the whole world?" Nan asked, as she stitched a bodice seam on a nightgown. She bit off the thread and knotted it with nimble fingers before turning the garment over to begin again on the other side.

Jolie watched as a garter snake slithered through the green grass. The front yard was dotted with the yellow faces of dandelions and smelled pungently sweet, since Deuter had given it a recent trimming with a scythe. "I guess—well, I'd like to have a baby."

Nan grinned coquettishly. "You'd best get busy, Mrs. Beckham, if you hope to keep up with me. Joe and I are going to do just that, come the middle of March."

Delighted tears brimmed in Jolie's eyes, and she nearly skewered herself on Nan's needle in her eagerness to embrace the woman. "That's wonderful!"

But Nan's look of pleasure had turned to a thoughtful frown, and she shuddered visibly. "There are so many things that can happen to a child in the country. Ella Cupcough's little girl fell down a well and drowned last year, and the summer before that, there was an outbreak of measles . . ."

"Those things could happen anywhere," Jolie reminded her friend gently. She surveyed the rippling wheat with loving eyes. "I want my children, if God sees fit to trust me with any, to grow up right here. The boys will work in the fields and the barn, because one day this place will belong to them."

"And the girls?" Nan inquired in a teasing tone, looking a little less troubled than before.

Jolie laughed. "They'll marry fine men with land adjoining Daniel's, naturally!"

Just then, Joe came around the side of the house, having finished the afternoon chores, and Jolie's expression went solemn as she recalled how close he'd come to dying without even knowing he was in danger. A lump formed in her throat as the lanky farmer picked two tea roses from the bush next to the porch and offered one to each woman.

It was the first time any man had ever given her a flower, and Jolie was both touched by the kindness of the act and stricken because the gesture hadn't come from Daniel. She watched with an emotion just shy of envy as Nan flushed prettily and thanked her husband with a slightly saucy smile.

All too soon, the Culleys climbed into their wagon and rattled away down the road, practically invisible because of the wheat.

Jolie took her rose into the house and set it in a bowl of fresh water, which she put in the middle of the table. Every so often, while she was preparing her supper, she paused to bend down and draw in its lush scent.

By that night, Jolie had almost forgotten that she'd had a very disconcerting visit from two men who were on the run from the law. She washed her hair and combed it dry in front of the bedroom window, and began to think in terms of which new dress she would wear for Daniel when he finally returned from his travels.

He came home in the middle of Friday afternoon, while Jolie was in the garden picking string beans. She was wearing her old clothes, her hair was stuffed up inside her derby hat, which she'd reclaimed from the scarecrow to keep the sun off her face, and she knew her chin and cheeks were smudged with dirt.

So much for winning Daniel's heart by looking her prettiest.

She approached shyly, dusting her hands off on her skirt, watching as Daniel climbed down from the wagon box and spoke to Deuter. The back of the rig was loaded with various supplies and covered by a canvas tarp, and Jolie thought she saw a movement underneath.

She was too glad to see Daniel to take the time to investigate, however. In fact, it was all she could do not to fling herself into his arms and beg him to take her upstairs.

His blue eyes twinkled as he touched the tip of her nose with an index finger. "Hello, wildflower," he said huskily, and for one breathless moment, Jolie thought he was going to kiss her right there in the barnyard. Instead he told her, "I brought you something." And then he reached into his pocket and brought out a simple gold wedding band, taking Jolie's hand and sliding the ring onto the proper finger.

No gift could have meant more to Jolie, and there were tears in her eyes when she looked up into Daniel's face. "I took good care of the place," she said, because for the life of her she couldn't think of anything else.

He grinned and lifted his gaze to the window high above their heads, where the bedroom curtains fluttered in the hot wind. "I'll want to turn in early tonight, Mrs. Beckham."

A thrill jolted through Jolie, but she didn't forget her dignity. "I imagine you're tired."

"I didn't say that," Daniel replied.

7

Although the warm glow of Daniel's tacit promise still thrummed in the depths of her, Jolie's smile faltered on her lips and then faded. Once Daniel learned that Rowdy and Blake had slept in his barn and eaten his food, he would be furious. All the ground he and Jolie had gained would be gone in an instant.

She took her husband's arm in an attempt to urge him toward the house, where they might talk without the myriad distractions of the barnyard. But a very distinct movement underneath the tarp covering the wagon halted her.

"Daniel . . ." she narrowed her gaze and frowned, then rounded the rig to stand behind it and lift the canvas. She jumped when she found two sets of very wide eyes staring back at her. "Tarnation," she muttered, tossing aside the tarp to reveal the most raggedy pair of children she'd ever encountered.

A tiny girl with long, straggly blond hair and sky blue eyes—she looked to be about four—crouched close to a boy of the same coloring. Their clothes were rough-spun and tattered, and their feet were bare.

Jolie's heart softened instantly, and she reached out for the girl, who burrowed against the other child's side to avoid being touched. "It's all right," Jolie said softly. "No one's going to hurt you."

"Hellfire and spit," said Daniel, coming to stand beside his wife and push his hat back on his head at the sight of the stowaways. "Where did you two come from?"

Jolie continued to hold out her arms in invitation to the smaller child, speaking to Daniel out of the side of her mouth. "Mr. Beckham, you are scaring these babies." Her gaze rested warmly on the small faces. "My name's Jolie, and I'll bet you'd both like something to eat, wouldn't you?"

The boy cleared his throat and looked warily through lashes as thick and sooty as a chimney sweep's broom. "We are a mite hungry, ma'am," he conceded, with a formality surprising in one so young. "I'm Hank, and this is my little sister, Gemma."

Daniel was frowning mightily, but he did Jolie the courtesy of keeping quiet.

"Come to me, Gemma," Jolie said gently, beckoning with curled fingers.

Gemma took one more look at Hank, who nodded, then allowed herself to be drawn into Jolie's arms. "I have to go real bad," she said, rubbing one eye with grubby knuckles.

Jolie took the child to the privy, and then they both washed their hands under a flow of clear, icy water from the pump. Inside the house, Jolie found Hank sitting at the table, his face freshly scrubbed and his corn silk hair slicked back, tucking into a tall glass of milk and a wedge of chocolate cake Daniel had cut for him.

Gemma's eyes widened at the sight of the food, and she practically catapulted herself away from Jolie's side to join in the feast.

Mrs. Beckham frowned. "Really, Daniel . . . cake? Lord only knows how long it's been since these children have eaten a proper meal. You'll have them sick as sailors, giving them sweets on an empty stomach."

Daniel ignored the lecture and caught his wife by one elbow, squiring her into the seldom-used dining room. "The boy tells me their uncle left them behind in Spokane, after he lost his job at the sawmill. Two different families were willing to take one of them in, but they didn't want to be separated. They ran off from the preacher's place and hid in my wagon."

Jolie's heart bobbed painfully, like a small boat moored upon a stormy sea. She knew what it was to be abandoned, and she could well understand the bond between siblings. As a child, she'd longed for a sister or a brother with all her heart.

"What kind of man would go off and leave two little ones on their own like that?" Daniel muttered, shoving one hand through his sweaty, dust-encrusted hair. "Hell, they're neither one of them big enough to spit over the top of a sawhorse."

"Maybe he'll change his mind and come looking for them," Jolie said, but even as she spoke the words, she doubted the idea. Her pa would never have given her another thought, after dropping her off on his sister and brother-in-law's doorstep, if he hadn't needed help with a new wife and family.

"I'll take them back to Spokane tomorrow," Daniel

decided, and Jolie could see a vein pounding in his neck. It was nearly time to start the harvest, and he could ill afford the time it would take to make the return trip.

Jolie's reaction came as a surprise even to her. She grabbed hold of her husband's rock-hard forearm and pleaded in a desperate whisper. "Please, Daniel . . . let Hank and Gemma stay until after the wheat is in! They're little, I know, but both of them could be a help with simple chores, like tending the garden and taking care of the chickens . . ."

The big man's gaze searched Jolie's face. "You'll get used to them. When they have to leave, you'll suffer and so will they."

She looked away for a moment, knowing Daniel's words were true but unwilling to send the children back into the cruel and callous world alone. Tears of frustration brimmed in her eyes.

Gently, unexpectedly, Daniel laid his hands on her shoulders. "There now," he said, flushing a little and averting his eyes for a moment. "There's no call to fuss. Hank and Gemma can stay until we're through harvesting." At Jolie's happy smile, he hastened to add, "But it's only temporary, mind."

Impulsively, Jolie threw her arms around Daniel's neck and kissed him soundly on the cheek. "Oh, Daniel, thank you. I promise they won't be any trouble at all, or get underfoot . . ."

A wry expression curved Daniel's lips for a moment, but then he released Jolie and turned away, rubbing his nape with one hand. "I've got things to do," he said, with a sort of remote politeness, and then he was gone.

Jolie hurried to the kitchen, where Hank and Gemma were just finishing off their pieces of cake. She refilled their milk glasses from the crockery pitcher and gave them each a slice of bread, some good yellow cheese, and a bowl of canned peaches. While they were eating, she heated water and brought the washtub in from the well house. Once again, her skirt caught on the same loose board.

She tugged it free with care, making a mental note to hammer the plank into place later, then hurried back to the house.

Hank eyed the tub suspiciously. "I done had a bath Saturday afore last," he announced.

"You have need of another," Jolie replied briskly, checking the water in the reservoir. "Do either of you have any clothes besides the ones you're wearing?"

The children shook their heads in concert.

She decided to put them each in one of Daniel's shirts so that she could wash and mend the ragtag garments they were wearing. Tomorrow, she'd see about getting them outfitted properly.

Once his hunger had been satisfied, Hank assured his small sister that he'd be nearby and left her to be bathed.

Jolie held back tears as she peeled away the child's dirty clothes and scrubbed her thin little body clean. Gemma's hair gleamed, the soft gold of morning sunlight, once it had been washed and brushed.

Practically swallowed up by one of Daniel's cambric shirts, Gemma settled herself on Jolie's lap and rested her head on her breast, one thumb jammed into her mouth. When Daniel came in, followed by Hank, Jolie raised a warning finger to her lips, and both males were surprisingly quiet.

Once she'd carried Gemma upstairs and settled her comfortably on the bed in the spare room to nap, Jolie went back to the kitchen. Daniel had emptied the washtub and was standing in the open doorway, drinking thirstily from a glass of cold well water.

Jolie gathered up the kettles and started for the pump, brushing against Daniel as she passed. She wondered if he recalled that he'd planned to retire early that night, and why, and a blush rose in her cheeks.

"You'd better bathe this one, Mr. Beckham," she said, minutes later, when she'd returned and set the kettles on the stove to heat. "I don't think he'd put up with it from me."

"Damn right I wouldn't," Hank replied, in earnest tones.

"We don't swear in the presence of ladies," Daniel said. Jolie watched as he moved to ruffle the boy's hair, then stopped himself at the last moment.

Hank looked at Jolie and turned red. "She'll have to go. I don't want any womenfolk staring at me."

When Daniel met Jolie's gaze, his mouth was solemn but his eyes were laughing. "You heard the man, Mrs. Beckham," he said. "No women."

Jolie shrugged and went out into the warmth of a summer afternoon. She could see a transparent moon in the sky, even though it would be hours before sunset.

A large, dusty conveyance with a crooked chimney poking through its shingled roof had been brought from some shadowy corner of the barn, and Deuter was whistling inside. Every few moments, a cloud of dirt would billow out through the open door at the back of the wagon.

Jolie went to the milk-stool step and coughed. "Deuter?"

He appeared in the doorway, holding a broom and greeting Jolie with a grin and a nod. "Afternoon, Miz

Beckham. I don't mind saying I've got a mean hankering for a whole passel of your cooking."

Frowning, Jolie ignored the remark. There would be meat and vegetable pie for supper, and she had no doubts that the men would make short work of it. "What is this thing?" she asked, waving a hand in front of her face to dispel a lingering fog of dust particles.

Deuter beamed, evidently pleased to impart any sort of information. "This here's the cook wagon, Miz Beckham. Dan'l told me to bring it out and get it cleaned up for you. How are those two little sprouts holding up?"

"Gemma is asleep, and Hank is having his bath," Jolie answered distractedly. "Deuter, did you say you were getting this wagon ready for . . . me?"

He nodded, leaning on the broom handle. "Yes, ma'am. She's all yours," he said proudly. "You can even sleep in it, though most folks favor stretching out underneath because the place gets kind of close with the cookstove going and all."

A painfully familiar sense of dispossession came over Jolie, but she wouldn't let it show. "I guess I wouldn't want the harvest hands tracking field dirt and manure into my kitchen," she said with careful dignity.

Deuter set the broom aside and came down to stand facing Jolie. "The place is wanting a woman's touch," he told her simply, and then he began unloading supplies from the buckboard and carrying them inside the cook wagon. Leviticus came and curled up on the threshold, but Deuter stepped over the tomcat without even breaking his stride.

Jolie tended to the chickens, and when she'd finished, she saw Daniel moving toward the well house, carrying the empty washtub. She ventured into the kitchen, but there was no sign of Hank.

After a few minutes of searching, Jolie found the boy in the spare room, curled up beside his sister on the bed. He was wearing one of Daniel's summer undershirts, and he was sound asleep.

A bittersweet tenderness swept over Jolie as she bent to kiss each child lightly on the temple and went out again.

She washed their clothes after supper and hung the garments over the backs of kitchen chairs to dry.

"You'd best take them to town for some decent duds tomorrow," Daniel said, frowning at the tears in Gemma's small, faded dress.

Jolie looked at her husband through lowered lashes, feeling incredibly shy and full of questions. Did Daniel expect her to share his bed that night, or was he consigning her to the cook wagon until after the harvest? Had she really felt him pull away from her after they'd discovered the children hiding in the buckboard, or was she just imagining it?

"Deuter did a nice job of sweeping out the cook wagon," she ventured. She'd have given what little she possessed for something to do with her nervous hands, but the supper dishes were done and the kitchen was clean. And she didn't know what was expected of her.

Daniel shrugged and poured himself a cup of coffee, and Jolie turned her brand-new wedding band slowly with a thumb and index finger. Now was the time to tell him about Blake and Rowdy's visit, but she found the words wouldn't pass her throat. She was just too afraid of what Daniel's reaction might be.

"I'll sleep out there in the chuck wagon until it's time to go into the fields," he said, nodding toward the darkened window. Even through the walls, Jolie could hear crickets and frogs singing their night chorus.

She reached out and clasped the back of a chair, Hank's threadbare little trousers and shirt moist beneath her palms. "I thought . . ."

Daniel turned to face her, and there was a fierce look in his eyes. "We can't share a bed with children in the house," he said.

Jolie swallowed. She couldn't think why she wanted to argue the case; it wasn't fitting. But argue she did, however circumspectly. "Mr. Beckham, we're husband and wife."

"Are we?" Daniel retorted hoarsely. Then he snatched his hat from the peg beside the door and disappeared into the night.

Jolie didn't need the bright wash of the moon on the landscape to tell her he was on his way to Ilse's grave. She was bitterly aware of the fact.

Setting her shoulders, Jolie caught up her skirts and whisked through the house to the stairway. After looking in on Hank and Gemma, she marched into the master bedroom and resolutely closed the door.

And she waited.

Daniel didn't come to their room at all, and Jolie was left to stew in shame and need, over flames fueled by guilt. It wasn't right for a woman to be yearning for a man so wantonly, whether he was her husband or not. And she'd as good as asked Daniel straight out if he meant to lie with her that night.

Jolie's cheeks throbbed in the darkness, and she stirred restlessly beneath the top sheet, the only covering she could bear in the muggy August heat. There was no denying it; she'd been downright forward.

And then there was the matter of telling Daniel that

outlaws wanted for murder, as well as robbery, had eaten under that very roof. They'd watered their horses from Daniel's well and bedded down in his haystack and, worst of all, they'd threatened his life.

Jolie squeezed her eyes shut against a sudden image of Daniel walking behind a plow, taking a bullet between the shoulder blades, falling. She saw blood spread over the back of his shirt in a crimson oval, and barely caught the scream that rushed into her throat.

She sat bolt upright in bed, still haunted by the picture of Daniel lying facedown in a freshly tilled field, and wrapped her arms around her knees in an effort to stop herself from trembling. Her skin was clammy with sweat, and fear gnawed at her insides.

Whatever the consequences, she had to warn Daniel.

She forced herself to lie down again, and to close her eyes. By some miracle, she fell asleep, only to awaken hours later, when a small form climbed into bed beside her and snuggled up. Jolie didn't need to see moonlight glittering in pale gold hair to know her visitor was Gemma.

Before settling in to sleep, the child whispered, "I habbed a bad dream."

A sweet ache filled Jolie. Already, she loved Gemma and Hank, but before a month was out, she would be forced to give them up. She sighed and stroked Gemma's hair back from her face. "You're safe now," she whispered, but even as she spoke she wondered how true that promise really was.

Jolie rose early the next morning, and she was in the kitchen when Daniel came in from the cook wagon, making breakfast for him and Deuter. Lamplight flickered in the predawn darkness, and the warmth from the stove was a comfort rather than a bother, as it would be later in the day.

Daniel helped himself to a cup of coffee, reaching past Jolie for the blue enamel pot, and neither of them spoke until he'd taken several swallows.

"The men we hired to help with the harvest will start showing up today," he said. "They'll be hungry when they get here, so I'll bring a ham in from the smokehouse."

Jolie only nodded and peppered the eggs she was frying.

Daniel went to the window over the sink and gazed toward the east, drawing thoughtfully on his coffee. "Put the things for the children on my account at the general store. They'll need shoes, and clothes for Sunday."

Scooping the eggs out onto a platter, Jolie set the food on the table, along with fried potatoes and a small mountain of crisp bacon. "I'd like to get them each a toy . . . just something small."

"Fine," Daniel agreed indifferently, as Deuter came in.

"If I had you for a wife," he said, with his customary abandon, running his eyes over Jolie, "I sure as hell wouldn't bed down in no cook wagon."

Daniel gave the younger man a quelling look but Deuter appeared unaffected, as usual.

The men consumed their breakfast while Jolie kept their coffee cups full. They left at first light to do chores and make more preparations for the harvest, and Jolie put out food for Gemma and Hank.

Once the children were fed and dressed, with their hair combed, Jolie went outside to find Daniel.

"We're ready to leave for town now," she said, wondering if he noticed that she'd washed with perfumed soap and taken extra-special trouble with her hair. It didn't appear so, since he seemed to be concentrating on the firewood he was chopping.

"Then go," he said, his shirt transparent with sweat, clinging to his back and chest.

She hadn't expected to brave Prosperity again quite so soon, not without Daniel beside her, at least. "Surely you don't mean, Mr. Beckham, that you expect us to go to town alone?"

He stopped working, finally, and mopped his brow with one sleeve. "That's exactly what I mean."

Jolie took one step closer and lowered her voice until it was barely more than a whisper. "Have you forgotten that I was nearly *hanged* in that town, only a week ago?"

Daniel looked exasperated, as though he resented having his wood chopping interrupted over such a petty concern as nearly being executed. "The trouble's all over now, and you're my wife. Nobody will bother you."

She thought of Rowdy and Blake making themselves at home on the farm but said nothing. The time for that confession would come later, when the long day was over and she and Daniel could sit quietly in the parlor and talk. Jolie sniffed. "Very well, then, I'll take my chances," she said. "But it'll be on your conscience if I'm lynched!"

She thought she heard Daniel chuckle as she turned in a whirl of crisply starched calico and stormed away.

Out in front of the barn, Deuter had just finished hitching a stout gray and black dappled horse to the buckboard. Hank and Gemma, wearing their clean but tattered clothes, were already settled in the back, their bare feet dangling.

Disgruntled, Jolie allowed her husband's hired

hand to help her up into the box and unwrapped the reins from the brake lever. She'd driven a wagon before, but she was more accustomed to walking or riding horseback, and taking charge of the buckboard was intimidating.

Nonetheless, Jolie managed to turn the horse and rig in the direction of the gate and soon she and the children were rattling down Daniel's rutted driveway toward the main road. Hank hurried to open the gate, riding along gleefully as it swung back on its hinges, then climbed over and closed the latch. Jolie felt that little ache in her heart again, but she didn't let herself dwell on the fact that Hank and his sister were only passing through her life. The prospect of walking into the general store in Prosperity and ordering clothes and shoes put on Daniel's account was daunting enough.

Once or twice, as the wagon jolted along between Daniel's wheat fields, Jolie glanced back to make sure the children were all right. Hank kept a protective arm around Gemma's thin little shoulders.

By the time they reached Prosperity, it was already hot, even though the sun was still at least two hours from its zenith. Flies swarmed around the horses, and the clang of the blacksmith's hammer rang through the open doors of the livery stable. Twangy piano music escaped the saloon, along with occasional bursts of male laughter.

Jolie brought the wagon to a stop in front of the general store, carefully setting the brakes and securing the reins. She carried Gemma to the wooden sidewalk, so she wouldn't have to walk in the street barefoot, but Hank wasn't about to endure such a humiliating courtesy. He was the first one inside the store.

While the streets had been virtually deserted, the mercantile appeared to be a haven for plump matrons and men past the age for work. At Jolie's entrance, it seemed that everyone turned to stare.

Although she didn't recognize any of the faces turned toward her, Jolie knew many of these people had been present at her trial and near-hanging, and panic washed over her in a cold rush. For a moment, she was actually dizzy, and the hazy light in the store went dimmer still. Then she took a deep breath and lifted her chin.

"The children will require shoes and clothing," she announced, to the general assembly.

Mrs. Craybrook came briskly forward, her lips pressed together so tightly that a network of tiny wrinkles ringed her mouth.

"Where is Daniel?" the woman asked, after a long perusal of Jolie's person. Somehow, Mrs. Craybrook managed to look down her nose at Jolie even though Jolie was taller.

"Mr. Beckham is busy preparing for the harvest," Jolie answered, raising her chin yet another degree.

The widow Craybrook's gaze turned to the children and narrowed. "These urchins yours?" she asked.

"I wish they were," Jolie replied, in all truth. "But they're just visiting for a while."

Although the widow clearly wasn't thrilled to have Jolie in her store again, she was even less eager to turn away what might amount to a substantial sale. She undoubtedly did considerable business with Daniel throughout the year, too, and would not wish to offend him.

"This way," she said stiffly, turning toward a shelf displaying shoes of various sizes.

Even if there had been a choice, Jolie would still

have selected the sturdy black shoes she bought for both Gemma and Hank, out of pure practicality. She purchased two pairs of short pants for Hank, along with shirts and stockings, and nice tweed trousers and a matching jacket for church. For Gemma, she chose cotton pinafores and a Sunday dress made of daffodil yellow lawn.

When all the necessities had been wrapped in a large bundle and securely tied with string, Jolie took both children by the hand and led them to the window, where a flock of toys lazed in the dusty sunlight. She watched with pleasure as their eyes roamed over dolls and fire wagons, jump ropes and balls.

Gemma finally turned to look up at Jolie questioningly, while Hank reached out with a cautious hand to touch a large red wagon with wooden rails and black iron wheels.

Jolie answered the little girl's unspoken query with a nod of her head, and Gemma's azure blue eyes went wide with disbelieving pleasure. Then she selected a rag doll with hair of yellow yarn—shyly, as though expecting someone to wrench it from her arms—and held it close.

"Please add the wagon and the doll to Mr. Beckham's bill," Jolie said, allowing herself just a shade of smugness when she saw the look of stern disapproval on Mrs. Craybrook's face.

The older woman turned and marched off to the counter, where she'd left her order pad. Jolie helped Hank lift the wagon from the window, then the two of them went outside and hoisted it into the back of the buckboard. Once both children were securely seated again, she returned to the store for the other parcels.

"Are those two some kin of Daniel's?" Mrs.

Craybrook demanded, gesturing toward the fly-specked window. Gemma and Hank were clearly visible on the other side.

"They're orphans," Jolie said, nettled at the reminder that she would have to give them up one day soon. "Gemma and Hank will be staying with us until after the harvest."

The widow's lips pursed for a moment, putting Jolie in mind of lemonade before the sugar has been added. "I don't know what this world's coming to," she fussed. "First Dan Beckham hauls off and marries a criminal, then he's spending money before the harvest is in to buy toys for a couple of children who don't even belong to him."

"We'd be happy to put everything back if you don't welcome our purchases," Jolie said, leaning closer but making no effort to lower her voice.

The recollection that she was in business to sell merchandise registered visibly in Mrs. Craybrook's face, and she hastened to add a doll and wagon to the account book. Jolie was glad the woman hadn't called her bluff, since she wouldn't have been able to ask Gemma and Hank to give back their gifts.

"You're very welcome," Jolie sang out cheerfully, from the door, even though Mrs. Craybrook had not said a thank-you. The lady storekeeper pretended not to hear, snatching up a feather duster and whisking it over a pyramid of canned salmon.

When Jolie, Gemma, and Hank arrived at the farm, Daniel was standing shirtless next to the pump. The skin on his arms and chest, only slightly paler than his face and hands, sparkled with little diamonds of water. He wasn't wearing his hat, and his hair was attractively rumpled.

Jolie felt a familiar stirring deep inside and revised

an earlier opinion. Perhaps Daniel Beckham wasn't handsome, in the classic sense of the word, but she felt a wrenching pull toward him, almost as though he'd reached right in and taken hold of her soul.

He put his shirt on slowly and approached the buckboard, lifting Hank's toy wagon in his strong arms. After that, he helped Gemma down, but his blue eyes never once left Jolie's face.

Her heartbeat quickened as the full weight of the love she bore this man settled upon her.

"I'll start dinner," she said, in a flustered effort to hide her reaction.

But Daniel caught hold of her arm when she would have gone into the kitchen. Gemma went to sit on the step, cradling her doll in her arms, and Hank pulled his wagon wildly around the dooryard. Jolie stared into Daniel's eyes, and the sensation was reminiscent of a time when she'd stood on the edge of a high cliff and dared the wind to lift her and set her flying.

"Someone was here while I was gone to Spokane," he said, in a low, raspy voice, shoving a familiar leather tobacco pouch under her nose. "Who was it?"

8

Jolie swallowed. "I think we should talk about this in private," she said, glancing nervously toward the children.

Daniel's grip on her arm tightened, and he thrust her quite unceremoniously onto the milk-stool step and into the shadowy interior of the cook wagon. As her eyes adjusted, she made out a sizable stove, the outlines of cabinets and bins, and a cot covered with a rumpled quilt.

Only a little while ago, she'd realized that the tempestuous emotion she felt for Daniel Beckham was real love. Now, she was going to lose him.

Despair struck Jolie's spirit like a mallet put to a gong and reverberated through her entire being, but she raised her chin and kept her shoulders straight as she looked up into Daniel's accusing eyes.

He was holding the damning tobacco pouch in one hand; probably, he'd found it in or around the barn.

"I meant to tell you," she said, and the words bore a tone of defiance because she was so certain they wouldn't be believed. "It was just that the moment never seemed right."

A vein in Daniel's neck pulsed as he waited, glaring down at her.

Jolie ran the tip of her tongue over dry lips. She sighed the self-condemning words. "Blake was here, with Rowdy. They spent the night in the barn."

Daniel shoved splayed fingers through his wheat gold hair, and his eyes narrowed. The small quarters seemed filled to pulse with the force of his annoyance, and Jolie knew the gathering storm had nothing to do with the weather.

For all of that, his words stunned her.

"Did they hurt you?" he demanded.

Jolie gaped at him, drew in her breath when his hands gripped her shoulders. "No," she finally managed to get out. "I was scared, b-but mainly for you and for Joe Culley." Haltingly, Jolie explained how the outlaws had gotten into the house, even though she'd blocked the doors with chairs. She closed her eyes against the memory of Joe walking into the barn, whistling, never suspecting he was in mortal danger. But she related that too, and, after drawing a deep breath and letting it out slowly, she finished the dismal tale. "Blake threatened to kill you—he said I'd be a rich widow if he did."

Daniel's sun-bronzed face appeared pale in the half-light of the cook wagon. "Why the hell didn't you tell me this before, when there was still some chance of catching up with those bastards?" he breathed furiously.

She glanced away, made herself look back. "I was afraid," she admitted. "Not just for you, but for myself, too. I knew you'd be angry."

He pushed past her, bent on leaving the close

confines of the wagon, but Jolie grasped his sleeve and held on. Although he paused, Daniel did not turn to meet her eyes.

"There's something twisted inside Blake," she said, barely able to force the hoarse words past the constriction in her throat. "He'll kill you if he thinks he can gain by your death. And Rowdy would drop you just for the sport of it, like he did that man at the bank. Watch your back, Daniel."

As though released from some invisible bond, Daniel sprang through the doorway of the wagon into the bright sunlight.

Jolie's eyes were wet, so she dried them with the back of her hand and sniffled a couple of times before she stepped onto the threshold. Half dazzled by the glare, she gripped the doorjamb and looked around at the sturdy house and outbuildings, the garden, the children, the wheat standing so still in the hot, heavy air. It was a good place, that farm, as close to heaven as Jolie hoped to get before she'd been judged by her Maker, but she didn't belong there.

It was because of her that Daniel was in danger.

Gemma's laughter chimed through the air, like the peal of a crystal bell, and Jolie's bruised heart wedged itself into her throat as she watched Hank racing through the high green grass, pulling Gemma behind in his wagon. If Blake was still nearby, and instinct told Jolie he was, it wouldn't be long before he realized that Daniel wasn't her only vulnerability.

Jolie's step faltered a little as she climbed down from the wagon and made her way toward the house. In the kitchen, she stoked up the fire and set about preparing a substantial midday meal of fried chicken, mashed potatoes with gravy, and green beans cooked up with onions and chunks of bacon. When she called out that the food was ready, Deuter, Hank, and Gemma came running, but there was no sign of Daniel.

"He's in the barn," Deuter said, before she'd asked the obvious question, as Jolie set the platter of chicken in the middle of the table.

Jolie smoothed her hair and tugged on her apron until it was straight. Then she marched outside, down the steps, and across the yard to the barn.

Daniel was picking a stone from the hoof of the dappled gray that had pulled the buckboard when Jolie and the children went to town.

"I didn't cook that food so you could waste it, Daniel Beckham," she said forthrightly.

Her husband looked back at her over one shoulder, and the expression in his eyes was so cold that Jolie felt as though someone had upended a bucketful of creek water over her head. "I'll eat in town," he said. "I want to have a few words with the marshal and send a wire to the preacher who was looking after Gemma and Hank in Spokane."

Jolie took a step nearer, though she didn't dare get too close. "You think I didn't tell you about Rowdy and Blake because I wanted to protect them, don't you?"

Daniel sighed, let go of the horse's foot, and went to the barn wall to take the buckboard harness down from its pegs. "It doesn't matter what I think, Jolie."

"It does," she insisted, wrapping her arms around her middle. Hearing her first name from Daniel had a piercing sweetness that brought a sting to her eyes.

Her husband led the big gray toward the wagon and began hitching the animal to the rig. Either he hadn't heard what Jolie said, or he was ignoring her.

"I'll be leaving soon," she said clearly, and her voice

trembled just a little. "It's the only way to keep Blake from using you and the children to get me to do what he wants."

At last, Daniel stopped his puttering. He stared at Jolie through narrowed eyes. "You're not going anywhere," he countered in a lethal rasp. "I paid five hundred dollars for you, and *by God* you'll stay right here on this farm until you'd worked off every cent!"

Jolie would not have denied to anyone besides Daniel that her primary sentiment in that moment was relief. It was certainly no compliment, however, that he saw her as a *purchase,* like a draft horse or a threshing machine. "Slavery's been abolished, Mr. Beckham, in case that's escaped your notice," she pointed out, keeping a hold, however tenuous, on her dignity. "You cannot buy people!"

He came to stand before her, his nose an inch from hers. "I bought you," he pointed out, with acid succinctness.

Helpless rage swelled up inside Jolie. "You damn fool!" she burst out. "Can't you see I'm trying to keep you from getting shot?"

In the next instant, Daniel's right arm stole around Jolie's waist, and he hauled her against him, lifting her feet clear off the barn floor. "I can take care of myself," he breathed, his lips so close to Jolie's that she could feel the soft warmth of them, "and you, too."

Daniel's mouth was the only thing about him that could possibly have been described as "soft." Jolie's senses came suddenly to life, making no sound and yet as shrill in their intensity as the steam-powered saw at Mr. January's mill. She was only too aware of the tamarack-hardness of Daniel's thighs and middle and, most especially, his manhood.

As he kissed her, first lightly and then with a sort of sweet violence, Jolie's blood raced to her head and then back to her feet in a single crimson wave. He took her thoroughly with his tongue, then allowed her to slide down the length of him until her feet touched the solid earth again.

"Daniel," she whispered, but when she would have laid her hands to his heaving chest to steady herself, he turned away and left her swaying in his wake.

He began hitching the gray to the buckboard, his movements swift and practiced. "Don't wait supper for me," he said, without looking at her again. "I may be late."

There was a woman in town, one who would be only too happy to meet Daniel's needs. The reminder induced a sharp sting. "And what am I supposed to tell the farm workers when they start arriving?" Jolie asked.

The muscles in Daniel's back and shoulders rolled gracefully beneath the fabric of his shirt as he finished coupling the horse and wagon and led the enormous animal toward the open doors of the barn. "That they're to sleep in here, as usual. They'll have their own bedrolls, but you'll have to feed them."

Jolie's temper was simmering again. She followed Daniel and the rig into the barnyard and glared at him, her hands on her hips, while he settled himself in the box and took up the reins. "How much of my debt to you will that repay, Mr. Beckham, my cooking for your field hands?"

"About a dime," Daniel answered caustically. Then he released the brake, slapped down the reins, and drove off.

Jolie watched him go, remembering the kiss and hating him for the power he had over her. Much to her secret chagrin, she wished with all her might that he'd come back and make love to her.

Fortunately for her, the demands on a farm wife's time were legion, and there was little time to stew. Jolie put Gemma down for a nap, settled Hank quietly at the kitchen table with an old reading primer she'd found on a bookshelf in the study, and listened as he struggled through several pages of simple prose.

At least, whatever else he'd lacked in his six years on earth, Hank had had a few months of education. And he was bright.

"You know," Jolie ventured, as she stood at the sink, peeling potatoes for the expected crowd of field hands, "you haven't even told me your last name."

Hank's eyes were a tender blue, like Daniel's, and that seemed like a good omen to Jolie. Which wasn't to say she didn't realize she was being dangerously fanciful. "I didn't reckon it was important," he said, closing the primer.

Jolie sliced a misshapen spud into halves and dropped it into a big kettle of cold, salted water. "Daniel—Mr. Beckham—means to send a wire to the people who were taking care of you and Gemma in Spokane. Just to let them know you're all right."

The child stared blindly at the woodbox next to the stove for a few moments. "They don't want us," he said. "No more than our uncle did."

A ruckus in the barnyard told Jolie that the men Daniel had hired for the harvest were beginning to arrive. Deciding to greet them later, she closed the kitchen door and sat down across the table from Hank. "Tell me about your father," she urged softly, folding her hands on the checkered tablecloth. "Do you remember him?"

Hank swallowed visibly and shrugged his thin shoulders. "Pa liked to drink and gamble. He tried, after Ma left, but I think it just got to be too much for him, seeing to Gemma and me. Last we heard, he'd got himself kilt."

The boy's words struck close to the bone with Jolie, not only because they were heartrending, but because she'd had a father much like Hank's. Dennis McKibben had been weak and self-indulgent, far more concerned with his own comforts than the needs of a half-grown daughter. He'd left Jolie with her aunt and uncle when greener pastures beckoned and, just when she'd come to love Nissa and Franklin and feel she had a real home at last, he'd showed up again and dragged her off to fetch and carry for his new wife.

She reached out to lay one hand over Hank's. How she wished she could promise him a permanent place on Daniel's farm, but she didn't dare. In the first place, the gift wasn't hers to give and, in the second, experience had already taught her that most situations were temporary, whether they were good or bad.

"I'd still like to hear your whole name," she said quietly.

"It's Wagner," Hank confessed.

Jolie offered him a handshake. "How do you do, Mr. Hank Wagner?" she smiled. "I'm Jolie McKibben Beckham, and it's grand to know you."

A shy grin broke over Hank's face. "I wish Gemma and me could be Beckhams, too," he admitted, and Jolie took him into her arms and held him. She wished the same thing, but she didn't hold out much hope that Daniel would change his mind about sending Hank and Gemma back where they came from. He probably had all he could do to put up with an outlaw wife, without stirring two abandoned children into the mix.

"I reckon I'll go and see if we missed any of the eggs when we gathered them this morning," Hank said, when Jolie ruffled his hair and released him from her hug.

"You do that." She smiled.

It was only after Hank was gone that she allowed herself to cry.

By supper time, there were a dozen men milling around in the yard, smoking cheroots and pipes. Jolie set out a hearty meal of fried ham, boiled potatoes, biscuits, and buttery corn, and the workers loaded up their plates and went back outside to eat in the grass. Over the sound of their laughter and talk, Jolie listened for the clamor of Daniel's wagon trundling up the drive.

When the sun went down, a little after nine o'clock, lantern light flickered cheerfully in the barn windows and one of the men played a sad ballad on a mouth harp. It gave Jolie a mournful feeling, even though she had Gemma and Hank for company.

Once she'd told them a made-up story, however, and tucked them into bed for the night, the loneliness grew more poignant. Jolie went to stand in the darkened parlor, at the window, glumly watching the empty road.

"Damn you, anyway, Daniel Beckham," she muttered, and just as she would have turned away, she saw a jostling light in the distance. A soaring sensation lifted her heart, but that didn't dampen her indignation at the way she'd been treated.

She was sitting in the kitchen, wearing a cotton nightdress and brushing her waist-length hair by the glow of a single lamp, when Daniel came in and hung up his hat. His gaze skittered past her, never quite touching.

"I see the men are here." He went to the stove, opened the door of the warming oven, and peered in.

Jolie smiled to herself. He was becoming accustomed to having a woman around again, even if it was only to cook and clean. And no smell of whiskey or perfume clung to his clothes. "I didn't save you anything to eat, Mr. Beckham. You said you'd be having supper in town."

"They give you one puny pork chop and two green beans in that place and call it a meal," he muttered, frowning as he wrenched open the bread box to find only a few crumbs inside.

"What place is that?" Jolie asked sweetly, brushing her hair again.

"The Jefferson Hotel." By the time Daniel replied, he was in the pantry, and his voice echoed off the walls. He came out carrying a jar of pickles, a wedge of cheese, and four oatmeal cookies.

Jolie sighed nonchalantly, just as though they'd never had words. "It was my understanding that they offer food in all the saloons," she observed. *As well as bawdy women,* she added in her mind.

Daniel pulled back a chair with one foot and sat. "I didn't have time for that," he said distractedly, glowering at the loot he'd spread on the table. "Great scot, woman, will you find me something decent to eat?"

She took leftover ham from the larder, along with a loaf of bread, and quickly made sandwiches. "I'll get the milk from the well house," she said, reaching for the doorknob.

The chair Daniel had been sitting in scraped against the floor as he rose with lightning quickness and grasped her by the wrist. "Not dressed like that, you won't," he hissed. "There are *men* out there."

Jolie was secretly pleased. "I forgot," she lied, with a bright smile. Actually, she'd figured the field hands were all in the barn, sleeping.

"Stay right here!" Daniel ordered, waggling a finger under her nose. He got out the crockery pitcher and left the house. When he returned, Jolie had finished grooming her hair, and she knew it gleamed like new honey in the soft lantern light. She did an inner pirouette when Daniel ran his eyes over her and then turned hastily away. "I thought you'd be in bed by now," he said hoarsely.

His wife engaged in a broad and somewhat theatrical yawn, then made a crooning sound as she stretched her arms high above her head. "I guess I should be," she agreed good-naturedly. "After all, breakfast time comes early, and I've got to earn my keep. Good night, Mr. Beckham."

"Jolie."

She stopped and waited in silence, afraid to turn around and meet Daniel's gaze because she could feel it burning into her back.

There was a long pause, and then he bit out a reluctant, "Good night."

Too proud to reveal her disappointment, Jolie left the kitchen without replying and made her way up the stairs to her empty bed.

She was filled with confusion and hurt as she lay down, and when she heard the kitchen door close in the distance, she rose and hurried to the window. In the moonlight, she saw Daniel standing outside the cook wagon where he'd slept the night before. He glanced in the direction of the maple trees guarding the graves of his lost family, and Jolie stepped back just as he lifted his gaze to her. When he started toward the house, she stopped breathing.

She was pretending to be asleep when the door creaked open, but she could see Daniel from under her lashes, standing in the chasm, his towering frame bathed in the thin silver gleam of the moon. When he crossed the room, took her arm, and yanked her out of bed, Jolie gasped in surprise.

"Stop it!" he ordered, through his teeth. "Damn it, whatever it is you're doing, *stop*. God help me, I'm losing my mind!"

Even though he hadn't hurt her, Jolie resented being dragged so rudely to her feet, and she wrenched free of Daniel's grasp. "I'm not doing anything!" she sputtered, in an angry whisper, smoothing her nightgown with the palms of her hands.

His strong fingers clasped her chin, and his normally serene eyes glittered as he searched her face, as if expecting to find something there to damn her with. "There are children in this house," he said despairingly, and Jolie knew Daniel was reminding himself of that fact, not her.

Jolie sensed that silence would make her case better than any argument, so she held her tongue.

Daniel surprised her yet again by sweeping her suddenly up into his arms. Without so much as a word of explanation, he carried her out of the bedroom, down the stairs, through the dining room and kitchen, and then into the night.

Stars shimmered and twinkled overhead, and crickets filled the air with their peculiar chattering chirp. The field hands weren't stirring in the barn, but a single, low lament from the milk cow came through the weathered boards.

Daniel stared down at Jolie for a long moment, as

131

though thinking he should know her from somewhere but couldn't recall just where, then carried her inside the cook wagon and laid her on the cot.

A pulse leaped at the base of Jolie's throat. "Daniel, what . . ."

The door closed, and the inside of that wagon was instantly and completely dark. Daniel didn't answer, but she heard his boots thump against the floor as he kicked them off, and there was a jingle of change in the pocket of a discarded garment. When he stretched out over her, careful not to crush her under his weight, she felt the dry warmth of his skin even through her nightgown. Her body, held in a state of frustrated arousal all through the day, thanks to one kiss in the barn that morning, caught fire in the space of an instant.

Jolie bit her lip to keep from moaning in anticipation when Daniel guided her gown up over her hips, waist, and breasts, then pulled it over her head and tossed it aside. With a disconsolate murmur, he kissed his way across the width of her collarbone and then took her nipple hungrily into his mouth.

Her response was primitive and completely involuntary. She arched her head back, gasping for breath, and gave a long, guttural groan. When she raised herself to Daniel, he took her in a long, smooth stroke that made her eyes open wide. The sides of her knees peeled away from his hips, and Daniel covered her mouth with his just in time to muffle her unrestrained shout of pleasure.

Jolie's traitorous body writhed beneath Daniel's; she flung her very soul into every parry, and her flesh quivered with longing each time he pulled back from her. While the strange joy reached its crescendo, Daniel nibbled idly at Jolie's neck, holding one hand over her mouth so that her ecstasy could remain a private thing.

When at long, long last she was still with exhaustion and satiation, Daniel smoothed her damp hair back from her face with both hands and drank kisses from her lips. Jolie felt his arms move past her head to grip something, and after every withdrawal, he thrust himself into her again. Each contact was deeper than the one before, and Jolie was sure their spirits fused when a great shudder finally racked Daniel and he released his seed.

It seemed an eternity had passed before she was able to think clearly again, but when that faculty returned, a singular, venomous pain came with it. Daniel had wanted Jolie, and he had plainly enjoyed having her, but even though he'd made his vows and signed a legal paper, he didn't consider himself truly married to her. If he had, he would have felt no need to make love to her outside his house, as though there were something illicit in their intimacy.

Only when he turned to kiss Jolie's cheek did he feel the tears on her face.

"What is it?" he asked, and Jolie had to give him credit for sounding like he really gave a damn. "Jolie?"

She didn't want him to know she was weeping for him; her entire body shook with the effort to hold in her sobs, even though it was already too late.

Daniel sighed when she didn't answer, and shifted so that he was lying on his back on the narrow cot. In almost the same motion, he lifted Jolie so that she sat astraddle of his hips. When she was settled on his masculinity, he slid calloused hands gently up her rib cage to cradle her breasts, then down to caress her bottom.

All the while, Jolie continued to cry.

"Tell me," he urged gruffly.

She didn't dare frame her misery into words even in the privacy of her mind, let alone speak of it aloud. She dashed at her eyes with the back of one hand and still the tears came.

Lord knew, Jolie's life had been tangled enough before she'd met Daniel. Now, she would have to hurt until the end of her days, knowing he was ashamed of her, that she was a concubine to him, not a wife.

Finally, he closed his fingers over Jolie's hips and raised her to the tip of his shaft. Then he lowered her slowly onto him. "If this is the only comfort you'll let me give you," he said, "so be it."

Jolie trembled as a flood of new sensation crashed over her, bent forward to grasp Daniel's shoulders lest she go plunging skyward like an arrow shot from a strong, taut bow. She was sure she couldn't bear the fierce sweetness of giving herself so thoroughly again. The response was already starting, building momentum with each stroke of his rod.

Her breathing became labored, and a thin film of perspiration broke over her flesh. Jolie knew she was going to explode within seconds, and she feared she would never be able to gather herself back into a single being again. *"Daniel!"* she cried, and her nails delved deep into his skin as she fought to hold back the tide of her own responses.

It was hopeless, and she buckled violently on top of Daniel, a low, continuous cry rumbling from her throat. He raised her high off the cot when his time came, with one powerful thrust of his hips, and Jolie reveled in his involuntary cry of surrender and rode his passion into a white-hot blaze of release.

She wasn't sure how much time had passed when

she finally returned to her right mind and realized that Daniel had pulled her nightgown over her head again, that he was lifting her, carrying her through the now-quiet darkness toward the house. She was too dazed to ask questions, of him or of herself. She could do no more than rest her head against his shoulder and close her eyes again, for Daniel had demanded all her stamina, and she had given it.

He brought her up the stairs to his room and laid her gently on the bed.

More than anything in the world, Jolie wanted Daniel to prove her earlier perceptions wrong, to lie down beside her, enfold her in his arms, and go to sleep. Instead, he covered her with a light blanket, bent to graze her forehead with his lips, and walked out.

She whispered his name, but then her eyelids fell and she dropped to the depths of consciousness, as though weighted by stones.

In the morning there was no time to grieve for her shattered hopes; fourteen men were awaiting a meal. Before they'd finished their coffee, Joe Culley arrived, driving a team of eight mules and pulling a cumbersome threshing machine behind him. Beside him was Nan, wearing a calico dress and a practical bonnet, clearly ready to help with the work.

She helped Jolie load the last of the supplies into the cook wagon, and the two women walked along behind as Deuter drove it deep into the fields. Hank and Gemma were riding inside, peering out through the window in the rear and waving.

"Fast work," Nan said with a grin, gesturing toward the children. "Anybody who didn't know better would think they belonged to you and Daniel."

Just the mention of his name made Jolie's heart

twist painfully, and she didn't even have to look at that blasted cook wagon to remember how expertly Daniel had loved her on its narrow cot.

"I wish they were ours," she said numbly. And then she explained how Hank and Gemma had stowed away in the wagon before Daniel left Spokane, since she and Nan had been too busy washing and packing dishes before.

Nan smiled sadly. "Dan hardened his heart, after Ilse and the babies died. He went right on going to church and all, but I'm pretty sure he stopped believing in just about everything and everybody." She paused to retie her bonnet strings, her expression thoughtful. "The Good Book says the Lord works in mysterious ways, and it would be my guess that He's up to something right here in Prosperity."

9

The cook wagon rumbled to a stop in a little copse of fir trees, where a spring bubbled and a load of firewood had been stacked. Shading her eyes with one hand, Jolie turned her attention to Daniel and the beginning of the harvest. Cacophony reigned, what with the braying of at least a dozen mules, the shouts of men, and the creaking metal wheels of the big wheat-cutting machine. An apparatus Jolie pegged as a thresher was also being erected, and more strange equipment was arriving by the moment, heralded by great clouds of dust.

After sternly cautioning Gemma and Hank about going near the machinery, Jolie sent them to carry firewood and then set about preparing her first cook-wagon meal. It would be noon before she knew it, and all those men would be ravenous.

Keeping the door of the closed vehicle open, despite buzzing flies, Jolie put kindling and old newspaper into the stove and struck a match to it. While she was doing that, Nan started getting out the plates and platters and pans they'd packed so carefully at the farmhouse.

Gemma and Hank brought ample wood, as requested, then scampered off to wade barefoot in the spring.

"They act just like they belong here," Jolie murmured, gazing through the wagon's one window and smiling as the children played happily near the small, shallow pool. The spring fed a creek, which provided natural irrigation for some of Daniel's land, no doubt making him one of the most prosperous, and envied, farmers in that part of the territory.

Nan was briskly making up the rumpled cot, a task Jolie hadn't gotten around to, and memories made her blush. At the head of the bed was a locked cabinet, with metal handles—the same ones Daniel had gripped when he was making love to Jolie, using them to pull himself deeper into her.

For a few torturously sweet moments, she relived the dizzying sensations, and her blood heated even more. She hurried outside the wagon, desperate for a breath of fresh air, and Nan followed.

"Are you all right?" the neighbor woman asked, touching Jolie's arm.

Since there was no way she could gracefully explain, Jolie worked up a feverish smile and nodded. "It was a little close in there, that's all."

Nan sighed ruefully. "Just imagine how it's going to be in the heat of midday, with the stove fired up like the boiler in a locomotive."

The prospect made Jolie weary, but she shored herself up. She'd worked hard all her life, under varying circumstances, and she wasn't one to waste badly needed energy on dread. All the same, she couldn't help reflecting that, by the time the day was over, a blast from hell's furnace would feel like a spring breeze.

Resolutely, she fetched a bag of fresh-picked green beans from the wagon and she and Nan sat side by side in the fragrant grass, snapping the curved stalks and tossing them into a big kettle. In the meanwhile, dust roiled everywhere, tumbling toward the sky and filling Jolie's hair and each pore of her skin with grit. The men yelled and swore and the mules brayed and by some miracle, the confusion coalesced into the beginning of harvest.

Daniel passed Jolie and Nan, driving a water wagon toward the spring, without so much as glancing in their direction, and the slight did Jolie profound injury, though she tried her best to hide it. When she looked at Nan, she realized she'd failed.

Her friend was smiling with a certain spicy sweetness. "It's like that with Joe and me, too," she said, her cheeks pinkening slightly beneath their sprinkling of freckles.

A handful of beans thumped against the side of the kettle as Jolie tossed them in. She was mightily embarrassed, but it was nice to know regular people had similar feelings; that made her feel less like a wanton strumpet hot for the touch of a man. She bit her lip and continued snapping beans.

"There's a story about Daniel," Nan dared, in a breathless whisper. She went right on working with the vegetables, and she didn't meet Jolie's eyes.

"What?" Ordinarily, she didn't go in for idle talk, but this concerned Daniel and that made it important.

"A certain soiled dove at one of the saloons in town is grieving because he got himself married. It's said that Daniel knows more about pleasuring a woman than most men do."

Jolie's face burned, and she snatched up another handful of beans with more energy than the task called for. "Nan Culley, how on earth would you manage to hear such a thing?"

Nan's voice was a saucy whisper. "Joe told me. Don't you believe it when men claim they don't gossip, because they surely do. Daniel knew a . . . a *foreign woman* a long time ago, in San Francisco, and she taught him how to—well, she taught him how."

It was impossible for Jolie not to turn and crane her neck in Daniel's direction. The muscles in his arms and shoulders moved gracefully as he handed buckets of springwater up to Deuter, who sat astraddle of the water wagon's black tank, pouring the precious liquid through an opening.

Jolie's heart leapfrogged over one beat. It was a frank relief to hear Nan's words, since Daniel barely had to touch her before she set to carrying on. She'd thought it meant she was a bad person, of lesser morals than other women. "Oh," she said, and her voice sounded as weak as she felt.

Soon after, Jolie carried the kettle to the spring, along with a ladle, and Nan came too, bringing buckets. Reaching the bank, Jolie knelt and began dipping water to fill the pot, doing her best to pretend she didn't notice Daniel standing only a stone's throw away.

When she finally had no choice but to lift her eyes to him, she felt an intangible blow strike her midsection. Although the sensation could not have been described as pain, it quite literally knocked the breath from her lungs.

Daniel was filthy from head to foot, his hair, skin, and clothes coated with dust, and he looked at her with a mixture of fury and blatant desire. Wounded by the former and painfully aroused by the latter, Jolie scrambled awkwardly back to her feet and hurried toward the cook wagon without even waiting for Nan to finish filling the buckets.

As Nan had predicted, the wagon was almost unbearably hot by noon, and she and Jolie were glad to escape it. The workers came in from the fields, black with dirt except for white circles around their eyes, and ate hungrily of the food the women had prepared.

Immediately after the hands had gone back to work, Jolie and Nan began washing dishes. As soon as they'd finished that, it would be time to start getting ready for supper.

Gemma and Hank were curled up in the cool, dandelion-sprinkled grass underneath the wagon, sound asleep and as dirty as any of the field workers. Jolie smiled, feeling a pang of affectionate envy for them, and went on with her work.

At sunset, she and Nan served fried trout, caught downstream by Deuter and a well-rested Hank, along with potatoes and boiled carrots. As soon as the heat subsided a little, the men washed in the creek and sat smoking and talking under a banner of stars. Nan and Joe said their good-byes and went home for the night.

Looking at the narrow cot, Jolie thought with longing of the wide, comfortable bed in Daniel's room back at the house. Since she'd had enough of the inside of the cook wagon to last her for a while, she tucked Gemma and Hank into either end of the narrow berth and took two blankets and a pillow outside.

She was making a bed under the wagon, in the sweet-smelling, bruised grass, when Daniel suddenly appeared, kneeling beside the rig to scowl at her.

"What do you think you're doing?" he demanded.

Jolie sighed. She loved this man, and Lord knew, she couldn't deny wanting him, but he could be downright exasperating at times. "I should think it would be perfectly apparent, even to you, Dan Beckham, that I'm making a place to sleep."

In a sidelong glance, she saw his Adam's apple travel the length of his throat and down again, and she held back a smug smile as he swallowed visibly. He leaned toward her, his dirty hands resting on the strained fabric covering his thighs. "I won't have my wife sleeping out here in plain sight of God and everybody!" he whispered hoarsely.

Jolie went right on spreading and smoothing her blankets. "I'm afraid there's nothing else I can do," she said, over the steady thrum of the crickets. "Gemma and Hank are in the cot, and there simply isn't room for me as well."

Daniel glanced over one shoulder toward the two dozen or so men he'd hired to help with the harvest. Due to the fact that it was too hot a night for a fire, and the moon was a thin fingernail paring in the black sky, only the vague outlines of their prone forms were visible. "You can go back to the house, then. I'll take you there myself."

She yawned, patting her mouth with straight fingers, then sat cross-legged on the makeshift bed to begin unlacing her shoes. "I couldn't leave the children," she said distractedly, though in truth she was feeling anything but nonchalance. "Besides, I need to be on hand early to get breakfast started."

Jolie took off her dress, confident that no one

besides Daniel could see her, and crawled between the blankets in her muslin chemise to stretch luxuriously. It felt wonderful to lie down and rest her aching muscles, and the sights, sounds, and smells of the night offered a tender comfort.

With a muttered curse word, Daniel wrenched off his boots, then his shirt, then his trousers. He tossed aside the blanket and lay down close to Jolie.

"You're filthy, Mr. Beckham," she said with a sniff, to hide the fact that she'd gone all warm and moist at the feel of his gritty flesh against her. "And you smell. You'd best sleep on the floor of the wagon."

He moved deftly over her and parted her legs with a motion of one knee, and she felt his manhood resting against the delicate skin of her thighs. "I'll decide where I sleep, Mrs. Beckham," he countered, in a low whisper.

Jolie felt herself expanding to accommodate Daniel, and her undeniable need of him was humiliating. "You should have a bath," she said.

"Here's what *you* should have," Daniel replied brusquely, and then, in simultaneous motions, he covered Jolie's mouth with his own and glided into her depths.

Just before dawn, shivering with early morning cold, Jolie hastened into her dress and shoes and climbed out from under the wagon. Daniel had not been beside her when she awakened, a fact that nettled a little, even though it didn't surprise her.

He had built up the fire in the cookstove, however, and he'd left warm, clean water so Jolie could wash. As soon as she performed her ablutions, she hastily brushed her hair and wound it into a loose knot at her nape.

She was returning from the spring, a heavy bucket of water in each hand, when the sun suddenly blazed over the horizon, spilling gold and crimson light onto the wheat. Jolie drew in her breath at the beauty of the sight, then hurried on toward the cook wagon.

After filling a metal basin with eggs from the crock full of water in the corner, Jolie started breakfast cooking. She'd already served the men and was in the process of brewing the third huge pot of coffee when Joe appeared on the milk stool outside the door, hat in hand.

"Mrs. Culley regrets as she won't be over to help this morning," he said, in his shy, friendly way. "She's feeling poorly."

A pang of anxiety twisted in Jolie's stomach. "It's not—"

Joe interrupted with a smile and a shake of his head. "Nothing a person wouldn't expect," he said. "She's fixing to be a mother, you know."

Jolie nodded, shy of discussing such a topic with a man, and went on about her work. She worried about Nan intermittently throughout that long, busy day, but there really wasn't much time for reflection. No sooner had she finished cooking one meal when it was time to start another, and what might she had left over she needed to keep Gemma and Hank under some semblance of supervision. The children ran from morning until night, dirty as savages, and they thrived.

Daniel was careful to avoid any personal contact with Jolie, and she knew he regretted lying with her the night before, in the sweet grass. After supper, she closed herself away in the wagon, where she took a warm sponge bath and brushed her hair before changing into a clean calico dress.

The men were sitting in a circle, swapping yarns by the light of a few carefully watched kerosene lanterns. Gemma and Hank sat on either side of Daniel, their heads resting against his sides, and his arms resting lightly around them.

Jolie blinked back tears and bent to lift Gemma, who was sound asleep. "It's time they were in bed," she told Daniel, and the storytelling went on as he got to his feet, hoisting Hank up onto one hip. He followed her to the wagon without a word.

Only when the children's faces and hands had been washed and they had been tucked in at the separate ends of the cot did Daniel speak.

"About last night," he began, shoving the splayed fingers of one hand through his hair.

They were outside the wagon, facing each other across the step, and Jolie reached up to touch Daniel's mouth with the fingers of her right hand. To silence him. She couldn't bear to hear him apologize for what had happened between them.

"Shhh," she said.

Daniel's lips moved, soft and pliant, against the pads of her fingers. "But . . ."

"I know, Daniel," Jolie whispered, with miserable practicality. "You're not in love with me, and you still care for Ilse."

He didn't deny her words when she finally lowered her hand to her side. She knew without his telling her that he would gladly have died in Ilse's place, rather than see his first love perish.

"I'm sorry," he said, after a long time.

So am I, Jolie thought brokenly, but she didn't dare speak aloud for fear of betraying her grief.

He bent slightly and kissed Jolie's forehead.

She slept fitfully that night, alone under the wagon,

with Daniel resting a dozen feet away. The next day, she worked even harder than she had before.

That Saturday evening, after dinner, Daniel took his small, improvised family back to the main house. No work would be done in the fields on Sunday, and those men who had not gone to town would be expected to cook for themselves.

Jolie saw that both Gemma and Hank had baths and shampoos before settling them in the spare room to sleep. Once she'd told them a long, involved story, Jolie went downstairs to start heating water for her own tub.

She was pleasantly surprised, and a little moved, to find that Daniel had already done the job for her. She took a thorough bath and put on a nightgown, but she had no real hope of seeing Daniel again before breakfast. He'd probably paid a formal call to the little graveyard yonder, no doubt apologizing to Ilse for his lapses, and then made himself a bed out in the barn.

Far too exhausted to pursue the matter, Jolie towel-dried and braided her hair, then dragged the bathtub onto the step and emptied it. The thing was too heavy to carry any farther, so Mrs. Beckham had to content herself with flooding the dooryard in soapy water.

She was stretched out in bed, tired enough to weep, when she heard Daniel climb the stairs and pause outside the door. She held her breath, too exhausted to receive him but yearning to lie peacefully in his arms. Moments later, however, his footsteps moved along the hallway again. She heard the door of the bedroom next to hers open and then close.

Jolie reached up and touched the wall with one palm, knowing Daniel was on the other side, keeping himself separate from her. A few moments passed, and she heard the bedsprings creak under his weight.

Even though she was exhausted, Jolie thought surely she'd cry if she lay still, so she got up and went across the hall to check on the children. Hank was sleeping soundly, but Gemma was tossing and turning.

Jolie got the little girl up to use the chamber pot, then put her gently back to bed. When she returned to the hallway, she could hear Daniel snoring in the third bedroom. She smiled sadly and climbed back into her own lonely bed.

In the morning, she made a simple breakfast of toasted, buttered bread, hot oatmeal and milk, and apricots from a jar in the pantry. Then Daniel brought the buckboard around to the front of the house and handed Jolie and Gemma up into the box, both dressed in their Sunday finest.

Hank rode manfully at the back of the wagon, with his feet dangling down over the dusty road. Jolie just hoped his stockings and knickers wouldn't get too dirty before they reached town.

Every long, hard bench in the little clapboard church was filled that morning by the time the congregation began to sing the first hymn. Jolie privately thought it was a wonder any of them could keep their places in the songbooks, the way they were stealing looks at her and Gemma and Hank.

The Reverend Blackborrow told the story of Adam's two sons, dwelling dramatically on the part where God heard Abel's blood calling out from the ground. It was a stirring tale and, even though Jolie had heard it countless times in Aunt Nissa and Uncle Franklin's church back in Nebraska, her eyes were wide by the time it was over.

The children were plainly relieved when the long service finally ended. Gemma and Hank ran off to play with the others while their elders shook hands with the reverend. Jolie learned that Mrs. Blackborrow suffered from a nervous condition and her husband had insisted she stay home that morning and rest herself.

Verena Dailey made a point of coming up to Jolie and embracing her, though all the other women were keeping noticeable distances. "I do hope you'll stay for the picnic this afternoon," she said.

Jolie had noticed the baskets and boxes resting in the backs of various wagons that morning, but she hadn't thought beyond that. Now, seeing the eyes of her neighbors skitter away without making contact, she knew she would not have been invited if it hadn't been for Mrs. Dailey.

They were outside in the sunshine now, and Jolie could see the children playing chase between the gravestones in the churchyard. She smiled. "We have dinner waiting at home," she lied, speaking clearly and brightly in hopes that no one would guess how much she wanted to be accepted.

Verena took Jolie's arm and, at the same time, winked up at Daniel. "I guess you'll just have to eat it later," she said. "I brought plenty of chicken and roast beef sandwiches for all of us." With that, she pulled Jolie into the circle of tight-lipped women and proceeded to introduce her to each and every one.

The older ladies remained coldly reserved, but, as the afternoon progressed, some of the younger ones began to show signs of friendliness. Of course, Jolie thought philosophically, they were probably just curious about her and the children. After all, the three of them *had* come into Daniel's life in rather unconventional ways.

While Jolie sat on the grass under an elm tree,

delicately nibbling at a piece of crisp chicken and listening as a young matron went on about how her little Jack kept losing the buttons from his knickers, Daniel joined in a game of horseshoes with the other men.

With un-Sunday-like pride, Jolie thought how he was the finest looking one of them all, towering over all his companions. To her, his back seemed broader, his smile warmer, his eyes friendlier. Her heart ached with the secret longing for his love.

When the picnic was over, Daniel hoisted both the children into the fresh hay in the back of the wagon. By the time he climbed into the box, Jolie had already taken a seat there, without assistance from him. For just this one precious day, she reflected, she and Daniel and Gemma and Hank had been like a real family.

At the house, Daniel went upstairs and changed into his work clothes, and Jolie packed more food—meats from the smokehouse, eggs, milk, butter and cheese from the coolness of the shed that protected the well, flour and sugar and other condiments from the pantry, vegetables from the now-neglected garden. While Daniel did the chores—either he or Deuter came back to the farm to tend to these duties twice a day—Jolie had the children put up their Sunday things and exchanged her brown sateen for a comfortable blue calico.

The four of them ate a light supper around the kitchen table, then set out for the camp in Daniel's buckboard. Even though a week of hard work lay ahead of her, Jolie was glad to be back. She liked the feeling of working close by her husband's side.

The evening air was cooler than usual, and the wind was picking up. Jolie noticed that Daniel kept taking uneasy glances at the sky, and the men built a bonfire close by the creek and roasted sweet potatoes in the embers.

Nan and Joe came by, in Joe's wagon, and while Nan looked a little peaked, Jolie was relieved to see her up and around.

The two women sat in the doorway of the wagon, sipping the bracing tea Jolie had made for the occasion.

"I'm sorry I haven't been here to help you," Nan said, lowering her eyes.

"I don't need you underfoot anyhow," Jolie teased, touching her friend's arm.

Nan gave her a surprised look, saw the twinkle in her eyes, and laughed. "In that case, maybe I'll just lounge around the parlor with my feet up for the rest of the harvest, Jolie Beckham," she replied.

Jolie's expression had turned solemn. "Maybe you should do exactly that," she said. "After all, no harvest is as important as a baby."

But Nan shook her head. "Daniel and Joe have a bargain that goes way back—he helps bring in our crops, and we help with his."

After that, the women lapsed into a thoughtful silence, watching the flickering orange light of the bonfire and sipping their tea as night settled over the land. Jolie was filled with wonder at her wealth, however transient. She had a pair of beautiful children she could believe were hers, if not in her head, in her heart. She had a home, plenty of food, and decent clothes, for the first time since her father had dragged her away from her aunt Nissa's side. And now, two genuine friends had entered her life . . . Nan and Verena.

Jolie supposed a woman couldn't rightly ask for

more, but there was one thing she still wanted . . . for Daniel to love her with his whole soul, the way he'd surely loved Ilse.

Soon, it was time to put Gemma and Hank to bed. Joe and Nan drove off toward home, their way lighted by a lantern swinging from the side of the wagon. The field hands spread their bedrolls on the ground around the fire and talked in muted tones of people and places that were far away.

Jolie was sitting in the doorway of the wagon, reading a book of poetry she'd purloined from a shelf in Daniel's parlor before they'd returned to the fields when her husband suddenly appeared. As always, to her chagrin, her breath caught in her throat and her heartbeat speeded up, just at the sight of him.

"Hank and Gemma are asleep," she said, because nothing else came to mind. She wondered what it was about this man that enabled him to shake her so thoroughly just by standing nearby.

Daniel was gazing up at the sky, his expression troubled, and Jolie knew without asking that he was afraid it would rain before the harvest was in. Although she had very little practical knowledge where crops were concerned, she was aware that a storm would be a major catastrophe. He braced one hand against the corner of the cook wagon and just looked at her.

Jolie was uncomfortable. "Was there something you wanted to say?"

His voice was hoarse when he answered. "It was nice, having you and Gemma and Hank around today."

She lowered her head to hide the smile of pleasure she was certain was wavering on her mouth. He was referring to the church picnic, and Jolie was delighted to learn he'd paid attention to something besides the sermon and the subsequent horseshoe tournament. "They're good children," she said, hoping Daniel would consider that when he went to take Gemma and Hank back to Spokane.

Daniel cleared his throat before speaking again. "I've been thinking about something you said," he went on. "About how you can't buy another human being."

Although Jolie certainly had no quarrel with this train of thought, she sensed some ominous undercurrent to his remark. "I was under the impression we'd resolved that, as a nation, during the Great Civil Conflict," she said, hoping he wouldn't notice that her hands were trembling as she smoothed her skirts.

Her husband's scowl reminded her, too late, that he'd been born and raised in North Carolina and had quite possibly been of the Confederate persuasion. After one thunderous moment, however, his manner became gentler. He even smiled, his teeth white in the gathering darkness, but his eyes looked sad. "So we did," he agreed. "My family never had slaves anyway. We couldn't have afforded to feed them."

Jolie still sensed the approach of something hurtful, and she wanted desperately to avoid it. "Did you fight in the war?" she asked softly.

He sighed and gazed off into the starry distance, his arm still braced against the cook wagon. "Yes, Jolie," he answered, after a long time. "I slept on the ground, like everybody else, and I ate biscuits filled with weevils. I must have walked half the length of Dixie in the same old worn-out pair of boots. And when the war was finally over, I was glad as hell to walk away whole—a lot of men on both sides weren't so lucky."

Jolie was silent. Lots of people still had bitter

feelings where the war was concerned, and it was apparent that Daniel numbered among them.

He reached out and took her hand, pulling her from the doorway of the wagon. "You're a very beautiful woman," he said reluctantly.

No one had ever told Jolie that before, and she was so moved that she couldn't even manage a thank-you. Her throat worked, but no sound came out.

He lifted his hand to her face and traced her jawline lightly with the calloused pad of his thumb. "I'll miss you when you go," he said.

Jolie swallowed. "When I go?" she echoed plaintively.

Daniel nodded. "You were right before—I don't own you. And I think you deserve a chance to start over somewhere else." The caress stopped, and his hand fell back to his side. "As soon as the harvest is over, I'll send you to San Francisco. I have friends there who can help you get a divorce and make a new life for yourself."

10

The memory of Jolie's stricken expression followed Daniel as he turned and walked resolutely away from the cook wagon. He wanted to take back everything he'd said about sending her to California, but he couldn't let himself do that. It was bad enough that he'd raised false hopes by making love to Jolie, and by letting Hank and Gemma stay instead of taking them straight to Spokane the moment he'd discovered them hiding in the wagon.

He walked along the banks of the creek, the wheat rustling in the darkness as he passed, until the dying fire and the camp were far behind him. Then, sitting on a rock, he reached down and picked up a pebble to toss into the water.

The stream glistened like a ribbon of ebony marble in the thin light. Daniel drew in the subtle scent of the crops, ready to be harvested, threshed, bagged, and sold.

Guilt chewed at him like an animal with small, needle-sharp teeth. He'd betrayed his gentle and delicate Ilse, who had lost her life trying to give him sons and daughters.

Daniel tossed another pebble into the creek, his eyebrows drawn together in a frown. More than remorse troubled him, however.

Although the loss of his wife and two children had devastated Daniel, had hollowed out parts of him that would probably still be void when he reached the far side of forever, his suffering had left him with a certain invulnerability. The worst had already happened to him, he had lost what he valued most in all of creation. Anything else that might occur, a plague of mice or grasshoppers in the wheat, his own sickness or even death, would be minor by comparison.

Now, he was faced with a new danger—caring about Jolie and those two skinny, unwanted little kids who'd stowed away in his wagon. To love them, to throw his whole soul into creating a new family, would be to lay himself open to unbearable pain all over again.

He sighed and shoved one hand through his dusty hair. He guessed he hadn't been thinking straight when he'd told Jolie he wanted children by her. Lord knew, he hadn't had a truly logical thought from the moment he'd seen her standing there in Hobb's hay wagon, looking pitiful as a wet kitten thrown to the dogs. He slapped his hands down on his muscled thighs, sighed again, and stood, rotating his shoulders in a vain attempt to relieve some of the lingering strain of a day's work.

He'd been walking a fine line with Jolie, giving in to the sweet temptation of that lush and supple body of hers, letting himself dream of a houseful of laughter and children and love. It was time he pulled in his horns and faced cold reality: He simply couldn't allow himself to care about another woman. The price was too high.

The grinding work went on, and on. The backs of Jolie's hands were splattered with small burns from cooking, while her palms were blistered and sore from chopping wood for the insatiable stove. Her clothes hung loose on a form that was leaner and firmer than ever before, and she couldn't remember the last time she'd been truly clean. Nan had taken to fainting in the heat of the day, so she no longer came to help with the work, but she had taken Gemma and Hank to stay with her until the harvest was over.

Despite her fatigue, Jolie missed the children, begrudging every moment she could not be with them. Daniel had been avoiding her for days, barely speaking to her even when she handed him a plate at mealtime, and she had no doubt at all that he meant to relieve himself of one very troublesome family the moment he'd harvested, threshed, and sold the last of the wheat.

There was always a lump in Jolie's throat, and she was forever on the verge of tears, but she was too stubborn to let Daniel know she was grieving. She smiled at the men as she served them and, at night, she joined them around the campfire, singing and clapping her hands as one of the field hands played spritely tunes on his mouth harp. Ballads always sent her fleeing into the hot, empty cook wagon, though, for songs like "Shenandoah" and "Red River Valley" brought her unruly emotions too close to the surface.

Work was her solace and her salvation, and occasional visits with Hank and Gemma, at Nan's small, tidy farmhouse, sustained her. Still, the thrumming pain inside her, pulsing in time with her heartbeat, never subsided.

When Sunday morning came, Jolie launched a minor rebellion and refused to attend church with Daniel. He drove off alone in the buckboard, probably planning to stop off at the Culleys to pick up Gemma and Hank for the services, and Jolie did her level best to go back to bed and sleep.

But it was hot enough to smother a body, and there was a fly buzzing somewhere in the room. The world looked hellfire red through her eyelids.

Jolie gave up and rose from the mattress she'd longed for so many nights when she'd slept under the cook wagon, or on the narrow, lonely cot inside it. She'd grown so used to working, she decided, that she couldn't feel comfortable lying still. Too, laboring on a Sunday, with apologies to God, of course, seemed an excellent way to get back at Daniel for his stubborn and mean-spirited ways.

She was in the garden hoeing, her skirts hiked up and her hair stuffed inside the old derby hat, when she heard the nicker of a horse. At first, Jolie wasn't concerned—this was a farm, after all—but then she realized that Daniel had taken his gelding, and there were no animals about except for old Leviticus and the black-and-white milk cow, Daisy. All the mules, like the cumbersome equipment, had been left at camp.

Jolie leaned on the handle of her hoe, eyes squinted against the relentless sunshine, and wiped one sleeve across her sweaty brow. A shift in the wheat to the west of the house drew her gaze, and Jolie nearly choked on her own indrawn breath when Rowdy and Blake rode over a low rise.

157

Their grins seemed unusually white against the backdrop of their filthy faces.

Silently berating herself for not keeping the shotgun close at hand, Jolie tightened her fingers around the heavy wooden hoe handle and tested its weight with an almost imperceptible upward motion of her elbows. If need be, she could do plenty of damage with that plain garden tool before it was wrested away from her.

"You've got a lot of brass, coming here," she said to Blake, as he dismounted and walked toward her. Rowdy got out of his saddle, too, but then he shed his dirty, sweat-stained canvas duster, hung it over his saddle horn, and walked off in the direction of the well house and the barn.

Jolie kept her eyes on Blake, every muscle perfectly still, ready to use that hoe to dig a furrow in the side of his head if that was what she had to do.

Blake stopped, a few feet away, one booted foot planted on either side of the wilted pea plants Jolie had been cutting down. He pushed his hat to the back of his head in a cocky motion and hooked his thumbs through his belt loops. The six-gun strapped to his hip looked particularly ominous in such an ordinary, everyday setting.

He ran his insolent gaze over her. "The sun's turned you brown as a nut," he said. "Don't you know a lady's supposed to keep her skin whiter than the keys on a new piano?"

Jolie swallowed and tried not to let on just how tightly she was gripping the hoe. "What do you want?" In the near distance, she heard a door creak on rusty hinges, but she didn't dare take her eyes off Blake long enough to trace the sound. She longed for

Daniel's return and, at the very same time, prayed that the reverend's sermon was running to the lengthy side that morning.

She began to sweat again, between her breasts and shoulder blades and along her upper lip, but now it was fear that spawned the reaction, not the merciless August sun.

Blake scratched the back of his head, making his hat wiggle on his crown. After that, he spread his hands wide of his torso in a gesture of astonishment. "What do I want?" he echoed. "Well, that's a fine how-do-you-do, when Rowdy and I have come all this way just to pay a Sunday call on you."

Jolie's gaze strayed anxiously toward the road, even though she did her darnedest to stare straight at Blake the whole time. "You and Rowdy must *want* to get yourselves caught and hanged," she observed, bravado lending a defiant lilt to her voice. "Otherwise, why would you still be hanging around Prosperity like a couple of flies on a cow-pie?"

The man she'd once believed was her friend smiled indulgently and took another step toward her. "You're making me feel unwelcome," he scolded.

She hoisted the hoe like a claymore and held it ready. "I'd rather see mice three deep in the wheat than you in my garden," she breathed. "Get out of here, Blake, and don't come bothering me again. There's no point in your bedeviling me, because Daniel—Mr. Beckham—means to send me away as soon as the harvest is in."

Blake folded his arms across his chest and, although he didn't seem daunted by Jolie's words or her weapon, he maintained his distance. He sighed philosophically and tilted his head back for a moment to study the sky. When his gaze met Jolie's again, though, the sweat dried instantly on her skin and a chill bit through to her very soul.

"I reckon that just means we've got to see that you inherit this place real soon," he drawled, after a long, deadly silence.

"Do you think I'd let you do that? Do you actually believe I'd allow you to gun down another innocent man and ride out of here with the deed to this farm in your hand?" Jolie burst out, at the end of her patience. From the corner of her eye, she saw Rowdy approaching, pulling Hank's cherished wagon along behind him like he thought he was doing something real clever, and her terror deepened. She summoned the last of her courage to hide the fact. "Daniel'll know you've been here, even if I don't tell him—which I will, I swear by God's vest buttons. He'll get the marshal and some of the men from town and they'll track you down like they would a couple of mad dogs."

By that time, Rowdy had brought the red wagon to the edge of the overgrown, neglected garden. He and the toy made an incongruous picture.

"Did you think we didn't know about the kids, Jolie?" Blake asked, with ominous good will, waggling his index finger at her.

Jolie felt a shiver spiral down her spine. "You just go near them, either of you, and I'll kill you," she said, in barely more than a whisper. Then, firmly grasping the handle of the hoe, she advanced on Blake.

He scrambled backward, grinning the whole time, his hands raised, palms out, in a bid for peace. It was a morbidly ironic parody of the way the bank president had tried to back away from Rowdy's bullet—or had it been Blake's?—that dreadful day. "Easy, now,

160

Jolie-girl," he scolded. "I got no objection to raising up a couple of kids. We'll start us a brand-new life someplace far from here, you and me, and they can go along. That way, we'll look more like a real family."

Jolie's stomach roiled at the comparison, and she gulped back the wash of acid that flooded her throat. In another sidelong glance, she saw that Rowdy was frowning, probably pondering the obvious gap in his friend's plan.

"I'm warning you both," Jolie said, keeping her shoulders straight and her voice even. Blake's suggestion didn't deserve answering. "Get out of here, and don't come back."

Rowdy fidgeted anxiously, his neck craned, his eyes fixed on the plume of dust billowing far up the road. "For chrissakes, Kingston, somebody's coming!" With that, he sprang into the saddle and reined his tired, spindly horse back in the direction from which they'd first appeared.

Blake mounted too, but his movements were damnably slow and methodical. He touched the brim of his hat in a mock-cordial gesture as he regarded Jolie's upturned face. "You be sure and tell the big man we were here," he said pleasantly. "But don't get any crazy ideas about trying to trap me or something like that. Wouldn't be smart, because even though I'd like for you and me and those kids to take up the honest life someplace far away from here, I'll kill them both if you cross me." He paused to glance calmly in the direction of the approaching rider or wagon. "And I know where to find them, Jolie-girl. They're at the Culley place most times, and there's no man around during the day."

With that, Blake rode after Rowdy by way of the garden, his horse's hooves trampling the last of the tomatoes and then cutting a destructive swath through the squash patch. But Jolie wasn't thinking about ruined vegetables as she dropped the hoe and raced through the tall grass toward the privy, both hands clamped over her stomach.

When she stumbled through the outhouse door, minutes later, gasping for fresh air, she found Daniel waiting on the path, his arms folded.

"Ilse used to get sick when she was carrying," he observed, glowering down at her as though she could make a baby all by herself and had probably done so just to spite him.

Make a baby. Jolie wrapped her arms around her middle and held on. She was shaking, and probably white as bleached flour. It hadn't occurred to her that she and Daniel might have made a child, and the prospect filled her with a strange mingling of dizzying hope and pure terror.

She shrugged, even though her feelings were anything but nonchalant. "That wouldn't be anything to worry about, would it, Mr. Beckham?" she challenged. "You could just turn the little thing over to some orphanage in Spokane as soon as the birthing was through and pretend the baby and I never existed."

Daniel's face clouded and Jolie knew in that instant that if he'd been a man to strike women, he'd have slapped her back on her heels. *"Is* there a baby?" he demanded, in a dangerous undertone.

Jolie bit her lower lip, taking a mental count. "I don't know," she finally replied, with a sort of saucy forthrightness. "It's too soon to tell." She was stalling, giving Rowdy and Blake time to escape so Daniel wouldn't go after them and get himself shot.

As if he'd somehow looked into her head and read her thoughts, Daniel swung his gaze toward the garden. He muttered a swear word and strode over for a closer look at the hoofprints in the rich, dry dirt. Inevitably, he turned and glanced back over one shoulder, seeing where the two outlaws had trampled down the wheat when they rode off.

He bolted toward the buckboard and began unhitching the big gray, and Jolie ran after him and grabbed his arm, her mind filled with horrible visions of blood and death.

"Daniel, no! They'll kill you!" she screamed, fighting like a wildcat to hold on even as her husband flung her away, into the soft grass. *"Daniel!"*

He had freed the draft horse of its harness and swung himself up onto the animal's powerful back. He glared down at Jolie for a long, torturous moment, then urged the gray into a burst of motion.

Jolie was horrified to see how fast the beast could run, and she sat there on the grass-cushioned ground, watching Daniel ride away and praying that God would overlook her failure to attend church and answer *just one* little request. "Please," she pleaded aloud, in a despairing whisper, "don't let Mr. Beckham be shot."

After a while, Jolie got herself up from the ground and started pacing the yard, watching the distance, waiting for some sound or sight that would tell her Daniel was on his way home to her, safe and sound. She didn't care if he hollered at her or forced her to sit through a three-day tent revival, she just wanted to see him ride in.

At dusk, Jolie fed and milked the cow and gave Leviticus his cream, and there was still no sign of

Daniel. She sat on the back step and waited, her chin propped in one hand, her eyes aching and burning, as if she'd kept them open through a desert sandstorm.

When someone finally appeared, it was only Deuter, who'd walked over from the harvest camp to see if anything was wrong. Jolie couldn't bring herself to tell him just how very wrong things really were. He might feel compelled to go after Daniel, and that would put him in terrible danger.

So Jolie made up a story—like all effective lies, it was very close to the truth—claiming that she and Daniel had had a dreadful argument and he'd gone off to town to see Pilar at the Ivory Rose Saloon. Deuter nodded sympathetically, as though such behavior would be the natural way of things, and then he lit a lantern and he and Jolie started back toward camp together.

"We'll be moving the cook wagon in the morning," the red-haired young man told her companionably. "Right after breakfast. It'll be a busy day for you, Miz Beckham, so you might want to get extra sleep."

In the privacy of the wagon, Jolie heated water and gave herself a sponge bath, then put on a clean nightgown. Every few minutes, though, she had to pull aside the curtain on the rig's only window and peer out, desperate for the sight of Daniel.

When the pounding sounded at the wagon door, Jolie was unprepared. "Who is it?" she asked, in a shaky voice, trembling in the shadows even though the place was hot enough to choke her.

Instead of answering, her caller just opened the door and stepped right in. Even without the frail light of the kerosene lantern, Jolie would have known her visitor was Daniel because her senses immediately went to riot, her breathing got short, and there was a tight ache in the pit of her stomach.

"You didn't catch them," she said, and closed her eyes, sagging with relief to sit on the edge of the cot's thin, hard mattress.

The pitch of Daniel's voice was softer than Jolie had ever heard it. And far more lethal. "What did they want?"

Jolie had braided her hair earlier, after washing and combing it, and she pushed the plait back over one shoulder. "To scare me," she answered, after several moments of struggle. "To let me know they're still around."

"Why?"

"I told you. Blake wants your farm, Daniel—or, at least, he wants the money it would bring."

Without warning, Daniel sat beside Jolie on the cot and wrenched her astraddle of his lap. Her nightgown was stretched taut across her thighs, and her breasts strained against the thin muslin, thrust forward by his fierce grasp on her shoulders. "Damn you, Jolie, if you're lying to me I'll see you hanged myself!" he hissed.

The quiet expulsion of words hurt more than a shout could have, more even than a slap. Jolie's eyes filled with sudden, stinging tears. "I'm trying to save your life, you big-dumb-farmer!" she sobbed. "God help me, *I love you!*"

Daniel stared at her as though she'd said something too horrible to credit. "No," he said, his voice a scratchy rasp.

"Yes!" Jolie cried. She wanted to pummel him with her fists and would have, if he hadn't stayed the blows by grasping her wrists. His hands felt huge and impossibly strong as his fingers curved around fragile bones, and while Jolie couldn't have escaped to save her life, he wasn't holding her tightly enough to hurt her.

"No," he repeated, almost desperately, and at almost the same moment he locked his hand behind Jolie's head and crushed her mouth to his.

In that enchanted time and place, Jolie had no pride. She gave a small, strangled whimper and threw her arms around Daniel's neck, returning his kiss. Sweet power sang through her bones and muscles and danced like St. Elmo's fire on her flesh, and their tongues writhed together as lovers might.

Jolie flung her head back and gasped when Daniel freed a plump breast from the confines of her nightgown and stroked the nipple with a work-roughened, skillful thumb. When his mouth closed around the tingling nubbin, warm and wet, Jolie moaned aloud.

Daniel broke away with a breathless gasp. "We can't—" he choked out. "The way I feel, the way I need you, this wagon would bounce so hard it'd set the springs to creaking."

Her need for him was deep, grinding and shifting painfully inside her, but Jolie raised herself from Daniel's lap and straightened her nightgown. Then, without a word, she got a basin down from a nail on the wall and carried it to the stove, where she labored for so many hours every day. She filled the basin from a kettle cooling at the back and set it on the floor next to the cot.

After that, she fetched a clean cloth and dipped it into the water. With a gentleness born of fiery passion, she began washing the dust from Daniel's face and neck. Then she slowly unbuttoned his shirt and pulled it off, one sleeve at a time.

His blue eyes smoldered as he looked down into her face, but he made no attempt to stop her from removing his clothes. Tossing the shirt aside, she carefully cleansed his chest and sides and arms. Presently, kneeling beside him on the cot, she washed his back, too.

That done, Jolie pulled his boots off and tossed them aside, but it was Daniel himself who unbuckled his belt. When his trousers were gone, Jolie got another basin and continued bathing her husband. Daniel's powerful muscles rolled and trembled under her hands, but he endured the washing, his eyes closed now, his chest rising and falling unevenly as he struggled to submit.

Memories of the pleasure he'd given her made Jolie bold. She set aside the water and cloth and bent forward to touch Daniel with her tongue.

He murmured a protest even as his hands cupped the sides of her head, urging her to stay. He groaned when she took him, and Jolie ran her hands up and down his rough, stony thighs, enjoying a rare, sweet dominion. Daniel's hips began to undulate, and his breathing grew quicker, harsher.

Jolie didn't want to let him go, but he finally gave a strangled gasp, wrestled her free and stood, thrusting her against the opposite wall. She felt a velvety chill caress her skin as Daniel pulled her nightgown off over her head and tossed it away.

She was drunk with the knowledge that she'd been the stronger, at least for a few minutes, and with the fierce kisses that followed. When Daniel hoisted Jolie off the floor and let her take his full length in one long, slow glide, her shoulders resting against the wall of the wagon, she sought his mouth feverishly. Had it not been for the passionate mating of their tongues, Jolie was certain she would have cried out her pleasure loudly enough for the stars to hear.

It was not a gentle coupling, the joining of Daniel and his bride, for it had its roots in anger and despair as well as longing, but there was no pain. Daniel's hips slammed powerfully against Jolie's soft inner thighs, and her nipples blossomed against the hairy expanse of his chest. Jolie clenched her legs around him when her climax began, and Daniel intensified the experience by locking his hands under her knees and holding them wide apart while he gave her a thorough taking. She bit her lip to keep from shouting as her body buckled helplessly upon Daniel, a living sheath rippling around its sword.

She felt his warmth surging into her even as he groaned into the moist flesh of her throat, and she stroked his hair and his back, comforting him. Comforting herself.

Finally, he laid her on the cot, without her nightgown, and then laid a blanket lightly over her. She was still quivering with delicious little aftershocks. He used some of the water to wash himself—even doing that he was magnificent—then put his clothes back on and made his way to the stove. He didn't look at Jolie as he poured coffee and lifted the cup to his mouth.

"It doesn't change anything, what just happened between us," he said, after a long interval.

Jolie's languid sense of well-being was instantly replaced by fury and hurt. "It might have changed a great many things," she said, just to spite him. "For example, you might well have put a baby inside me tonight, if you haven't already."

He turned to stare at her, the cup forgotten in his hand. "Don't say that."

"It's quite true," Jolie insisted. And for better or

worse, it was. Only God knew whether or not their passion had drawn a new soul toward earth.

Even in the unsteady light of the lantern, Jolie could see the color drain from Daniel's face.

"You must have known it could happen," she said airily, plucking primly at the blanket.

He shoved a hand through his hair with such force that Jolie feared he'd uproot a thatch. "Of course I knew, but . . ." His voice trailed off.

Jolie sighed and settled into the pillows, carefully arranging the covers to hide her breasts. "Well, let me tell *you* something, Daniel Beckham. If there is a baby—and I'm not saying there is, mind you, but there *could* be—I absolutely refuse to let you leave the poor little thing on the doorstep of some orphan's asylum."

"I would never do that!" Daniel whispered angrily, and shrugged his broad shoulders in a way that made Jolie think he was trying to draw himself inward, to somehow become smaller. It was plain that he'd remembered the men outside, and didn't want to draw attention to the goings-on inside the cook wagon.

"You'd send Gemma and Hank back to penury," she said, hoping *penury* meant poverty, as she guessed it did. She collected words the way some people gathered seashells, and she didn't always know how to categorize them.

Daniel bent slightly forward at the waist, glowering. "There are probably lots of families who want to give them a good home."

"They aren't puppies, Daniel," Jolie pointed out, folding her arms across her bosom and drumming her fingers on her elbows. "They're children. And there are 'lots of families' who are just looking to bring home a slave to wash their dishes and scrub their floors."

Daniel shook his head in resigned frustration, for all the world as if he'd offered a convincing argument and been rebuffed for his trouble. "You've been reading Charles Dickens," he said, with a sigh.

Jolie wasn't about to confess that she'd never gotten beyond McGuffey's Reader. "What if I have?" she inquired tartly, hoping he wouldn't expect a demonstration of her knowledge. All she knew about Mr. Dickens was that he'd been an Englishman and that he'd passed on several years before.

Her husband set his coffee mug down on the stove top with a clanking thump. "I can see there isn't any point in talking about this tonight," he said with an air of disdain that made Jolie want to spring across the wagon's dark, crowded interior and throttle him where he stood.

In the next instant, as he reached for the doorknob, a swift, smothering panic engulfed her. While her body had wanted, even needed, Daniel's attentions, her spirit cried out for another kind of closeness. It would be bliss to have Daniel lie beside her and hold her in his arms.

"Don't go," she whispered.

Daniel looked at her for a long time, during which Jolie thought sure he must hear her heartbeat, it was so loud. But then he opened the door and went out into the darkness. Jolie caught the scent of smoke from the campfire and heard the plaintive music of a mouth harp.

She'd never felt more alone in all her life.

11

The sky was heavy with clouds the next morning, and there was an ominous weight to the air, but the dreaded rain did not come. Wagons rumbled through the denuded fields to be loaded high with burlap sacks full of new wheat, and there was so much dust that Jolie was occasionally forced to cover her mouth and nose with a corner of her apron in order to breathe. By the middle of the day, the camp had been moved onto another section, where there was no creek. From then on, they would have to depend on the water wagon.

Jolie was resting in the shade of her traveling kitchen, during that short but blessed lull between washing up from breakfast and putting dinner on to cook, when Verena Dailey turned up driving a buggy. With no apparent regard for the heat, she was dressed in her usual black sateen and sporting a veiled hat. Just looking at her made Jolie want to topple over into the dry grass from heat prostration.

Instead, she rose politely as the older woman got

herself down from the rig, secured the reins, and approached, waving a silk fan trimmed in ivory under her chin. The men were harvesting and the threshing machine was making a loud clatter, while patient mules labored around and around a large gear made of metal and stone to generate the necessary power. Every once in a while, a spark from the wheel would ignite the dry wheat, someone would give a raucous shout, and all available fieldhands would rush to stomp out the blaze. The process always put Jolie in mind of Indians doing a war dance.

She smiled listlessly as Verena finally drew near enough to give her a brief embrace.

"I've brought the makings for lemonade," she announced, raising her voice to be heard over the general cacophony of the harvest. With that, she turned and trundled back toward the buggy, leaving Jolie to look after her with a watering mouth.

Mrs. Dailey returned with a basket of lemons, a bag of sugar, and a crock of transparent, sawdust-speckled chips from her icehouse. Inside the cook wagon, she and Jolie hastily brewed lemonade and gathered metal cups for the men to drink from.

The incessant dust settled just a little as the dirt-blackened field hands stopped their work to consume the lemonade in grateful gulps. Even Daniel, who had been about as talkative as a cigar-store Indian since walking out on Jolie a few nights before, grinned as he handed back his empty cup.

There was a pink glow under Jolie's sun-browned cheeks as she turned away to carry back the empty bucket and the ladle she had used to serve the thirsty workers. When she returned to the cook wagon, she found a cup of the tart, icy drink awaiting her. She and Verena sat side by side on the edge of the cot, as straight backed as two duchesses having afternoon tea.

Their conversation, however, was less formal. Verena reported that Mrs. Dunntwiddle had gone to Spokane via the stagecoach to have a blue mole removed from the side of her nose and that the new schoolmaster had arrived early and taken the attic room in Alverna Krayper's boarding house. He was a small man, it seemed, who sneezed constantly and wore spectacles with thick lenses. Verena allowed as how the poor man would probably bump his head on the slanted ceiling every time he stood up straight, despite his diminutive size.

The chat was interrupted by a sharp shout from the fields, a cry audible even over the incessant noise, instantly followed by a pistol shot. Verena and Jolie raced outside, Verena moving almost as rapidly as Jolie did, to see that the work had stopped and the fieldhands had gathered into a tight cluster, staring at something—or someone—on the ground.

Jolie knew there had been an accident, and she swept the bent heads with frantic eyes, looking for Daniel.

Her relief when she saw him shoving his way through the crowd was so intense that it made her head light and her knees weak. The shot echoing in her skull, she searched for signs of Rowdy or Blake, but if they were around, they were well hidden.

She lunged toward the scene at the edge of the wheat field and elbowed through to Daniel's side.

Joe Culley lay on the ground, his face deathly pale under its coating of dirt. Sweat made muddy rivulets on his forehead and cheeks, and his breathing was quick and shallow.

"Take it easy," Daniel was saying, as he knelt beside

his friend in the stubble of wheat stalks, cutting a rent up the side of Joe's trouser leg with a pocketknife.

"What happened?" Jolie gasped.

The man beside her was only then sliding his pistol back into its holster. "Snake," he answered simply. Sure enough, the carcass of a diamondback rattler lay nearby, in two distinct pieces.

Jolie shuddered, but her attention was centered on Daniel and she took a step nearer, wanting to help, not knowing how.

"I need a strip of cloth," Daniel said, revealing an angry red wound on Joe's knee as he ripped aside the trouser leg. Although he hadn't so much as glanced in Jolie's direction, she knew his words had been addressed to her.

Quickly, she bent to lift the hem of her skirt and tear off the bottom-most ruffle on her petticoat. She handed this to Daniel and watched as he tied a tourniquet around Joe's leg, then polished the edge of his pocketknife on the inside of his own shirt sleeve.

"Somebody get some whiskey," he ordered, but he was already cutting an X-shape on Joe's badly swollen knee. When crimson blood beaded on the lanced skin, Daniel bent and put his mouth to his friend's flesh. He sucked hard, turned his head and spat, sucked again.

Joe gave a raucous, defiant shout of laughter, holding himself upright on his elbows, his head back. But his face was contorted with pain and fear.

The process continued for several more minutes, with Daniel loosening and tightening the tourniquet at intervals. Finally, one of the field hands broke through with the requested whiskey, and Joe took a long, thirsty gulp. Then, before sagging backward to lie flat in the dirt, he handed the bottle to Daniel.

Mr. Beckham filled his mouth, spat into the dirt, poured more whiskey past his lips, and swallowed. Then he shoved the bottle at Jolie, again without looking at her, and again loosened the cloth around Joe's leg.

"Deuter," Daniel said, finding his friend in the cluster of grimy men. "Get a buckboard and take Joe home. Seems he insists on lying around in his bed while the rest of us work." At last, the blue eyes swiveled to Jolie's face, and Daniel rose to his feet as he spoke. "You'd best go along. Nan will need you."

Jolie nodded. She wanted to help the Culleys in any way she could. "What about the cooking?"

Daniel's expression was unreadable, but his gaze hadn't wavered from her face. He opened his mouth, but no sound came out.

In fact, it was Verena who answered. "I'll take care of everything around here," she said, in brisk, efficient tones. Then she turned to wave her arms at the gathered men like a crow flapping its wings. "Now, get back to work, the lot of you. Good heavens, it's a wonder poor Joe can breathe, what with all of you standing so close and sucking up the air."

Deuter had already brought the buckboard over, and the men were wandering back to their jobs. Still, Daniel and Jolie just stood there, staring at each other like a couple of fascinated strangers.

Finally, Daniel broke the strange spell by dragging one shirt sleeve across his grit-covered face, expelling a heavy sigh, and turning his attention back to Joe. Several workers were hoisting the half-conscious man into the bed of the wagon.

Daniel gripped the ankle of Joe's good leg and gave it a slight shake. Jolie, not knowing what else to do, scrambled into the back of the wagon to ride beside her friend's husband, cross-legged, with her skirts tugged modestly into place.

The road to the Culley place was not really a road at all, but just a worn path abutting the wheat fields. Deuter drove the rig, bumping and rolling, over land that had already been harvested.

One of the men came running after them with a blanket; Jolie unfurled the scratchy woolen in the muggy air and spread it carefully over Joe's inert frame.

Deuter spoke to her over one shoulder, shouting to be heard above hooves and harnesses, threshers and mowers. "You see to the Culleys, and I'll go on into town for the doc."

Jolie nodded, wishing she'd thought to bring along some water; Joe's throat was probably dry. Just during that short ride to his farmhouse, he fluctuated between wild fits of shivering and copious sweats. His teeth were chattering when he told Jolie, "Daniel got most of the poison out. I know he got most of the poison out."

Jolie touched his forehead and forced herself to smile. Daniel had reacted quickly and calmly to the crisis, but she'd seen more than one person die of snakebite during the trip west with her pa and his new wife. And most of them had looked better than Joe did.

"I can't die," he said, as if he'd seen right into her mind. "Nan needs me, and we got that little baby coming next March . . ."

"You'll be fine," Jolie insisted, past the lump in her throat. She had to turn her head for a moment, so Joe wouldn't see the tears shimmering in her eyes.

The Culley farm was smaller and more modest than

Daniel's, boasting only a weathered frame house and a barn. There was a stone well with a little roof over it, a vegetable patch, and a grassy knoll. Gemma and Hank came running over the crest of the slight hill at the approach of the wagon, their golden hair glinting in the sunshine, a black-and-white sheepdog yipping at their heels.

Simultaneously, Nan came out of the house, wearing a brown calico dress and wiping her hands on her apron. Jolie felt a stab of pain when her friend saw Joe lying prone in the back of the buckboard and raced across the yard.

Nan caught back a scream with an audible gasp and immediately scrambled into the wagon bed. "Jolie, what happened?" she croaked, kneeling at Joe's other side and cradling his head.

"Snake," Deuter answered, before Jolie could get out a word. "Let's get him inside as quick as we can. I'll go fetch the doc."

Nan nodded somewhat frantically and clambered down from the wagon, along with Jolie. Both women hung back while Deuter hauled the smaller man onto his feet and helped him toward the house.

"Is Joe gonna die?" Hank asked, tugging at Jolie's skirts. Behind him, as always, was Gemma, her eyes big with uncertainty and a wariness that made Jolie's heart ache. These children were no strangers to trouble; they knew it only too well.

Jolie pulled both Hank and Gemma close while Nan hurried ahead into the house, with Deuter and Joe. "I don't know," she said honestly, because to mislead them would be only a temporary kindness. "Joe is very sick. Nan and the doctor and I will do all we can to help, but there's only so much that can be done." She bent to kiss both grubby, sun-warmed faces. "I know I can depend on you to be very good children so that Joe can get the rest he needs."

Hank and Gemma nodded solemnly and Jolie ushered them to the porch, where they sat side by side, their bare feet dangling over a bed of thirsty pansies. Jolie was touched to notice that Hank was holding his sister's hand in a reassuring grip.

Nan's house was really more of a cabin, with a fireplace, a stove, a table, and two chairs in the main room. The bedroom was actually a lean-to with a slanted outside wall. Nan was just tucking a colorful if somewhat worn quilt around Joe, and Jolie nearly collided with Deuter in the doorway.

He nodded briefly in farewell and returned to the wagon.

Joe talked constantly, but his words were no longer coherent, and he was thrashing back and forth on the bed.

"I think we'd better clean that wound," Jolie said matter-of-factly, sounding confident even though she wasn't. All she really knew was that it wouldn't do any earthly good for her and Nan to stand around and fret. "Do you have whiskey?"

"There's probably some brandy left from when I made the Christmas fruitcake," Nan offered, her normally serene eyes frantic with the need to be of some help to her husband.

"Get that," Jolie told her friend, pushing up her sleeves. "We'll need hot water and soap, too, and clean cloths—some for cleaning and some for bandages."

Nan looked relieved to have a mission and bustled out to the stove. Jolie followed, snatching up a bucket and heading for the well. Gemma and Hank were still keeping their vigil on the porch.

Jolie smiled at them, despite the seriousness of the circumstances. "I didn't mean for you to sit there like a couple of knots on a log." She nodded toward the sheepdog, who was sitting nearby, panting. "Looks to me like your friend there is real anxious to play."

Hank spared the animal a slanted grin, reluctant and fleeting. "All right," he agreed manfully, shunting himself down from the porch and over the flower bed, then lifting Gemma after him. "But he'll have to be *quiet.*"

Jolie nodded and went on to the well as the children and the dog scampered away into the lush, waving grass again. Like at Daniel's place—Jolie never thought of the farm as her own in any way—the Culley land seemed to be mostly in wheat. She filled the bucket and returned to the house, where she poured the water into a big kettle waiting on the stove. After that, she went back for more.

By the time they'd heated enough water, and Nan had found the brandy, Joe was completely delirious. He laughed raspily and talked to Daniel, as though the two of them were working side by side in the wheat fields. It was an eerie experience, but Jolie concentrated on washing the wound thoroughly. Once she'd done that, she treated it with generous dollops of liquor—this made Joe bolt upright and swear colorfully even though he clearly didn't know where he was or what was happening to him. Satisfied that the snakebite was as clean as she could make it, Jolie bandaged the leg with strips of cotton torn from Nan's best sheets.

An hour later, there was still no sign of the doctor—given the fact that his was a country practice the man could be miles away—but Joe had quieted down and seemed to be resting a little more comfortably. At least, Jolie *hoped* he was resting; she knew people sometimes lapsed into an unhealthy kind of sleep just before death.

It was then that Nan fell apart. She flung herself down on Joe's chest and sobbed, clutching his shoulders and pleading with him not to die and leave her alone.

Gently but firmly, Jolie pried the woman away and, with a strong arm around her shoulders, led her into the next room.

"You hush yourself this minute, Nan Culley," she scolded, in a loud whisper, pressing her friend into a chair at the scarred oak table. "We don't know how much that man can hear, and we certainly can't have him thinking we've all given him up for dead!"

Nan paled at the reprimand and sagged back in her chair while Jolie used the last of the hot water on the stove to scrub her hands. When she felt reasonably clean, she went outside to the well with a bucket, then returned to put the tea kettle on.

The day was sweltering, but Jolie had been so busy she'd forgotten the heat. Weather notwithstanding, the situation called for a cup of strong, sweet tea.

"If he dies I don't know what I'll do," Nan said, her voice a subdued wail. She was still whiter than Great-aunt Gussie's ghost, and she rocked back and forth in her chair as though she couldn't stop moving, but she'd stemmed the worst of her panic. "Out here, all by myself, with a baby coming—"

"Why, you'd do what you had to, grieve and then get on with your life," Jolie broke in, finding cups and a crockery teapot on the shelf. "And you're not 'all by yourself'—you've got Daniel and me."

Nan looked at her with bleak eyes. "You're a kind woman, Jolie Beckham, and your Daniel is a fine man.

But I'd just as soon Joe and I went right on like we have been."

Jolie didn't have an answer, so she just touched Nan's hand again and went about brewing the tea.

When the doctor finally arrived, Joe's flesh was the waxy color of death, and his breathing was so shallow that his chest barely moved. The crusty old physician examined the bite, said Daniel had done the right thing by drawing out the poison and Jolie by cleaning the wound, and walked out of the little lean-to bedroom, shaking his head from side to side.

He was headed directly for the door, but Nan blocked his way and took hold of his sleeve with one hand. "Joe's going to get better," she said, in a strained voice, as though the intensity of her feelings could make it so.

The doctor shook his grizzled head. "I'm sorry, Mrs. Culley," he said hoarsely. "The venom has spread through his system. I don't look for your husband to pull through."

Nan didn't say anything in reply, but her straight back stooped a little as she let go of the old man's arm. Without looking to the left or the right, she slipped back to Joe's bedside.

Jolie's sadness swelled in her throat, but if there was one thing she'd learned in her eventful life, it was that sometimes all a person could do was just keep putting one foot in front of the other. She mixed up a batch of corn bread and put it in the oven to bake, then heated a jar of beans from Nan's shelf of goods.

Her friend refused to eat, but Gemma and Hank were hungry. Jolie sat with them on the Culley's rickety stoop and forced herself to swallow a share of the food.

Daniel rode up on the big gray draft horse, just as

the sun was blazing its last rebellious battle against the night sky. Jolie's aching heart was eased a little by the way he swept Gemma up to ride on his shoulders and ruffled Hank's hair as the boy scrambled along at his side, but the feeling was short-lived.

"Go and see to my horse," Daniel said to the children, when he finally stood facing Jolie, his eyes as wary and unfriendly as ever. He set Gemma down, and she rushed off to help, as eager to please Daniel as her brother was. "Mind you don't get behind him," the big man called after them, looking back over one hulking shoulder.

"The doctor says Joe's going to die," Jolie said, in a voice ragged with misery, when the little ones were out of earshot, leading Daniel's horse to the trough out in front of the barn.

Daniel sighed and pushed back his hat to shove one hand through his dirty hair. "How's Nan bearing up?" he asked quietly.

Jolie shook her head. "She's not. I tried to get her to eat something—I was thinking of the baby as much as Nan herself, but she wouldn't touch a bite. All she wants to do is sit there holding Joe's hand and staring at him as if she can make him live just by willing it."

Memories contorted Daniel's strong features for a moment, and Jolie didn't need a crystal ball to figure out what he was thinking. There was no doubt in her mind that he was recalling his own vigil beside Ilse's deathbed. He looked straight through Jolie, just as if she'd turned invisible, as he walked on into the house without a word of reply, his hat held respectfully in one hand.

Jolie wanted to follow after him, but that would have been an intrusion of sorts, so she smoothed her skirts and remained where she was, watching through blurred eyes as Hank and Gemma brought a bucket of oats from the barn for Daniel's horse.

Just as the sun gave up its struggle and sank behind the wheat in a burst of crimson fire, Joe Culley passed on. Jolie knew it had happened by the wail of grief from inside the cabin, and the sounds of Daniel trying to lend a shy man's inept comfort. Murmuring a brief prayer, Jolie got to her feet and carried the plates and utensils from supper back into the cabin.

Nan was huddled close against Daniel's chest, sobbing. The wildness of her pain and fury pulsed in that little house like a heartbeat.

Jolie felt an agony of her own: the inability to help her friend in any solid way. Indeed, it was Daniel who seemed to hold things together.

He took Gemma and Hank back to camp with him, and sometime later, well after dark, Deuter arrived, bringing Verena Dailey.

"The little ones are at my place," Verena told Jolie, who had come out to greet her in the light of the lanterns swaying on either side of Deuter's wagon. "Essie Sue Philpot is with them—she's the postmaster's daughter. Where's Nan?"

Jolie gestured sadly toward the house. "Ever since Daniel left, she's been sitting in the rocking chair, talking to Joe just as if he could hear her."

Verena let out a heavy sigh and adjusted her proper black gloves. "Well, we've got to see to the laying out. The weather's too hot to wait long for the burying, and besides that, it's harvesttime."

Apparently, Jolie thought, with a twinge of bitterness, even a tragic death like Joe Culley's couldn't be allowed to interrupt the bringing in of the crops. She followed Verena into the house.

Inside, the widow removed her veiled hat and laid

aside her gloves. "You go on back," she said to Deuter, with a wave of one age-spotted white hand. "We women will see to things here, and I dare say Mr. Pribbenow will arrive with a coffin first thing in the morning."

Deuter hesitated, his hat in his hands, his dust-coated face a study in misery. "I could draw some water and haul it in before I go," he offered, glancing in Jolie's direction and apparently finding her a pitiful sight.

Verena was already on her way into the lean-to, where even then Nan could be heard talking with frantic good cheer, to her dead husband. "We'll need water for washing the body," she said, with a thoughtful nod. Then she went to Nan and laid both hands on the young woman's trembling shoulders.

Jolie built up the fire, even though the cabin was already unbearably hot, and when Deuter brought the water in, she had kettles ready to heat it.

Somehow, Verena persuaded Nan to sip a glassful of the homemade blackberry wine she'd brought from her place. Nan went into a sort of trance after that, and sat out on the front porch, staring up at the stars and singing in an odd, eerie voice.

Meanwhile, Verena and Jolie saw to the necessary task of preparing Joe Culley for a final wagon ride to the churchyard. They were not repulsed by the work —the laying out of the dead was a task women were called to do, like bearing children and cooking for their men. Still, it was a sad interval, and tears slipped down Jolie's cheeks as she helped Verena strip away Joe's torn, dirty clothes, wash his waxen flesh clean, and dress him up again in his Sunday best.

When his hair was slicked down and combed,

Verena laid pennies on Joe's eyes to hold them closed and led the way out of the bedroom.

She and Jolie washed thoroughly, neither one speaking, and went out to sit on the stoop, on either side of Nan. They each took one of her hands and there the three of them sat, through the long, chilly hours of the night, waiting for Philias Pribbenow to drive up in his wagon and collect Joe Culley's remains.

Jolie was half-blind with fatigue and despair when she returned to the wheat camp the next day. A dark-haired woman was there, cooking for the men, and her Latin eyes swept over Jolie with an expression of hot disapproval, but she offered no explanation for her presence. And Jolie asked for none.

Verena had taken Nan home with her, after Mr. Pribbenow and his assistant had carried Joe away in his new pine-board coffin.

Jolie wasn't aware of Daniel's presence until he took her elbow to help her up the cook-wagon steps.

"The funeral?" he asked, his voice barely more than a rumble.

"This evening, soon as it cools off a little," Jolie answered, without looking at her husband, sighing and pushing a sweat-soaked tendril of hair back from her face. "Nan's with Verena."

Daniel halted her progress when she would have gone on into the wagon, where she'd intended to splash her cheeks and throat with tepid water and start preparing the next meal.

"Look at me, Jolie," he said.

She had no strength left to rebel, so she met Daniel's gaze and saw that he was regarding her gently. That was almost her undoing. "Nan's going to sell the farm and go live in town until after she's had the baby," she said spiritlessly, because she knew Daniel expected words from her.

"I'm taking you home," he said decisively. "You'll be able to rest there." Despite his husbandly statement, there was a certain distance in Daniel's manner. He let go of her arm and stepped back. "Get your things."

"I have all these men to cook for," Jolie said, wondering what she'd done to displease Daniel now.

He shook his head. "Pilar will see to that. I won't have you pushing yourself into a state of collapse, Mrs. Beckham, and that's final. Gather up whatever you need—Deuter will take you back to the house in a few minutes."

Pilar. The name had a stinging familiarity, though Jolie was too exhausted and distraught to piece together why the very sound of it bothered her so. She put the poetry book she'd been trying to read into her satchel, along with her spare dress, her nightgown, and the brushes she used to groom her hair and clean her teeth.

When Deuter appeared with a wagon, Daniel hoisted Jolie up into the seat behind the hired man.

"Don't bother with the chores," Daniel ordered his wife quietly. "Just get yourself something to eat and lie down and rest."

Jolie nodded dumbly, and her distracted gaze wandered back to the stranger, Pilar. The woman's hard yet singularly lovely face was turned toward her, and as Jolie watched, the full lips formed a small, triumphant smile.

When she and Deuter reached the farmhouse, Jolie didn't even want to go inside. She yearned to stretch out in the cool, fragrant grass under the poplar trees instead, close her eyes, and not have to entertain another painful thought for years and years. She was sitting cross-legged on the shady ground when Deuter brought her icy well water in a metal cup.

"You see that I don't miss that funeral," she said, with all the sternness she could manage, after she'd taken a long drink. "Mrs. Culley will need all her friends around her."

Deuter took the cup gently from her hand, his voice low and quiet. "Don't you fret, Miz Beckham. I'll look out for you."

Jolie McKibben Beckham lay right down, weary as Eve after the flight from Eden, and slipped into a sound and desolate sleep.

12

Daniel left the wheat early that day, in order to wash off a couple of layers of field dirt and put on clothes fit for bidding a permanent good-bye to a friend. He grieved deeply for Joe, and for the young, frightened wife he'd left behind, but there was yet another process working inside Daniel, fomenting in the very core of his spirit.

It was fear.

No one knew better than Dan Beckham did that life was dangerous and difficult and sometimes downright cruel; he could point to the graves out by the maple tree as proof of that. And now, just before sunset, he would see one of the best friends he'd ever had put into the ground—a man who'd been alive and well, working and dreaming, only a day ago.

Once again, Daniel was witness, in Nan Culley's fierce pain and bewilderment, to the terrible cost of caring. In the muggy, pungent privacy of the barn, he fed and watered his horse. And despite his formidable strength, he could no longer fight off the fact he'd been holding at bay for twenty-four hours.

It might have been Jolie who'd been bitten by that snake, or one of the children.

The knowledge so terrified Daniel that he gripped the railed sides of his hay wagon and held on for a long moment. An onslaught of gruesome images swept over him in a thundering wave. His shirt, already stiff with dirt and dried sweat, was instantly drenched.

Once that moment had passed, however, the wash of fear subsided, leaving a raw void in its wake. Daniel ran his shirt sleeve across his forehead and strode out of the barn.

That was when he saw Jolie curled up under one of the poplar trees. Although she was not a small woman, she looked so vulnerable lying there, like a doll left out by a forgetful child, and at the sight of her Daniel's insides clenched painfully.

He longed to gather Jolie up, carry her inside the house, and stand guard day and night for the rest of her life, to make sure nothing and no one ever hurt her. It was an impossible proposition, never mind that Jolie wouldn't have put up with it for a moment.

Daniel searched inside himself, sorting through a tangle of emotions until he found a safe one: anger. Damn it, did the woman *want* to be bitten by a rattler? Hadn't she told him herself that those two outlaws she'd been running with were around someplace, just waiting to start trouble?

He was about to hook one arm around Jolie's waist and yank her unceremoniously to her feet when the sound of a pistol being cocked brought him up short.

"Don't touch her, Dan'l," a voice said evenly. "Not unless you mean to do it in a kindly fashion."

Deuter was sitting just a few feet away, on an upended fruit crate, and he was pointing Daniel's own Colt .45 in an ominous direction.

"Damn you, Deuter," Daniel burst out, in a furious whisper, "put that thing down!" He still wasn't over the shock of having Deuter—of all people—challenge him so brazenly. Besides, protecting Jolie Beckham was *his* job.

The farmhand sighed and laid the pistol down in the deep grass without comment.

Evidently awakened by the stir, Jolie sat up, yawning and rumpled. Daniel saw the realization that he'd come to collect her for a funeral dawn in her face and wished there had been some way he could shield her.

"Is it time to leave?" she asked.

That dreaded sensation threatened to sweep over him again, but Daniel shored himself up. "Get yourself tidied up, Mrs. Beckham," he ordered gruffly. "We're expected in town."

With that, Daniel strode away to pump himself some water for a bath.

Jolie gave Deuter a sad smile as she got to her feet. She knew he'd been sitting nearby, practically the whole time she was sleeping, and she was touched.

She didn't bother to heat water to wash with. Instead, she got herself a cloth and soap and a towel, along with fresh underthings and her brown sateen church dress, and bathed herself out in the well house. The cool bite of the water, pumped from the depths of the earth, braced her up for the ordeal ahead.

Or perhaps it numbed her. When Jolie and Daniel arrived in town in the wagon, an hour or so after she'd awakened from that dreamless sleep in the fragrant grass, she had an odd sense of unreality. She pinched the tender skin on the inside of her forearm, on the off chance that she wasn't in town to see Joe Culley buried at all, but still slumbering underneath the poplar tree.

The churchyard was surrounded by buggies and wagons and lone horses tethered to the picket fence. Most of the mourners were dressed in their work clothes, having just left the sawmill or the harvest, the bank or the livery stable.

Daniel lifted Jolie down from the wagon. There was comfort in the solid strength of his arms and despair in the careful holding-away as he made sure their bodies didn't touch.

Gemma and Hank appeared, their dandelion gold hair bright in the last fiery sunshine of the day, their blue eyes filled with fear and questions as they looked up at Jolie. She hugged them both close for a moment, and kissed each one on top of the head.

"Have you been minding Mrs. Dailey?" she asked, her voice husky.

"Yes, ma'am," Hank said staunchly. "We surely have. But Gemma and me, well, we've got a mind to come home with you, if that's all right with you."

Daniel's big frame stiffened at the word *home*, but Jolie pretended not to notice.

"We'll be getting on with the harvest tomorrow, I'm sure," she told the child. "Frankly, I could use somebody to carry water and pick berries and catch trout for the men's dinner."

The two worried little faces brightened. In that remarkably subtle way he sometimes had, Daniel herded his brood toward the graveside, where Joe's other friends were gathered.

Although she would not have thought to lean on him, Jolie took blessed assurance from knowing Mr.

Beckham was standing directly behind her, as solid and well-rooted as a cedar tree. She looked on, dry-eyed and oddly distant from the proceedings, while the minister said Bible words over Joe's pinewood coffin.

All around her, women wept softly, and Jolie wondered if it was some lack in her spirit that let her endure the ceremony so stoically. Nan's thin shoulders were moving with the force of silent sobs, and Verena's eyes were suspiciously bright behind her black net veil.

This was what it all came down to, Jolie thought dispassionately. A person worked and hoped and dreamed and suffered for whatever number of years the good Lord had allotted to them. Then, if they'd lived a respectable life, a few friends would show up to cry for them when they were lowered into the ground some summer day—harvest allowing, that is.

Jolie raised her eyes to the pink and gold and crimson sky for a moment, wondering if there really was a place for folks to go after they'd left this world, like the preachers claimed.

When she looked at Nan again, and it took some doing to get up the courage for that, she was startled to see Ira January standing beside the new widow, holding her arm. The millowner was handsome, in an oily sort of way, but the sight of him made a shiver roll under Jolie's skin, like it did when she saw Blake Kingston or Rowdy Fleet.

In due time, Nan Culley was led away from the grave, and the women of the Methodist Church, normally at odds with those of the Presbyterian persuasion, served a picnic supper to the mourners. Jolie ate, knowing she needed the sustenance, but the food seemed to have neither taste nor texture, and it didn't come near to filling the hollow place inside her.

Nan had made up her mind not to return to the farm, except to fetch her things, and it was said that Mr. January had rented her a room at Mrs. Krayper's boarding house. He was sure enough sticking close by her side during the funeral supper.

When he finally went off to smoke with the other men, under a leafy oak tree, Jolie approached Nan. She'd already said all the words of consolation she knew, so she just asked the question that was uppermost in her mind. "Is Mr. January some kin of yours?"

Nan raised her chin a notch. She was pale as winter moonlight, and her eyes looked like two burnt holes in a blanket. Her beautiful auburn hair was hidden under a dark bonnet. "He's a friend," she said stiffly. She looked away for a moment, and her ivory cheeks flushed apricot. "I'm not strong like you, Jolie," she finished, giving the words a defiant tone.

If anything, Nan's confession heightened the sympathy Jolie felt for her, but it certainly didn't inspire the disapproval Nan seemed to expect. Jolie took her friend's arm in a gentle grasp and lowered her voice to a whisper. "You mean, he's going to be your—protector?"

"A woman needs a man to survive," Nan replied, and there was a desperate glint in her eyes. "I have a baby coming—"

"You have a farm to sell," Jolie reminded her friend, certain the proceeds from the sale of the land would allow Nan to support herself and her child.

But Nan shook her head. "There are too many debts," she answered. "And Joe and I had just barely proved up on our claim when—" She stopped. "Mr. January will see to it that I have a place to live for the time being, and after—after a year—"

After a year, Nan and Ira January would be married. Jolie was about to protest that no woman should wed a man under such circumstances, but she stopped herself at the last moment. Who was she, Jolie McKibben, to lecture someone else on the proprieties of marriage? She'd had no say in the matter of her own wedding; Big Dan Beckham had plucked her out from under that hanging tree like he would a sparrow from a rain barrel.

Jolie took Nan's cold hands into her own and squeezed them reassuringly. "Don't make the mistake of thinking Mr. January is your only friend," she warned kindly. "You've got Daniel, and me, and Verena, and all these other folks."

Tears brimmed in Nan's eyes. She bit her lip and nodded.

A few minutes later, the Beckhams left the churchyard. Hank and Gemma were asleep in the back of the wagon, replete with food and the excitement of a community event, funeral or not, and crickets sang in the grass. Daniel had lit the lamps that swayed on either side of the buckboard, though there was a moon, and he seemed so deep in thought that Jolie didn't even attempt a conversation.

They returned to the wheat camp, rather than the farmhouse, and Jolie heard the lonely sound of a mouth harp even over the creaking of the harnesses and fittings and the braying of mules. It all flowed together to make a sad refrain—Joe Culley would never come whistling up to the Beckham's back step again.

* * *

Daniel had forgotten all about asking Pilar to come and cook for the men while Jolie was helping over at the Culley place. When he brought the wagon to a halt at the edge of camp, though, he was bluntly reminded.

Pilar came sashaying toward him in one of those Spanish blouses that didn't cover her shoulders and a ruffled skirt of such a bright shade of red that it showed plainly in the dark. Her hands rested on her full hips, and her eyes caught sparks from the bonfire as she looked at Jolie.

"Get your things," Daniel said to Pilar, "and I'll take you back to town."

Pilar's chin jutted to a downright mulish angle but, after a moment, she smiled vindictively and shrugged one fire-lit shoulder. "I guess I've got no call to be surprised," she said, watching Jolie, who was standing stock-still, like a furious cat in that split second before it turns tiger and commences to screaming and clawing. "When Big Dan Beckham has no more use for his women, he just tosses them to one side and goes on to find another."

Daniel started to speak, but Jolie cut him off.

"Pilar," she breathed, glaring right back at the woman like she was about to let loose with a right swing. Just when Daniel thought he was going to have to restrain Jolie, she turned and looked up at him, and despite the darkness he could see the wounded fury in her eyes.

Obviously, she'd pieced together the facts: Pilar was a saloon woman, and her lush body had been a sweet comfort to Daniel on many a bleak night.

It was clear enough that Jolie believed Daniel had brought Pilar to camp for some other reason than cooking.

Pilar's smile widened—she'd done what she'd

aimed to do with only a few words—she was evidently satisfied. She swished over to the cook wagon and climbed the steps to collect her things.

Daniel started to defend himself, then decided it was probably better if Jolie thought he was low-down enough to sleep with one woman when he was married to another. That would make it easier for her to head off to San Francisco when the harvest was over and make some sense of her life.

After setting her jaw and favoring Daniel with a look hot enough to melt the ice off Onion Creek on the coldest day in December, Jolie swept the skirts of her church dress up in both hands and stomped off to see to the children.

Keeping himself from going to her and swearing he hadn't sullied their vows was one of the hardest things Daniel had ever been called on to do. As he helped Pilar into the wagon and then handed up her carpet-bag, he reasoned that it didn't really *matter* if he kept his promises to Jolie or not. Their marriage ceremony hadn't had any real meaning, after all; he'd only been trying to save the woman from being hanged.

The wagon springs creaked as Daniel climbed up into the box and took the reins. Come to that, Jolie could just go ahead and think whatever she wanted.

He turned his mind to the Culley farm, waiting to be harvested, and despite the genuine grief he felt at the loss of a good friend, he coveted the rich land and the sturdy little house with an intensity that shamed him. If he bought those acres—and he couldn't because of the money he'd spent to save Jolie from the noose—his farm would be the most substantial piece of land between Spokane and the Oregon border. Better still, his younger brother, Enoch, could finally bring his family west and settle in at Joe's place.

Then, Daniel and Enoch would be partners and neighbors, as well as brothers.

There were other advantages to the idea, too. After Jolie and the children were gone, Daniel's big place wouldn't seem so empty. Not with Enoch and Mary and the little ones just across the fields . . .

After putting Hank and Gemma to bed in the cot inside the cook wagon, Jolie fetched blankets and a pillow and made herself a pallet underneath. The grass was flat and dry beneath her bedroll that night, and it had lost its sweet fragrance.

Jolie closed her eyes, glad to see the last of that wretched day, but a grim kaleidoscope of scenes blossomed in her mind, driving away any hope of sleep.

She saw Nan standing beside Joe's newly dug grave, wringing her hands and weeping, with Ira January hovering at her side. Jolie sat bolt upright with such speed that she thumped her head against the bottom of the wagon.

Rubbing her aching crown with one hand, Jolie whispered a string of curse words she'd thought she'd forgotten. She was going to have a goose egg the next day, but that didn't matter in the scheme of things, and neither did a little pain. It had just occurred to her that Mr. January might be courting Nan because he expected to get the deed to her farmland along with a bride and another man's baby.

Jolie sank back onto her blankets. She didn't know the millowner well enough to be making such judgments, she told herself, but her instincts insisted the man was a skunk and a scoundrel.

Maybe Nan hadn't told him about the debts. Maybe she was that scared, that desperate.

She rubbed her sore head with one palm, and her throat tightened as she fought down a powerful urge to weep. Not for poor Joe, God rest him. No, the reason Jolie wanted to cry was a far less noble one: Daniel hadn't put aside his saloon woman, even though he had a wife to turn to when the needs of a man were upon him. He'd been brazen enough to bring a prostitute right to that camp, with all the field hands knowing who she was, while Jolie wasn't around to look after her interests.

The mournful rhythm of the harmonica filled the night, seeping into Jolie's soul like smoke.

She tried to sleep, tried desperately, but as the hour grew later and later, and she didn't hear the sound of a returning wagon, she could no longer deny what she knew to be true. Daniel was spending the night with his mistress, brazen as brass, with his wife and all the field hands knowing.

The hurt and humiliation were almost more than Jolie could bear. She felt shamed, as if she'd been the one to do something wrong.

Presently, she turned onto one side, watching through tear-blurred eyes as the stars twinkled above the moon-washed wheat, bright as rhinestones on dark cloth.

She vowed by all that was holy that no one would ever guess how deeply the pain of her husband's betrayal had pierced her. Especially not Daniel.

The next morning, Jolie rose before the sun, as usual, and the instant she opened her eyes, the hopelessness was there to greet her. Breakfast was well underway, and the men were finishing off the second pot of coffee, when Daniel finally turned up, driving his battered wagon. He was clean and dressed in fresh work clothes, and he silently dared Jolie to ask where he'd been.

She didn't.

Instead, Jolie dished up a plate of ham and eggs, poured coffee into an enamel mug, and held them out to Daniel. She hoped it was plain that, from her point of view, Mr. Beckham was just another hired hand.

Daniel had not slept in that cluttered little room over the Ivory Rose Saloon the night before, though that was what he wanted Jolie to believe. Instead, he'd sat up until all hours, jawing with the jaybird who'd replaced Hamish Frazer as head of the Fidelity Bank. Then he'd gone home to the farmhouse to have himself a bath and lie tossing and turning in his lonely bed until dawn broke.

He'd been half hoping Jolie would fly into a magnificent rage when he showed up in camp, but she'd disappointed him as well as the harvest crew by treating him just like anybody else. Hell, she'd hardly batted an eyelash.

The day's work began soon after he'd handed back his plate, and Daniel took solace in that, just as he had all his life. For all the backbreaking demands of the harvest, the need of Jolie and the comfort she might have lent echoed within him like the wind trapped in a canyon.

The smell of supper was in the air as nightfall approached, and the men and mules were exhausted from cutting and threshing wheat. Even though he was hungry as a bear waking up in the dead of winter, Daniel didn't stay to eat, and he didn't speak to Jolie.

Back at the house, he did the evening chores and gave old Leviticus a saucerful of creamy milk. Then Daniel wolfed down a quart of canned venison and half a loaf of stale bread, both scavenged from the pantry.

He was still starved when he washed up out by the pump and put on his doing-business suit, which also served for church on Sundays, but there was no helping that. Daniel had finally managed to make up his mind about one of the dilemmas in his life, and he was a great believer in doing one thing at a time.

He just hoped Enoch and Mary would be able to make the trip west before the snow flew.

Much to Jolie's surprise and, though she wouldn't have admitted as much, her relief, Daniel returned to camp that night. She was playing checkers with Deuter, a stump serving as a table, upside-down stew kettles for stools.

"What's going on here?" Daniel demanded, as though he'd caught Deuter and Jolie wearing each other's clothes.

Jolie didn't look up from the board, but it wasn't because she was being coy. She couldn't let Daniel see the flush of color pounding in her cheeks. "Just whiling away a summer evening, Mr. Beckham," she answered, as coolly as if he were a peddler offering shoddy wares.

Out of the corner of one eye, Jolie saw Daniel's gaze swing to Deuter. "Go and see to the mules," he said evenly.

Deuter was considering a move on the gameboard, one brawny hand rubbing his chin. "The mules have been seen to," he replied.

This time, there was no mistaking the tone of Daniel's voice or the set of his shoulders. "See to them again," he said.

For all his other shortcomings, Deuter was no fool.

He rose from his seat on the upturned kettle and strolled off toward the rope corral, whistling as he moved through the warm summer evening.

Daniel took his place across from Jolie, crouching down to face her after edging aside the cooking pot with one foot. He sighed, clasped his hands together, unclasped them, took off his hat and put it on again.

"He would have beaten you," he said presently, surveying the red and black game pieces between them.

Jolie suppressed a smile. "Thank you for telling me that, Mr. Beckham. I must confess that, for a while there, I was indulging in foolish hopes."

Daniel flung his hat aside, into the dry grass, and let out his breath in an impatient huff. "I bought the Culley place," he blurted out. "And that means—well, it means I won't have the money to set you up in San Francisco until after another harvest. You'll have to stay here in the meantime."

A whirlwind, made up partly of pure joy and partly of bruised pride, threatened to lift Jolie off that old cast-iron kettle and spin her through the air like the down of a dandelion. She anchored herself to the ground by wrapping both arms tightly around her knees and remembering how it was to face the workers and serve their food, knowing they were aware of Daniel's visits to Pilar.

"I don't have to stay anywhere, Daniel Beckham," she whispered when, at long last, she thought she could control her renegade emotions enough to speak. "I've been on my own before and I'm not afraid to take to the road."

Daniel leaned toward her, and she knew he was seething by the meter of his breathing. "You wouldn't dare."

Jolie arched an eyebrow and looked straight into his eyes. "Wouldn't I?" she countered sweetly, and then she moved to stand, meaning to round up Gemma and Hank and send them off to bed.

But Daniel took her arm in a hard if painless grasp and set her right back down again. "Damn it, woman, you'd best not try," he warned, in an undertone. "No wife of mine is going to go traipsing around the territory, with nobody to look after her!"

She pulled free of him. "That's exactly what I am," she responded, with an airiness she didn't feel. "No wife of yours."

This time, he didn't stop her from walking away.

Hank and Gemma were over by the fire, listening as the men told stories. Although they grumbled when Jolie told them to see to their private business and wash their faces and hands in the basin she'd set on the cook-wagon steps, they obeyed readily enough. And both of them were sound asleep almost as soon as they'd climbed into the cot.

Jolie smoothed back their dusty golden hair and kissed their foreheads, then blew out the lamp and got her blankets together. The fire was out and the camp was quiet, except for the snuffling of the mules and the snoring of the exhausted field hands, when Daniel joined his wife underneath the wagon.

"Go away," she whispered.

"Not likely," he said, and settled into the blankets beside her, stripped to his summer underwear.

"Don't you dare touch me," Jolie warned, even though a wanton part of her ached for Daniel's possession.

Without a word, he unbuttoned the front of her dress and, heaven help her, she couldn't so much as raise her hands to stop him. It was dark underneath that wagon, and the scents of Daniel and the grass and the fertile earth filled Jolie with primitive needs and feelings. She longed for his weight to settle upon her, and for the fierce, blissful fire of his taking.

"Daniel," she whimpered, torn between desire and her own vast pride.

He laid aside the front of her dress, pulled up her camisole until her plump breasts were bare, and bent his head to lightly kiss one distended nipple.

"Daniel," Jolie repeated, knowing she was lost.

When Jolie awakened the next morning, feeling sated and more confused than ever, she was alone. She washed in the limited privacy of the wagon, put on the cleanest of her dirty calico dresses, and went out to fry up plattersful of salt pork, cold boiled potatoes cooked the night before, and the eggs Deuter had gathered for her back at the farm. She put coffee in the crimson embers of the fire to brew and smiled sleepily while the men simultaneously ate and teased her about her cooking.

Only Daniel was stubbornly silent and unsmiling, and Jolie wished she dared snatch the brimming plate out of his hand and empty it right over his head. He was the most confounding, mule-headed man she'd ever had the sorry luck to run across.

More's the pity, she thought, with an inward sigh, that she loved him so much she sometimes felt sure she wouldn't be able to contain the emotion.

That day carved the groove into which the future flowed. The harvest went on, in a dizzying spindrift of days, and Jolie worked until even her spirit was numb. At night, she played checkers with Deuter, or struggled with her reading, or sat around the fire and listened to the songs and stories the men carried with them like bedrolls and likenesses of the ones back home.

Sometimes, Daniel joined her beneath the wagon, when the rest of the camp was quiet and dark, always taking her into his arms and loving her into sweet madness, always treating her like a distasteful stranger the next morning. Jolie was ashamed of her ready compliance, but her need for Daniel went far beyond the physical, into realms she didn't begin to understand, and she could no more have spurned him than refused her next breath or stopped her heartbeat. She took the bittersweet moments her husband allotted her, and she cherished them, despite her brave words about taking to the road one day.

13

On September fourth, the day after Daniel and his crews had finished harvesting wheat for those neighboring farmers who'd contracted for the service, the rain came in a pounding deluge. It thundered against the roofs of the barn and house and made pockmarks in the stubbled fields, turning dry dust to mud. What remained of the garden was battered to the ground, and the scarecrow's hay-stuffed limbs sagged.

Daniel hoped it was an omen, the storm holding off until after the crops were in, that it meant God approved of his buying Joe Culley's land and sending for Enoch and his family. Daniel was a practical man, however, and square in the center of his mind he knew it was raining because nature had decreed that it should. Period.

A few of the men who'd worked for him were holed up in the barn that afternoon, waiting for the storm to let up so they could get back to their own places. Some would spend part of their wages for stagecoach passage, but the majority planned to make the journey home, in whatever direction it might lie, on foot. Most were depending on the money they'd earned to see them and their families through a long and bitter winter, so they economized however they could.

In the meantime, Jolie would continue to cook for them.

The farmhouse kitchen glowed with the light of kerosene lanterns, and a warm fire crackled in the stove. Jolie had wrestled Hank onto a high stool in the center of the floor and was trying to cut his hair. The boy squirmed, his blue eyes baleful as they regarded Daniel from beneath the rim of a crockery bowl. Gemma, in the meantime, was sitting in the rocker in a warm corner, quietly rocking her baby doll.

A bittersweet feeling unfolded in Daniel's heart and, after a moment, he resolutely snatched his hat and canvas coat from their pegs beside the door. He should have taken those little whippersnappers back to Spokane the moment he found them crouched in the back of his wagon.

Now, because he'd given in to Jolie's dictates, the parting would be a painful one.

"I'll be in the barn," he said, without looking back.

"Mind you stay covered up, Mr. Beckham," Jolie responded, in a matter-of-fact tone, her shears making a rhythmic sound. "You could catch your death in this weather."

In spite of himself, Daniel smiled a little. Odd as it seemed, one of the things he'd missed most after Ilse died was having a woman fuss at him. *Keep yourself warm, Mr. Beckham . . . Come have your supper while the food's still warm . . . Take off your shirt, please, and I'll tighten that third button . . .*

A gust of wind met Daniel as he opened the door and, for a moment, he thought better of leaving the warm kitchen. In the end, though, he decided the cold and wet might bring him back to his senses, and he proceeded through the downpour toward the barn.

Jolie's spirits were heavy as she put away her sewing shears—actually, they were really Ilse's, like so many things in that house. Like Daniel.

Gemma stopped her rocking, holding her china "baby" protectively, to regard Jolie with solemn eyes. Hank had wriggled off the stool and raced out of the kitchen the moment the bowl had been lifted from his head.

"Elsie's hungry," the child said, nodding toward the doll in her arms.

Jolie smiled, carrying the dish towel she'd draped over Hank's shoulders earlier to the door for a shaking out. She felt an achy little twinge halfway between her stomach and her heart. "I guess we'd better see that she gets a little something to eat, then. Do you think she'd like a cinnamon roll?"

The little girl nodded again, eagerly. "Yes, ma'am, I do," Gemma answered.

After fetching a fresh roll from the pantry—she had baked only that morning, because she was fidgety and needed some way to keep her mind off what she knew was coming—Jolie brought the pastry to Gemma on a luncheon plate.

"There you are, Elsie," Jolie said to the doll, with a little curtsey.

Gemma giggled and kept up the pretense of feeding the roll to her doll, snatching bites for herself when she thought Jolie wasn't looking. Jolie did her best not to watch, because it depressed her mightily to know that in a day or a week or, at the most, a month, Gemma and Hank would no longer be part of her life.

Her throat constricted, and she raised her chin another notch and stirred the chicken and noodles she was stewing for supper with more energy than necessary.

That night, after they'd eaten, Jolie put the children to bed early and told them a story she'd invented, about a band of gypsies. Hank was so enthralled that he nearly—though not quite—forgave her for the haircut, which, he avowed, had been an even worse trial than his Saturday bath.

Jolie's eyes were burning when she kissed Hank and Gemma good night after their prayers, turned down the wick in their lamp, and went out.

She found Daniel in the study, the only room in the house where clutter was ever permitted, working over his ledger books. Maybe it was Jolie's sense of impending heartbreak that gave her the brazen courage to approach him. Except for claiming his husbandly rights on a fairly regular basis, and taking his meals in the kitchen, Daniel avoided Jolie. He had been keeping his distance from her, emotionally if not physically, ever since Mr. Culley's death two weeks before.

He looked up when she entered the room, sighed, and shoved one hand through his hair. "I've been wanting to talk to you," he said, with gruff resignation.

Somewhat insolently—because on occasion behaving in a sassy manner kept embarrassing tears at bay—Jolie flopped down into the wing-backed leather chair facing Daniel's desk. She arched both eyebrows and folded her arms. "Well, Mr. Beckham," she asked, "have you found the money to get rid of me after all?"

Daniel regarded his unwanted wife with narrowed

eyes for a long moment, rubbing his stubbly chin with one hand. "I told you. You'll have to stay until after the next harvest."

Jolie was slightly relieved, though she would have hunted down Blake Kingston and kissed his feet before admitting as much. She bent the fingers of her right hand and studied her broken, peeling nails.

Her husband cleared his throat, averted his eyes for a moment, then met Jolie's gaze squarely. "I'm taking Gemma and Hank back to Spokane, soon as the rain lets up. You're welcome to come along if you want."

She turned her head quickly, to hide her reaction to Daniel's words. Even though his announcement had come as no surprise, Jolie still felt as though she'd been gored by an angry bull. Practically the last thing in the world she wanted to do was look on while Daniel handed the children over to strangers, but to avoid seeing them go would have been pure cowardice.

"I'll go along," she confirmed in a murmur, looking down at her hands now. They were knotted in her lap and the skin around the knuckles had gone milk white.

"Jolie." Daniel's voice contained a gentle reprimand. *"I warned you this would happen."*

She raised her eyes—they glittered with tears—but all she had left now was defiance. "Damn you, Daniel," she burst out in a raw whisper. *"Damn* you and your frozen heart!" With that, Jolie thrust herself out of the chair and dashed out of the study.

Out on the porch, she gripped the railing with both hands and sobbed as the rain fell.

It was a surprise, feeling Daniel's strong hands close over her shoulders. He turned her gently to face him, curved a calloused finger under her chin, and lifted. "Maybe it would be best if you just stayed here," he said, his voice hoarse.

Jolie tried to dash away her tears with the back of one chapped hand, but they seemed to fall as steadily as the raindrops bouncing against the porch roof and rustling in the shrubbery. "No," she said staunchly. "I want to see this through to the finish. I won't walk away from those children *one moment* before I have to."

Daniel's work-roughened palms came to rest against Jolie's wet face, and his thumbs caressed her cheekbones. He started to speak again but, before he could get the words out, Jolie pushed free of him, moving a little distance along the railing.

"You just keep your distance, Mr. Beckham," she said. "You won't be quieting my objections and having your way with me tonight!"

Remarkably, Daniel looked amused rather than annoyed. In the light flowing out through the parlor window, Jolie saw him smile slightly as he folded his arms across his chest and leaned back against one of the two posts that supported the porch roof. "I've never forced you, Jolie," he pointed out reasonably. An unspoken *I didn't have to* trembled in the misty night air. "I'm not about to start now."

Jolie nodded briskly, not knowing quite how to respond to Daniel's statement and edging farther away. It was quite damnably true, what he said . . . he had only to touch Jolie in an intimate way and she would catch fire under his hands.

"Good night, then," she said.

"Good night," he answered.

* * *

Later, Jolie waited for Daniel to come into their bedroom, silently vowing to horsewhip him if he so much as set foot over the threshold. As it happened, however, he didn't even try the doorknob. Jolie lay there, aching and too warm and insisting to herself that she was relieved, until just before the rooster crowed.

Like always, the stove was lighted and the lamps were pushing back the early morning darkness when Jolie reached the kitchen. The coffeepot had already been set over the fire, and the pungent aroma lent a moment's encouragement.

When she went to the door to peer out and check the weather firsthand, she encountered Deuter, mounting the steps with a basket of brown eggs in one hand. With the other, he touched the slouchy brim of his old hat.

"Looks like the rain stopped," Jolie remarked unnecessarily. If Deuter heard the worried note in her voice, he didn't comment.

"Yes, ma'am," he said, stepping past her into the kitchen and hanging his hat on its customary peg.

Jolie could dimly make out the shape of a wagon, out by the barn. She heard the jingle of harness fittings and the braying of mules. "I guess Mr. Beckham must be getting ready to head for Spokane," she said, near tears as she thought of how it would be, never seeing Gemma and Hank again, never hearing their laughter.

"No, ma'am," Deuter answered, setting the basket of eggs on the worktable near the sink. "Dan'l's got meetings in town today. About selling the crops and the like. He'll be signing papers to buy the Culley place, too."

So Daniel wouldn't be taking the children back to

Spokane . . . at least, not that day. The respite added vim to Jolie's step as she prepared to fry up a panful of eggs to go with breakfast. Mention of the Culley farm set her to wondering if Nan had changed her mind about marrying Ira January, now that Daniel was formally buying the land.

She began slicing bacon and dropping the pieces into her largest skillet. By the time Daniel came in, bringing the four hungry hired hands who still remained, she'd made up her mind to go ahead and ask if she could ride into town with him.

Jolie didn't speak to her husband until Deuter and the others had finished eating and left the house. Daniel lingered, sipping his coffee.

"Will you be seeing Mrs. Culley today?" she asked, helping herself to a cupful of the strong brew and sitting down to her own eggs, bacon, and toasted bread.

"I imagine so," Daniel allowed, a little distantly.

"Then I'd like to come with you."

"I'll be leaving in half an hour," he said, with a shrug. Then he carried his plate and mug to the sink and went out.

It hadn't exactly been a warm invitation, Jolie reflected, as she hurried up the stairs to wake Hank and Gemma, but it would have to do.

The children looked rumpled and worried as they sat up at opposite ends of the spare-room bed.

"Are we leavin' today?" Hank asked.

Gemma scrambled the length of the bed, on her knees, to huddle close to her brother and look up at Jolie with fearful eyes.

Jolie's throat tightened. "Not today," she managed to say, after a moment of inner struggle. Then she clapped her hands together once, smartly. "Hurry, now. Mr. Beckham won't wait for us, and you still have to dress and eat a little something."

Gemma and Hank rode in the back of the wagon, their faces bright from scrubbing and from excitement, while Jolie took her usual place beside Daniel in the box. He said almost nothing from the time they left the farm until they reached Prosperity.

Mr. January was waiting on the wooden sidewalk in front of the Fidelity Bank when Daniel brought the wagon to a stop. Even though the millowner was leaning one shoulder against a pillar and smiling, his jawline was set.

"Hello, Daniel," he said cordially, pushing himself away from the post and approaching, his thumbs hooked under his belt. He nodded in Jolie's direction. "Mrs. Beckham."

Daniel's manner was less than friendly, and he didn't take the trouble to smile. "You have business here?" he asked, in a brusque tone.

Mr. January adjusted his modish hat with a suave motion of one hand and shrugged one shoulder. "I don't have to have a reason for walking on a public street," he said, and though he was still showing his teeth in a broad grin, there was an edge to his voice. "I have as much right to be here as you do."

Jolie wondered why Daniel disliked the other man so intensely but, of course, that was neither the time nor the place to ask. She did her best to ignore the tension buzzing in the warm September air as Daniel reached up to help her down from the wagon.

In the instant his hands closed around her waist, however, Ira January and the quiet street and even the two children scrambling out of the wagon bed no longer existed for Jolie. She'd seen a look of worry in Daniel's spring sky blue eyes when he touched her, there for only a fraction of a heartbeat, then gone again. A look that turned the whole world cold.

It was Nan who distracted her, coming out of the millinery shop across the street, properly mournful in the heavy black garb of a widow.

"Hello, Jolie," she said, with a wan smile. Nan looked pale, and too thin for someone with another life growing inside her. She greeted the others with a nod. "Daniel, children."

Daniel's gaze shifted grudgingly from Nan's face to Mr. January's and then back again. "Hello, Mrs. Culley," he replied, as Hank crowded close to him and Gemma clung to Jolie's skirts. Their eyes, Jolie noticed, were fixed warily on Ira.

"Mr. January has very kindly agreed to look out for my interests, where this sale is concerned," Nan said, but she didn't look any too happy to have him there. In fact, it would have been Jolie's guess that her friend wanted to lift her skirts from the ground and run.

Daniel removed his hat and opened the bank door, gesturing for Nan to precede him inside, along with Jolie and the children. "Do you think I'd cheat you?" he asked his friend's widow.

Nan looked away. "No, Daniel, of course not," she replied, in a hushed, hurried little voice. "Mr. January is just being . . . attentive, that's all."

Daniel gave the other man a look Jolie didn't envy. "Yes," he responded evenly, "I imagine he is." When Daniel made a gesture with his right hand, Gemma and Hank scuttled over to sit quietly on a bench next to the window and wait, their feet swinging high off the floor.

"How did you do that?" Jolie muttered. Gemma always minded her just fine, but Hank had to be tracked down and dragged into the house by one earlobe whenever Jolie wanted him to take a bath or have his hair trimmed or just sit quietly. Why was it that he'd obeyed Daniel without so much as a moment's hesitation?

Mr. Beckham was still staring down Mr. January. "Mrs. Culley and I have agreed on a price," Daniel said. "We won't be needing any help from you."

Mr. January's expression was sullen and stubborn. He stood his ground, pulling a cheroot from his pocket and striking a match against the bottom of his boot to light the tobacco.

It seemed that Jolie had been spun around like someone blindfolded for a game, stumbling from one dreadful realization to another. First, there had been the infinitely painful knowledge that she was about to lose the children, then the cold shock she'd gotten looking into Daniel's eyes while he was lifting her down from the wagon, and now the awareness that Nan was still keeping company with Ira January.

The banker, Mr. Niddly, a young man with bright yellow hair and sideburns, came forward, smiling. He offered his hand to Daniel, then to Nan, then to Mr. January. He neglected to greet Jolie in the same fashion, though his manner was pleasant enough.

Chairs were drawn up in front of Mr. Niddly's desk, and everyone sat down. The meeting began.

Nan shifted nervously in her seat, and Jolie began to wonder if her friend had mentioned to Mr. January that she had debts to pay from the proceeds of the farm sale.

"Daniel is purchasing all the tools and equipment, as well as many of the household furnishings, one cow, and a team of two sorrel draft horses," Mr. Niddly said. "Is that correct?"

Nan nodded, her already milk white skin going a shade lighter. "Yes, sir," she answered.

The banker was clearly in a jovial mood. He opened a ledger book, wet the tip of his index finger, and paged through the records. "Once your debts have been cleared, Mrs. Culley," he said cheerfully, "you will still have the sum of one hundred and fourteen dollars to do with as you like."

For a moment, Jolie felt hopeful, because one hundred and fourteen dollars was an awful lot of money, but then she caught sight of Mr. January's face and realized her earlier fear had been a justified one. Nan's eager beau had not known there were debts to be settled.

First all the color seeped from Mr. January's face. Then, in the next instant, he was flushed red with surprise and annoyance.

"Debts?" he asked, in a deceptively soft voice.

Daniel actually smiled at the man—something Jolie would not have done. At least, not while Mr. January was wearing that six-gun strapped to his hip. "Debts," he confirmed.

Ira glowered at Nan, pushed back his chair, jumped up, and stormed out, slamming the door of the bank behind him. Nan covered her face with both hands and let out a loud, wailing sob.

Jolie immediately moved to console her friend, sitting in the chair beside Nan and wrapping an arm around her shoulders. "There, now," she said. "You don't want the likes of him anyway."

"I need a husband," Nan snuffled, while Daniel produced his handkerchief and Mr. Niddly shifted in his seat, obviously uncomfortable.

"Nonsense," Jolie responded briskly, patting Nan's back. "Husbands are nothing but work and trouble, anyway." She paused to pass Daniel a defiant look and snatch the handkerchief out of his hand. "What you should do is take your hundred and fourteen dollars and strike out for new horizons. You could probably find work in Seattle, in the cannery—"

"Let's just sign those papers, shall we?" Daniel interrupted, his voice as rusty as an old tin tossed down beside the trail somewhere.

Out of the corner of her eye, Jolie saw Mr. Niddly slide the documents toward Daniel with haste and relief.

Daniel signed and pushed them along the desk to Nan, who tearfully added her own signature. She'd calmed down a little by the time Mr. Niddly wrote out her bank draft and waved it delicately back and forth to dry the ink.

Nan folded the draft, tucked it into her threadbare handbag, and got out of her chair. Mr. Niddly and Daniel rose too, out of politeness, and Nan muttered something and left the bank.

The army had bought the bulk of Daniel's wheat for their installation at Fort Deveraux, and their representative had settled the account with Mr. Niddly. When the banker went off to get their draft from the safe, Daniel turned to Jolie. "Exactly what did you mean," he demanded, "when you told Nan husbands are nothing but work and trouble?"

Jolie tugged at her gloves and tilted her chin slightly to one side. "I might have added that they're stubborn and unreasonable, too," she answered primly, "if I'd just thought of it."

Daniel opened his mouth to say something, then thought better of the idea. Mr. Niddly was coming toward them, carrying the check from the army.

Growing restless, Jolie glanced toward the bench

where they'd left Hank and Gemma to see if the children were behaving themselves.

They were gone.

While Jolie's reasoning mind knew they'd probably just crossed the street to look at the toys in the window of the general store or to use the public privy behind the Ivory Rose Saloon, another part of her was wild with fear. She hadn't forgotten Blake Kingston's easy threats to use them to get what he wanted.

Heart hammering against the base of her throat, Jolie excused herself from the proceedings and hurried out the door.

Hank and Gemma hadn't gone to the privy, nor were they inside the general store or the millinery shop or either of the churches. Jolie didn't check the saloons; she would send Daniel to do that after he came out of the bank.

By the time he did, she was practically frantic, and she almost got run down by the midday stagecoach when she hurried across the street to meet him.

"I can't find Gemma and Hank anywhere!" she cried.

Daniel sighed and looked up and down the road with a slow turn of his head. "They're all right, Jolie," he said. "Deuter gave Hank a penny this morning, and they're probably buying candy."

The hair on the back of Jolie's neck was standing up. "I already checked the mercantile, Daniel," she said, making an effort to be calm. She touched his arm. "Will you look in the saloons?"

"Yes," Daniel replied, and he managed to pack a lot of comfort and reassurance into that one simple word. He steadied Jolie a little by gripping her shoulders for a moment. "You go to the schoolhouse, down that way." He indicated the direction with a thumb.

"There's a swing out back. If you don't find them playing there, try Mrs. Krayper's boarding house, right behind the Presbyterian church. She loves kids, likes to sit them down on her porch step with a glass of lemonade and a cookie."

Jolie nodded, praying Gemma and Hank would turn up in one of those safe, ordinary places, and turned to hurry off in search of them.

Daniel kept Jolie in sight until she'd turned a corner and disappeared. Women, he thought, with an inward sigh. A man could give them clothes, a roof over their heads, and food to eat, and how did they repay him? By saying he was nothing but work and trouble!

Scowling, Daniel started toward the nearest saloon, though he doubted he'd find Gemma and Hank inside. They'd have been thrown out of either the Lone Wolf or the Ivory Rose, since they weren't tall enough to see over the top of the bar.

There was a lot of noise inside the Lone Wolf. Men were already drinking and playing cards, and the piano was tinkling away loud enough to beat sin. If those kids were in there, he promised himself, he'd give them a talking to they'd still remember when they had wrinkles and gray hair.

His mood softened, though, as he thought of Hank and Gemma hiding in the back of his wagon that day, with their dirty faces, ragged clothes, and big, hungry eyes.

Just as he was about to walk into the Lone Wolf, he noticed the covered wagon across the street, in front of the mercantile. A young woman in a bright calico dress was offering a handful of grain to one of the plow horses hitched to the rig, her bonnet dangling down her back. Her husband was probably inside the store, haggling over the price of a keg of nails or a jug of molasses.

Daniel figured the couple for homesteaders, and he felt a pang as he watched the woman stroking the horses' necks and talking to them. He and Ilse had come to Prosperity in a rickety old wagon, too, with their love, a fifty-pound sack of beans, and a handful of dreams. . . .

He crossed the road and touched his hat brim politely to let the woman know he was a gentleman. "Morning, ma'am," he said.

She smiled and answered in a soft, familiar drawl that was soothing to Daniel's Southern ears. "Good morning, sir."

A movement under the canvas caught Daniel's eye, and inspiration struck. "You have some little ones traveling with you?" he asked.

"Yes, I do," she replied, walking away from the horses. "They're inside the store, with their papa."

Daniel rubbed his chin. "If you're sure of that, ma'am, I'd like to take a look inside your wagon, if you'll permit me. I happen to be missing a couple of barn monkeys, and they've been known to hide in other folks' rigs."

The woman smiled again and nodded, patting her stomach. Daniel hadn't noticed how her middle bulged until then. "Lord knows, Enoch and I have all the children we can look after as it is, and another on the way. Last thing we need is an extra pair."

Daniel was around behind the wagon before the full meaning of her words registered.

"Your husband's name is Enoch?" he asked, leaving the canvas flap untouched and stepping back into the street to stare at her.

Just then, a man with dark, curly hair and a ready

smile came out of the mercantile, with one child at his heels and another in the crook of his arm. "The store-mistress says Daniel lives a few miles east of here," he started.

Daniel's voice was hardly more than a croak, and his heart was hammering. This was his brother, one part of him reasoned, the boy who'd followed Daniel down the road, crying, when he left home that long-ago day, meaning to head west. Yet practicality told him Enoch couldn't have gotten his letter and made the trip from North Carolina in such a short time.

"Daniel?" the other man asked, setting down the child and pushing back his hat to reveal familiar features and mischievous hazel eyes.

"Enoch," Daniel replied, in a ragged whisper. And then he laughed right out loud, for sheer joy. "Enoch!" he shouted.

14

There had been no sign of Hank and Gemma at the schoolhouse swing, nor had Jolie found them sitting on Mrs. Krayper's porch, eating cookies and drinking lemonade. She was in a near panic, certain that Blake and Rowdy had added kidnapping to their list of crimes, when she reached the main street of town and saw the covered wagon.

Jolie supposed it had been there before she'd run off to look for the children; she'd just been too agitated to notice. Daniel was standing in the street, talking to a man and woman in poor clothes that had obviously seen much wear and washing, and he appeared to have forgotten he was supposed to be searching.

She stopped to take a deep breath, square her shoulders, and try to bring her raging fear under control. Since she couldn't restrain the emotion entirely, it burst forth as anger.

"Daniel Beckham, those children could be *miles* away by now, and here you stand, palavering with strangers!"

There was surprise in Daniel's expression when he turned to see what woman dared to treat him in such a way . . . as if he hadn't guessed who would be standing there, with her arms akimbo and her face burning hot.

Mild amazement gave way to humor, and Daniel smiled and cocked his left thumb toward the wagon. "Have a look in the back of the rig. My guess is, you'll find Hank and Gemma staring back at you."

Jolie swallowed hard as the powerful backwash of her own fright and frustration struck, leaving her shaken. The man and woman who had been talking with Daniel were looking at her, but she couldn't quite bring herself to meet their eyes. She scurried around behind the wagon and lifted the canvas flap.

Sure enough, Gemma and Hank were crouched inside. Gemma looked just plain scared, but Hank's expression was defiant as well as apprehensive.

Before Jolie could say a word, however, Daniel materialized beside her, his hands resting on his hips, his gaze narrowed on the small boy and girl before him.

"Just exactly where did you two figure on going?" the big man demanded sternly.

Hank raised the set of his chin by a notch or two and put his strong little arm around Gemma's shoulders in a protective gesture. "We was headed someplace where folks wanted us," he answered straightforwardly.

In a sidelong glance, Jolie saw Daniel flinch. Clearly, he'd convinced himself all along that Hank and Gemma didn't *know* he was planning to shuffle them right out of his life, the way he would a mule that refused to be broken to harness.

Or a wife he'd never wanted in the first place.

Daniel recovered quickly, and chuckled as he lifted his hat and settled it right back the way it was before. "You wouldn't have gotten far with these people." He looked at Jolie for a moment, then went on. "This is my brother, Enoch," he said. "And that's his wife, Mary, and his little ones, Ruthie and Holt. They're going to stay with us for a few days, then take over the Culley place."

Jolie's emotions were all a-tangle. She was happy that Daniel's beloved brother would be with him at last, and she was also a little jealous because he was so darned glad to see Enoch and Mary. Mostly, though, she was thankful that Gemma and Hank were safe and sound. Jolie held out her arms, and Gemma sprang into them and clung to her neck with wiry little arms.

As the child trembled against her, obviously just as relieved as Jolie was, Jolie closed her eyes tightly. *We women,* she thought, *are always being dragged somewhere we don't want to go, just because some man decides it's time to move on.*

"The boy's welcome to ride with us," Enoch said easily, when Daniel moved to help Hank down from the wagon. Daniel's brother was a good-looking, even-tempered man with mischievous hazel eyes, and Jolie couldn't help liking him.

A tentative, sunbrowned hand touched Jolie's sleeve. "You must be Daniel's wife," the pretty blond woman said, with a sort of shy hopefulness. Her green eyes were round and guileless, and filled with the tender hope that she'd be liked and accepted in this strange new place. "We hoped he'd remarry."

Jolie shifted Gemma onto her hip and smiled in a warm, welcoming fashion. This was no time to be explaining that she wasn't *really* Daniel's bride, but

224

more of a fallen housekeeper. "I'm Jolie," she said, offering her hand.

"Mary," replied Enoch's wife, with a little nod of acknowledgment.

It was much later, when the kitchen was cozy with lamplight and warm from the dying fire in the stove, when the children were all tucked away for the night and the men were in the barn, that Mary explained their unexpected arrival.

"It was a relief to Enoch and me to find out Daniel had sent for us," she said, gazing down at her tea, which she'd been consuming in delicate sips, as though it were ambrosia and the taste of it might never touch her tongue again. "Times are hard back home, and we just couldn't scrape out a living anymore. We came out here on the hope that we could homestead somewhere nearby." Tears brimmed in Mary's eyes, and Jolie's heart softened even more. Mary had probably done without even the simplest comforts of life for some time. She was expecting, with two little children to think about, and she hadn't known what she'd find in Washington Territory.

Jolie reached out to squeeze her sister-in-law's hand, and an infinite sadness swept over her. She and Mary might have been such good friends, sharing secrets, stitching quilts and making clothes for the children, putting up pretty cinnamon and mint pears to give to friends and neighbors at Christmastime. Instead, Mary would stay here, with a husband who clearly adored her, and Jolie would be sent off to faraway San Francisco. Out of sight, out of mind, that was Daniel's philosophy where she was concerned.

Mary was drying her eyes with the back of one small, calloused hand. "Is something wrong, Jolie? You looked mighty sad, just for a moment there."

Making herself smile, Jolie shook her head. She could not, *would* not burden this weary young woman with her troubles. "Would you like more tea?" she asked, and her voice sounded brittle instead of bright, as she'd intended.

Mary hesitated, then nodded eagerly. "Oh, yes. Please."

Jolie refilled Mary's cup from a cream-colored crockery pot with a blue stripe around its middle and set her chin in one hand. "You must be exhausted," she said, "coming all that way by wagon."

"We traveled as far as St. Louis by train," Mary said with a shrug, as though that changed the journey from a long, rigorous trek to a Sunday afternoon outing. In the next instant, though, her pretty eyes took on a haunted expression. "It took practically all the money we had to buy that wagon and outfit it. I was so scared we wouldn't get over the mountains before winter set in."

"But here you are," Jolie reminded her gently. "Safe and sound. And believe me, Daniel won't let you lack for anything. I'm sure this is the first happy surprise he's had in a good long while." She was sad again, wishing she and Gemma and Hank could have had the same effect on him.

Mary's fingers tightened around her teacup, then relaxed again. "It must have been dreadful for Daniel when poor Ilse and the new baby passed away, after they'd lost the little girl and all. He surely suffered, being so far from his loved ones."

The subject of Ilse, Daniel's *chosen* bride, was an uncomfortable one for Jolie, but she made no attempt to skirt it. "Yes, he suffered," she reflected, looking past Mary, seeing an image of Daniel standing at Ilse's graveside, hat in hand. "He loved her very much."

Mary ran the tip of her tongue over wind-chapped lips. "But he has you now. And he seems happy."

Jolie smiled, just to keep herself from crying. She simply didn't have the emotional energy to tell Mary that she'd been married to Daniel only because he didn't want to stand by and see a woman hanged. "For as long as he wants me," she said, so softly that Mary didn't seem to hear.

That night, Jolie and Daniel slept together in their bedroom, with Mary and Enoch just on the other side of the wall, in the extra room. Jolie folded her arms and stared up at the ceiling, wondering if Daniel was trying to give his brother and sister-in-law the idea that things were even remotely normal around that place.

"Did you tell Enoch about me?" she asked, in a soft, wary voice. "About how I'm an outlaw and everything?"

Daniel's chest moved abruptly, and he made a sound that might have been either a chuckle or an exasperated sigh. "You're not an outlaw, Mrs. Beckham," he replied, in a tone she couldn't read. It was too dark to make out his expression, so Jolie had to go on supposition.

"But you did tell him they were going to hang me?"

There was a long silence, then a reluctant, "Yes."

The mortification of that made Jolie's cheeks throb with heat, and she was glad of the darkness.

"It's the truth," Daniel said reasonably, after another significant pause. "Besides, he and Mary would have heard about it anyway. We don't have that many women come to Prosperity to get themselves hanged."

Much as she yearned to, there was no way Jolie could deny her husband's words. *I hate you, Big Dan Beckham,* she reflected, knowing the thought for a lie from the moment she conceived it. "I don't suppose you took the trouble to mention that I was innocent?"

Daniel shifted to lie on his side in the big, sturdy bed, and Jolie blushed again as the bedsprings creaked under his weight. She devoutly hoped Enoch and Mary wouldn't think she and Daniel were *doing* anything. She saw his white teeth flash as he smiled, trembled as his finger slowly traced the circumference of her nipple, making it go taut against the crisp cotton of her nightgown.

"I've never seen anybody hanged that didn't swear they were pure as the first snowfall in heaven," he teased, and Jolie thought grudgingly how much she loved the warmth and substance of him, the re-strained strength, even the sun-dried-linen scent of his skin.

She slapped his hand away from her breast, precise-ly because she wanted him so much, and because he was the most damnably presumptuous man she'd ever encountered. For all of that, she was already stretch-ing her toes languidly toward the foot of the bed.

"Leave me alone," she whispered, hoping he wouldn't notice how halfhearted she'd sounded.

He leaned down to nibble lightly at the base of her throat, causing the nerve endings to leap under their fragile layer of flesh. In the meantime, one of his big hands traveled along her thigh, dragging the soft cloth of her nightgown upward.

"If you say so." He breathed the words, bringing his mouth to one covered nipple even as his palm came to rest against the moist center of her femininity. "Do you say so, Mrs. Beckham?"

Jolie moaned as all her most personal muscles tightened in anticipation of the pleasure Daniel had taught her to want. His mouth was warm over her nipple, making the cotton of her nightgown moist, and the small morsel strained to nourish him. Her hips began to move, seemingly of their own accord, pressing her intimate place against the calloused flesh of his hand.

He opened the buttons at the front of her gown with fingers that were remarkably nimble, considering their size, and bared the breast he'd been teasing. "Mrs. Beckham?" he prompted.

"They'll—hear us," Jolie gasped, already dizzy with the sweet ferocity he was arousing in her. "The children—Enoch and Mary—they'll think . . ."

"They'll think I'm having my wife," Daniel finished for her, in a low, husky tone, and then his lips closed around her nipple and one of his fingers ventured inside her.

Jolie arched her back and bit down hard on her lower lip to keep from crying out in startled ecstasy. The passion always came as a surprise, because of its suddenness and its force, even though Daniel had made love to her often. He never used pretty words, but there was poetry in the way he made Jolie yearn for satisfaction and then quietly gave it.

She reached up to clasp the underside of the headboard in her fingers when Daniel pushed her nightgown up beneath her arms to make free with her breasts and her belly and, finally, the silken delta nestled between her thighs. Again and again, he brought her to the very precipice of glory, only to let her fall away at the last second like a dying star tumbling through the night sky.

Finally, Jolie could no longer endure the needing. "Daniel," she sobbed, and the name was a plea, a surrender, an order.

He nudged her legs apart with one knee and settled

himself upon her, letting her feel his length and hardness and power. "Say you want me, Jolie," he rasped, caressing her cheek with one hand, brushing aside the moist tendrils of gold that clung to her skin.

"You know I do!"

"Say it."

"I want you—*damn* you, Daniel, I want you."

His fingers curved gently over her mouth, muffling the cry of pleasure she could not hold back as he slid inside her, stoking inner fires that were already raging out of control.

Afterward, Jolie could not have said whether she carried on, or whether the bedsprings squeaked fit to wake all those awaiting the trumpet call in the churchyards of Prosperity. She just lay there, nestled against Daniel, waiting for her heartbeart and her breathing to slow down, her flesh drenched from the effort of meeting each thrust and parry with every shred of strength she possessed. She felt as though her muscles were soaked in warm honey, and she was unable to marshal the necessary reflexes to speak or move.

Daniel held her close, and his lips brushed her forehead. "Oh, Jolie," he mourned raggedly. "What is it about you that makes me forget every decent promise I've ever made to myself?"

She couldn't have mustered the strength to respond even if she'd had an answer to offer him. Daniel's lovemaking had left her with all the physical stamina of a pool of melted wax. But then, she knew Daniel didn't really expect a reply, because for all of it he'd been addressing himself more than her. She didn't dare suggest, or even entertain the fancy, that he couldn't resist her because he loved her. Just as she loved him.

When the even meter of Daniel's breathing told her

he was sleeping, Jolie closed her eyes and drifted into a sunny place where lush dreams awaited her.

It seemed only a moment later that Daniel awakened her with his customary nudge and raised himself to sit on the edge of the bed. She moved to touch his broad back but withdrew her hand at the last moment.

"I think there's a baby growing inside me," she said, and the announcement was obviously as much a surprise to Daniel as it was to her. She hadn't planned to think such a thing, let alone say it, but all of the sudden the words were just there, between them. "I was supposed to have my woman-time, but it didn't come."

He clasped her chin firmly in one hand and looked at her as though she'd just confessed to burning down a field of ripe wheat. "There's no mistake?"

Jolie counted in miserable silence. She'd never been much better with numbers than she was with the written word, but this was a sum she could cipher up easily. "No mistake," she said.

Daniel muttered something, released his hold on her, and stood.

Raising herself on her elbows, Jolie glowered at her husband. "You're a farmer, Daniel," she said tartly. "You, of all people, should know how babies get started."

He was busy wrenching on his clothes, and his only reply was an unintelligible grumble.

Jolie tossed back the covers, wounded and angry. Her eyes were stinging with hot tears. "Tell me, Mr. Beckham—did you see me as a whore? Did you think I was like they are, like Pilar, that I somehow knew how to keep myself from conceiving a child?"

Daniel stopped to stare at her and, for one frightening moment, Jolie actually thought he was going to strike her. "I didn't think anything of the sort," he breathed furiously. "And we've already talked about Pilar. That subject is settled!"

She bounded out of bed to stand toe to toe with Daniel, fists clenched at her sides, jaw set. "Just because *you've* decreed it?"

"Be quiet!" Daniel commanded. "You'll wake the whole house!"

"You weren't worried about that last night!"

He shook a finger under her nose. "Jolie, I'm warning you . . ."

"About what?" Jolie demanded fiercely, standing on tiptoe now. "You're nothing but a hypocrite, Daniel Beckham! You go to church every Sunday and pretend to be a pious man, but the plain truth is, you don't give a damn who gets hurt as long as you have your meals cooked, your clothes washed, and . . . and regular doses of wifely affection!"

A hoot of merry laughter sounded on the other side of the wall and, in the gray light of dawn, Jolie actually saw Daniel blush.

"So help me, I will not abide a fractious woman!"

Jolie snatched his shirt from the back of the rocking chair, where she'd carefully draped it the night before, and slammed it against his hard middle. "Not another word out of you," she burst out. "I'm going to have your baby and I'll be damned if I'll let you deny this child the way you've denied me!"

With that, Jolie grabbed a dress from the armoire and stockings and underthings from the bureau and slipped behind the changing screen. Her movements were awkward and fury was still pounding at every pulse point, but she managed to put on her clothes.

When she came out, Daniel was gone.

Muttering, Jolie washed her face, brushed her hair,

braided it into a single plait, and pinned it up in a coronet. Reaching the kitchen a few minutes later, she found Mary already there, with the stove going and the coffee perking. Pancake batter awaited pouring onto the griddle, and fresh bacon had been sliced for the skillet.

"It's good to work in a real kitchen again," the other woman said quietly, averting her eyes for a moment and then looking earnestly into Jolie's face. "I hope you don't mind my taking the liberty."

Jolie knew what it was to cook beans and wild game over a campfire alongside the trail for weeks and months on end, and she had only empathy for Mary. "Fact is, it's kind of nice not being the one to make breakfast, Mrs. Beckham," she said.

Mary smiled, and her green eyes twinkled merrily. "Then we're agreed, Mrs. Beckham," she responded.

By the time Daniel, Deuter, and Enoch came in from attending to the morning chores, their faces and hands glowing red from a scrubbing in icy well water, the meal was on the table. Daniel didn't once look at Jolie, even though she sat right next to him, and that was just fine by her.

Enoch occasionally glanced from Daniel to Jolie and back again as he ate, and seemed barely capable of containing his amusement. His eyes danced and it was obvious he wanted to laugh, that inside, he *was* laughing.

Jolie was mortified anew, recalling how she'd tossed and moaned beneath Daniel the night before, and the things she'd said that morning in their room.

It was a relief when the men finally finished eating and went outside to hitch up Enoch's team. The children trailed sleepily downstairs, first Hank and little Holt, then Ruthie and Gemma.

When Enoch stuck his head in the door to announce that they'd be heading over to the new place to "get situated," though, all four scrambled to empty their plates and dash out to the barnyard.

"Home," Mary murmured, emerald eyes alight, as she put on her bonnet and tied the calico strings carefully under her chin. "We're going home."

Jolie smiled. Lord knew, she had plenty of troubles of her own, but it was uplifting to see someone else feeling so happy. Hastily, she put the last of the dishes in hot, soapy water to soak—leaving them was unheard-of, but this was a special day—hung up her apron, and followed Mary outside into the sunny September morning.

Given the rutted road and the worn-out springs on Enoch and Mary's wagon, it was easier to walk the distance to the neighboring farm than to ride. Mary and Jolie strolled along behind, chatting, while Hank and four-year-old Holt rode astride one of the horses pulling the rig. Ruthie was perched on Enoch's shoulder and, when Gemma looked longingly from the man and girl to Daniel, he smiled and scooped her up and carried her the same way.

Jolie felt a sense of celebration, mixed in with all those other emotions, mostly conflicting ones, that made such a tangle inside her. It was fall, the crops were in and, for this little while, anyway, she and Gemma and Hank could pretend to be part of the Beckham family.

Nan had taken her personal things, clothes and brushes and wedding Bible and such, from the little house, but the basic furnishings were still there. Jolie felt an ache inside as she and Mary dragged the feather mattress outside to air and took the flour-sack curtains down from their hangings of droopy baling twine for washing. Life had a way of changing, like the course of a rushing river, and sometimes it happened in a split second.

"Enoch tells me Mr. Culley was bitten by a snake," Mary ventured, sometime later, when the men were carrying in crates and chests and barrels from the overloaded wagon.

Jolie nodded, a lump thickening in her throat. She missed Joe, with his good-natured whistling and easy manner, and she often pined for the warm chats she and Nan had enjoyed. "It could have been Daniel," she said, voicing a terror she'd never fully faced before.

"On the way out here," Mary said, bracing herself with her forearms against the split-rail fence that enclosed the small corral next to the barn, "a little girl drowned in a river we were crossing. Up by Fort Deveraux, we buried a whole family that died of influenza." She rested one hand on her protruding stomach and surveyed the crystal blue sky. "I admit to wondering why the good Lord would bring those people through Indian attacks and windstorms and trail accidents, just so they could perish within a stone's throw of where they meant to get."

The remark put Jolie's troubles into perspective, at least for the moment. "I guess about all we can count on in this life is things changing," she said. The insight made that lovely, blue-gold day in early autumn seem especially precious, something to be stored away in the heart and cherished during the bitter winter to come.

Later, Daniel and Enoch went to town to get supplies, taking the boys along, and Mary and little

Ruthie curled up together on the sun-warmed feather mattress to nap. Deuter was busy nailing up some loose boards inside the barn.

So it was that Gemma and Jolie set out for home alone, hand in hand, their black shoes scuffing up dust as they walked.

"Me and my brother will be going away soon," the little girl announced, stringing more words together in that single sentence than Jolie had ever heard her use all at once.

Jolie was careful not to answer too quickly. "I see," she said, when they'd gone a little distance and the familiar farmhouse was in sight. "I guess that was why the two of you were hiding in Enoch and Mary's wagon yesterday."

Gemma nodded solemnly. "Hank figured they was going to Californy."

"Umm-hmm," Jolie replied, her tone thoughtful, her manner inviting more confidences.

The child looked up into Jolie's face, her weathered little soul clearly visible in her eyes. "I reckon you and Mr. Dan don't want us," she said, shrugging one small shoulder as though not being wanted didn't matter.

Jolie averted her eyes, silently cursing Daniel Beckham, once again, for his stubborn will and hard heart. It was a long time before she could trust herself to speak. "There isn't a better little girl in the whole of this earth than you," she finally said. "So don't you go thinking no one wants you. It's just that, well, sometimes people can't have what they wish for, even if it's the fondest hope of their heart."

Gemma's fingers curled around Jolie's, grubby and strong. "Maybe you could take me back to that church place," she said, with touching dignity. "Hank says the Jesus-man lives there. You and I, we could find

Him and ask if He wouldn't change Mr. Dan's mind about us staying. Then we could go to school and everything."

A tear slipped down Jolie's cheek, no doubt leaving a trail in the layer of dust covering her face. She wiped it away quickly with the sleeve of her dress. "We'll just bring the subject up when you say your prayers tonight," she promised.

At home, Jolie made ham sandwiches and dished up bowls of canned peaches, and she and Gemma sat down on the back step to eat. Leviticus wandered over and meowed plaintively until he got a share of the tangy smoked meat. Gemma was generous, and when both she and the tom had had their fill, Jolie put the little girl down on the parlor settee for a short nap.

She was standing by the mantlepiece, looking at the framed picture of Daniel and Ilse on their wedding day, when she heard the back door open and close again. And in spite of the harsh words she and Daniel had exchanged, in spite of the fact that he would rather have a paper likeness of Ilse than a living, breathing wife, Jolie's heart did a little leap at the prospect of seeing him again.

"Daniel?" she called, her voice soft because Gemma was already sleeping, smoothing her hair and turning toward the doorway with a smile she just couldn't keep to herself.

But it wasn't Daniel towering in the passage between the dining room and the parlor. No, Blake Kingston stood there, one shoulder braced against the woodwork, looking like the downtrodden outlaw he was in his filthy canvas duster, worn boots, and seedy old hat.

Jolie instantly positioned herself between Blake and the child lying on the settee.

"What are you doing here?" she demanded, in a stunned whisper. She felt as though all her blood had drained away into the floorboards, leaving her weak. A glance into the oval mirror over the fireplace told her her skin was waxen.

Blake pushed himself away from the doorjamb, sparing Jolie a foolish, cocky little smile, and strolled across the floor to bend down and twine some of Gemma's golden hair around one finger.

The child stirred slightly but didn't awaken, and Jolie's heart hammered to a stop, then started again.

"She looks enough like you," Blake speculated, still hovering over Gemma, "that folks would believe she was yours."

"Get out," Jolie breathed, taking his arm. "Now, before Daniel comes back and finds you here . . ."

"I'm not worried about that," Blake answered, grinning as he allowed himself to be steered out of the parlor and back toward the kitchen. "Rowdy's out in the barn, keeping a lookout from the loft window."

Jolie shivered, just as though a ghost had run an icy finger down her spine. It didn't take much to make Rowdy kill—he'd proved that by shooting down the banker the day of the robbery—and Daniel and Hank could step into his sights at any moment.

15

Blake smirked at Jolie as he drew his pistol from its holster and gestured toward the stove. "Pour me some coffee," he said.

Jolie smoothed her skirts with sweat-dampened palms and obeyed with as much dignity as possible. "I declare, you and Rowdy must *want* to be caught," she fretted, taking a clean mug down from the shelf.

The man she'd once believed to be her friend swung a kitchen chair around backward and sat astraddle of the seat. He pushed the brim of his hat back with the barrel of his forty-five. "You might put a little whiskey into that, if the farmer keeps any around."

Inspiration struck Jolie in the instant after he'd spoken. "There's some in the pantry," she said easily, hoping the idea she'd just had wasn't glowing in her face like a beacon as she moved toward that small room.

Blake was clearly thinking about the liquor he craved, rather than the fact that Jolie would be out of his sight for a few moments. "Just hurry it up." He thrust his pistol back into the holster. "Me and Rowdy get a mite nervous hanging around here."

In the privacy of the pantry, Jolie added a generous dollop of liquid from a brown bottle Daniel had once shown her, then poured in three fingers of whiskey in the hope of masking the taste of the other ingredient.

"Then why do you keep on coming back?" Jolie inquired moderately, carrying the mug to the kitchen and pouring in strong coffee from the pot on the stove.

Blake helped himself to both sugar and cream when Jolie set the cup down in front of him, and she was pleased, but she was also scared. She was taking a tremendous risk, trying to trick the outlaw this way, and there was no telling what he'd do if he figured out what she was up to.

He took a sip of the brew and closed his eyes. Jolie stared at him, holding her breath and praying he wouldn't taste the laudanum in the coffee.

Only after the fact did Jolie pause to wonder what Rowdy might do if her plan to drug Blake into insensibility succeeded. She could only hope the other man would stay at his post in the barn until she got Blake's pistol away. As for the distinct possibility that Daniel would return at the worst time imaginable, well, Jolie had to leave that to the Lord's discretion.

Presently, Blake began to yawn, but he swallowed the potion in a series of greedy gulps, then thumped the mug down hard on the tabletop. "That's the worst coffee I've ever tasted," he muttered. "This time, just give me straight firewater."

Figuring whiskey could only help the laudanum along, Jolie hurried obediently into the pantry and snatched up the bottle. By the time she returned,

Blake was facedown on the tabletop, snoring fit to rouse Moses himself.

Fearing a trick all the while, heart hammering, Jolie crept close and hastily snatched the pistol from his holster. Blake snuffled and tried to sit up, but the effort was too much for him, and he collapsed again with a thump. His hat rolled across the table and sailed to the floor.

Just as Jolie stepped back, the heavy firearm wavering between her clammy palms, the door opened and Rowdy appeared in the chasm.

"Blake's caught," Jolie said bravely, prepared to shoot if that was what she had to do. "There'll be no saving him, Rowdy Fleet, or yourself either. So you'd better just lay down your gun and put your hands up."

Rowdy was shaking his head and grinning feverishly as he backed out the door. A muscle underneath his left eye twitched the whole time. "No woman's capturin' me," he said. "I'd ruther be shot."

Since Jolie knew she wouldn't be able to keep a proper eye on two such dangerous men until help came—even if one of them *was* only partially conscious—she didn't even attempt to stop Rowdy from escaping. Only moments later, she heard the sound of pounding hoofbeats and breathed a sigh, grateful that her brash impulse hadn't gotten her killed. Or Daniel.

Gemma wandered in, rubbing her eye with the back of one hand and sleepily surveying the unexpected guest passed out at the table. When she looked in Jolie's direction and saw the forty-five clasped between her hands, her small body stiffened with surprise.

"Go out to the barn straight away, Gemma," Jolie

said evenly, "and fetch me some baling twine. As much as you can find."

The child glanced once more at Blake, who was staring at Jolie with the empty eyes of a deadman, apparently unable to move. Gemma gave him a wide berth as she hurried across to the back door.

Jolie ran the tip of her tongue over dry lips. "If you see any sign of Deuter or Mr. Beckham, you tell them to get in here as quickly as they can!" she called after the little girl.

Blake blinked a few times, as though struggling against the drug, and then lapsed back into noisy slumber.

"I didn't see Mr. Dan or anybody," Gemma said, minutes later, when she returned with enough twine to tie down two Gullivers and a Paul Bunyan.

After setting the gun down on the worktable, far out of Blake's reach if he should awaken, Jolie hastened to pull his hands behind him and bind them, separately, to the outside rails of the chair back. She tied each of his feet to a table leg and then, just to be sure, she bound him around the waist, too.

No sooner had she finished the task when she heard a team and wagon clatter into the dooryard. Some husband and protector Daniel Beckham was, showing up when all the excitement was over.

Carrying the forty-five in the folds of her skirt, Jolie stepped out onto the back stoop to watch Daniel and Deuter climb down from the wagon box while Hank bounded from the back. The minute she saw them, it came to Jolie how scared she'd really been, and she realized for the first time that the front of her dress was soaked with perspiration and tendrils of her hair were clinging to her face and the back of her neck in damp little clumps.

Before she'd given the matter any further thought, Jolie rushed down the steps and across the yard to fling herself into Daniel's arms. Gemma was close behind.

"There's a man in there tied up at the table," the child announced solemnly, pointing toward the house. "His horse is in the barn."

"Thunderation!" Hank yelled, heading in that direction only to have Deuter catch hold of his collar and yank him back.

Daniel frowned down at Jolie, more in puzzlement than displeasure, and gingerly pried the pistol from her fingers. "Now, Mrs. Beckham," he teased, "you're not the best cook in the world, but I wouldn't think you'd have to go to quite those lengths to scare up a supper guest."

Knotting her hand into a fist, damnably grateful for the feel of his strong arm around her waist, Jolie moved to strike Daniel in the chest. She stopped herself at the last moment. "It's not funny, Daniel," she sputtered, gesturing wildly toward the door. "Blake Kingston's in there."

All amusement and quite a lot of the color faded from Daniel's face. After glancing at Deuter, he checked the chamber of the forty-five and then started for the house.

"You and Gemma stay here," he ordered, without troubling to look back.

Gemma and Jolie disregarded the command and followed the men into the kitchen.

When Deuter saw the way Jolie had tied Kingston, he gave an irreverent hoot of laughter. "I seen a man trussed up like that once before," he said. "It was in a whore house, down at Tekoa . . ."

Daniel silenced his hired hand with a stringent

look, clasped Blake none-too-gently by the hair, lifted his head, and scowled into the insensible face. "What the hell did you do, Jolie, crown him with a skillet?"

Calmer now, Jolie folded her arms. "Do you see any blood?" she retorted. "I gave him a dose of medicine with some whiskey and the coffee left over from this morning." She frowned. "You don't think it'll kill him, do you?"

Daniel let Blake's head roll back to the tabletop. "Your coffee?" Daniel replied, deadpan. He grinned when Jolie's face reddened at the insult, then he took out his pocketknife and began to cut away the twine that bound Blake. "I'm surprised she didn't run a line from his neck to the pump handle," he said to Deuter.

Jolie's eyes had gone so wide they hurt. "You're not letting him go!"

The men exchanged a look that Jolie preferred not to interpret.

"No, Mrs. Beckham," Daniel replied, at his leisure. He hauled Blake to his feet as easily as Gemma would have grabbed up her doll. "We're taking him to town for a little visit with the marshal."

Jolie moved toward the door, as if she could bar Daniel from passing through it. "Rowdy's out there somewhere," she hissed. "He's probably just waiting for you to drive by in the wagon so he can shoot you and take off with Blake."

"She could be right," Deuter allowed. He made the idea sound incomprehensible, and Jolie didn't appreciate that. "Maybe I should ride into Prosperity and bring the marshal and a few of his men back here."

Jolie glanced anxiously at Daniel, knowing the final decision would rest with him. Praying that, for once in his life, he wouldn't be too boneheaded to listen to reason.

"All right," he said, after a good long interval of consideration. "I guess I'd rather keep an eye on things here anyhow. On your way into town, stop by and tell Enoch to keep Mary and the kids close to the house."

Deuter nodded, went to the study for a rifle, and left by the front way.

Daniel tossed Blake into the pantry, closed the door, and propped a chair under the knob. Then, as though it were an everyday experience to come home and find a wanted man tied to his table with baling twine, Mr. Beckham ruffled Hank and Gemma's hair and said easily, "You two run along upstairs and make sure you have clean clothes to wear to school. The term starts tomorrow."

The children didn't pause to question the order—they never did, with Daniel—but raced through the house to the stairway.

Daniel poured himself coffee from the pot that had been sitting on the stove all day, took a sip, made a face, and tossed the contents of his cup into the sink. "You make a habit of entertaining outlaws, Mrs. Beckham?" he inquired moderately, after opening the door to toss the potful of rancid brew into the yard, grounds and all.

Jolie watched as he filled the kettle with water from the bucket on the edge of the sink and added fresh coffee grounds. "No, Mr. Beckham," she replied, just as formally, though her very blood stung with indignation. "I make a habit of staying alive. I didn't invite Blake and Rowdy here, they just showed up. Besides, I *told* you they were still hanging around this part of the country, and you wouldn't listen."

"I was busy with the harvest," Daniel said, setting the coffeepot on the stove and adding wood to the fire.

245

Jolie was in no mood to hear excuses. "I declare, Daniel Beckham, sometimes you are as dense as a kettleful of yesterday's beans," she huffed, gathering up the twine he'd cut away from Blake's hands, feet, and middle. "Do you honestly think Mr. Kingston was *company*, that I was expecting him? Have you ever come into this kitchen and found Nan or Verena all bound up like a rolled roast?"

Daniel chuckled, leaning back against the sink and folding his arms. "Simmer down, Jolie," he said. "It's something of a strain on a man to come home and find a killer in his kitchen. I spoke without thinking."

"Seems to me you do a lot of that," Jolie replied, whisking by him with the twine in her hand. He'd cut the stuff in such a way that it was of no earthly use, and she meant to burn it in the stove.

Her husband surprised her by taking a gentle grip on her arm and turning her so that she had to look up at him. "You did a brave thing," he said. "Stupid, but brave."

Jolie drew a deep breath to protest the word *stupid* but stopped when she saw the mirth twinkling in Daniel's bright blue eyes. "My choices were somewhat limited," she said primly, after several charges of electricity had shot up her arm from Daniel's hand. "After all, Blake would never have let me get behind him with a skillet."

Daniel grinned, laid his fingers to one of Jolie's cheeks and his thumb to the other, and lifted her face for his kiss. "Neither would I, Mrs. Beckham," he muttered, his lips warm and soft against her mouth. "Neither would I."

He swept the tip of his tongue lightly over her lips, skillfully preparing her. Then, when her mouth had opened for him, he kissed her with a thorough grace that left her feeling shaken.

Jolie was still clinging to the front of Daniel's shirt with both hands, struggling to regain her equilibrium, when Hank and Gemma thundered back into the room. In their excitement over the prospect of attending school, they'd evidently forgotten all about the dangerous man now imprisoned in the pantry.

Gemma was wearing her Sunday finery, and Hank had put on his jacket and knickers and made an effort to groom his hair.

Their eagerness to be like other children, attending school, having folks and a home place, tugged at Jolie's heart.

"What time are we supposed to be at school tomorrow morning?" Hank asked breathlessly.

"Eight o'clock," Daniel said, and when Jolie went to move away from him, he held her in place.

"But we was supposed to get sent away," Gemma reminded Daniel, her eyes big with confusion.

Hank elbowed her lightly in the ribs.

Daniel smiled—a little sadly, Jolie thought. "You'll be staying here until I can work out what to do with you. Now, we've got chores to do, so you two had better get out of those fancy duds and lend a hand."

As always, Daniel got immediate obedience. The children scurried off to do as they'd been told.

"What made you change your mind?" Jolie asked softly, her breath catching at the sensations Daniel could make her feel just by holding her close to him. "About taking the children back to Spokane right away, I mean?"

Daniel was winding a strand of her hair lightly around one finger, and he seemed to find the process fascinating. "Seeing Enoch's little ones, I guess," he reflected hoarsely. "It would be pretty quiet around here without Gemma and Hank. Besides, if they got wind that I meant to take them back, they'd probably head for the high country—and God only knows whose wagon they might end up in this time."

Jolie shivered just to think of those children alone on the road, at the mercy of Rowdy Fleet and the likes. "It's no kindness," she said, "getting Hank and Gemma's hopes up only to smash them later."

"I figure some decent, solid people will come through in the spring, looking to homestead. Somebody looking to take in a couple of little ones."

She let out a sigh. Reasoning like Daniel's could surely try a body's patience, but the children weren't leaving and they were all safe. For Jolie, that was enough to ask of one day.

Gemma and Hank came downstairs in their everyday clothes and followed after Daniel like scampering kittens as he strode through the thickening twilight toward the barn. Jolie set the table for five, because she was used to feeding Deuter, and went out to the well house for cream, eggs, and butter. After carrying those things inside, she headed for the smokehouse, to cut down a small ham.

Tonight, they would celebrate.

When the cured meat was warming in the oven, Jolie decided to make a cake to go along with supper. She glanced uneasily toward the pantry door. The chair was still wedged under the doorknob.

Of course, she wouldn't think of going inside. She'd just wait until Daniel came back, and have him get the flour and spices she needed, along with some potatoes to boil and maybe a few rutabagas to cut up and put in with the ham. . . .

Daniel was busy with the chores, though, and precious time was wasting, time when the potatoes could be simmering away on the stove and the cake could be baking. Surely Blake hadn't awakened yet, Jolie decided; she'd given him enough whiskey and laudanum to knock out an ox.

Biting her lower lip, Jolie approached the pantry door. "Blake?" she called out, in a cordial, quivery voice. "Blake?"

There was no answer.

Jolie considered her dilemma for several moments, then moved the chair.

Which was a near-fatal mistake.

She was reaching for the knob when suddenly the pantry door was flung open, and Blake loomed over her, wild-eyed and furious. He held the big carving knife high above his head, and an ugly word hissed between his teeth as he lunged at her.

Jolie's shock was so great that it seemed to take a long time, not to mention extraordinary effort, to scream. But scream she did, dodging Blake's maniacal attempts to stab her.

Only moments later, Daniel came hurtling through the kitchen doorway. He and Blake fought in earnest; this was no friendly brawl behind the Grange Hall.

Blake fully intended to kill Daniel.

Heart pounding, Jolie grabbed the skillet handle in both hands and tried to get within range of Blake's head. Despite the fact that the outlaw was smaller than Daniel, he was putting up the kind of fight only a madman could. Jolie danced around behind him, waving the pan.

When Blake managed to open the front of Daniel's shirt, the carving knife leaving a crimson trail as it passed, she let out a shriek of fury and fear and swung wildly. She missed, and the skillet made reverberating contact with the corner of the stove.

The force of the blow practically loosened Jolie's teeth.

In the meanwhile, Daniel gave a raging growl, rather like an angry bear, and knocked the blade from Blake's hand with a blow. The next one made solid contact with the outlaw's midsection and sent him crumpling to the floor.

"Why in the name of God's great-aunt Minnie did you let the bastard out of the pantry?" Daniel yelled, as Jolie steered him over to the sink and opened his torn shirt. Daniel was cut from near his left shoulder almost to his right hip, and the wound was bleeding, but it wasn't deep.

Gemma and Hank huddled in the doorway, round-eyed and scared.

"Everything is all right," Jolie said, glancing only briefly in their direction but speaking in a firm tone of voice. "Run down to the road and see if Deuter and the marshal are coming."

Reluctantly, the children went off to obey.

"Damn it," Daniel muttered, flinching as Jolie began cleaning the cut with cold water and the corner of a dish towel. "What possessed you to let him out?"

"I wanted to make a cake," Jolie answered, as though the answer to Daniel's question would have been perfectly apparent to an idiot. "When I called Mr. Kingston's name and he didn't reply, I assumed he was still unconscious."

She crossed the kitchen again, stepping over Blake's prone form, and fetched the iodine from a high shelf in the pantry.

Daniel swore roundly when she began dabbing medicine on the wound. In addition to her husband's unsolicited opinion of her nursing skills, Jolie heard the sound of horses from the road.

Within a few minutes, the kitchen was filled with men—Enoch was there, along with the marshal and a couple of drunks he'd probably recruited from the Lone Wolf or the Ivory Rose as a sort of ragtag posse. Deuter, Enoch explained, had stayed at his place to look after Mary and the kids.

The marshal dragged a rummy Blake to his feet and handcuffed him, exchanged a few words with Daniel out on the back step, and rode off toward town. His band of tattered deputies followed.

Jolie sent Gemma upstairs for a clean shirt for Daniel and calmly righted the butter churn and the chairs the two men had overturned while they were fighting. She was trembling the whole time, and when she gave a little wail of frustration and delayed fear, Enoch put his hands on her shoulders and pressed her into a chair.

Kindly, he poured coffee and set it down in front of his sister-in-law. "There now," he said. "Sip on that while I find something to give it some kick." He was pouring in the whiskey he'd found in the pantry when Daniel returned.

"Are we going to have supper?" Hank inquired, sniffing at the rich aroma of warm pork.

The child's question broke some of the tension, for Jolie at least, and she burst out with a foolish little giggle. Daniel looked at her coffee, rife with liquor, and raised one eyebrow.

Things happened in a flurry of movement and color after that. Somehow, while Jolie sat, shaking so hard she could barely drink her pungent coffee, the ham got taken out of the oven and someone opened two jars of green beans and heated them. Someone else sliced bread, while yet another person poured milk, and there was a meal on the table.

Jolie ate, listening as Daniel and Enoch talked back and forth and never absorbing a word, but the minute the last bite went down her throat, everything else started right back up. She ran outside and around the corner of the house, nearly tripping over Leviticus.

When her stomach finally stopped rebelling, Jolie became aware that Daniel was standing beside her. He handed her a mugful of cold well water, and she rinsed her mouth and spat, then drank gratefully. When she'd swallowed the last pure, icy drop, she hiccuped and then sobbed, almost simultaneously.

"You'd better get yourself off to bed before you fall apart like a flour sack with the seams cut," Daniel said in a quiet voice. He was still close, but he didn't move to touch her.

Jolie sagged against the wall of the house, her back shuddering with the effort to hold back sobs. It had been too much for her, all of it—Joe Culley's death, her pregnancy, the strain between herself and Daniel, the frantic search for Hank and Gemma, the whole experience with Blake. She simply had no strength left.

Tentatively, Daniel touched her shoulder. "You'll feel better tomorrow, Jolie," he promised. "Come along inside now and get some rest."

She nodded, unable to do more, and allowed him to lead her around the house and inside. She was relieved that they came in through the front, so she didn't have to pass Enoch looking as though she'd just faced a banshee.

Daniel stopped at the bottom of the stairs, one hand resting on the newel post, and Jolie could feel his eyes following her as she mounted the stairs. Although she knew the rigors of lovemaking would be too much for her that particular night, she longed to lie down beside Daniel, his great strength guarding her like a wall, and feel his arms around her.

At the top of the steps, she turned to look down, and found that Daniel had quietly slipped away. Moments later, she heard his voice from the kitchen as he talked with Enoch.

Jolie looked in on Gemma and Hank and found them sleeping, their best clothes carefully draped over the footboard of the bed and the back of a rocking chair. She kissed each of them lightly, offered a silent prayer that God would go before them and make their way smooth, and left the room.

After washing up and putting on a nightgown, Jolie went to the window to look out on the freshly harvested fields. She wondered if Rowdy Fleet was hiding somewhere nearby, maybe in someone's barn, or if he'd taken to the road. Jolie wanted to believe the outlaw had put the territory behind him forever, and maybe he had. With Blake in jail, he wouldn't have to divide the money they'd gotten robbing the bank. He could keep it all for himself and ride out for California or Mexico.

Jolie felt a little better.

When light from the open door flooded the area surrounding the back steps, her attention shifted. She watched as Enoch and Daniel parted with a handshake, and a slight, shivery thrill went through her. Daniel would bank the fire now, turn down the lamps in the kitchen, and climb the stairs to their room. . . .

In the glow of the moon, she saw Enoch mount one of the horses that had pulled his wagon west from St. Louis, wave his hand, and ride off toward his own place.

Jolie held her breath, but instead of turning around to come back inside, Daniel paused for a long moment and then walked slowly toward Ilse's grave.

After watching him as long as she could bear to, Jolie turned away from the window, put out the lamp burning on the bedside table, and crawled into bed.

Daniel never joined her.

Gemma and Hank were up and about uncommonly early the next morning, their faces scrubbed pink, their hair slicked down with water and vigorous brushing. Daniel came in through the back door just as they were finishing their oatmeal.

Ignoring Jolie, except for one bemused glance, Daniel took his regular place at the table. Minutes later, Deuter appeared and claimed his own chair.

"I hated school," the hired hand told the children. "Couldn't wait to get out of that place."

Jolie set his cup of coffee down in front of him with slightly too much force. "Deuter," she reprimanded.

As usual, Deuter was undaunted. "One time, me and Jesse Bachel drew *x*'s on the teacher's chair with India ink, and she walked around all day long with blue marks on her behind."

"Deuter," Jolie repeated.

Daniel hid a smile behind the rim of his coffee cup, and Jolie narrowed her eyes at her husband to let him know she didn't approve of his attitude.

Hank laughed at Deuter's account of the prank, but Gemma just looked puzzled.

Jolie busied herself putting up lunches for the children in tin lard pails she'd found in the well house and thoroughly washed. When they set off for town, riding importantly on either side of Deuter on the wagon seat, a knot rose in Jolie's throat. Daniel would go about his work, tending the animals and such, and she would have no one to talk with the whole day through.

"I'd like to go into Prosperity," she announced, smoothing her hair. "I believe I could walk the distance, since it isn't very far."

"You'll do no such thing," Daniel responded immediately. "Fleet is still out there somewhere, and if he has a list of favorite people, Mrs. Beckham, you're nowhere near the top."

Jolie raised her chin, prepared to be as mule-stubborn as necessary. "I want to pay a call on Nan Culley and purchase a length of pink ribbon for Gemma's hair, and neither you nor Mr. Fleet is going to stop me."

Daniel's jawline whitened, and he gave Jolie a narrow look, but then he sighed. "I'll hitch up the wagon," he said.

He and Jolie drove into Prosperity together.

16

As Jolie was settling herself into the wagon seat, she bumped something with the toe of one shoe and looked down to see a rifle lying on the floorboards. Even though it was a warm day, bright and glimmery gold, she shivered at the reminder that Rowdy might be somewhere nearby, waiting and watching.

"I don't see why it's so all-fired important for you to go to town now," Daniel grumbled, as he took up the reins.

Jolie drew in a breath filled with the sweet, peculiar pungency of the country. "No one's forcing you to come along," she pointed out. "I would have been perfectly content walking to Prosperity."

Daniel didn't reply; he simply scowled at her and gave the horse an unnecessary slap with the reins.

Long before they arrived in town, the shrill screaming of Mr. Ira January's steam-powered saw reached their ears. The mill was in full operation, and it seemed remarkable to Jolie that she'd never noticed the intensity of the noise before.

"You don't care much for Mr. January, do you?" she said to Daniel, mostly to make conversation.

He gave her a sidelong look from under the brim of his everyday hat. "I don't give him much thought, as a matter of fact."

"But when you *do* think of Mr. January," Jolie persisted, unwilling to let Daniel put off her question so easily, "you get irritated."

"That happens with a few other people, too," her husband responded dryly.

Jolie squared her shoulders decisively. She would simply repeat her original question until Daniel answered it. "You don't care much for Mr. January, do you?" she echoed, in dulcet tones.

Daniel sighed, and she saw a muscle tighten in his jawline. "No, Jolie," he replied, tacitly conceding defeat, "I don't like the man."

The sound of the school bell chimed melodiously over the screech of the saw. "Why not?"

Mr. Beckham looked very put-upon indeed. "You won't be partial to the answer," he warned.

"I still want to know." A combination of bravado and pride made Jolie say those words; inwardly, she had a suspicion she'd do better to remain in ignorance.

Daniel's gaze was direct. Almost defiant. "January used to pay a call on Pilar now and then. I had a few objections to the way he treated her, and he and I . . . exchanged words."

Jolie looked away, but she knew there was no hiding the indignant color that rose in her neck and then pulsed in her cheeks. Men had mistresses and frequented houses of ill-repute; it was a fact of life, but knowing that didn't make images of Daniel in the arms of a prostitute one whit easier for Jolie to live

257

with. Other women's husbands were other women's husbands, but Daniel was hers, and that changed her entire perspective on the matter.

They had reached the center of town, and Daniel brought the wagon to a stop in front of the mercantile. "I have some business at the Ivory Rose," he said, but he nodded toward the general store. "If you need anything, just tell them to write it on my page in the ledger book."

Although she had prided herself on her toughness all her life, Jolie was near tears as she climbed down to the rough-board sidewalk. Lately, she seemed to have about as much control over her emotions as she would have had over a runaway boxcar on a downhill track.

Daniel secured the team and then walked across the road toward the saloon, never pausing to look back. Jolie watched him until he disappeared through the swinging doors, into the decadent, mysterious swirl of smoke and music beyond, then reminded herself that it was Nan she wanted to see.

Her friend answered the door when Jolie mounted the steps of Mrs. Krayper's porch and knocked. There were deep circles under Nan's eyes, and her formerly vibrant complexion had gone sallow behind its smattering of freckles.

"Jolie," she said. The name rushed out of her mouth as a hoarse whisper.

Jolie took Nan's hand. "How are you?" she asked quietly, though there was no doubting the reply to that question. Nan seemed to be on the verge of collapse.

Nan linked her arm with Jolie's and started down the walk toward Mrs. Krayper's front gate. "Ira's decided not to marry me," she confided, when they were safely away from the house. Tears brimmed in her brown eyes. "He thought he was getting our farm . . . or the proceeds from its sale . . . as part of the bargain."

They paused by the fence, where the leaves of a lilac bush offered a semblance of privacy, and Jolie chose her words carefully. "You don't need him anyway," she said. "Surely you could sell goods at the mercantile, or make beds at the hotel . . ."

Nan stopped Jolie with a shake of her head, but she didn't meet her friend's eyes. "Not with a baby to care for." With visible effort, she made herself look at Jolie. "I'm fresh out of choices, it seems. What little money I've got will be gone soon, and although Alverna Krayper is a good woman, she can't afford to let me live under her roof without paying. Jolie, I'm moving in with Mr. January tomorrow. I'm going to be his . . . his housekeeper."

Jolie felt the color drain from her face. "You mean . . . ?"

"Yes," Nan answered miserably. "I'll have to do more than cook and clean. But at least I won't end up working in one of the saloons."

Jolie figured the two options weren't so very different from each other. She clutched Nan's arm desperately. "Let me speak with Daniel," she pleaded. "Perhaps there's some way he can help."

Nan raised her chin, and her eyes glinted with proud fire. "I'd rather take a room upstairs at the Ivory Rose than become a burden on my friends," she said fiercely. "And if you drag Dan Beckham into this, I'll never forgive you." Having made this pronouncement, and there was no doubt she'd meant every word, Nan gathered up her skirts and whisked back to the gate, up the walk, and into the house.

Jolie stood alone on the sidewalk for a long time, digesting what she'd heard, feeling as though someone had just struck her square across the middle with a heavy board. In one moment, her ire took in all men, and she hated them for the power they held over women. In the next, her fury was trained on Ira January, hot and ruthless, like sunlight streaming through a magnifying glass onto dry parchment.

The incessant shriek of the mill saw broke Jolie's inertia; the sound seemed to pull her along that quiet, small-town street, as surely as if it were a rope tied around her waist. Her fists were clenched at her sides, her jaw was set, and she looked neither to the left nor right as she passed through Prosperity proper.

Reaching Mr. January's mill, which occupied a place at the opposite end of town from where the mercantile and saloons stood, Jolie passed an unattended team and buckboard. There was a horsewhip coiled on the seat, and she appropriated it without hesitation.

The mill owner must have seen her approaching, for he strolled out of a nearby clapboard building beaming as broadly as if Jolie had brought him an applesauce-plum cake and all good wishes. He stopped about ten feet from where she stood, folded his arms and drawled, "Well, hello there, Mrs. Beckham. What can I do for you?"

Jolie thought of her bereaved friend and how cruelly this man meant to take advantage of her. Her palm grew moist where she gripped the handle of the whip, and various muscles in her shoulder and forearm tensed in preparation. She'd learned to wield a lash while journeying west with her father years before—the cracking sound scared tired teams of oxen into moving on when they wanted to stop—but of course she'd never used one on a human being. This was the first time she'd ever even been tempted to do that.

"You can leave Mrs. Nan Culley alone, that's what you can do," Jolie answered.

Looking entirely undaunted, Mr. January spread his hands. "I'm offering the woman a home and a decent way to earn a living."

The handle of the horsewhip seemed to leap in Jolie's fingers. "Kindly don't use the word *decent* in regard to the sort of life you're offering Mrs. Culley, Mr. January," she said evenly. "It's hardly fitting."

January gave a gruff guffaw and ran his eyes insolently over Jolie's person. His smile didn't waver. "My, my, Mrs. Beckham, you've come a long way. Only a short time ago, you were convicted as a bank robber and about to hang. Now you've become a moral crusader. Tell me, was this salutary change due to the influence of your upstanding husband?"

Color stung Jolie's face. "I'm no more an outlaw than you are, Mr. January. And now that Blake Kingston has been captured, everyone will know the truth soon enough." Even as she uttered the words, however, it occurred to Jolie that this cherished theory held any number of potential flaws. For one thing, Blake might decide to lie about her involvement, in order to pay her back for capturing him.

She gave the whip a skillful crack, just to let the millowner know he wasn't dealing with a person of puny convictions. "You're wasting your time, trying to change the subject," she said, calling on all her aplomb just to keep from turning around and running like a mouse headed for a hole.

"Exactly what is it you require of me, Mrs. Beckham?" January asked cordially and Jolie realized, to her further mortification, that a crowd was gathering. If word of the incident chanced to get back to Daniel . . .

"I demand that you stop bothering my friend, as I said before," Jolie stated evenly, keeping her gaze fixed on Mr. January. "If you don't, I'll peel the hide off you like the scrapings from a carrot!"

This threat produced a ripple of laughter in the small throng pressing in around them.

January grinned and took another step toward Jolie. "I do believe I've been pursuing the wrong woman," he said, in a voice clearly intended to carry. "I should have snatched you out of the back of Hobb Jackson's hay wagon myself, instead of leaving you for Dan Beckham."

His meaning was as clear as a high mountain stream in early springtime, and Jolie was roundly insulted. The whip whistled through the air as she drew it back, but before she could snap its tip at Mr. January's boots and scare the holy how-much out of him like he deserved, a strong hand closed around her wrist and stayed her.

Her colliding senses told her Daniel had arrived a seeming eternity before she dared turn and look up into her husband's furious blue eyes. She opened her fingers and let the whip fall to the ground, though her bearing was anything but docile.

"Get in that wagon," Daniel seethed, pointing one hand toward the rig drawn up at the edge of Mr. January's property. "Don't give me any guff, just *get in that wagon.*"

By his very officious manner, Daniel had made it impossible for Jolie to obey and still retain her self-respect. After all, practically the whole town was looking on, just the way they had been on the day of her near-execution.

"I will not," she replied, with dignity.

"That's a fiery little lady you've got there," Mr. January remarked companionably, evidently deeming it safe to approach now that Jolie was disarmed. "Taming her would be a most enjoyable process, I'm certain."

Daniel's ferocious gaze swung from Jolie's face to Ira's. "I'll thank you to stay out of this," he said, in low, deadly tones. "It's none of your concern."

"I'll be happy to leave," Jolie announced magnanimously, "as soon as Mr. January promises to let Nan Culley be."

"His promises aren't worth a puddle of spit," Daniel replied, and there was something in the timbre of his voice that made Jolie wish she'd sacrificed her pride and gotten into the wagon when he'd first issued the order.

"My offer to give Nan . . . Mrs. Culley . . . a proper home stands," January said. His eyes flicked from Jolie to Daniel and back again. "Unless, of course, I can persuade you to take over my household, Mrs. Beckham. Daniel means to get rid of you, anyway, from what I hear. This will save him untold aggravation—not to mention train fare."

Jolie had never encountered such brazen effrontery in her life, but before she could comment, Daniel took Ira by the lapels of his shirt and flung him backward against the side of a nearby freight wagon.

Mr. January smirked even as he struggled to catch his breath after impact. "Isn't that what you told Pilar, Daniel?" he asked, wiping his mouth with the back of one hand. "That things would be back to normal between the two of you after you sent the current bride packing?"

The words stung Jolie's spirit like so many furious

bees. She'd known Daniel wanted to get rid of her—
he'd told her so on several occasions—but she hadn't
dreamed the whole town knew, or that he'd discussed
the matter with Pilar.

Stiffly, with her head held unnaturally high, Jolie
turned and made her way to Daniel's wagon. Pretending not to hear the townspeople whispering, or to see
them pointing, she climbed up into the box and sat,
smoothing her skirts over her knees.

Aunt Nissa had once told her to assume the virtues
she needed and they would eventually be her own. In
that moment of utter disgrace, Jolie draped pretended
dignity around her like a cloak.

Daniel said something to Mr. January—what it
was, she couldn't hear—then walked over and
climbed into the box to sit beside Jolie and take up the
reins.

"Just exactly what did you hope to accomplish back
there?" he asked, when the wagon was moving away
from the noisy mill. "Besides making me look like a
damn fool, I mean?"

Jolie curled her lower lip back against her teeth for a
long moment, willing herself not to cry. She'd wanted,
somehow, to help Nan, though she saw now that her
actions had been ill-advised and plainly impulsive.
She'd reacted to the situation without thinking first.

"I refuse to explain myself to you, Mr. Beckham. As
far as I'm concerned, you are no friend of mine."

"You're right, Jolie . . . I'm not your friend. I'm
your husband. And I have a right to know what
possessed you to make a public spectacle of yourself
that way."

Jolie shrugged, lending the gesture as much impu-
dence as she could. "I would be unwise to trust you

with any such confidence," she said coolly. "You would undoubtedly go straight to Pilar with the details, like some gossipy old maid. Pretty soon the whole town would know."

Out of the corner of her eye, Jolie saw Daniel's jaw muscles tighten. "January just wanted to rile you," he said, after a long interval had passed. Instead of driving straight on out of town, Mr. Beckham brought the wagon to a halt in front of the marshal's office. "I didn't say any of those things to Pilar or anybody else."

Jolie folded her arms. "Then how did he know how anxious you are to be rid of me?" she demanded, in a furious hiss.

Daniel sighed. "I don't know, Jolie. Maybe someone overheard us talking and spread the word."

She eyed the weathered front of the jail house with some trepidation, having spent so much time there waiting to be hanged. "Don't think for one moment that I'm accepting your apology," she said. "I'm taking it under advisement, that's all."

Her husband set the brake lever and swung gracefully to the ground. "I don't recall apologizing for anything," he replied, sweeping off his hat and wiping his brow on one sleeve.

Jolie narrowed her gaze as she stared at the squat, ugly building. There were aging wanted posters nailed to the outside wall, edges curling, print fading. "What are we doing here?"

"The marshal wants to talk to you, that's all." Daniel rounded the wagon and reached up to lay his hands on the sides of Jolie's waist. "There's nothing to worry about."

Only a person who had never expected to swing

from the end of a rope could have made such an observation. Jolie ran moist palms down her skirts to dry them. "Daniel . . ."

Her husband's grip on her arm was reassuring, rather than forceful. "I won't leave you," he said.

The marshal, an old man with rheumy blue eyes and one enormous freckle in the middle of his bald pate, didn't take the trouble to rise from his chair when Daniel and Jolie entered. He spared Daniel a nod and rolled the matchstick he was chewing from one side of his mouth to the other.

"Mornin'," he drawled.

Jolie supposed her panic was too great to disguise completely, but she was trying. She stayed close to Daniel, never letting her eyes stray toward the two barred cells at the back of the single large room. She couldn't help recalling the fear she'd endured during her captivity, the frustration, the lack of privacy.

"Have a seat," Marshal Wilcox said, still speaking as though Daniel were the only other person in the room.

Instead of sitting down, however, Daniel surprised both the lawman and his wife by walking around behind the desk, gripping Wilcox by the back of his collar, and hauling him to his feet.

"I like a man to stand when Mrs. Beckham walks into a room," he said companionably.

Marshal Wilcox looked flustered, but he rallied quickly enough. He greeted Jolie with a warm, "Mornin', ma'am," and watched warily as Daniel rounded the desk to stand behind his wife's chair. One big hand rested lightly on her shoulder.

Feeling at least moderately safe, Jolie risked a glance toward the cells. Blake was in the one on the right-hand side, his fingers curled around the bars, watching Jolie with an unsettling glint in his eyes.

The lawman cleared his throat in what could only be described as a nervous fashion. Then he sat back in his chair and rubbed his stubbly white beard with one hand. "Kingston will go on trial soon as the circuit judge comes through again," he said. "You'll be asked to tell what you know about the robbery, and the killin'."

"I already told you, during the first trial," Jolie pointed out reasonably. "It's just that none of you would listen."

"You stickin' by your story that you didn't know Kingston and Fleet meant to hold up the bank?"

"Yes. The whole thing came as a terrible surprise. All Mr. Kingston told me was that he had some business inside. I was to wait and hold the horses."

Daniel's hand slipped away from Jolie's shoulder, and she felt that simple separation like the loss of a limb.

"Why don't you tell the truth, Jolie-girl?" Blake spouted from his cell. "You knew what I was doing. We needed money, you and me, to stake ourselves to a new start in Mexico."

Jolie ignored Blake, the way she would have ignored a buzzing fly. "Couldn't we go home now?" she asked in a small voice, looking up at Daniel.

His face was closed to her, as surely as a gate guarding private property, but he nodded. "We'll be leaving," he said.

The marshal remembered his manners, such as they were, and scrambled to his feet. "We'll let you know when the judge gets here, Mrs. Beckham," he said.

Jolie didn't take the trouble to answer. She just

made her back as straight as a fireplace poker and swept toward the door.

"She's a liar!" Blake called out, as Daniel stiffened but did not turn around. "A liar and a thief and a killer! Remember that, every time you turn your back on her."

Daniel wrenched open the door and waited, without a word, for Jolie to step through ahead of him. Outside, she climbed into the wagon seat unaided, marveling that it wasn't even noon yet and already the day was a disaster.

Neither Daniel nor Jolie spoke throughout the ride home. Once they arrived, Jolie went straight into the house to make a midday meal for Daniel and Deuter, wondering all the while she worked how she'd managed to get her life into such a tangle.

After the food had been served and eaten and the kitchen set to rights again, the men went out to the barn. Jolie climbed the stairs and entered the little room next to the one she shared with Daniel. Her intention was to lie down on the bed and rest for an hour, in a place where there were no memories, but for some reason Ilse's pinewood chest caught her eye, and she was drawn toward it.

She'd found a dress inside, soon after coming to that house as Daniel's bride, but she'd never felt it would be proper to go through the contents one by one. Now, with her spirit feeling strangely disjointed, she knelt in front of the large box and lifted the lid.

Slowly, she laid aside folded items of clothing, a shawl, a pillowcase with an unfinished trim of delicate crochet. Underneath was a framed likeness of Daniel as a much younger man, wearing a tattered Confederate uniform and looking duly solemn. The two top buttons of his flimsy coat were fastened, the bottom ones missing entirely.

Jolie touched the guileless face with a fingertip, feeling a certain kinship with Ilse Beckham because she knew what it was to love Daniel. In giving him her body, she had unwittingly handed over her soul as well.

She turned the frame and saw a flourish of words on the back. "My brave, darling Daniel."

Laying the photograph carefully on top of a stack of lavender-scented underthings, Jolie reached farther inside the chest. This time, her fingers closed on the binding of a book.

She lifted the volume out and saw that it was a very fine book indeed, bound in rich leather, with a blue ribbon attached for marking pages. Feeling more as if she were reading a letter addressed to her rather than invading another person's privacy, Jolie opened the cover and recognized Ilse's flowing, confident handwriting.

This was the first Mrs. Beckham's private journal.

Jolie closed the volume and started to set it aside, then opened it again. A warm September breeze ruffled the lace curtains at the window and the scent of lavender wafted from inside the pinewood trunk. It was almost as though Ilse had joined her in that quiet, simple room, perhaps sitting on the edge of the bed or lingering in the doorway.

The first words that caught Jolie's attention were, "I'm glad I didn't know Daniel when he was a soldier. I could not have tolerated the thought of losing him to an enemy's bullet for even a moment."

Because of the ornate handwriting and her own shortcomings as a reader, Jolie had to work to make out what Ilse had written, but she persisted, reading a little here, a little there.

Finally, she came to the day Daniel and Ilse's firstborn child had died.

"I don't want to live," Ilse had written, and the wild rawness of her grief and pain was clearly visible in the slant of her letters. "There is no point in it, when all one loves can be snatched away in the span of a heartbeat. Perhaps what they say about heaven is really true. Perhaps if I die, I will once again be with my precious little Eugenia."

Jolie's vision had blurred, and she paused to sniffle and wipe her eyes with one sleeve. She flipped ahead a few pages, hoping to find that Ilse had rallied.

"I'm going to have another baby. I've told Daniel, and I know he's pleased, thinking this will finally bring his wife back to him. I dare not tell him that I have forgotten how to hope . . ."

Unbearable sadness tightened Jolie's throat. She closed the book and put it back in the chest, along with the photograph of Daniel and the clothes Ilse had worn.

When Gemma and Hank arrived home with Deuter, jostling happily in the back of one of Daniel's wagons, Jolie gave them oatmeal cookies and listened with genuine delight while they told her all about school.

Hank figured on staying around until he'd mastered numbers, while Gemma felt that letters had a greater appeal. She had already mastered the word *cat*.

It was during supper, while Daniel and Deuter were talking about the spring planting and the children were yawning over their plates, that the loud, imperious knock sounded at the front door.

Frowning, Daniel pushed back his chair and stood.

Hank and Gemma both scampered after him when he went to answer the summons.

"I hear you almost horsewhipped Ira January this morning," Deuter commented, evidently unruffled by the prospect of a visitor, as he scooped a third helping of boiled turnips onto his plate. "Too bad Daniel came along and interfered, to my way of thinking."

Despite everything, Jolie smiled. Deuter had a charm of his own, unpolished though he was. "It seems Mr. January isn't a very popular man around these parts," she said, rising to test the coffeepot for warmth with the tips of her fingers. "Except maybe with Pilar."

Deuter shook his head. "She don't like him, either. He blacked one of her eyes once." He frowned and took a bite from a slice of thickly buttered bread. "A man has no call hitting a woman," he reflected sagely, his mouth full.

Jolie heartily agreed, but it didn't seem necessary to say so. She got down mugs for herself and the men and poured coffee.

The sound of voices came to her from the other end of the house, Daniel's and one she didn't recognize, that of another man. Something about it made her uneasy.

When Daniel returned a few moments later, his expression was solemn. But then, that was nothing new.

"You'd better come into the study," he said to Jolie. "The children are upstairs packing their things."

In that instant, the bottom dropped out of Jolie's stomach. She even felt dizzy, and had to set the heavy coffeepot down with a thump and grip the back of a chair until her knees got some starch in them again.

"What?" she whispered, as anguished at the idea of

losing those children as she would have been if nature had knitted each of them under her own heart.

But Daniel only gestured for Jolie to precede him to the study.

A handsome blond man was sitting in front of Daniel's desk, consuming brandy as greedily as if he never expected to flop a lip over the rim of a glass again. He needed a haircut and his clothes were ragged and filthy, but those were things Jolie was inclined to accept about a person because she knew only too well how easy it was to fall on unfortunate circumstances.

"This is Bill Springer," Daniel said gruffly.

The visitor may have been concentrating pretty heavily on his drinking, but he stood and nodded a greeting to Jolie. "Ma'am," he said.

"Mr. Springer claims he's Gemma and Hank's uncle."

Jolie stared at the empty snifter in Mr. Springer's hand. "And now he's come to take them away," she said. In those moments, she fully understood the black despair Ilse had revealed in her journal. Jolie wouldn't have loved Hank and Gemma any more if they'd been born of her own loins, and losing them might well be the experience that finally knuckled her under.

17

"Do you have papers, some kind of proof that you're truly kin to these children?" Desperation made Jolie mulish. Hank and Gemma were precious to her, and she couldn't let them go without a struggle. Furthermore, she resented Daniel's apparent willingness to be done with them so easily.

Mr. Springer chuckled and tugged at a lock of his fair hair. Even through the road dust that dulled it, Jolie could see it was exactly the same shade as Gemma and Hank's. "No papers, ma'am. Just this hair and this face. You see, the nippers' ma was my sister, Shallie."

Jolie knew he was speaking the truth—there was simply no denying the resemblance—but she still had serious doubts about his motives. "Taking proper care of children requires some doing, Mr. Springer. They need regular meals and clean clothes and warm beds to sleep in."

The visitor's gaze shifted to the bottle of brandy sitting on Daniel's desk. He ran his tongue over wind-burned lips and his fingers tightened around the empty snifter. "Yes, ma'am. But family's family, and the kids and me, we belong together."

Jolie opened her mouth to pursue the subject, but Daniel silenced her by laying a gentle hand to her arm.

"You'd best go up and see how Gemma and Hank are faring," he told her.

The prospect of saying good-bye swelled in Jolie's throat, and no words, be they friendly or hateful, could have gotten past. She simply nodded and hurried out of the room.

Hank and Gemma were in the room they shared, seated side by side on the bed. Gemma rested her head against her brother's small shoulder, clutching her cherished doll in both arms.

"I'll leave my wagon," Hank said manfully. "You and Mr. Dan are bound to have a boy sometime."

Jolie looked away for a moment, her eyes burning. Then she knelt on the floor in front of the children, taking one of their hands in each of her own. "This man, this Mr. Springer . . . do you know him? Is he kind?"

A tear trickled down Gemma's cheek, but she didn't answer or even look Jolie in the eye.

It was Hank who answered. "He's like pa was. He drinks and he womanizes some. I reckon he'll leave us behind someplace one day soon." The boy's small, freckled face brightened. "Maybe Gemma and me could find our way back here if he did that. We'd both be bigger and stronger, and Mr. Dan might figure we could be of help around the farm."

Jolie swallowed. She'd seen the likes of Mr. Springer before—her own father had been the same sort of man—and she knew his reasons for wanting his sister's children were probably less than noble. With-

274

out a word, she got to her feet again, turned, and walked resolutely down the stairs.

Daniel was still in the study with Mr. Springer, frowning as their guest downed what must have been his third or fourth snifterful of brandy.

"I'm sorry," Jolie lied briskly, when she entered the room, "but Gemma and Hank won't be able to leave tonight. Mr. Beckham and I will need to see some proof—other than the color of your hair, Mr. Springer—that the children will have proper care."

Jolie didn't dare glance at Daniel. She could only pray that he would agree with her, and the chances of that seemed pitiful in the extreme, given his oft-voiced desire to live in peace as a single man again. After all, it wasn't as though the Beckhams were in accord about anything else; there had been that unfortunate episode at Mr. January's mill in the morning, and Jolie had reason to believe that Daniel cared far more for a certain prostitute than he did for her.

Springer shoved splayed fingers through his matted hair. His smile was ingratiating, and his manner somehow reminded Jolie of a hungry dog wriggling at their feet. "It's true there ain't no money," he said. "A man can't move on without that."

Jolie tensed inwardly, though she focused all her inner powers on appearing calm. She'd never cared much about money, but in that moment she wished she were a woman with the means for bribery. If she understood him correctly, Mr. Springer was saying he was willing to *sell* the children, and the very idea filled her with a mingling of jubilation and rage.

Daniel moved to take up the brandy bottle and refill Mr. Springer's glass, but Jolie saw no sign of reaction in either his manner or his bearing. "You're saying, then," he began, his tone idle and even, "that you'd be

willing to part with Gemma and Hank permanently
. . . for a certain sum?"

Springer looked around him and once again flashed
his groveling-dog grin. "This is a nice place and I can
see you're good, decent folks. Yes, sir, it would be a
comfort to my poor dead sister, if'n she were alive to
know, of course, that her little ones were growing up
in peace and plenty."

Except for the slight tautness Jolie saw between
Daniel's shoulder blades when he turned away, he
revealed no hint of his true feelings.

As for Jolie, her heart was thundering so hard with
excitement and hope she marveled that the others
didn't hear it. At one and the same time, she wanted
to choke Mr. Springer for his base and decadent ways.
She opened her mouth to say what she thought, but
Daniel silenced her with a ferocious look.

When he took a thin black wallet from his desk
drawer and extracted a twenty-dollar note, Jolie's
breath caught in her throat, and she swayed slightly,
fearful that she was only imagining the gesture. Or
that she'd misinterpreted Daniel's intentions.

Mr. Springer ran his tongue over his lips again as
Daniel held out the money; the desire to pounce and
snatch away the currency showed in every line of the
wanderer's body.

"Mind my words, Mr. Springer," Daniel warned,
with quiet sincerity. "The bargain you and I make
tonight will be binding until Hank and Gemma are
grown. If you trouble them in any way, if you so much
as set one foot onto my dirt again, I'll find you and I'll
hurt you. Is that absolutely clear?"

Springer reached out and grabbed the note, crushing his ancient hat to his chest with his free hand. In
the next moment, he was easing toward the door,

wearing the same smile as before . . . one as sweet as fudge when it sugars. "It's clear, Mr. Beckham," he replied hastily. "You won't see me again."

"Wait." Even the bravest soul wouldn't have dared disobey Daniel's order, not in the tone it was uttered, and Springer hardly measured up to the standards of most cowards.

He froze in the study doorway. "Yes, sir?"

"Are there any more . . . family members out there, or are you the last of them?"

"There ain't nobody else," he answered. "The nippers' pa, he got himself kilt a couple of years ago, up at Tylerville."

Jolie gripped the back of the leather chair where Daniel liked to sit reading some nights, all but swept away in a torrent of sadness and joy. She was sorrowful because Gemma and Hank had lost their father, whatever sort of man he might have been, and exultant because they were staying.

She turned to Daniel, after hearing the front door close smartly behind Mr. Springer, with tears brimming in her eyes. "Thank you, Daniel," she said.

He refused to meet her gaze. "Don't go reading anything into this, Mrs. Beckham," he warned, in his stern way. "I've got no more intention of raising up those children than I ever did, but I won't see them given over to a coyote like Springer." Daniel sat down in his desk chair and opened his ledger as calmly as if he'd been discussing the price of grain with Deuter. "There's school tomorrow. You'd best see that they're tucked up in bed."

His standoffish attitude was no barrier to Jolie's relief and happiness. She strolled over to his side and bent down to kiss him soundly on the cheek. "I love you, Dan Beckham," she said, and it was only when she'd left the room that she grasped the full implication of her own words.

Her cheeks ached with embarrassment as she gathered her skirts and started up the stairs to tell Gemma and Hank that Mr. Springer had gone away.

The moment the words were out, Gemma flung her arms around Jolie's neck and kissed her face repeatedly, like a small, eager puppy, and Hank gave a whoop of delight. Jolie escorted her charges to the privy, then supervised the washing of faces and teeth in the kitchen. When all the ablutions had been completed, she sat in the rocking chair across from the stove and took Gemma onto her lap, while Hank sat cross-legged at her feet.

Soon as they were both settled, and properly attentive, Jolie told them a long, made-up story about a gruff but gentle giant who lived alone in a cottage in the middle of a forest. At the beginning of the tale, the giant was irritable and lonely. By the end, he had a wife and two children who loved him very much, and everyone lived happily ever after.

Jolie was sitting in front of the bureau mirror, plaiting her just-brushed hair for the night, when Daniel came into the room. As always, her pulse quickened, though she went right on humming and braiding and pretending not to notice he was there.

The charade became unworkable, however, when he came to stand directly behind her, his hands resting on her shoulders, his eyes frowning as he stared down at her in apparent puzzlement.

"I don't want to love you, Jolie McKibben," he said in a husky voice, when a very long interval had passed. "And I won't, ever. But I think it's about time we both came to terms with the fact that we need each other."

Jolie let go of the shimmering rope of golden hair, letting it rest against her bosom. Beneath the cotton of her nightgown, her nipples jutted in response to a cool breeze from the window. Or was it a reaction to Daniel's nearness?

"What are you saying, Mr. Beckham?"

"I want you to stay right here, as a sort of partner. You'll share my bed and we'll bring up any children the Lord sees fit to send along."

If the whole thing hadn't sounded so much like a business arrangement, Jolie would have been thrilled. As it was, she had distinct reservations. "You'll have someone to cook and clean," she said evenly, rising to her feet. "You'll never want for the comfort only a woman can lend. But what do I get from this, Daniel? And don't say a roof over my head, clothes to wear, and food to eat, because any of a hundred other men would give me those things."

Jolie didn't quite dare remind Daniel of Ira January's scandalous offer that very day, but then, there was no necessity of it. The knowledge drew a white line of fury around Daniel's lips and along his jawbone.

"I don't know," he finally answered. "My house, my land, my name . . . I've got nothing else to offer you."

Jolie thought of the wedding picture still displayed on the parlor mantelpiece, of Daniel's practice of visiting Ilse's grave at regular intervals. She answered in a soft but bold voice. "Yes, you have, Dan Beckham. But I'll wait, like a good farmer's wife, until the seeds grow."

Daniel's eyes slipped unwillingly over her ripening figure. "If you ever decide to go, you'll leave my son here."

"Your son," Jolie replied, without missing a step, "might well be a daughter. And before I make any promises, Mr. Beckham, I want one from you."

He arched one eyebrow and studied her suspiciously. "Such as?"

"Such as, you have to swear by all that's holy that you won't go near the saloons and have truck with women like Pilar." The force of Jolie's conviction carried her past the wall of trepidation that so often kept her from challenging Daniel.

Her husband considered her statement for entirely too long a time, it seemed to Jolie. "A man has—"

"Don't you dare say a man has needs!" Jolie interrupted, in an outraged whisper. "So does a woman, and the freedom to trust her husband is one of them!"

Daniel reared back slightly and grinned, pretending she'd struck him. Then he was serious again. "As long as you're a proper wife to me," he said, "I'll be a good husband to you. That's as close to a promise as I care to get."

Jolie was by no means satisfied with his answer, but it was still a night of breathless jubilation. Daniel had changed his mind about sending her away and, with any luck at all, he'd grow so attached to Gemma and Hank that he wouldn't be able to let them go, either. She reached up to open a button of his shirt. "I'd be interested to hear your idea of a 'proper wife,' Mr. Beckham," she said.

The warm, hairy flesh of his chest quivered almost imperceptibly under her fingers as Jolie undid yet another button. "Jolie . . ."

She continued unbuttoning Daniel's shirt until it gaped to his midriff, and he made no effort to stop her. When she pushed the fabric aside and brazenly flicked a masculine nipple with the tip of her tongue, he let out a low groan.

"Tell me about proper wives, Daniel," she teased, in a purring tone, making a little circle of kisses around the taut nubbin. "What do they do?"

Daniel's big hands gripped her shoulders, and he pressed her to the bed with a gentle ease, her legs dangling over the side of the mattress. In a single motion, he stripped away her nightgown and tossed it aside, and her partially braided hair unfurled like a glistening banner across her breasts and belly.

"They give," he said hoarsely. "They give and they take and they give some more." He peeled off his shirt while he was kissing her, while he was claiming and exploring her with his tongue, but later she had no recollection of how he shed the rest of his things.

He gripped her ankles in his hands and knelt beside the bed, murmuring that the lamplight looked like spilled honey on her skin. When he began to taste that honey, to savor it, Jolie was utterly lost.

Her heels delved deep into the mattress as she raised herself to Daniel in fevered offering, and he enjoyed her without hesitation. Finally, he turned her, so that she was kneeling, and made her ride the tip of his tongue into the very core of creation. He weighed and fondled her breasts with his hands while her body performed its ancient dance of pleasure and surrender.

Jolie was still responding long after the peak of satisfaction had been reached, and Daniel allowed her that sweet interlude. He stretched out on the bed with her, holding and caressing her while she floated through the different stages of descent.

When she was utterly relaxed, Daniel settled himself between her thighs. They both knew she would ignite like a brushfire the instant he entered her; no matter how thoroughly he'd attended her beforehand, Jolie always went wild when their bodies were joined.

That night was no exception. What was different, however, was that Daniel made no effort to muffle her cries of ecstasy as he usually did. It was an interval of enchantment, a time out of time.

There was a chill in the air the next morning, and a shifting layer of snowy fog lingered over the land long after Deuter had taken Gemma and Hank off to school in the wagon.

Daniel had apparently finished the morning chores when Jolie carried a jug of cream to the well house for chilling. He followed her, and lifted her skirts, and tended thoroughly to her pleasuring. The cold, dank air turned to tropical heat as Jolie moved in concert with the ancient rhythm.

Around midday, Verena Dailey dropped by in her buggy, a large basket at her feet. "Let's go and greet these new neighbors I've been hearing so much about," she called to Jolie, who was scattering feed for the chickens. "I know I could make their acquaintance on Sunday, but I can't wait that long."

Smiling, Jolie nodded and hurried into the house to get one of the two rhubarb cobblers she'd baked that morning.

Enoch was hammering industriously in the barn when the two women arrived in Verena's rig. Mary came out of the house straight away, with a shy smile lighting her face and her children clutching at her skirts.

Jolie made introductions, and Mary accepted the basketful of preserves from Verena, as well as the rhubarb cobbler from her sister-in-law, seeming sincerely pleased. The three of them were chatting happily when Enoch came in to wash his hands and eye the cobbler with undisguised interest. As always, that mischievous light was dancing in his eyes.

He was properly presented to Verena, and she was charmed by his good looks and easy manner.

"We'll be expecting you and Daniel for dinner Sunday, after church," Mary said, as Jolie and Verena were preparing to leave. "Please say you'll join us as well, Mrs. Dailey."

Verena smiled and accepted graciously.

"There's nobody like a Southerner when it comes to winsome manners," the older woman observed, as she took up the reins of her buggy. "That Enoch could smile the garters right off an old maid, and Mary makes a person feel like she's just been *living* for them to come calling."

"They're nice people," Jolie said, but she couldn't help the way her mind shifted to Nan. She wondered if her friend had really gone and moved into Mr. January's household as planned.

"But?" Verena prompted gently, confident as she guided the single horse pulling the rig.

"The Culleys were fine folks, too," Jolie said, twisting her hands together in her lap. "They were happy, just like Enoch and Mary are now."

Verena nodded her understanding of Jolie's sentiments, but her words were typically practical. "There are some things we have to accept at face value, Jolie, trusting that it will all come right in the end. I reckon the good Lord figures there's a lot we plain don't need to know, and I'd guess He's right."

Jolie was beginning to comprehend Daniel's reserve more clearly; something inside her feared taking the risk of caring for Enoch and Mary and their little family the way she had for Nan and Joe Culley. Life was so short for some, and fragile as a wisp of dandelion fluff. "I believe Daniel and I are going to have a child," she announced, in order to shift her mind to happier things.

"When?"

"Sometime in May."

With a smile, Verena nodded. "You've been good for Daniel," she said. "From the glow I see about you, Mrs. Beckham, the pair of you have been getting along for once."

There *was* a quiet, fragile happiness unfolding inside Jolie, though she knew her marriage would never be the stuff of storybooks. "We've been getting along," she confirmed, looking away to hide the slight blush rising in her cheeks.

The days that followed were some of the most joyous Jolie had ever spent. While Daniel and Deuter prepared the fields for spring, she cooked and cleaned and sewed. Her stomach grew rounder and Blake Kingston was trundled north to Fort Deveraux because the army wanted a word with him about some horses they were missing. She and Mary formed a fast friendship.

The only thing that really troubled Jolie during that blissful period was the fact that Nan had indeed taken up residence in Mr. January's fancy house. Every time Jolie had tried to pay a call, the doll-size Chinese houseboy Ira had brought in from San Francisco had come to the door with a note that said Mrs. Culley "wasn't receiving."

Jolie's life was full and busy and, after a while, she left off the visits because they were always unproductive.

By the time the end of October rolled around, and

the first flakes of snow came wafting down from a gray afternoon sky, Jolie had almost forgotten that Rowdy Fleet existed. She was driving the buckboard to town to meet Gemma and Hank in front of the schoolhouse when the outlaw rode out from behind a stand of poplar trees fronting an abandoned homestead and blocked her way.

Instantly, a mist of perspiration covered Jolie's skin, but she was damned if she'd let that devil's house pet see that she was scared. She raised her chin and the forty-five hidden beneath the folds of her skirt in simultaneous motions.

Rowdy laughed as he looked down the steady barrel of the pistol. "Fiery lady like you almost makes a man yearn for the honest life," he said. If he was afraid, he was hiding his fear as well as Jolie was hers. His horse moved fitfully in the rutted path Daniel and the others generously referred to as a road, perhaps sensing some agitation in its master. "Where did he hide the money, Mrs. Beckham?"

Jolie wrinkled her nose, forgetting her fear for a moment of true bewilderment. "Where did who hide what money?"

Rowdy spat, and the gesture was rife with furious frustration. "Kingston. He stashed the five hundred dollars we got from the bank in a barrel in your barn. I went back to get it, and every cent was gone." Ignoring Jolie's pistol, he drew his own and cocked it. "The two of you planned this, didn't you? You and Blake. He talked a lot about the both of you starting over someplace else, and that money would have made a mighty hefty stake."

It was news to Jolie that Rowdy and Blake had hidden the loot from the bank robbery on Daniel's property, but the discovery did explain why the two of them had kept coming back the way they had. They'd been checking on saddlebags full of federal notes.

"Whenever Blake started talking about making a life with a woman, he was just dreaming," she reasoned, with a tranquility she certainly didn't feel. "You knew that long before I did, Rowdy. And you also know he'd never trust me enough to tell me where the money was. He obviously planned on cutting you out and keeping everything for himself."

A muscle flexed under Rowdy's stubble of beard. "He won't get away with this."

Somewhere, Jolie found the audacity to shrug. "Looks like he's already done that."

The noise of an approaching wagon made Rowdy's horse downright jittery, and its rider waved the forty-five threateningly. "I'll be hiding in them trees over there. You tell whoever's comin' that you've seen me, and I'll drop 'em right before your eyes. And as soon as I've pulled back the hammer again, I'll shoot you, too."

Jolie swallowed. Rowdy had killed at least once before, and she knew he wasn't making an idle threat, like some men would. "All right," she agreed, and held her breath as he rode toward the shelter of the popular trees.

After a moment's hesitation, she realized it would look strange for her to be just sitting there in her wagon, square in the middle of the road, and whistled softly to get the horse moving again.

Enoch's buckboard came over the rise only an instant or so later, and he drew up alongside her as the two wagons came abreast. A wispy layer of gossamer snow glistened on the boxes and bags in the bed of Enoch's rig and along the brim of his hat. His grin showed teeth every bit as white as the flakes tumbling down around them.

"If you're going after Hank and Gemma," he said, "don't trouble yourself. They're over at the mercantile with Daniel, chewing on peppermint sticks while he stands around the fire jawing about the best time to plant."

Jolie's smile was a bit thin and brittle; she was too conscious of Rowdy lurking only a few yards away to carry on a normal conversation. The outlaw was probably thinking about shooting Enoch through the heart or the head, just for the sport of it. "I'll just go along and join them," she said, in a voice she barely recognized as her own. "I need a jug of molasses and some blue thread anyhow."

Enoch touched the brim of his hat, released the brake lever he'd been holding with one booted foot, and drove off. It took all Jolie's strength not to turn and watch him go, and her entire body was stiff with tension as she got her own rig moving again. She expected to hear a shot at any moment.

By the time Jolie brought the buckboard and the big draft horse to a stop in front of the general store, the snow was falling in earnest and she was shaking like a feather in a high wind.

She entered the mercantile, huddling inside her heavy woolen cloak, her cheeks stinging from the cold, and sought Daniel out with her eyes. He was standing next to the stove, drinking coffee and listening politely while Elden Small went on about the good old days before things got so "derned modern."

Her lips formed his name, but she never knew for sure whether she'd spoken aloud or not. She didn't always have to, with Daniel; oftentimes, he heard things she was only thinking about voicing just as if she'd said them aloud. The phenomenon worked in reverse, as well.

His brows knitted themselves together for a moment, in a ponderous frown. Then he set the metal coffee mug on top of the potbellied stove with a clank and approached.

"What is it?" he asked, his hands closing around her elbows, supporting her, feeling blessedly good and strong. "Jolie, what's happened?"

She imagined herself telling Daniel about her encounter with Rowdy Fleet and was immediately filled with new fear. If she breathed a word of what had happened, Daniel would rush right out to track the outlaw down. Despite his formidable physical strength and substance of character, Mr. Beckham would be no match for such a man; he could never comprehend Rowdy's devious ways and animal cunning.

She thought quickly, desperately, and blurted out on impulse, "I went by the school to fetch Hank and Gemma and they weren't there."

It was a very poor lie, and Jolie knew it, but it was the best she could do on such short notice. If Enoch mentioned meeting Jolie on the road, and he and Daniel worked together almost every day, he might well say he'd told her the children were with his brother at the mercantile.

Daniel's eyes still looked a little troubled, though he smiled. "They're here," he assured her quickly. "Safe and sound."

Jolie lowered her eyes, not wanting Daniel to see that she'd deceived him, that her surprise and relief were all pretense. "Thank heaven," she said. She meant those words with her whole heart—she and

Daniel and the children were safe for the moment—
and her trembling was entirely real.

"Sit down," Daniel ordered quietly, ushering Jolie
into the circle of men that surrounded the stove and
pressing her into a chair. Bold as she was, she would
not have dared to breach the invisible masculine
boundary on her own.

It was the purest agony, enduring Daniel's kindness
while knowing all the time how utterly furious he
would be if he knew Rowdy Fleet was riding free
because Jolie hadn't mentioned her encounter with
him. Men thought in wholly different terms than
women, she'd learned that much, and there was no
reason to believe Daniel would understand that she'd
had to lie to save his stubborn hide.

Through the front window, she watched the snow
coming down, thick as feathers shaken from some
huge pillow. When Daniel summoned the children
from the back of the store—they'd been watching a
litter of speckled puppies being born—Jolie gathered
her scattered wits and stood, pulling her cloak tightly
around her.

She'd done the right thing not to tell Daniel about
Rowdy, she assured herself, over and over again,
following behind her husband's loaded wagon as they
drove homeward through the mounting blizzard.

Yes, she'd definitely done the right thing.

18

Daniel had ridden his big draft horse to town, so he led the way home through the thickening snow, with Hank perched in front of him, gripping the saddle horn. Jolie and Gemma followed slowly in the buckboard.

As they passed the stand of poplar trees where Jolie had encountered Rowdy earlier, she shivered, not just with cold, but with remembered fear. Other emotions churned in the pit of her stomach, too . . . remorse for one, confusion for another.

By the time they reached the farm, snow was coming down so thick and fast that Jolie could barely make out the edges of the house.

"Take the kids and go inside," Daniel ordered, hoisting her down from the buckboard in his usual forthright fashion. "I'll see to the horses."

Jolie would have preferred to stay with Daniel, despite the biting chill of that Halloween wind, but she knew her husband's suggestion made better sense.

Taking Hank and Gemma under the folds of her cloak, she hurried toward the house.

Deuter was in the kitchen, and he'd brought two enormous pumpkins up from the cellar. Hank whooped with delight, while Gemma looked at Jolie in bewilderment.

"Are we going to carve jack-o'-lanterns?" Hank cried, peeling off his coat, hat, mittens, and scarf.

Jolie was helping Gemma out of her cold-weather gear when Deuter answered.

"Yep. And we'll make 'em fierce-looking enough to scare off any witches or ghosts that might come sneakin' around here tonight."

How about outlaws? Jolie thought miserably. *Would two jack-o'-lanterns frighten Rowdy Fleet away?* "Daniel could use some help putting the buckboard away and taking care of the horses," she said in a quiet tone, pulling chairs nearer the stove and hanging their snow-dampened things to dry.

Deuter wasn't wearing his hat, being inside, but he touched an invisible brim all the same. "Yes, ma'am."

Hank had explained something of the process of carving pumpkins to Gemma by then, and both children were so excited at the prospect that they were practically jumping up and down. Jolie settled them at the table, where they could admire the orange giants, and made hot chocolate to chase away the chill.

While the children were having their cocoa, Hank maintaining all the while that nobody in the territory would have bigger, more frightful jack-o'-lanterns than they would, Jolie peeled potatoes and sliced smoked ham for supper.

The kitchen was warm and tidy and full of good smells when Daniel and Deuter came back from the barn. Jolie's heartbeat quickened when she heard Daniel stomping the snow from his boots on the back step.

She moved the pumpkins to the pantry for the time being and set out dishes and silverware for supper. Jolie had filled the stove reservoir earlier, so there was warm water for the men to wash in. They performed their exuberant sudsings and splashings and sat down at the table to drink the hot, aromatic coffee Jolie had brewed for them.

Mrs. Beckham's tender conscience and natural bent toward practicality made war on the battleground of her spirit while she served up the food. Sure, Daniel would be in danger if he went after Rowdy, a thing he would certainly do if he learned the outlaw was lurking about. But perhaps being unaware of the threat put him in even greater peril.

During supper, Daniel's glance kept straying to his wife's face, as though he sensed she was hiding something, and each time Jolie averted her gaze. She had that familiar feeling that if she let Daniel look squarely into her eyes, he would read her secret on the pages of her soul.

Once the meal was over, Jolie and Gemma cleared the table, and while Jolie washed the dishes, the pumpkins were brought from the pantry. The good cloth was folded and put away, and newspaper put down, so that the carving could be done.

Gemma and Hank watched with big eyes as Daniel spat on a whetstone and began sharpening his hunting knife. Deuter showed the little ones how to draw a pattern on the pumpkins so that a face could be shaped, and they fell to their tasks with such exuberance that they trembled.

Beyond the window, big wisps of snow drifted

down, resembling little ghosts in the flickering lamp-light. Jolie's throat tightened and she had to hold back tears because this was all she'd ever wanted, children and a home and a good man to love, and someone like Rowdy Fleet had the power to take it all away.

The kitchen brimmed with light and laughter, Daniel's quiet and deep, the children's merry and musical, like the chiming of church bells on a clear summer morning. Jolie sat down in the rocking chair in the corner of the room and took up the mending basket, repairing a hole in the toe of a gray woolen work stocking. For now, for tonight, she would not go wandering into the future, with all its frightening possibilities. Nor did she allow herself to stray into the past, with its unhappiness and pain. She had *this moment,* that was all, and she intended to cherish it.

Hank and Gemma were still with her, and she was carrying Daniel's baby in her womb, and they were all safe and warm inside a sturdy house. Those things were enough.

Finally, after much ado, the jack-o'-lanterns were finished and plump tallow candles were found to put inside them. Black smoke curled from the tiny vents in their bristly handled lids, and light shone through their eyes and their zigzag smiles. The pleasant smell of charred pumpkin tinged the air.

Jolie allowed Hank and Gemma to stay up a little later than she normally would have, so they could enjoy their handiwork. Still, when the time came, they went off to bed under protest.

When Jolie returned from hearing the children's prayers and tucking them in, Deuter had left the house for his room in the barn and Daniel was banking the fire in the stove.

After lifting off their tops, Jolie blew out the jack-o'-

lanterns and the aroma of burned squash seemed to intensify for a few moments.

"Thank you, Daniel," Jolie said quietly.

Her husband, who had taken the coffeepot to the door to toss its contents into the snowy yard, looked at her only after he'd rinsed the kettle and filled it for morning from the bucket of well water next to the sink. "You're welcome, Mrs. Beckham," he answered, "but I admit to not knowing what it is you're thanking me for."

Jolie turned her back and looked out the window into the night, even though she couldn't see more than a few yards. She rested one hand on the firm side of a grinning Halloween pumpkin—it was still warm to the touch—and swallowed.

"You and Deuter gave the children a happy memory. One that will probably sustain them later."

Although he was a big man, Daniel could move with graceful silence, and Jolie stiffened in surprise when his hands came to rest easily on her shoulders. "How about you?" he asked, turning her to face him, speaking with a soft gruffness. The hard, gentle power of his nearness all but took her breath away. "Are you happy tonight?"

She remembered her vow to remain in the moment, swallowed a knot of emotion, and nodded. "Yes. No matter what happens, I'll never forget the sight of you and Deuter and Hank and Gemma carving pumpkins. It's hard to say whose faces were shining brighter, the children's or the jack-o'-lanterns'."

Daniel's lips brushed her forehead, and his hands came to rest at her sides, just under the curve of her breasts. She drew in a sharp breath in anticipation; with just a motion of his thumbs, he could stroke her eager nipples and make them jut with readiness against her camisole and dress.

He chuckled, but there was caution in the sound. Wariness. "Something's deviling you, Mrs. Beckham, and I'll expect you to tell me all about it in the morning. For tonight, though, I want you warm and soft and naked in my bed."

Jolie trembled, not with scandal but with the prospect of pleasure so keen it was often nearly unbearable. When Daniel's mouth descended to hers, when he gently prodded her lips apart and swept her mouth with his tongue, all thoughts of trouble and fear were driven from her mind. All that existed was the fire that flickered and then roared to life inside her, all that mattered was Daniel's kiss and the weight of his hands on her plump breasts.

He pulled away from her, just when she thought she'd surely die of the yearning, and turned down the lamps. The kitchen settled into cozy darkness, and Daniel took Jolie's hand.

She expected him to take her upstairs, to their bed. Instead, he led her through the hall and into the leather-and-woodsmoke-scented room he used for reading books and doing accounts. The air was dark and a little chilly, since there was no fire on the hearth, but those things only gave the place a sense of celebration and magic, as did the fat puffs of snow wafting past the window glass.

Slowly, and with quiet ceremony, Daniel undressed his wife. He started by letting down her hair and combing it with his splayed fingers. Next, he unfastened the line of buttons at the front of her calico dress and pushed the fabric back over her shoulders.

Jolie trembled as the cool air and Daniel's glittering

gaze touched her naked skin, and her nipples made hard little knots against the thin muslin of her camisole. One tiny button at a time, Daniel opened this last barrier to her warmth and bounty.

When her breasts were bare, he stroked them, his touch light and almost reverent. Jolie felt like a goddess, bathed in silvery moonlight and iridescent snow, and she tilted her head back in silent surrender to Daniel's will.

Presently, one arm curved around her waist to support her, one hand cupped beneath a full breast, he bent his head and took suckle from her. A low groan of pleasure escaped her throat, and she entangled her fingers in his hair, caressing him as he drew from her generous womanhood.

Some way, though she never knew exactly how because she was too enchanted to think, Daniel stripped away the rest of her clothes. And his shirt must have been gone, too, for later she could recall the feel of his bare chest against her palms and the tips of her fingers.

The big leather chair creaked as he settled into it, pulling Jolie down onto his lap. She closed her eyes while her body slowly took him inside. He groaned and let his head fall back as her feminine muscles cherished him.

"Jolie," he rasped, clasping her hips in his work-hardened hands in a desperate move to stay her from rising and falling along his length.

She was well beyond the ability to reason by then however; her most primitive feminine instincts had taken over, and her body was making all the choices on its own. An ancient cry, a cry of glory and sweetness and white-hot fusion, came from her throat. She escaped Daniel's grasp and rode him mercilessly.

Jolie heard Daniel's choked gasp, and of course she felt the unrestrained force of his thrusts as he gave in to her seduction, but she couldn't see his face because she was blinded by the dazzle of rapture that encompassed her.

They reached the summit of their passion at the same moment, their mouths blending, their tongues battling. And each swallowed the triumphant shout of the other.

Jolie sagged against Daniel's chest the moment her body had stopped convulsing in reckless response, and his arms enfolded her. In some ways, that was the sweetest thing of all.

Next morning, Jolie overslept, and when she opened her eyes, the first thing she saw was frost glistening on the window in fanciful curlicues and fan shapes. Beyond, she discovered later, when she'd made herself presentable, peeked in and found the children's room empty, and hurried downstairs, was a world formed of pure white marble and dusted with glimmering crystal.

The kitchen was warm and the coffee was simmering on the stove. Jolie poured herself a cup, wrapped her woolen cloak around her shoulders, and ventured outside.

Tracks and wheel marks in the otherwise perfect snow told her Deuter had probably taken Hank and Gemma to school in the buckboard. The rhythmic sound of an ax striking wood rang bell-like in the crystalline air.

Jolie followed the noise to the woodshed, where she found Daniel chopping fuel for the fire, his breath making a white cloud every time he exhaled.

"Why didn't you wake me?" she demanded, taking

a defensive stand just in case Daniel decided to lecture her on the duties of a farm wife. "Goodness, half the day must be gone!"

Daniel didn't pause in his work, but a grin pulled briefly at the corner of his mouth and his pale blue eyes danced as he glanced in his wife's direction. "You looked pretty as a ripe peach in August lying there. I just couldn't bring myself to bother you."

Jolie stepped into the fragrant, shadowy confines of the shed, and the bite of the cold day was less brutal. A flush pulsed in her cheeks as she recalled the wanton way she'd responded to Daniel, in his study of all places, and later on in his bed. He'd kept her awake and busy for a good long time. The memory made her insides turn warm and achy.

"If I didn't already have your baby growing inside me, Daniel Beckham," she said saucily, "last night would have accomplished the purpose."

He continued chopping, and his grin was downright rascallike, purely unsuited to a God-fearing Presbyterian. His words were even less so. "I wouldn't recommend that you go on teasing me," he said. "Just remembering makes me want to bend you over the woodpile and get you to breathing hard and hollering again."

Jolie could see herself doing exactly that, right there in that woodshed, and the image made her start and then jump a step backward. "I *didn't* holler," she insisted in breathless indignation, spreading splayed fingers over her bosom.

The grin intensified to a positively devilish degree. "You did holler, Mrs. Beckham," Daniel answered. "Would you like me to repeat what you said?"

"No!" Jolie gasped, remembering that as well as the lovemaking. Polite women didn't listen to such phrases, even if they'd uttered them themselves only the night before, in a frenzy of passion.

Daniel laughed and drove the ax head deep into the chopping block. He faced Jolie, his hands on his hips, his head tilted to one side, at a mischievous slant.

"Come over here, Mrs. Beckham," he said.

Jolie tried to resist him, she truly did. But the pull was as mysterious, as elemental as lightning or thunder, and in the end she had to obey it.

There was still a telling warmth in her cheeks two hours later, when Jolie was busy in the kitchen, making sandwiches and pies for the midday meal. She dipped her fingers in the water bucket and laid them to her face in an attempt to cool it when she saw Mary approaching on horseback.

Holt, the older of the two Beckham children, rode behind Mary, his arms clasping her thickening middle. The little girl was in front, huddled inside her mother's frayed woolen cloak.

Daniel came out of the barn to help his sister-in-law from the saddle just as Jolie made her way carefully down the icy back steps.

"Where's Enoch?" Jolie heard her husband ask, and she noticed the concern in his voice even if Mary apparently didn't.

"He's home with his feet by the fire, drinking a potion of honey and lemon," Mary answered brightly. "He's got a touch of the grippe, you know." She beamed, taking in a deep breath and looking around her as though she'd stumbled into some magical kingdom from a storybook. "Me, I just couldn't stay inside those walls another moment. It was too purely beautiful out for doing home things."

Daniel swung both children down from the horse's

back, making them giggle with dizzy delight, but he was gentle as he extended his hands to Mary, and Jolie was touched by the sight. It was pure, glorious luck that Daniel Beckham, the best man that side of the Mississippi River, had chanced to rescue her from the noose and bring her home to tend his kitchen and share his bed.

In the next moment, though, she remembered Rowdy's existence, and the thought of him shadowed her spirit like a dark cloud. Her smile faded.

Mary and the children might have encountered the outlaw between their place and Daniel's. Jolie shuddered inwardly as she imagined the scene, knowing that, if anything happened to them, not only would Daniel never forgive her, she'd never forgive herself.

Mary stayed for the noonday meal, which she referred to as dinner, in the way of Southerners. She was fine company, and Jolie heartily enjoyed the visit, but she was edgy the whole time, too, worried Mary wouldn't be safe on the way home. She wondered how she could tell Daniel, without revealing too much, that his brother's wife should be escorted across the fields.

By the time her sister-in-law had her children bundled up and was ready to leave again, however, Deuter was back from town. He tied Mary's horse behind and drove her and the little ones home to Enoch in the buckboard.

The sun was bright and the snow was melting as Jolie stood in the dooryard, watching the wagon move away over ground that would soon turn to mud, one hand shading her eyes. Daniel startled her.

"You've been nervous as a cat on a flapjack griddle ever since yesterday," he said. "What's bothering you, Jolie?"

So, he'd finally gotten around to asking her to account for her odd mood the day before. Jolie ran her tongue over her lips and looked up at Daniel, sure and certain her heart must be showing plain in her eyes.

"I don't like to tell you," she confessed, smoothing her apron and starting back toward the house, "but I suppose I don't have much of a choice now." Jolie waited until they were inside, with the door closed. She stood behind a chair as she spoke, her hands clasping the back, and Daniel sat opposite, his arms folded on the table's edge. "I saw Rowdy yesterday, on my way into town. It seems he and Blake hid the stolen money in the barn, but Blake apparently moved it and he's come back to look."

All the color drained from Daniel's flesh and, for one horrible moment, Jolie could imagine what he'd look like dead, laid out for burying. He rose slowly from the chair, his fists clenching and unclenching at his sides.

Jolie didn't retreat; she knew he'd never strike her even if she shamed him in front of the whole territory. But her grip on the back of the chair tightened. "I was on my way to town and passing that abandoned homestead . . . the place that's part of your land now . . . when Rowdy rode out of the poplar trees and held a gun on me. He told me about the money and wanted to know if I'd found it, and he said he'd kill you if I told you anything." She paused, took a deep breath, and studied the checked pattern of the table-cloth as though hoping to find the perfect explanation woven into the fabric. "Rowdy'd no sooner told me that than we heard a horse and wagon coming. He said he'd shoot me *and* whoever it was if I gave him away, and when the rig came over the rise I saw it was Enoch driving. I was so afraid Rowdy was going to kill him, I could hardly think straight . . ."

"Sweet God in heaven," Daniel rasped, turning away and striding off into the hallway.

Jolie scrambled after him, wide-eyed with fear as he wrenched a rifle down from the rack behind his desk in the study, checked the chamber, and loaded it.

"Pack some things for you and the children," he ordered, hardly even glancing at Jolie as he pushed past her and strode back toward the kitchen.

Jolie's heartbeat seemed as loud to her as a mallet striking a brass gong. The worst was happening. Not only was Daniel going after Rowdy, he was sending her and Hank and Gemma away, probably forever. He was fed up.

"We don't want to go anywhere!" she cried, frantic to stop Daniel and at the same time knowing there was no way to do that. "We belong here with you!"

"Not while Fleet is on the loose. I can't track him and protect the three of you at the same time. Now, get your things ready. I'll drive you to town and get you a room at Mrs. Krayper's place." He set the rifle down to put on his coat and hat. "Like as not, Enoch will want Mary and their little ones to do the same."

Under any other circumstances, Jolie would have been faint with relief just because Daniel hadn't decided to ship her off to San Francisco and the children to some orphanage after all. As it was, she was still practically consumed with terror because Enoch and Daniel could so easily be shot to death.

She tried reason, even though she knew before she uttered a word that the effort would fail. "Rowdy's like a mad dog, Daniel. He *likes* killing."

"That's just why I'm going to bring him down,"

Daniel answered. "Do as I told you, Jolie. I'll be back for you as soon as I've spoken with Enoch."

It wasn't Daniel who drove into the dooryard an hour later, though, it was Deuter. He was silent as he loaded up the things Jolie had packed for herself and the children. She gave the jack-o'-lanterns, which now looked a little lopsided and forlorn, one last look before leaving the house.

Soon, Jolie was settled in a cramped room at Alverna Krayper's boarding house. Gemma and Hank sat on the narrow bed across from hers, their feet dangling, their expressions gloomy. The only element of cheer was the fact that Mary and her little ones were squeezed into the room across the dark hallway.

Suppertime came and the two women and the children joined the other boarders in the dining room. Jolie felt as though she were back in the schoolhouse, standing trial again, the way the landlady and her tenants kept stealing curious looks at her.

The evening was only tolerable because Mary kept up a running patter, deliberately provoking an argument with the new schoolmaster by insisting that left-handed children should not be forced to use their right hands. After that, she proceeded to tell the circuit preacher, who was just passing through on his way to Fishtrap, that she didn't see what Saint Paul could possibly have been thinking of when he decreed that women shouldn't be allowed to speak in church.

The snow was gone by nightfall, dissolved by the warmth of an autumn sun, and Jolie was restless. After she'd put the children down for the night, she went across the hall to ask Mary to look in on them while she took a short walk.

Mary's son and daughter were already sleeping, and

she was reading by the light of a single kerosene lamp. She frowned. "Daniel and Enoch said we should stay right here," she pointed out. "No matter what."

"I won't be long," Jolie pressed, desperate to breathe fresh air and have room to move her elbows freely, if only for a little while. "And I promise I won't go far."

Mary shrugged and lowered her eyes to her book again as Jolie stepped back and closed the door.

The air outside was almost springlike, and there were stars scattered across the sky like clear marbles on a carpet. Jolie kept her skirts from the mud as she made her way along the wooden sidewalk, enjoying the lights and inwardly keeping time to the bawdy music coming from the saloons.

Ira January's house looked as imposing as always, since it was the biggest place in town, but Jolie opened the gate and glided up the walk anyhow. It had been a while since she'd tried to call on Nan, and this seemed as fitting an occasion as any.

Mounting the porch, grateful for the light of the fat candles burning in the brass lanterns affixed to either side of the door, Jolie gave the bell knob an authoritative twist. She waited, arms folded, tapping the toes of one foot, and then rang again.

She was about to turn away, resigned to yet another defeat, when the door creaked open and Nan's waxen face peered at her around the edge. Mrs. Culley's manner was furtive, like that of a doe driven from some hiding place by hunger or thirst.

"Come in," she said, whispering the words, looking back over one shoulder as though she expected someone to stride up and countermand her words. "Hurry!"

Nan clasped Jolie's hand and pulled her into a

darkened parlor, where heavy velvet drapes were pulled against the night. Only when the two women were huddled behind an ornate Oriental folding screen did Nan speak again.

"Oh, Jolie," she murmured raggedly, "you were right! I should never have come here . . ."

"That's an easy problem to solve," Jolie said, making no effort to keep her voice down. "We'll simply leave, right this moment. I'm sure Mrs. Krayper could find a place for you, or perhaps Reverend and Mrs. Watman would take you in until we can decide what to do."

Nan was already shaking her head, her finger raised to her lips in a bid . . . no, a *plea* . . . for circumspection. "You don't understand. He'd come after me. He'd drag me back here and it would be worse than if I'd never left!"

Jolie felt cold horror as she gazed into Nan's eyes and realized her friend had already given up. Only God knew what had prompted her to finally admit Jolie to the house and confide in her, even as little as she had.

"I won't leave you here," Jolie whispered, furious because she hated having to hide from Ira January to protect her friend. She wanted nothing so much as to walk straight up to him and spit in his face. "It isn't decent. And look at you . . . you're narrow as a fence picket, and there are big circles under your eyes!"

Nan dug her heels into the expensive Persian rug when Jolie tried to pull her toward the door. "I've got to stay," she said. "I won't have the medicine if I go. I *need* the medicine!"

"What medicine?" Jolie asked, as a new fear rose around her like dirty floodwater. "Nan Culley, has that man been giving you laudanum?"

Nan ran her tongue over her lips, and her eyes looked feverish and glazed. "I don't know what it is. It makes me sleep, and when I sleep, I'm with my Joe again."

This time, Jolie was brooking no refusals. Nan was strong, or had been once, but Jolie was stronger, and if she had to drag her friend out of the house by the hair, she was going to do it.

She hoped it wasn't an omen of things to come that Mr. January was coming through the front gate, whistling, just as she hauled a protesting Nan over the threshold.

Jolie had no weapon but bravado. "Please step out of our way, Mr. January," she said formally. "Mrs. Culley is leaving, and she's never coming back."

Ira's gaze glittered, making the moonlight seem harsh, and he folded his arms. "Go back into the house, Nancy," he said evenly. "I'll tend to your little rebellion later."

To Jolie's furious horror, Nan broke free of her grasp and dashed to obey. The door clicked shut behind her, and Jolie knew if she tried to gain entrance, it would be barred.

She eased her way past January, giving him a wide berth. "If you hurt Nan or her baby," she cried, "you'll account for it, not just to me, but to Daniel as well!"

The millowner laughed. "I'd just as soon not deal with Daniel at all," he responded blithely. "But 'accounting' is only one of the things I'd like to do to you. And when it comes to Nancy, the law is squarely on my side, so don't go pestering the marshal with this. She should no longer be addressed as 'Mrs. Culley,' you see. As of today, her name is Mrs. January."

19

Jolie swayed slightly, sickened by the news that Nan had *married* this monster. The house loomed behind her, sinister and gloomy, as though it were the landing at the top of a stairway leading straight into hell. Some innate evil seemed to pull at her, trying to draw her back inside.

Somehow, Jolie managed to find the courage to stand her ground instead of bolting and running, as every impulse urged her to do. "You told me you didn't want to make Nan your wife," she said. "You were angry because she had no property or money to bring to the marriage."

January smiled, his teeth gleaming in the darkness, as Jolie imagined those of a wolf would do. "I changed my mind," he said with a shrug. "That may be a woman's prerogative, but it doesn't belong to the feminine gender exclusively."

Jolie's hand tightened on the gate latch for a moment before she eased it open and stepped through.

"You needn't think I'm going to forget what I've learned tonight, Mr. January," she told him. "There is a way to help Nan, and rest assured, I will find it."

The gambler laughed. "The law says a man's wife belongs to him, like property or livestock. I can do what I like, Mrs. Beckham, and we both know it." With that, he went up the walk, opened the front door, and stepped inside the house.

Jolie stood on the sidewalk beyond the fence, trembling. There was no telling what unspeakable things he might do to Nan to punish her for her defiance, and the fact that Jolie could do nothing to help made her physically ill.

Sadly, Mr. January had been quite correct in his statements regarding his complete freedom to abuse Nan in virtually any way he liked. Wives and children both were possessions in the eyes of the law and, rather like house pets, could be disciplined in whatever way the man of the family might see fit to employ.

It occurred to Jolie, when the lights of Mrs. Krayper's boarding house came into view again, that she'd been fortunate indeed that it had been Big Dan Beckham who'd brought her home from the hanging that day. Dying would have been better than having to live with a fiend like Mr. January.

As it happened, Daniel and Enoch were waiting in the boarding house's small front parlor when Jolie slipped through the front door. She might have tried to make for the stairs, hoping to go unnoticed and thus be spared explaining why she'd defied her husband's orders to stay put, if Enoch hadn't spotted her first thing. He nudged his brother and pointed, and Jolie said a silent farewell to all hope of escape.

"Where have you been?" Daniel demanded, in a furious whisper, towering over Jolie like a human mountain now. He could surely be imposing when he chose.

"I'm glad you asked," Jolie responded, taking his arm. "Though I'm entirely certain you won't care for the reply." She led him out onto the porch, where there was at least a semblance of privacy. "Daniel, I went to visit Nan Culley tonight, over at Mr. January's place." She saw the light of outrage kindling in Daniel's eyes and held up her hands, palms out, in a bold request for silence. "You were certainly right about him . . . he's a very wicked man. He married Nan, after all that fuss because she didn't have land or money, and he's mistreating her. She's thin and she's terribly frightened and he's giving her some kind of medicine . . . laudanum, I think. Daniel, for her sake, for the baby's, we've got to help her."

Frustration was etched into every line of Daniel's powerful frame. "We can't," he said raggedly, after a long, explosive silence. "She's his wife."

Jolie was shocked, even though she'd known most men thought alike when it came to dogs, idiots, half-breeds, and women. "Daniel . . ."

"It isn't our place to interfere between a man and his wife," her husband interrupted, in a tone of firmness and finality.

"The hell it isn't!" Jolie retorted, arms akimbo, eyes flashing with temper. "We're her friends! Who's going to look out for Nan, if not us?"

Daniel sighed heavily, his gaze skirting Jolie's to search the night sky beyond the gingerbread trim of Alverna Krayper's porch roof. When he looked at her again, Jolie saw bleak resignation in his face. "Did Mrs. Culley ask for help?" he inquired, and Jolie knew by his tone that he'd already guessed the answer.

"No," she said, almost in a whisper, lowering her

head. At first, Nan had seemed to want Jolie's assistance, but when it came time to sort the matter out, the woman had lost her courage.

"Until she does, Mrs. Beckham," Daniel said, "you and I will be minding our own business. How are Gemma and Hank?"

Jolie sighed. "They want to go home to the farm," she replied. "Just as I do. Daniel, how long will it be?"

"I don't know," her husband answered wearily. "If Fleet's anywhere around Prosperity, he's keeping himself well hidden."

"Have you managed to round up any help, or is it just you and Enoch and Deuter doing all the looking?" For understandable reasons, Jolie had minimal confidence in the law-enforcement abilities of the local marshal. As far as she could tell, the man just sat around under that big freckle on the top of his head, content to hang whoever was handy.

"There's a posse," Daniel said, but the words were spiritless and Jolie knew a band of farmers and mill hands and saloon keepers would be no threat to a wily little snake like Rowdy. "If you want to call it that."

On impulse, Jolie went to her husband and clutched his upper arms. Her fingers could barely stretch across the hard expanse of muscle, let alone find enough purchase to get a good grip. "Daniel, leave it be. I'm begging you. Rowdy's mean as a badger with a thorn in its paw, and he'd shoot a man on sight if the idea struck his fancy!"

Daniel kissed Jolie's forehead lightly. "That's why we've got to find him," he said, with resignation. "Leaving Fleet to roam the countryside would be like letting a rabid dog run loose."

"But you're not a lawman," Jolie pleaded. "It isn't your responsibility—"

"Isn't it?" Daniel broke in. "I've got as much to lose as anybody. And I mean to protect what's mine."

There would be no reasoning with Mr. Beckham; Jolie could see that. She nodded, as resigned as he was, and it seemed there were no more words to say.

"Go inside," Daniel told her, after a long and difficult interval had passed. "It's getting chilly out here, and we can't have you catching your death."

An argument came to mind—she was no more susceptible to chills than he was—but Jolie held it back. "Good night, Daniel," she said, and went into the house.

Morning brought a crisp, golden orange day, typical of late fall. Jolie saw to Hank and Gemma's grooming, like always, and after they'd had a breakfast of oatmeal and cream in Mrs. Krayper's kitchen, she walked them to school. Gemma and Jolie held hands, scuffing up crunchy leaves from the maple trees lining the town's single residential street, while Hank kept himself a little apart. He watched Jolie and his sister with affectionate disdain, shaking his head once in a while so anyone who happened to be looking on would immediately know he thought girls were plain silly.

As she was returning home from the schoolhouse a few minutes later, deep in troubled thoughts of Nan's situation and the singular threat Rowdy represented, the idea burst upon her like the Light that surrounded Saint Paul on the road to Damascus.

The outlaw was concerned about one thing, and one thing only, and that was the money he and Blake had taken from the bank on that portentous day in late spring. The two had hidden the loot in Daniel's barn and then, without telling his partner, Blake had moved it. Rowdy was bold, and he was cunning, but he clearly didn't know when to cut his losses and run, or he wouldn't be burrowed in somewhere nearby, waiting.

Jolie actually smiled as she hurried toward the boarding house. She'd turn over every board and rock on Dan Beckham's place if she had to, but she'd find that money, and she'd hand it over to Rowdy. He was greedy and feral, like a rat, and probably desperate enough to try snatching the cheese from a trap.

She didn't want to think about some of the other things Fleet might be desperate enough to do. Jolie had a great deal at stake, and no matter how frightened she might be, she couldn't afford to huddle docilely inside Mrs. Krayper's boarding house and wait for the men to set things right.

Then there was the matter of Nan's tragic circumstances. *That* certainly couldn't be left to the masculine population of the town.

Using some of the household money Daniel had given her, Jolie hired a horse and buggy from the livery stable and set out for the farm. Clinging to the adage that mighty forces precede the bold, paving their way, she drove straight down the center of Prosperity with her chin held high and her gaze fixed straight ahead.

Out of the corners of her eyes, she saw a few people pause to watch her drive past, but no one tried to stop her, and for that Jolie was devoutly grateful.

She went right by her own place, though she longed to have those walls around her again and that sturdy roof over her head, and headed for Verena's.

Jolie found her neighbor dressed in black, as usual. Verena's tidy house was quiet except for the ticking of an old clock on the parlor mantelpiece. Her eyes narrowed when she admitted her unexpected caller.

"Why aren't you at Alverna's, where you belong?"

"I don't belong at Mrs. Krayper's boarding house," Jolie replied briskly. "Any more than you do."

Verena sighed and gestured toward a cushioned rocking chair in front of a sun-filled window. "I've never heard such a fuss as Daniel made about me staying out here alone," the older woman said. "But I won't be driven from my own land by some flea-chewed saddle bum, and that's all there is to the matter. May I get you some tea?"

Jolie shook her head, smoothing her skirts nervously over her lap. "I've come about Nan Culley," she said. And then she told Verena everything she knew about their friend's situation. "Daniel says it isn't our business and we can't interfere," she finished, "but Nan is in dreadful trouble."

Verena looked sad. "Yes."

"I was thinking we could kidnap her, and bring her here. I'm sure after the medicine had worn off, Nan would come to her senses and listen to reason. She could just get on a stagecoach to Spokane and start all over again."

Mrs. Dailey stared pensively out the window for a long time, but Jolie knew she wasn't seeing the climbing rosebush on the other side of the glass. She was thinking.

Finally, she said, "It will take Nan some weeks to get better, and I don't have the first idea how we'll handle Ira January, but we've got to do something. If you can manage to get her out of that house, bring her straight to me."

Jolie reached out and squeezed her friend's hand in gratitude. "Thank you."

"Just don't underestimate Mr. January," Verena

313

warned solemnly. "He's not a man of kindness or graces and he can be ruthless."

A cold finger touched Jolie's spine. "I'll be careful, I promise."

After that, the two women talked of Jolie's unhappiness at being stuck away at the boarding house. Verena, hungry for company, brought out tea and lemon-butter cookies and things didn't seem quite so impossible to Jolie when she left.

Although the animals were still in the barn and Daniel lived in the house as always, the Beckham farm had a lonely, bereft feeling about it when Jolie drew up the rented horse and rig in the dooryard and climbed down. The experience would have been completely bleak if it hadn't been for the old tomcat, Leviticus, who meandered out of the barn to greet her with a raucous *meow.*

Jolie smiled sadly. "I'll wager you know where Blake put that money, don't you? You're probably privy to everything that happens on this place." She paused and sighed. "If only you could talk."

"Reooow," Leviticus responded charitably.

"I'm afraid that's of no appreciable help to me," Jolie answered, lifting her skirts and heading in the direction of the barn.

She looked in every logical place . . . checking for loose floorboards, peering behind sacks of grain, lifting saddles and the lids of crates. The light in the open doorway crept deeper into the barn, then began to recede again. And Jolie had still found nothing.

She went outside, dusting her hands together and looking around. Jolie doubted Blake would have had brass enough to hide the booty inside the house, but then he'd shown very little reticence about such things before his capture. Come to that, he would probably consider it a grand joke to stash the take from a bank robbery under the nose of one of the community's most prominent citizens.

Jolie stepped into the house, and its familiar sights and smells surrounded her like loving arms. Even though she'd only been away for a day, she felt a pang of homesickness so keen that it brought tears to her eyes.

As methodically as possible, Jolie searched every room. She looked behind the books on the shelves of Daniel's study, and under the cushion of the leather chair where he'd made such scandalous love to her not so many nights before. She checked his desk drawers and even lifted the corners of the rug.

She was going through the pantry, peering into every jug and sack, when the voice sounded behind her.

"I'll be damned if you don't have more gall than a monkey in mating season," Daniel said.

Jolie whirled to see her husband standing there, his forearms raised and resting against the framework of the pantry doorway. High color raced to her cheeks, but she kept her chin at an obstinate angle.

"What are you doing here, Jolie? Didn't I tell you not to leave the boarding house except to walk Gemma and Hank to and from the schoolhouse?"

"I had a yen for some oatmeal cookies," she said, after some wild considering. "You know how it is when a woman's in the family way . . ."

Daniel's look showed plain skepticism and no small amount of irritation. "Being 'in the family way' is all the more reason a woman should obey her husband," he said.

Jolie stood toe to toe with Daniel and looked straight into his eyes. "Even when that husband is wrong?"

"Yes," Daniel had the audacity to reply. "Of course, I'm not wrong."

"Of course not," Jolie retorted, her face hot with indignation.

He folded his arms and braced one shoulder against the doorjamb. "What were you looking for, Jolie? And don't say 'oatmeal cookies' or I swear I'll forget myself and turn you across my knee." Daniel leaned closer, his nose only a fraction of an inch from hers. "Don't lie to me, either."

Jolie bit her lip. Daniel did have an uncanny way of catching her in prevarications, and besides, she would eventually need his help if her plan were to work. The only problem was, he might decide the whole idea was too dangerous and forbid her to pursue it.

"I was looking for the money."

Daniel's brows knit together for a moment in a frown of suspicious puzzlement. "What money?"

"The five hundred dollars Rowdy and Blake took from the bank," Jolie replied, the words tumbling out in a rush. "They hid it in the barn, but then Blake decided to double-cross Rowdy and he moved the saddlebags. Naturally, he's not telling the law where, and Rowdy can't get close enough to him to find out."

Daniel's right index finger jutted toward the floor in a series of stabbing motions. "You mean to tell me that money has been on this land the whole time?" he demanded, in a furious undertone.

Jolie's aplomb was deserting her. "It's not as though I *knew* or anything like that." She paused, frowning. "Of course, Rowdy believes I was in cahoots with

Blake, and I suppose that makes him even more dangerous."

Daniel rolled his eyes, then backed out of the pantry doorway, but not before taking a light but inescapable hold on Jolie's arm. He pulled her right along with him and pressed her unceremoniously into a chair. "I'm assuming you haven't found anything yet," he said. "What were you planning to do if you turned up that five hundred dollars?"

"Bait a trap, naturally. Rowdy would come to collect it and you and Enoch and the rest of the posse would be waiting for him."

The expression in Daniel's eyes bore an odd resemblance to relief, though his tone belied that he was entertaining any such gentle sentiment. "Oh? And how did you mean to get in touch with him with this news? So help me, Jolie, if you've known where he's been hiding out all this time . . ."

"Rowdy will contact me again." She refused to stoop to Daniel's level by responding to the insinuation that she'd kept any of those dratted secrets to protect Fleet. It was Daniel she'd been looking out for, and Gemma and Hank. "Like I said, he thinks I know where it is."

Daniel muttered a swear word under his breath, sighed, then started toward the door. "Come along, Mrs. Beckham," he said. "We're heading back to town."

Jolie didn't move. She just sat there at the kitchen table, her arms folded stubbornly, waiting for Daniel to realize she wasn't trotting along behind him.

Sometimes he acted like he'd just been elected sheriff of a two-person county.

When Mr. Beckham discovered himself to be traveling alone, he turned back. "What now?" he snapped, from the doorway. "This is my home," Jolie announced. "It's the first real one I can remember having, except for a short while when I lived with my aunt Nissa and uncle Franklin. And I've just decided that no mean-spirited bantam rooster like Rowdy Fleet is going to chase me away from it."

Jolie thought she saw a glimmer of respect in Daniel's gaze, along with the expected annoyance.

He wasn't any better at giving ground than she was, however. "I can throw you over one shoulder and haul you out of here, Jolie. It's not like you have a choice or anything."

She was willing to allow that he was right. He was bigger than she was, and much stronger, but if he tried to carry her from this kitchen he'd raise a good sweat doing it. In fact, the task would roughly resemble attempting to stuff a wildcat into a meat grinder.

"You wouldn't let Rowdy run off your livestock or burn your barn down or trample your corn patch, would you?" Jolie demanded, mightily provoked. She waved both arms in wild emphasis. "Yet you're willing to drag the children and me . . . and we're the closest thing you've got to a family, Daniel Beckham, like it or not . . . all over the territory!"

To her surprise, Daniel came peaceably to the table, pulled back a chair, and sat. He set his hat aside and regarded her with solemn befuddlement. "It means that much to you . . . staying here, I mean?"

Jolie hadn't realized how that house and farm had spoiled her for other places until she'd been forced to take up residence in one of Mrs. Krayper's attic rooms. "Yes, Daniel," she answered quietly, "it means that much."

He sighed and scratched the back of his head. "It'll

be a risk. I can't be here all the time, looking out for you."

"I've looked out for myself most all my life anyhow," Jolie replied, "and my next breath is a risk. And my next heartbeat. We all have to take our chances, one way or another."

Daniel rubbed his chin, pretending to ponder the question, but Jolie knew he'd already made up his mind to let her and the children come back to the house. The sweet, unexpected joy of that was like a magnificent bird taking wing in that other world inside her, the realm of the heart and spirit.

"I reckon if I try to keep you at Alverna's, you'll just proceed to run off again and stir up more trouble."

Jolie's mouth quivered, but she didn't smile. "I reckon that's so, Mr. Beckham."

Her husband slapped the tabletop lightly with one hand. "All right, then," he said, in the tone of a long-suffering saint, "so be it. Just remember that I warned you."

Jolie nodded and then sprang happily from her chair. "I believe I'll just dust a little, and put together a dried apple pie or two for supper."

Daniel's blue eyes caressed her for a long moment, dancing with silent music and humor the way Enoch's sometimes did. Jolie felt an even greater love for her husband flow into her from some invisible source, quickening her step and bringing warm color to her cheeks.

"Keep this handy," Daniel ordered, handing his wife the loaded forty-five he'd brought from the study.

Jolie took the gun easily and tucked it away in the shallow drawer underneath the tabletop. "You needn't worry about me, Mr. Beckham," she assured Daniel brightly. "I'm a fine shot."

"Considering that some folks still believe you sent poor old Hamish Frazer over the next horizon the day of the bank robbery, I wouldn't go around calling attention to that if I were you."

Having washed her hands and put a crisply starched apron on over her dress, Jolie went into the pantry and came out with a crock full of dried apple slices. She was so happy that it was easy to be charitable and let Daniel's remark pass. "You will have Deuter pick the children up at school?"

"Yes," Daniel responded, still sounding beleaguered, "and I'll have him fetch your things from the boarding house, too."

"Thank you," Jolie said, peering into the woodbox beside the stove with plain disapproval. It was empty, except for a few slivers and chips of bark.

When Daniel left the house, Jolie followed, heading for the woodshed at a brisk pace. Her cheeks throbbed as she remembered being so thoroughly taken by her husband in that very place, and she was hasty as she loaded her arms with kindling and pitchy chunks of pine.

After smoke was curling from the chimney and water was heating in the reservoir, Jolie felt much better. She hummed as she mixed flour and lard and vinegar and water for crust.

While the pies were baking, she continued her search for the money Blake had hidden. She looked in every drawer and cache, under and behind every piece of furniture. She even slid beneath each of the beds on her back to make sure he hadn't slit open one of the mattresses and stuffed the currency inside.

When Deuter brought Hank and Gemma home that afternoon, he also brought their belongings from the boarding house. Both children immediately changed their clothes and proceeded to chase each other all over the dooryard, so exuberant was their pleasure at coming back.

Enoch and Mary came to supper, and Daniel killed a pair of fat chickens for the occasion.

"How did you manage it?" Mary whispered, while the two women were preparing the birds for frying. "Daniel and Enoch were both so set against our leaving the boarding house before that outlaw was caught."

"I just told Daniel I wasn't going to stay in that place another day," Jolie replied, a little pompously. Her wishes didn't often prevail over her husband's, and the good Lord would no doubt forgive her for taking a degree of pride in the small victory.

Mary smiled. "I try to mind what Enoch tells me," she confided. "But I can't always manage."

Daniel and his brother were seated at the table, oiling harnesses and arguing about politics as they worked. Enoch had a pipe in his teeth, and the smell of the tobacco was pleasantly masculine.

"I believe these women are plotting against us, brother," Enoch said, his eyes grinning as surely as his lips.

Daniel sighed philosophically and doused the cloth he was using with more of the pungent oil. "I don't reckon there's any doubt about that. Scares a man half to death just to consider what'll happen if they ever get the vote."

Enoch laughed. "All the saloons would be closed down, and the fast women would be sent to convents to mend their ways."

"There wouldn't be any more wars," Mary put in, with good-natured obstinance. "And children wouldn't have to work in factories from morning till

321

night." She glanced fondly at her own small daughter, who sat in the rocking chair playing with a rag doll. "Oh, yes, Enoch Beckham, it would be a better world if women had a say in things."

"I think women will be granted the vote eventually," Jolie dared to speculate.

Enoch chuckled again; practically everything in life seemed to be a cause for merriment as far as he was concerned. "Right about then, Congress will decide to levy a tax against a man's wages. The government will get a piece of his earnings before he ever sees them."

"They'd best not try that," was Daniel's rumbled response.

That evening, it began to snow again, and Jolie wanted Enoch and Mary to stay the night. They refused the invitation, having stock to tend and chores to do in the morning, and set out for home. Jolie stood at the window, watching as the lights swinging from the sides of their wagon soaked slowly into the stormy night and then disappeared.

The snow fell all night long and, by morning, it was so deep that Daniel had to wear snowshoes to travel between the house and barn. Gemma and Hank stayed home from school, of course, working their lessons at the kitchen table after breakfast.

Jolie set herself to baking bread, and while she worked, she considered the problems facing her. She hadn't given up on finding the robbery money, but she was running out of ideas for places to look. As she turned and kneaded buttery dough, it was Nan Culley who filled her thoughts. Somehow, she had to get her friend away from that dreadful man, at least long enough for Nan to clear her system of intoxicating medicines and come back to her senses.

The wintry weather continued, however, through

Saturday, when Hank and Gemma took baths in water melted down from snow and heated on the stove. Both the outside pump and the one inside the well house were frozen solid.

Sunday was so bitterly cold that even Daniel didn't feel inclined to make the journey to church.

On Monday morning, a frigid rain fell, leaving a crust of ice to coat the snow. Jolie was beginning to develop cabin fever. She'd done all the mending and made up all the fabric she had on hand, as well as cooking up every recipe she'd ever learned.

Tuesday night, the ice on the creek began to shift and crackle, and Wednesday's sun rose bright and fierce, accompanied by slightly warmer winds. Jolie drove Hank and Gemma to the schoolhouse herself, expertly navigating the buckboard around the deep mud holes that had formed in the road.

Passing the mill, she saw Ira January engaged in conversation with two men who had just arrived with a wagon loaded down with supplies. With her back straight as a flagpole, she headed straight for the fancy house where Nan was being held as a willing prisoner.

20

The motion of a curtain on the second floor of the January house told Jolie that Nan was probably aware of her arrival. It remained to be seen whether the Chinese houseboy would succeed in keeping the friends apart.

Jolie drew the buckboard to a halt at the front gate, set the brake lever, arranged her skirts as decently as she could, and climbed down from the box. Her heart beat faster with every step she took . . . through the gate, up the front walk, across the veranda to the door. Only the sure and certain knowledge that Nan, and her innocent child as well, would inevitably perish if something wasn't done kept her from losing her courage.

To Jolie's tremendous surprise, it was Nan herself who answered the repeated and energetic twists of the bell knob. She looked even more wretched in the harsh definition of daylight.

"Thunderation, Jolie Beckham," she hissed, showing at least a shadow of her former spirit, "have you gone mad? Mr. January made it very clear that he didn't want you around . . ."

Jolie took a hard grasp on her friend's elbow, making plain the fact that she had no intention of letting go. "Phooey on Mr. January," she said rashly, and she proceeded to half lead, half drag Nan down the porch steps and along the walk. Never mind that the misguided Mrs. January was wearing a white ruffled bed dress and her hair was sticking out in as many directions as there were minute marks on a clock. "You've seen the last of him *and* this mausoleum he calls a house."

Nan didn't try to resist . . . her experiences with Mr. January had probably long-since proven such efforts fruitless. She allowed Jolie to shuffle her through the gate and up into the buckboard seat. Seeing the other woman shivering in the crisp chill of the morning, Mrs. Beckham lamented the fact that she hadn't thought to find some kind of wrap for Nan.

At the same moment, the houseboy came bursting from the house, chattering foreign words in his agitation. Jolie set her jaw and brought the reins down sharply onto the horse's back, shouting a raucous command as she'd heard Daniel do.

The Chinese man raced down the road in pursuit, queue flying behind him, and stolen glances back over her shoulder gave Jolie a few moments of stomach-clenching fear. Several times, before she'd gotten the rig up to an adequate speed, the nimble little man had almost managed to catch them. It was only too easy to imagine him springing up into the back and forcing Jolie to stop the wagon.

By the combined graces of God and Jolie's own frantic driving, though, the gap between the houseboy and the Beckham wagon began to widen slowly.

"Hold on!" Jolie shouted to Nan, who just sat there, clinging to the wagon seat and looking bewildered. Even though their pursuer had dropped back, the two women would not be truly safe until they'd reached the farm. All the houseboy had to do was sprint to the sawmill and tell Mr. January what had happened, and men on horseback would soon be racing after them.

Tendrils of Jolie's hair whipped against her face as she urged the horse to greater and greater speeds, leaving Prosperity proper, and all its staring passers-by, far behind.

They were nearer Enoch and Mary's place than Daniel's when Jolie glanced back again and had her worst fears confirmed. Ira January and two other men were chasing the wagon on fast horses, and they were gaining.

Wildly, Jolie steered the horse off the hard-packed ruts of the road and the wagon went jolting and bumping over the fields. The smoke of Enoch's chimney twisted and swirled against a fiercely blue sky, like some transparent gray ribbon, serving as a beacon.

Jolie began to shout and whoop, praying the noise would bring Enoch running from the house or barn with a loaded rifle in hand. Mr. January and his friends were closing in fast.

Nan was staring straight ahead at the house that had been hers and Joe's, until such a short time before. Although she possessed neither the time nor the inclination to assess such things just then, Jolie thought she caught just a glimpse of reason behind the glaze that shrouded her friend's eyes.

Mr. January rode abreast of Jolie's horse and bent deftly in the saddle to take a firm hold on the harness.

Jolie let out a shriek of outrage and fear and, in that moment, she saw Daniel, Deuter, and Enoch running toward the house from the fields. Alas, it was Mary, obviously pregnant, her hair tumbling down over one shoulder in a heavy braid, who appeared on the step with what looked like a squirrel gun in her hands.

Expertly, she raised the weapon and drew a bead on Ira January's head.

Ira let go of the harness and glowered at Jolie. "Daniel won't stand behind you on this," he said evenly, his jaw clenching once in a spasm of annoyance. "Nancy is my wife and I can do with her as I please."

"Not on this land you can't," Mary pointed out reasonably, firing once into the air to show she meant business.

By that time, Daniel and the others had reached the scene, and Jolie eyed the breathless men with frank irritation. Good thing she hadn't had to depend on the likes of *them* for assistance.

"What the hell is going on here?" Daniel demanded, approaching the wagon. Although all his attention seemed to be absorbed by Mr. January, he somehow managed to reach up and lift Jolie unceremoniously down from the box.

At the same time, Deuter reached for Nan, and Enoch took the squirrel gun from Mary's hands and walked calmly over to back up his brother.

"This meddling little bandit you call a wife has just stolen my woman, that's what's going on here!" January spat, his face reddening with frustration and fury. The two men who'd accompanied him on the chase hung back, looking reluctant.

Daniel's glance at Jolie was about as sweet as fresh kerosene, but she still took enormous comfort from his solidity and strength. When she moved close against his side, he put an arm around her.

"Look at Nan, Daniel," Jolie pleaded. "Just *look* at what he's done to her. That's all I'm asking."

Mr. Beckham's sun-browned face paled a little when his eyes shifted to his former neighbor. Mary was wrapping a quilt gently around Nan's trembling shoulders, at the same time leading her toward the warm solace of the house.

"My God," Daniel whispered. His jawline tightened when he looked at January again, and Jolie could tell he wanted to wrench the millowner down from his horse and beat him senseless.

"I won't let you do this, Beckham," January spat, his tone and expression bitter.

"You've worn out your welcome, mister," Enoch put in smoothly. "You'd best be putting this place behind you."

January stood in his stirrups for a moment, assessing the fertile land and sturdy cabin that might have been his, then letting his eyes fall to Jolie. She saw an unmistakable threat in his gaze.

"Don't think we've settled this, Daniel," he said, finally looking from Jolie to her husband. Then he turned his horse and rode off, his two henchmen following at an eager pace.

"You've got some mighty fancy explaining to do!" Daniel told Jolie, when Enoch and Deuter had gone into the house, along with Mary and Nan.

"I hardly think so," Jolie replied. "You saw the condition Nan's in. It's perfectly clear that I had no choice but to take her away from that house any way I could manage."

"You might have gotten yourself *and* Nan killed," Daniel breathed, watching as January and his friends grew smaller and smaller in the distance.

"I had to do something," Jolie insisted, starting toward the house.

Nan was settled close by the fire, in a rocking chair, sipping tea from one of Mary's cherished china cups. "I lived in a place just like this once," she said, in a voice that sounded oddly like a little girl's.

Jolie glanced at Daniel, tears stinging in her eyes, and then crossed the small and crowded room to stand behind her friend's chair and lay her hands on Nan's shoulders. "Soon as you're all warmed up," she said soothingly, lending her voice a brightness she didn't feel, "Daniel and Enoch will take you to Verena's for a nice, long visit. You'd like that, wouldn't you?"

Nan nodded, although Jolie could see she didn't remember who Verena was, or understand anything that was happening.

Presently, the men went outside, and Mary and Jolie bundled Nan into a woolen frock Mary would wear to church on winter Sundays, once she'd borne her baby. They wrapped a cloak around her, too, and then, with Daniel driving the buckboard and Deuter riding along behind, keeping a sharp lookout, Jolie and Nan set out for Verena's farm.

The older woman came across the yard clucking and shaking her head at the condition Nan was in.

"Joe Culley must be rolling in his grave," Verena muttered to Jolie, long minutes later, when she and Jolie had led a trembling Nan upstairs and settled her in the spare room. A little spirit lamp provided some warmth while Verena hastened to put fresh linens and warm blankets on the bed.

Nan sat rocking slightly in her straight-backed chair and staring out the window, apparently unaware of the conversation . . . and even of the women having it.

Jolie nodded in response to Verena's statement. "Ira January chased us right to Enoch and Mary's door," she confided, in a whisper. "I haven't been so scared since the day I was supposed to hang." But she had been, she realized. Her encounters with Rowdy and with Blake Kingston had been powerfully frightening.

"I've no doubt that Ira'll show up here, once he works out that Nan isn't staying with you and Daniel," Verena replied, with a nod, as she smoothed the soft woolen blankets over the bed and then turned them back. "You'd better keep your wits about you, Jolie Beckham, because if Mr. Ira January gets his hands on you, you'll rue the day you ever crossed him."

Jolie didn't need reminding of that, but she tried to put the whole matter out of her mind while she and Verena dressed Nan in a warm flannel nightgown and tucked her into bed.

"I need some of my medicine," Nan announced, her eyes wide and vacant as she looked up into Verena's kindly face.

Verena patted her shoulder. "Of course you do, dear," she said. "You just settle in, all comfortable like, and I'll get you some." Without a word of explanation or even a look for Jolie, the older woman went out of the room, returning minutes later with a brown bottle and a spoon.

"You can't," Jolie protested, her eyes wide as she watched Verena pour a dose of laudanum to give Nan. "She's—"

"We can't just take it away all of the sudden," Verena interrupted crisply, spooning the medicine into Nan's mouth. "I've seen this problem before, and it's thorny to deal with. We'll have to wean her off gradually."

Jolie was heartsick, but she knew Verena was right. She nodded and kept her peace.

Nan settled back against the fluffy feather pillows, closing her eyes and sighing contentedly, like a sleepy child. Verena sat on the edge of the bed and gently smoothed Nan's hair away from her forehead, humming a hymn in soft tones.

When Nan was asleep, Verena put out the spirit lamp and she and Jolie left the room.

Daniel was downstairs in the kitchen, sipping coffee he'd helped himself to and waiting for the women to return. He rose from his chair when they entered the room.

"This is a dangerous thing you're doing, Verena," he said, as Jolie sat down at the table and their hostess set about brewing tea. "Ira January isn't a man to toy with."

"I might say the same to you, Dan," Verena answered, setting out a pretty teapot with roses and bluebirds painted on its sides. She spooned in fragrant tea leaves. "Maybe he wouldn't take you on in a regular fight, but he's got more money than most everybody in Prosperity put together, and he can make trouble for you and Enoch both if he has a mind to do it."

A glance at her husband told Jolie that Daniel knew Verena was right, and she felt a chill take her even though the kitchen was toasty warm. Not once had she considered that her actions might have an impact on Daniel, and for a moment she wished she hadn't been so reckless. "What could Mr. January do?" she managed. "To give you grief, I mean?"

Daniel studied his wife for a long moment before he answered. "He could respond in kind, Jolie, by taking you or the kids captive and holding you until I turned Nan over to him."

Jolie shuddered, but this was a possibility she'd mulled over already. "That would be against the law," she said.

Her husband arched one wheat-colored eyebrow. "And what you did isn't?" he retorted, without particular rancor.

She dropped her eyes. "Maybe," she conceded, "but some laws need to be broken enough times that they can't be put together again. They want sweeping out, like dirt on a fresh-scrubbed floor."

Daniel surprised his wife with a slight, distant smile, but it was Verena he looked at. "I'll leave Deuter to look out for you," he said. "All the same, you've got to be more careful than you've ever been."

Verena poured hot water into the teapot and carried it to the table, along with cups and saucers and fancy lumps of sugar. "I know that, Daniel," she said, in the kindly, tolerant tone of a schoolmarm addressing a first-day student. "Drink your tea."

"Why is it," Daniel asked, half an hour later, when he and Jolie were headed home in the buckboard, "that just when I think you're going to stay out of trouble for a day or two, you rush right out and stir up the nearest hornets' nest?"

He didn't sound angry; just beleaguered and curious. Jolie laid one hand to his arm as she answered, "It's just that there's so much that needs putting right."

Daniel sighed. "I ought to be furious with you, but I've got a certainty that Joe Culley would have looked out for you, if I'd been the one to die and you'd fallen in with the likes of January."

"I told you, Mr. Beckham, that Nan was suffering," Jolie pointed out, exasperated. "You said as long as she was Mr. January's wife, we couldn't interfere. What changed your mind?"

"Seeing her," Daniel answered, after a long moment of deliberation, during which he stared straight ahead at the road as if he didn't know it like his own barnyard and fields. "It was pretty easy to imagine you in her situation."

That was as close as Daniel Beckham had ever gotten to expressing tender feelings, and Jolie's spirit soared for a few moments, despite the exhausting demands of the day.

At home, she began washing shirts and long underwear and trousers, as she might have done on any other chilly but sunny day, and Daniel went about his business, too. When the sun reached a certain point in the sky, he ordered her away from the clotheslines and inside, where she was to remain until he returned from the schoolhouse with Gemma and Hank.

Jolie waited until the wagon rumbled out of sight, then carried another basketful of clean laundry down the step and across the frost-browned grass of the dooryard. There was only so much daylight left, and she didn't want a lot of clothes hanging in the kitchen around the stove that night.

Once she'd finished with the laundry, Jolie gathered eggs and went to the well house for some cream, because Daniel liked his evening coffee almost white. Her hem caught on a protruding board, as it nearly always did, and Jolie freed it with an impatient little tug before returning to the house.

Things seemed beautifully, wonderfully ordinary

that afternoon, when Daniel brought the children home and they rushed into the house to huddle by the stove and consume wide wedges of dried apple pie. The sweetness of it all, of just being there with Daniel and Gemma and Hank, filled Jolie's heart with a poignant achiness.

About an hour before sunset, just as Jolie was taking the last of the laundry from the clothesline, fat flakes of snow, half the size of hen's eggs, started to tumble from a slate gray sky. And Enoch arrived, riding one of the big plow horses that had pulled his wagon west from St. Louis.

"I guess it was the excitement," he said to Jolie, without preamble, swinging down from the saddle as Daniel came out of the barn. "Mary's fixing to have the baby."

Only presence of mind kept Jolie from dropping Daniel's clean shirts and trousers and union suits onto the ground. "And you left her alone!" she cried.

Enoch looked bewildered and that familiar, happy mischief was absent from his eyes. "I can bring a calf or a colt or a filly into the world all right," he allowed, swallowing nervously, "but I'm plain fuddled when it comes to humans."

Jolie shook her head and hurried toward the house with her burden of laundry, dumping it all on the parlor settee to deal with later. She'd helped with several births while traveling with the wagon train years before, but she was far from an expert at the task. As she recalled, the event was made up mostly of screaming, sweating, and blood.

"I'll go back to the farm with you," Jolie said to her brother-in-law, reaching for her cloak and tying the ribbon strings beneath her chin. Hank and Gemma were at the table, Hank working on his ciphers while

Gemma practiced writing the first five letters of the alphabet. Jolie met her husband's gaze as he loomed in the doorway. "Daniel, you'll stay here with the children. I'll be home in the morning."

Daniel opened his mouth to speak, but Jolie didn't wait around to hear what he'd meant to say. She followed Enoch outside and allowed herself to be lifted onto the back of the big draft horse. Enoch swung up behind her.

"Make sure Hank washes behind his ears," Jolie called to her husband, as Enoch turned the horse toward his own place, "and Gemma needs to use the chamber pot directly before she goes to bed!"

A look back over Enoch's shoulder showed Daniel standing in the middle of the yard, a shower of giant snowflakes whirling around him, waving farewell. His smile was crooked at one corner.

"There's chicken and dumplings simmering on the stove!" she added, feeling a tug at being separated from Daniel again, even for a single night. "You see that those children don't fill their stomachs with dried apple pie and turn up their noses at supper!"

Daniel nodded.

Enoch spurred the horse to a canter, and Jolie plunged both hands into the animal's coarse mane to hold on. It was fully dark by the time the lights of the cabin came into view, windows glowing in the blackness like bits of some golden quilt.

Jolie was on the ground and hurrying toward the house before Enoch had brought the horse to a complete halt.

The children were calmly eating their supper of corn bread and beans, too small to know that something of grave importance was happening. Jolie kissed each of them on top of the head and proceeded into the lean-to bedroom, untying and taking off her cloak as she went.

Mary lay on the bed, still wearing her calico day dress, her skin and hair soaked in perspiration. Her eyes were big with fear, but when she saw Jolie she smiled.

"It's been some day, hasn't it?" she managed to get out. When her bulging stomach contracted visibly under the fabric of her dress, however, she drew in a hissing breath, clutched the bedclothes in both hands, and arched her head back, surrendering to the pain.

"Yes, indeed," Jolie agreed, laying aside her cloak and opening a polished pinewood chest at the foot of the bed. "And it would seem it isn't over yet."

Mary gave a gurgling laugh even as she moaned in the grip of another contraction. She was breathing hard and deep when the pain passed.

Having found a clean nightgown in the chest, Jolie proceeded to help Mary out of her dress and into the gown.

"Please," Mary gasped, clutching Jolie's hand when she was just about to wring out a wet cloth and drape it over Mary's forehead. "Make sure Enoch and the babies are all right first."

Jolie nodded and returned to the main room of the cabin to do as she'd been asked. Enoch was sitting in the rocker by the fireplace, both children in his lap, rocking and staring distractedly into the flames.

Returning to Mary's bedside, Jolie found her sister-in-law in the throes of another contraction. Although she made only a low, groaning sound, the play of her muscles was so strong that, for a moment, only her heels and the back of her head seemed to be touching the bed.

Tenderly, Jolie soaked a cloth in cool water from a

basin on the upended crate that served as a bedside table and laid it over Mary's forehead, whispering soothing words. Mary relaxed, slowly, but that was due to the rhythm of nature, Jolie knew, and not to anything she'd done.

"Mrs. Culley," Mary struggled to say, during that short lull when her body was still, gathering strength for the next attempt to push the new baby out. "Is she all right? Did you get her settled at Mrs. Dailey's?"

Jolie was touched at Mary's concern for another, given the fact that Enoch's wife was probably in for a long and painful night herself. "When I left, Nan was sleeping," she replied softly.

A low sound of panic and dread flowed between Mary's clenched teeth, and once again her stomach knotted.

"You go right ahead and call out if you need to," Jolie said.

When that episode had passed, Mary turned to lie on her side. "My back hurts so bad," she confided. Jolie looked ahead to her own birthing time and wondered if she'd be as brave as Mary.

She moved around to the other side of the bed and began massaging the taut muscles at the small of Mary's back. She saw a tear streak its way down her sister-in-law's cheek.

"I'm real scared," Enoch's wife confided fitfully. "I don't want to carry on and frighten Holt and Ruthie, but maybe I won't be able to hold back. . . ."

"Don't try," Jolie scolded gently, bathing Mary's face again.

"But Holt and Ruthie . . ."

Jolie smiled. She would worry about Hank and Gemma, no doubt, when it came time to deliver Daniel's baby. "Enoch can come sit with you for a

337

while, and I'll tell the little ones a story and tuck them into bed. How would that be?"

Mary's effort to restrain herself from crying out was plainly visible. She took Jolie's hand and squeezed it once. "You're an angel, Jolie Beckham, sent straight from heaven. Having a sister makes it so much easier, starting over in a new place and all."

Once again, Jolie's eyes burned with tears. "If I came from heaven, I took the long way," she answered hoarsely. "And angels don't commonly find themselves standing in the back of a hay wagon with a noose around their necks." She bent and kissed Mary's damp forehead. "As for that other part, you're exactly the sister I'd have asked for if anybody had given me a choice."

Enoch looked up anxiously when Jolie stepped out of the tiny bedroom and lifted a nodding Ruthie from his lap. Holt was already curled up on his cot over by the wall, the firelight flickering over his handsome little face.

"It'll be a while yet," Jolie told her brother-in-law quietly. "But Mary would like to see you." The sweet-smelling child laid a small head on her shoulder and yawned, and Jolie's heart constricted at the wonder of all it was to be a woman.

While Enoch was in with Mary, Jolie helped the little girl into a nightgown, set her on a chamber pot, and then washed her hands and face and put her to bed. Then she removed Holt's plain black shoes and carefully covered his sleeping form with a warm quilt.

That done, Jolie emptied the slop jar, added a log to the fire, washed her own hands, and poured herself a cupful of leftover supper coffee. She was standing at the window, watching the snow fall, when Enoch came out again.

"Mary needs you," he said.

Jolie nodded and turned away from the window to follow him back into the tiny lean-to. Even though she was glad Enoch and Mary had come to live nearby, she couldn't help remembering that this had been Nan and Joe Culley's house first. If it hadn't been for a snake in the wheat field during the harvest, Nan would have had her child here in peace, with Joe to hold her hand.

Mary's labor had begun in earnest, however, and that fact distracted Jolie from everything else. There simply wasn't time to grieve for the Culleys.

Enoch spoke steadily, calmly to Mary as she struggled to bring forth his child, letting her grip his hands when she needed something to push against. After about two hours—Jolie knew that to be a relatively short interval for delivering a baby—the child's head appeared.

Smiling and crying at the same time, Enoch bent his head close to Mary's. "Almost done, darlin'," he whispered hoarsely. "Almost done."

Jolie wondered if Daniel would be kindly and attentive like Enoch when her time came, or if he would hide out in the barn or even go to town and swill whiskey while she was bearing his child. Some men just couldn't contend with the natural rigors of the process, no matter how strong-minded they were about other things.

"Push, Mary," Jolie commanded. And then the wonderous magic happened; there was a tiny head . . . shoulders . . . a thin little body.

Jolie caught the child gently in her hands. "It's a girl," she said, moved to the very core of her spirit by the mystical beauty of the experience. "A precious, perfect girl."

Mary sobbed with joy and relief, and tears coursed freely down Enoch's cheeks. Jolie cleared the baby's nose and mouth, then tied and cut the cord. After bundling the infant up warmly in a blanket she'd set out earlier, Jolie left Enoch and Mary alone with their new daughter.

She busied herself warming water at the stove, and when she'd scrubbed her hands and forearms, she carried a basin to Mary's bedside. Enoch, with his strong, farmer's hands, was gently bathing the baby when Jolie walked out of the room again.

Weary beyond all bearing, yet at the same time overjoyed at the sheer audacity of life, Jolie sank into the chair nearest the dying fire and stared into the smoldering embers. She laid her palms lightly to her abdomen and closed her eyes, dreaming of the day her own child would enter the world.

Daniel arrived early the next morning, his wagon wheels leaving dark lines in the deep powdery snow. A bundled-up child perched on either side of him, faces barely visible for their scarves and hats.

"I love you, Daniel Beckham," Jolie murmured, as she went out onto the step to watch him climb down from the seat of the buckboard and reach up for Gemma.

"Did the baby come?" Daniel called, and the pristine snow made his voice carry.

Jolie beamed, proud of her small part in the miracle. "Enoch and Mary have a fine new daughter," she replied, and when Daniel got up close, she surprised herself as well as him by flying straight into his arms.

21

Daniel's embrace tightened around Jolie's waist, just for a fraction of a second, before her arms fell away from his neck. She was breathless, and only when she was standing on the floorboards of the porch again did she realize he'd lifted her clean off her feet.

Warmth pulsed in her cheeks. "Come in," she said, averting her eyes from Daniel's steady and knowing gaze for a moment. She raised one finger to her lips, giving Hank and Gemma looks of affectionate warning. "But do be quiet, because Mary and the new baby are still sleeping."

Later, when Enoch and Daniel were back from doing morning chores and Jolie had made breakfast, the newest member of the Beckham family awakened. In order to let Mary rest, Enoch carefully carried the infant from the bedroom and laid her in the carved wooden cradle he'd brought in from the barn.

The four older children crowded around the rustic little crib for a look.

"Can we get one of these?" Gemma inquired of

Jolie, her eyes large and serious. It was clear she was referring to the baby, not the cradle, and Jolie felt her cheeks heat up again.

Daniel cleared his throat and looked away quickly, while Enoch let loose with one of his hooting chuckles.

Nobody really answered Gemma's question, though.

The snow was deep that day, but the sun was bright and warm, so Daniel drove Gemma and Hank on to school. Jolie spent the busy morning hours looking after the baby and Mary, who was already rallying from her ordeal. Mary had an appetite and a sense of humor, and she kept getting up and walking around even though Jolie pleaded with her to stay in bed.

It was around noon when Daniel returned, and Jolie was very glad to see him, even though she assumed an attitude of brisk indifference.

"I don't imagine you got much sleep last night," he said, his breath making clouds in the cold November air as they jolted toward home in his wagon.

Jolie sighed and shook her head. "Not much. I sat down in the rocking chair and closed my eyes for a few minutes."

Daniel nodded, but Jolie could tell he was thinking about something else entirely. His azure gaze kept sweeping the white velvet horizon and there was a rifle on the floorboards at his feet.

At home, Jolie prepared water for a warm bath while Daniel put the horse and wagon away in the barn. When he entered the kitchen, bringing a blast of cold air in after him, he found his wife sitting cross-legged in the tub, which she'd set in the middle of the floor.

His throat worked visibly as he swallowed, hovering there against the door as though he'd never seen a naked woman before. "You might have warned a man."

Jolie smiled, stretched out one leg, and squeezed warm, soapy water over her flesh from a sponge. "'Warned' you? I'm not frying bullets in hot bacon grease, Daniel Beckham; I'm only taking a bath."

Daniel thrust himself reluctantly away from the door, his manner wary. He fixed his gaze carefully on the coffeepot, which was sitting in its usual place on the stove, and gravitated toward it.

Something fundamental had been altered between Daniel and Jolie with the birth of Enoch and Mary's baby, in a way so subtle as to be almost imperceptible. Jolie couldn't be sure her husband had sensed the change, of course, but all her instincts said he had.

She settled back in the rapidly cooling water, making no effort to hide her bosom, and closed her eyes. Just being in the same room with Daniel was a stirring, strangely sensual experience, though she was really too exhausted for lovemaking.

"Don't be falling asleep right there for the whole world to see," Daniel grumbled. She heard him leave the room and when he came back he brought one of the good damask towels.

Tenderly, he took Jolie's arm and helped her to her feet. Warm sweetness unfolded deep within her as he dried her, for he'd never touched her more intimately, but he made no demands. Between the mad flight with Nan from Mr. January's house the day before, and the hours spent midwifing for Mary, Jolie Beckham simply had nothing left to give.

Daniel had brought a blanket, as well as a towel, and Jolie felt its wooly warmth fold around her. He lifted

343

her into his arms and she let her cheek rest against his shoulder.

His lips brushed her forehead very lightly. "You've earned your rest, Mrs. Beckham," he told her in a hoarse voice.

Jolie was in a daze of delicious weariness when he laid her down on their bed, pulled a flannel nightgown over her head, and tucked her beneath the heavy blankets. The woolens still smelled faintly of moth balls, even though Jolie had carefully aired them on the clothesline just after the harvest.

"Daniel," she said, and that one word was all she could manage, so it had to convey everything. Her eyes kept fluttering closed and her lips seemed too heavy to move.

He kissed her, not passionately, but with the promise of passion. "Rest," he told her, and then he left her and she heard the latch on the door click softly into place.

Jolie stretched luxuriously and turned over onto her stomach to sleep, and when she awakened, it was to the delicious aroma of stewed poultry. She opened her eyes to see Daniel trying to maneuver through the bedroom doorway with a tray in his hands; he'd heated leftover chicken and dumplings for her midday meal. But then, perhaps it wasn't noon, but morning, or evening.

She sat up with a yawn, pushing her hair back from her face with one hand and squinting toward the window. Either it was a cloudy, gloomy day, or twilight was already descending on the land, for the pane of glass had a charcoal sheen to it.

Jolie was immediately anxious. "Gemma and Hank . . . ?"

"Downstairs, minding their business," Daniel answered, approaching the bed. Apparently guessing that Jolie was about to toss back the covers and go see for herself, he stopped her with a look of mock sternness. "You're staying right there in that bed, Mrs. Beckham, so don't go getting any ideas."

She was frowning, thinking of all the things she'd meant to accomplish. "What time is it?"

"Eight-thirty," Daniel answered.

Jolie was horrified. *Eight-thirty.* She had shirts to press, and the parlor floor needed sweeping and scrubbing. Not only that, but Verena was taking care of Nan all alone, and poor Mary's household was probably in an uproar without a woman's guiding hand . . .

Daniel plunked the tray down across her lap. "Eat," he ordered.

Jolie could see that this wasn't an order that could be defied. Besides, her stomach felt as cavernous and empty as a canyon. She reached for the spoon.

"Verena and Nan . . ."

"They're fine," Daniel said. "Deuter's looking out for them. And Mary's doing well, too."

"Have they chosen a name for the baby yet?"

Daniel nodded. "Rachel Anne," he answered. "Mama's first name is Rachel, and Mary's mother was called Anne."

Jolie chewed a tasty bite of dumpling, thinking. "What are we going to call our baby?"

The question had been presented innocently; Jolie could not have guessed what kind of reaction it would provoke. Daniel bolted away from the bed, nearly upsetting Jolie's tray in his anxiety to be away from her, and stood with his back turned. She could see the quickness of his breathing in the motions of his shoulders.

"Daniel?" Jolie's voice was small, shaky.

He didn't answer her, nor did he look back. He simply left the room.

Jolie sat in bed for a long time, her appetite gone. She'd only *thought* things were different between her and Daniel now that he'd seen a baby come into the world healthy and strong and holding on tightly to life.

After a while, she set aside the tray, climbed slowly out of bed, and began putting on her clothes. While she was brushing her hair, she heard a horse nickering and went to the window just in time to see Daniel riding away from the barn.

She braided her hair and wound it into a tidy chignon, then proceeded downstairs.

Hank and Gemma were playing jacks on the parlor floor. The lamps were all lit and there was a crackling blaze in the fireplace, but still the place suddenly seemed about as warm and welcoming as a crypt.

"Did Mr. Beckham say where he was going?" Jolie asked lightly.

The children were plainly relieved to see her.

"Town," Hank said. "We're not supposed to let nobody in the house while he's gone."

"'Not supposed to let *anybody*,'" Jolie corrected, reaching for her mending basket. It was easy to imagine Daniel turning to Pilar for solace; after all, he had an outlaw bride who gave him one problem after another.

Jolie was braced for Daniel to stay away all night, as he'd done once or twice during the harvest, but he returned just after the downstairs clock struck one o'clock. His wife was back in bed by that time, with none of the lamps lit, pretending to be asleep.

She lay very still, breathing evenly, listening as Daniel's boots were set aside with a familiar *clump,* hearing his belt buckle jingle as he removed his trousers. When he stretched out in bed beside Jolie, she playacted like she was stirring in a dream and scooted closer to him.

He felt warm and solid beside her, as always, but he didn't smell of the spicy perfume she remembered Pilar wearing, or of any other, for that matter.

Jolie laid a hand on his thigh, felt the muscles tense powerfully beneath her palm. He knew she was awake now, there was no helping that, but she didn't speak because she was afraid she'd say the wrong thing and he'd bolt again.

"Blake Kingston broke out of jail," he told her. "The marshal figures he's probably on his way back here."

The news struck Jolie like a blow. It was bad enough having to fear Rowdy and now Mr. January. Adding a third man to the mix made her feel like a trapped animal. "Yes," she said, her palm making a slow circle against the flesh of Daniel's thigh, not because she wanted to arouse him but because his very substance gave her comfort. "Yes, he'll come back here to get the money. And Rowdy will be watching for him."

Daniel moaned distractedly, but he made no move to stop Jolie from touching him. The sound brought out some deep hunger in her, and she closed her fingers boldly around his burgeoning manhood.

"Jolie," he breathed.

She alternately squeezed and massaged his length, taking solace in this most natural, most elemental of caresses. She slipped beneath the covers to kiss his rib cage, his hairy chest, his quivering belly.

347

He rasped her name again, desperately.

Jolie knelt astraddle of his legs and bent forward to tease him with her tongue and the silky rope of her braid.

She twined her plaited hair around him, like ribbon around a maypole, and kissed the part of him still exposed. He arched his back and groaned, and Jolie used the tip of her tongue, at once disciplining him for his impatience and rewarding him for his sheer splendor.

Slowly, ever so slowly, Jolie took away the braid, unwrapping him like a gift, taking little nibbles of what she revealed. By that time, Daniel was so big and so ready that she could barely contain him.

Finally, with a fierce and primitive growl, he made it plain that he could tolerate no more of her teasing. He freed himself and locked his hands around her subtly broadening waist, lifting her easily over his head, taking the peak of one dangling breast between his lips.

Daniel goaded Jolie as relentlessly as she had done with him, now sucking at her nipple, now flicking it lightly with his tongue, leaving it pleading and straining while he turned to attend its mate.

Jolie sank her teeth into her lower lip to keep from calling out, but the loving had just begun. Daniel's right hand closed brazenly over her moist delta, and the hidden nubbin of flesh pulsed against his rough palm.

"Once won't be enough, Jolie," Daniel warned lazily, between forays with her nipple. "Twice won't be enough. When morning comes, you'll still be crowing louder than the rooster."

A thin film of perspiration covered Jolie's body, and

she wondered when Daniel had taken away her night-gown. Her breath came hard and fast, and her hips ground against Daniel's hand even though she had never consciously sent a command to the muscles involved.

"Oh," she whimpered frantically, as the parries grew fiercer and more desperate. "Oh, Daniel . . ."

He wasn't talking; he was too busy tugging on her nipple with his mouth.

Jolie curved her spine inward and threw her head back, letting Daniel take what he wanted of her, glorying in her very vulnerability to his hands and tongue. She groaned again, and then his fingers slipped inside her and her body exploded with spas-modic sensation. For a long time afterward, Jolie's sheath was still clenching and unclenching around the gentle invaders.

But Daniel had meant what he said about once not being enough, or twice, for that matter. He put Jolie through her paces, making her surrender to him over and over again, in a hundred, no, a thousand different ways.

She was certain, by the time he laid her on her back and parted her thighs, that he'd already drained every ounce of passion from her. Instead, he had only primed her for the final, colossal responses he in-tended to draw from the very depths of her being.

The moment he entered her, Jolie was energized, charged with passion all over again. She went wild, clawing at the bedclothes, flinging herself upward to meet Daniel's deep, measured thrusts. When he came, it was a violent surrender, and he covered her mouth with his own and sipped her cries of satisfaction as they burst from her throat.

Her body was still responding to its total conquering long after Daniel had withdrawn. Tiny, hidden muscles leaped and stretched inside her, and her descent was a dizzy one, for he'd sent her spinning far past the moon and stars.

Then his hand came to rest over her breast, and all the musical strings inside her were instantly pulled taut, vibrating. As quickly as that, she was ready to be played again, like some supple, resonating instrument from a heavenly band.

She performed for him, for herself, until sleep finally claimed her, no longer willing to be denied.

When Jolie awakened in the morning, the room was chilly but Daniel had filled the pitcher on the bureau with clean water, now gone tepid. She washed and dressed quickly, carrying the basin downstairs with her to be emptied in the backyard.

Six inches of new snow covered the ground, and the air was hard and sharp. Jolie hummed as she prepared breakfast and laid out clothes for Hank and Gemma to wear to school . . . on mornings like that one, they always came scampering to the stove the minute they got up, dressing in the shimmering glow of heat that surrounded it.

When Daniel came in with a bucket of milk, he had the smells of cold weather and manliness and freshly pitched hay about him, and something deep inside Jolie's wanton body tightened like a watch spring.

Daniel set the milk bucket on the table, took Jolie's hips in his hands, and pulled her easily to him. He chuckled as he bent to give her a commanding kiss.

"I'll have you again, Mrs. Beckham," he said, after totally mastering her with his tongue. "Soon as I'm done with the morning's business."

Jolie trembled as a wave of heat rolled over her, and her eyes drifted shut as she tilted her head back for another intoxicating kiss.

Instead, she got a playful pat and squeeze on the bottom and a jovial, "What did you cook for breakfast?"

Jolie's blood was hot with passion the whole time she fried pork strips and flapjacks, but there was nothing to be done because the children were up and about. Daniel's eyes followed her wherever she went, shining with devilment and promise, and she thought how remarkable it was that he'd awakened this other woman inside her. This woman she'd never dreamed she could be.

As usual, Daniel drove Gemma and Hank to school in the wagon. When he came home, he unhitched the horse directly and led it into the barn.

Jolie grabbed up her cloak and hurried out there, telling herself she only wanted to know if there was news from town. In truth, that spring inside her was pulled so taut it was about to break.

"Daniel?" She paused in the doorway of the barn, seeking out his familiar frame in the shadowy interior. There was a strain in him, she could make that out, and a peculiar tension.

Something was very wrong.

He hesitated a moment, then hung the harness rigging in its customary place and turned to face her. "January bought my mortgage from the bank," he said.

Jolie wasn't entirely sure what that meant, but she knew it was bad. She swallowed hard and stared at Daniel, waiting for him to explain.

Daniel pushed his hat back for a moment and

wiped his brow with one shirt sleeve, even though it was cold that day and the gray skies threatened still more snow. "There's nothing owing on this place, so he can't take it," he went on woodenly. "But Enoch's farm . . ."

She closed her eyes for a moment, sickened by the thought that Enoch and Mary could lose their home, after saying good-bye to most of their family and traveling so far. Their hopes and dreams could be dashed with the stroke of a pen.

Another silence pulsed in the barn, then Daniel continued. "I figure January will show up any time now, wanting full payment for the land."

Jolie thought she might vomit, she was so shaken. The worst part of all this was knowing it was her fault Daniel had been forced to spend his savings. "I guess you wish you'd never laid eyes on me," she murmured, looking down at the straw-covered floor.

Daniel crossed the long space between them, cupped one hand under Jolie's chin, and lifted. "I won't have you blaming yourself for any of this, Mrs. Beckham. A man takes chances in life, and sometimes he ends up on his face in the mud and manure."

Under other circumstances, Jolie might have smiled at Daniel's colorful way of putting things. As it was, she could barely keep herself from bursting into tears of frustration and regret. Her vision was a little blurred, as a matter of fact, when she gazed up into his eyes.

It was like looking at a summer sky.

"I'm so sorry, Daniel," she whispered. "I've caused you so much grief, when all I ever wanted . . ." But she couldn't finish, couldn't tell him what she'd wanted, because she would be too wounded when he turned away. Jolie had no illusions that her husband loved her the way he'd loved his first and true wife.

He kissed her forehead, very lightly and, in one and the same moment, released his gentle hold on her chin. Without another word, he turned away and stood gripping the side of the buckboard with both hands.

Jolie caught up her skirts and hurried out of the barn, cursing the day she'd thrown in with Blake Kingston. Her life had been going downhill on greased runners ever since.

She might have hidden in the bedroom all day, moping, but Verena and Nan arrived for a visit, escorted by a watchful Deuter. Nan was still not her old self, of course, but there was a pink tinge to her once-waxen cheeks, and her eyes were clearer.

After greeting her friends with a rather fragile smile, Jolie set about brewing tea and fetching cookies from the pantry. The three women sat in the parlor, as befitted a formal call, and Jolie noticed that Nan's gaze kept straying to the now-barren rosebushes beyond the window. No doubt she was recalling the summer day when Joe had picked two fragrant yellow blossoms and presented them to his wife and to Jolie with such courtly ceremony.

Jolie was certain she'd guessed correctly when Nan's eyes filled with shimmering tears. Mrs. Beckham reached out to clasp her friend's hand and give it a reassuring squeeze.

"Nan's been helping me trim a spring bonnet to send to my niece in Kansas City," Verena announced, over the rim of her cup. Behind her, Ilse Beckham looked down on the small company from inside the framed photograph on the mantel. Verena turned to look at Nan. "You've got a gift for millinery, my dear. You should have your own shop."

Nan merely lowered her eyes. She hadn't touched her teacup, and her hands were knotted together in her lap.

After that, Verena turned her attention to Jolie and frowned. "You're not looking very well this morning, Mrs. Beckham. Is there something wrong?"

Jolie couldn't bring herself to speak of Ira January and the threat he represented to Daniel, not in front of poor Nan, whose grip on composure was so tenuous. Neither could she lie to Verena, however, so she replied, "I imagine it will all work out."

In truth, she imagined nothing of the sort. Mr. January hadn't liked Daniel in the first place. Now, because of Jolie, the powerful millowner was hungry for vengeance.

Not that Jolie regretted snatching Nan away from that dreadful house. She felt remorse only because innocent people . . . Daniel, Enoch, Mary, and the children . . . were going to suffer over something they'd had no real part in.

As soon as Nan and Verena had started out for the Dailey place, with Deuter once again serving as their squire, Jolie resumed her search for the bank money. It was doubly important now that she find the loot before Rowdy and Blake did.

She fared no better in the enterprise than she had before, but giving up was not an option. It was because of her that Daniel faced the loss of the land he'd bought from Nan Culley, and she had to make things right. Somehow.

Ira January arrived that evening, riding as confidently into the dooryard as if he were a welcome guest. Daniel went out to meet him, and the two men talked in the twilight while Jolie watched from the window, her bruised heart stuck tight in her throat.

When Daniel came into the house a few minutes later, he tossed a folded document onto the kitchen table.

"He wants the money now," Jolie said wretchedly. Up until that very moment, she'd been nursing a vain hope that Mr. January would be reasonable about the matter.

It was as though Daniel didn't even see her. He left the room without speaking or even glancing in her direction, moving like a man in a daze.

The walls of the house seemed to move in closer in those moments, making Jolie feel crowded, almost smothered. She grabbed for her cloak and headed outside, and before she'd had time to think about what she was doing, she found herself under the maple tree, gazing down at Ilse Beckham's fancy marble headstone. The grave was awash in moonlight and fallen leaves.

"Tell me how to help Daniel," Jolie muttered, crouching to clear away some of the crisp scattering of crimson, orange, and gold. "Please. I love him so much."

"Now, that's right sweet," a familiar voice drawled from behind her.

Shooting to her feet, Jolie whirled, cast a frantic look back over one shoulder and saw Rowdy Fleet standing there in the shadows. There was no mistaking the fact that he had a pistol in his hand.

"Don't scream," he warned. "Beckham will have another wife to bury if you do."

Jolie's every instinct called upon her to protect the

child growing under her heart. That necessity made her appear calm, even though she was in the grip of wild panic.

"Blake said he'd tell me where he hid the money if I brought you to him, so that's what I'm going to do."

She swallowed and then lifted her chin. "I won't go with you."

He cocked the pistol expertly, and moonlight shimmered along the polished, blue-black barrel. "I didn't offer you no choice," Rowdy pointed out, gesturing toward a horse hidden in the dark shadow of the maple tree. "Now, git."

Jolie glanced longingly toward the house. If she screamed loudly enough, Daniel would come running, gun in hand. But before her husband could reach her, Rowdy would have ended her life, and her baby's as well. Daniel, at a disadvantage because of the darkness, would doubtless be the next victim.

"All right," she whispered, starting toward the nickering, nervous animal.

After Jolie was mounted, Rowdy climbed up behind her. She could feel the barrel of his forty-five prodding the small of her back. "Not so much as a peep out of you," he said, his breath foul as it moved through her hair and touched her face. He smelled as if he hadn't had a bath since childhood, and his closeness made Jolie's skin crawl.

Jolie said nothing at all. She just stared straight ahead.

"You're going to write Big Dan Beckham a letter," Rowdy informed Jolie fancifully, as the horse carried them farther and farther from everyone and everything she held dear. The chilly night seemed especially dark and menacing.

Jolie shivered, but, other than that, she didn't react.

She didn't want Rowdy to know just how frightened she really was.

Rowdy's voice rumbled past her ear. "You'll tell him farm livin' ain't for you, and say your farewells."

"Why?" Jolie couldn't hold the question back, even though she tried with all her might. It was really fate she was asking, not Rowdy.

"Blake wants you," the outlaw answered blithely, as if that were all that mattered . . . and, to him, it probably was. Good will had evidently been restored between Rowdy and Blake, and it seemed Blake was picturing himself as a husband.

Jolie's stomach would have churned at the prospect of being touched by any other man besides Daniel, let alone surrendering herself to the likes of Blake Kingston. She gulped back the bile that surged into her throat and squared her shoulders. "Surely you don't trust Blake, not after what he tried to do," she ventured, knowing she had only one real chance. She had to start trouble between the two men who meant to hold her prisoner, one for a few hours or days, one for a lifetime. "He would have taken that money and headed for the hills if it had been you that was caught instead of him. He planned to cheat you."

She felt the tension in Rowdy's small, wiry frame even before it erupted from his lips. "Hush up," he rasped, "or so-help-me-God I'll kill you right here, right now!"

22

Rowdy rode to the timbered side of Prosperity, where the dark mountain loomed behind the lumber mill. Jolie clung to the saddle horn, shivering, full of wild, quiet fear. She wasn't surprised when they approached a large house from behind; the place was so big, it could only have belonged to Ira January.

Jolie's mind rushed through the possible implications of that, and she fought down the new rise of panic that swelled within her.

Blake came out through a rear door, holding a lantern high in one hand, and he gave a low, delighted chuckle when he saw Jolie.

Rowdy swung down from the saddle and wrenched Jolie after him. Her ankle twisted painfully when she hit the ground, and acid pooled in the back of her throat.

As Blake approached, Ira January stepped through the open doorway and followed. Even in the thin light of the kerosene lamp, Jolie could see that both men were grim faced.

"All right, Kingston," Rowdy crowed, shoving the pistol he'd held on Jolie into his belt, "I brung her. Now, you gotta tell me where that money is."

A demonic grin stretched across Blake's face, and hatred glittered behind his eyes. "A deal is a deal," he said smoothly, gesturing toward the house with his free hand. "Soon as I've dealt with Mrs. Beckham, here, you and I will ride out and fetch the money."

Jolie retreated a step when Blake reached for her, only to collide with Rowdy, who gripped her arms above the elbows and thrust her forward again.

Blake's gaze burned into her face; he looked fanatical and rabid, like a mad coyote she'd seen once. He chuckled, probably amused that she'd even dreamed of escaping him, and raised his hand to curl his fingers around her cheek. His touch, though light, sent yet another charge of terror surging through her. "Who'd have thought my sweet little Jolie-girl was really a Delilah, willing to betray the only man who was ever good to her?"

Blake was referring, she knew, to her visit to the marshal's office that day when he was still in jail.

She eyed him with undisguised contempt. *"Good* is hardly the word I'd use for the way you treated me," she replied evenly. "First, you made it look like I was part of that robbery. Then you left me to hang for something I hadn't done."

January interrupted by clearing his throat. "Couldn't we discuss this inside?" he complained irritably. "I'd rather everybody in Prosperity didn't know I have company."

"Anything you say, boss," Blake answered. Then he buried his fingers in Jolie's hair, gripping it hard near the scalp, and propelled her toward the open doorway.

Neither Rowdy nor Mr. January seemed to think

treating a woman so roughly was at all untoward. They certainly didn't intercede on Jolie's behalf.

She was in pain and half-sick with fright, but Jolie's mind had snagged on one word Blake had said . . . *boss.* Rowdy and Blake had probably been working for Mr. January from the first, and while the marshal and Daniel and the others were searching the countryside for the outlaws, they'd been hiding in the fanciest house in town.

Jolie narrowed her eyes at Ira January when Blake flung her into a back hallway. The place was close and dark, lit only by the bobbing lantern in Blake's hand.

"It happens that I have a bone to pick with Mrs. Beckham myself," the millowner said, with a smug smile. "Tell me, Jolie . . . have you seen my wife lately?"

Color surged into Jolie's cheeks, and she raised her chin obstinately. She felt no remorse for kidnapping Nan. Even if there had been a way to go back into the past and change what she'd done, she wouldn't have taken it. "Nan was never your wife," she said, with a boldness that was all bluster. "She was your victim . . . just like poor Hamish Frazer at the bank."

January's eyes glinted with annoyance and he raised his hand to strike Jolie, only to have Blake step between them.

"She's my woman," the second man said quietly, and Jolie noticed a slight tremor in his voice. "I'll see to any correcting that needs to be done."

Relief that January hadn't struck her and offense that Blake regarded her as his woman collided within Jolie. The impact left her breathless, like some kind of silent explosion. *I'm my own woman, and Daniel Beckham's,* she thought fiercely, but she wasn't foolish enough to say the words out loud. It was beginning to dawn on Jolie, in fact, that she'd probably said too much already.

Blake loosened his hurtful grip on her hair, only to take another bruising grasp on her upper arm.

"Put her in the room off the cellar and make sure she's gagged," January said, sighing the words. His was the manner of a commander who must constantly deal with bumbling, rebellious troops. "Soon as Big Dan misses the lady, he'll come right to my door. Fleet, you see that the horses are out of sight."

"I want that money 'fore I go anyplace," Rowdy argued, figuratively setting his heels.

They went through a doorway at the end of the shadowy hallway and down a set of stairs. The dank smell of mildew and closed space rushed up to fill Jolie's nostrils and her throat. The soles of her shoes slipped on the stone steps and she could barely see to put one foot in front of the other, but she didn't fall because Blake was holding on so tightly.

In the cellar, Jolie made out shelves of canned and bottled goods, vegetable bins, and assorted clutter.

Her heart sank when January swung one shelf away from the wall—it creaked eerily on unseen hinges—and gestured grandly for her to precede him.

She stifled a shriek when Blake hurled her into the musty chasm, where rats and all manner of other vermin probably lurked. She could see nothing but shapes and shadows, and a spiderweb draped itself across her bosom.

Jolie brushed away the gossamer net with quick hands.

Blake followed her into the cell, bringing the welcome light of the lantern. She looked around, seeing only a stool and an overturned crate with an empty metal mug sitting on top of it. Not surprisingly, there was no other way out.

"Sit down," Blake ordered, setting the lamp on the crate table with an irritated thump. Rowdy was peering suspiciously into the dark cavern, not out of any concern for Jolie's safety, she was sure, but because he was afraid of somehow being cheated out of his share of the robbery money.

With dignity, Jolie took a seat on the dusty stool, smoothing her skirts as neatly as she might have done at a church social or a fancy tea party. The door disguised as a shelf ground shut upon them and Jolie could hear Rowdy and Mr. January arguing heatedly on the other side.

"A suitable place for a nest of rats to hide," she said, refusing to look at Blake when she spoke because that would have been an acknowledgment and she didn't want to give him even that much.

Blake's voice took on a tone that was at once sarcastic and wheedling. "Seems Mr. Beckham has changed your mind about me, Jolie-girl," he said, crouching in front of her and taking her hands with a tenderness that was calculated to be brutal. "I'm a heartbroken man."

Jolie's mouth filled with spittle, and she yearned to spew it into Kingston's face, but she didn't dare. "You're just being cussed, Blake Kingston," she said in a furious whisper, "and you know it. You don't want a woman . . . you never did . . . and this plan of yours to start over somewhere else with me as a wife is just plain spiteful."

He curved a hand under her chin and ran his thumb lightly over Jolie's lips. When Daniel did that, Jolie's most private places melted like so much candle wax, but Blake's touch was repulsive. "Consider your alternative, Jolie-girl . . . there's only one, you know. You've learned too much tonight, you see . . . you found out about this room, for one thing, and how me and Rowdy have a . . . business arrangement with Mr. January and all." He paused to rub his own chin thoughtfully, in the manner of a learned man pondering great questions. "There'll be more going on tonight, I reckon, that we wouldn't want you telling Mr. Beckham or the law about. What it all boils down to, pretty girl, is this: If you don't ride out with me when I tell you to, I'll have to kill you."

A shudder danced up Jolie's spine, but she kept her back straight and her chin high. She still wouldn't let her gaze link with Blake's, but this time it was because she didn't want him to see the fear in her eyes. For her baby's sake, as well as her own, she knew she had to keep her composure so she could be alert to any opportunity for escape.

"I guess it doesn't make any difference to you," she said evenly, "that I don't want to be your wife. I love Daniel Beckham, and no matter what you do to me or where you force me to go, that will never change."

"Enough," Blake rasped, entangling his fingers in Jolie's hair again. "You're mine. I won't hear sweet talk about Beckham or any other man."

Jolie bit into her lower lip to keep herself from blurting out that she was carrying Daniel's baby. Blake would probably not take the news well.

Blake leaned forward and touched his lips to hers, experimentally, awkwardly, causing the pit of Jolie's stomach to roll. It was an act of darkness, in no way resembling Daniel's warm kisses.

She drew back and dragged one sleeve across her mouth, and fury kindled in Blake's eyes in the same instant.

"Bitch," he ground out, and Jolie was sure he was going to strike her hard.

Voices in the main part of the cellar stopped him.

"I done what you and Blake told me to do," Rowdy was saying angrily. "Now, just give me my share of the money and I'll put this whole damn territory behind me."

Blake sighed, for all the world like a long-suffering preacher who has tried to lead his flock toward the Light only to have them wander off in all sorts of foolish directions. He rose to his feet, leaving the lamp on the crate top and Jolie on her stool, and turned away.

Jolie watched as he took a thin blade from the top of his boot and then pushed aside the hinged bookcase. Before she truly credited what was going to happen, it was all over.

Rowdy came at Blake in a rush of agitation and words, and Blake put the knife through his partner's throat as calmly as he might have slaughtered a pig. Blood spouted from Rowdy's neck, his eyes went blank, and his knees gave out beneath him.

A silent scream of horror tore itself from Jolie's throat, and she slapped both hands over her mouth.

January swore distractedly, as though he'd just looked down and seen manure on his boot. "You might have done that somewhere where it wouldn't make such a mess," he said.

Jolie had seen death before, she'd even seen murder, that horrible day in front of the bank in Prosperity, but she'd never witnessed such a callous dispatch of a human life. The shadows of the little cell pressed in close, and she felt herself swaying forward in a faint.

Blake caught her, his hands gripping her shoulders, and gave her a shake. She could smell Rowdy's blood on his skin and feel it tainting her dress where Blake held her. "I've got no time for mollycoddlin' a woman, Jolie-girl," he warned briskly. He let her go and she felt herself pitch toward him, the room and indeed the world beyond it dissolving into an utter blank.

When she awakened, probably only seconds later, the lamp was still burning on the crate and the room had been closed off from the cellar. Rowdy lay opposite her, rolled onto his side, facing the wall, and a rat the size of a small house cat balanced itself on his upper arm, sniffing.

Jolie scrambled upright, a scream surging along her throat with all the force of a night train racing through a tunnel, but no sound came out. Only then did she realize that rags had been stuffed into her mouth and secured with a bandanna tied around her head. Her hands were bound behind her back.

Making a whimpering sound, Jolie got to her feet and kicked at the rodent until it gave her a long perusal and then finally trotted away. She knew Rowdy was dead and thus would feel nothing—he'd perished when the blade of Blake's knife had pierced him—but not even he deserved to be left to the vermin.

Her next impulse was to vomit, and she fought it with every ounce of strength she possessed, knowing she would probably choke to death if she lost control. *Daniel,* her spirit cried, in silent desolation, as another soul might have called out for its guardian angel. *Help me, find me.* She thought of the innocent child nestled inside her. *Help us.*

She knew if Daniel could see her, he'd tell her to be calm, to collect her thoughts. So Jolie began to pace the length of that tiny, filthy room, drawing deep breaths in through her nose and mentally repeating an old nursery rhyme until her thoughts stopped their game of tag and settled into an orderly procession.

The sound of footsteps on the floorboards over her head was the first thing she noticed.

She stopped and looked up and somehow she knew Daniel was nearby, that he'd come searching for her, just as Ira January had said he would. Calling out was useless, because of the gag, and since her hands were tied, she couldn't make noise by beating on the back of the shelf with her fists.

When Jolie wriggled her toes, thinking of kicking one heel against the wood the way a mule might do, she realized for the first time that someone had taken her shoes. She didn't dare upset the crate in an effort to cause a clatter, because it still held the lamp, and she couldn't risk either darkness or fire.

Her choices had dwindled to one. She began flinging herself bodily against the back of the hinged shelf, praying the activity wouldn't hurt her baby. *Daniel,* she screamed inwardly. *Daniel!*

When the shelf swung aside, though, it wasn't Daniel who stood in the chasm, but Ira January. He was grinning as Jolie hung back, shoulders heaving with the effort to breathe after her exertion.

"I'm afraid your knight in shining armor has ridden back across the drawbridge without you, Princess," January said. "Any minute now, Mr. Beckham will come to the inevitable conclusion that taking up with a lady outlaw was a sorry bargain and he should have known better in the first place. Following that, he'll put you out of his mind and go right on with his life as though nothing had ever happened."

Jolie felt tears brim in her eyes. Revealing her emotions to this man shamed her, but there was no hiding her despair.

January crossed the room, after giving Rowdy's corpse one desultory look, and calmly untied the bandanna tied around Jolie's face. Next, he pulled the rags from her mouth and set them aside on the table.

"No use to scream, now," he warned distractedly. "Nancy used to shriek like a fishwife when I locked her up in here, and even the houseboy didn't hear her."

A chill swept over Jolie then, reaching deep into her bones. It was more than the dankness of the cellar; this was the stark, merciless cold of evil. "What did you say to Daniel?" she whispered, her eyes wide, her throat so sore that the words came out scratchy.

January smiled, apparently pleased with himself. "That you've been in love with Blake Kingston from the beginning, and that the only reason you'd marry a bumbling farmer like him was to save your skin. I said the whole town knew you were playing him for a fool all along, even if he didn't."

Jolie closed her eyes tightly for a moment. It was only too easy to imagine Daniel believing those cruel words, even though they'd come from a man who hated him. He would give them credence because they confirmed something he already accepted, deep down in his own soul.

She forced herself to look at January. "You've been in cahoots with Blake and Rowdy all along," she accused evenly. "Why would a man with your money and property want truck with outlaws?"

"Money isn't everything, Mrs. Beckham," January replied, in a tone of good-natured scolding. "There's vengeance, for instance. Blake and I have known each other for a long time, and when he showed up a few days after the bank robbery, looking for a place to hide out, it occurred to me that he and Fleet might be a big help in accomplishing my purposes."

"Which are?"

"I'm going to take away everything Beckham has," the millowner vowed, and there was no humor in his bearing now, only bitterness. "By the time I'm through pulling strings and calling in notes, he won't even have that little plot of land where his wife . . . pardon me, dearest . . . his *first* wife, is buried."

Blake appeared before Jolie could respond, casting a nervous glance from January to his captive and back again.

The master of the house laughed, as though there weren't a dead man lying a few feet from him. Jolie knew now what it was to live a nightmare.

"Relax, Kingston," January said. "While I find Mrs. Beckham very attractive, in a hoydenish sort of way, there isn't time for me to woo her properly. We've got to get Fleet out of here while it's still dark."

Blake nodded reluctantly, and he and January hoisted Rowdy's lead weight off the floor and carried him out. Jolie didn't even bother to hope they would forget to lock her in, but they did overlook the gag.

As soon as the two men and their grisly burden were gone, she began trying to squirm out of the thongs that bound her hands. The ties were made of rawhide and while they stretched a little, Jolie knew they wouldn't give.

Glancing at the lamp, which was burning low and would soon gutter out, leaving her alone in the darkness with the rats, Jolie was struck by a desperate inspiration. Kneeling beside the crate, she managed to dislodge the glass chimney from the lantern by bumping it with her shoulder.

The naked flame leaped free, then flickered as if it would go out. Praying she wouldn't set her dress on fire, Jolie turned and extended her arms backward, looking over one shoulder all the time. She felt heat against the sides of her thumbs, and then the flames began to lick at her skin. Just when she thought she wouldn't be able to bear it another moment, the rawhide thongs popped apart and she was free.

At least partially.

In the last failing light of the lamp, her hands and fingers so numb that she could barely work them, she searched the floor for a weapon. There was nothing to be had except the glass chimney from the lantern; Jolie grabbed that and smashed it against the crate, leaving a jagged end.

Breathing deeply, muttering every recitation she'd ever learned to keep from going completely mad with fright, Jolie held the chimney in both hands and hovered in the corner of the cell, waiting.

Presently, the wick in the lamp drew up the last of the oil. There was one brilliant flare of light, and then the musty chamber was completely dark. Jolie tried not to think about the rats, and the way Rowdy had looked in death. Instead, she fixed her thoughts on Daniel and Hank and Gemma, and how much she wanted to get back to them.

If she survived this night, she vowed to herself, she would go right to Daniel Beckham and tell him straight out that she loved him. Life was precious, and fleeting, she'd learned that now, and she was through waiting for fate to hand her what she wanted.

Whether an hour had passed, or a day, Jolie didn't know but, finally, when her dress was wet with perspiration, when the muscles in her arms were cramped and the lamp chimney felt slick in her hands, she heard footsteps approaching. Holding her breath, Jolie stepped back, held the jagged glass high, and waited.

The hinged shelf began creaking inward, and Jolie ran a dry tongue over her lips. Flickering light from a candle or a dim lamp trickled into the gloom, and by that time her heart was pounding so hard that the sound of it seemed to echo off the dripping walls of the cellar.

"Jolie?"

Jolie's muscles were already in motion before she realized the voice that had spoken her name had been a feminine one. At the last possible instant, she let go of the jagged lamp chimney and it clattered to the hard dirt floor. "Nan?"

Welcome light flooded the room as Nan swept in, carrying a lamp. She still looked wan, but the expression in her eyes said she was fully present, not wandering in some far country of the mind like she had been before. "It's all right, Jolie," she said, shivering a little as she looked around the cramped little cell where she too had been held prisoner. "You're safe now."

Jolie was shuddering so hard she could barely force her knees to support her. She stumbled past Nan, out of the room that smelled of rats and mold and death, and sank against an opposite wall, breathing deeply to keep from bursting into tears or hysterical screams.

"Daniel knew I was here," she managed, after a long time, as all the pieces began to fall together in her mind. "He *knew.*"

Nan nodded, taking Jolie's arm and ushering her toward the stone steps. "Yes. He came to fetch me at Verena's, reasoning that I'd know where to look for you."

"But Mr. January, and Blake . . ."

A golden square of light awaited Jolie and Nan at the top of the staircase. "When Daniel returned with the marshal and a posse, January and Kingston ran out the back way to their horses. Your husband and the others chased them into the high country."

Jolie felt sick, but she would not allow herself to fall apart. "In the dark?" she asked, in a choked whisper.

Nan walked briskly along the back hallway, probably as anxious to escape that house as Jolie was. "I won't pretend the danger is anything less than grave," Joe Culley's widow said evenly. "But we've got to trust that right will prevail."

Jolie had seen wrong win out many a time, at least in the short run, but she was determined to remain strong. Her own close brush with death had given her an unshakable resolve to live her life from an utterly new perspective. She followed Nan into a spacious parlor that smelled too thickly of pipe tobacco and bay rum.

Nan shuddered again as she looked around. "Daniel said we were to stay here, but I don't think I can bear that, Jolie. Let's hitch up one of Mr. January's rigs and head for your place."

Jolie would no more have stayed in that house willingly than danced down the banister on tiptoe, but her plan varied slightly from Nan's. "You may certainly do as you like, Mrs. Culley," she said, in formal tones. "But I'm going after my husband and make sure he's all right."

Nan's eyes went wide, then narrowed to slits. She

371

set the lamp on a table with a thump and placed her hands on her hips. "There are times, *Mrs. Beckham*, when I quite lose patience with you. This is no occasion to be headstrong and heedless. Nothing would suit Mr. January better than to get his hands on you again and use you as a weapon against Daniel!"

The truth of her friend's words was not easy for Jolie to accept, since her every instinct called upon her to mount the first available horse and rush off in pursuit of the posse. The only answer she could manage, in fact, was a nod.

Nan drove Daniel's buckboard capably, while Jolie sat despondently beside her on the hard wooden seat, aching from the very center of her soul. The night was dark and cold, and a light snow was falling, but Jolie was barely aware of her surroundings. Her thoughts were with Daniel, like her heart, in the thick timber on the mountain.

When the lights of Daniel's farm came into view, it was some comfort to Jolie. The moment she stepped over the threshold into the kitchen, Mary met her with a soft cry of relief and a strong embrace.

Jolie's eyes filled with tears, but her voice held a halfhearted rebuke. "What are you doing out of bed, Mary Beckham?"

Mary drew back far enough to meet Jolie's gaze, moisture sparkling along her lower lashes. Her hands were firm on Jolie's upper arms. "When there's trouble, family and friends have to shoulder each other's burdens. Enoch brought me and the children here so I could look after Hank and Gemma while the men were about their business."

Moving woodenly, Jolie went to the big wicker basket resting a few feet from the stove and looked inside. Tiny Rachel Anne slept soundly within, drawing in her breath to give a tiny, contented sigh.

Jolie thought of her own child, yet again, and laid both hands over her middle. God willing, Daniel would live to see not only the morning, but the little one that was bone of his bone and flesh of his flesh.

She went upstairs to look in on Hank and Gemma, kneeling beside their bed to kiss each one on the forehead, vowing that whatever happened, she would never be parted from these children. That, too, was a part of the new person she'd become by walking through the valley of the shadow.

When Jolie returned to the kitchen sometime later, her thoughts more composed than before, she found that Nan and Mary had prepared a hot bath for her. She scrubbed the dirt from her hair and skin and, wearing a nightgown and wrapper Mary had brought from upstairs, burned the dress she'd worn earlier. It was filthy with cellar dirt and with Rowdy's blood and, worst of all, with nightmarish memories.

As the night deepened, Nan went off to sleep in the spare room upstairs, and Mary stretched out in the parlor on the settee, covered with a woolen throw Ilse had probably knitted. Jolie, stiff with fatigue and fear, kept her lonely vigil at the kitchen table.

Dawn broke and there was still no sign of Daniel.

Jolie went right on waiting. Remaining there, in the warmth and safety of that farmhouse kitchen, was the hardest thing she'd ever done. For Daniel, and Daniel alone, she suppressed her desperate need to ride out in search of him.

The sound of weary whistling, carrying over a pristine blanket of new snow, jolted Jolie out of her fretful revelry. She jumped from her chair and rushed to the window over the sink.

Daniel, Deuter, and Enoch were dismounting in front of the barn. It was Deuter doing the whistling, Daniel and Enoch both looked tired and grim.

Jolie flung open the back door and ran heedlessly down the stairs, slipping and sliding like a camel on ice as she scrambled to meet Daniel.

His arms came around her, solid and strong, tightening fiercely.

"I love you, Daniel," she vowed, cupping her hands on either side of his face and staring straight into his eyes. "Do you hear me? I *love* you, and I won't be shut out of your life or sent away. I'm here for good."

Daniel surveyed her face solemnly, then kissed her lightly on the lips. "You're parading around the barnyard in your wrapper, Mrs. Beckham," he pointed out. "It isn't proper." After that, his mouth cracked into a crooked smile. He set Jolie on her feet and propelled her toward the house with a light swat on the bottom.

Jolie looked back over one shoulder as she hurried along. The breathless relief of having Daniel home, safe and sound, made her chatter. "Did you catch them? Blake and Mr. January, I mean? Blake killed Rowdy, you know . . . I saw it with my own eyes . . ."

"We found them," Daniel responded, pushing open the back door and guiding his wife firmly inside. "January's dead, and Kingston took a bullet in the kneecap, so he won't be breaking jail before they hang him."

"So it's over." Jolie sighed.

Daniel pulled her close and kissed her. "It's over," he replied. The feel of his hard, wind-chilled body heated Jolie's blood and made her heart beat faster. "Did they hurt you?"

She shook her head. "I was powerful scared, though," she confessed. "I thought I'd never see you again, never be able to tell you how I feel."

Her husband bent to take a nibbling sip at her lips but drew back as Enoch came in, stomping snow off his boots and grinning.

The rest of the morning was busy.

Deuter took Hank and Gemma to school, like always, and Enoch and Mary drove Nan back to Verena's and went on home after that.

Daniel was in the parlor when Jolie came in to tell him the midday meal was ready, and she watched, frozen, from the doorway as he took the photograph of himself and Ilse down from the mantelpiece. He looked solemnly at the faces of himself and his bride, other people, really, from another time.

He turned before Jolie could flee.

"She was a good woman," he said quietly.

Jolie's eyes stung with emotion, and her throat was tight. "Yes," she agreed softly. "I know."

Daniel put the picture into a large wooden box and closed the lid with a gesture of gentle finality. "I was a fool to ever talk about sending you away," he said. "I've loved you ever since I saw you standing there in the back of that hay wagon with a noose around your neck." He paused to chuckle ruefully. "I guess I figured I could keep myself from caring about you just by deciding not to, but it didn't work."

She stood on tiptoe to kiss his chin. "And Hank and Gemma? What about them?"

"They're staying, too, if they'll have us for folks," Daniel answered hoarsely. "I had a couple of empty corners in my heart, and those two kids filled them up real snug."

Jolie felt shy all of a sudden, and almost overcome with joy. She'd never known such happiness in all her life. "You must be hungry, Mr. Beckham."

Daniel only nodded, and Jolie raced up the stairs to put on a practical woolen dress and sturdy shoes, eager to please now that she was a genuine wife, loved and wanted. She rushed to the well house to fetch cream for Daniel's coffee, and while she was doing that, her hem caught once again on the same pesky board.

Frustrated, Jolie crouched to push the plank back into place, only to have a whirl of images spin in her mind like leaves caught in a fall wind. Biting her lower lip, her heart pounding, Jolie wrenched the weathered strip of wood upward and peered into the resultant hole.

A set of saddlebags had been stuffed inside.

Forgetting the cream she'd come for, Jolie grabbed up the bags and opened first one side and then the other. Sure enough, she'd found Blake's hiding spot after all . . . the satchels were filled with federal currency. Holding her skirts in one hand so she wouldn't trip over them, she raced back to the house.

"I found the robbery money!" she cried, flinging the bag down onto the kitchen table in bright-eyed triumph. She felt exonerated of her connection with Rowdy and Blake now; she'd made amends for taking part, however inadvertently, in their crime.

Daniel smiled, but he didn't ask Jolie where she'd found the loot, and he didn't open the saddlebags to count it. He just swept Jolie up into his arms and started toward the stairs.

"This calls for some celebrating, Mrs. Beckham," he said.

And celebrate they did.

Epilogue

Nan Culley never used the surname of January, but she did take over the mill she inherited at her second husband's death, along with the house and a sizable bank account. She gave birth to a beautiful baby girl in mid-March and named her Jolie Verena, for her two best friends.

Hank and Gemma were legally adopted into the Beckham family. Hank studied medicine when he grew up and became Prosperity's first real doctor. Gemma married a young man whose land bordered Daniel's and lived a long, happy life.

Jolie delivered Daniel Beckham, Jr., in May of 1878, and five more children followed, all boys except for the last, all healthy and strong.

At long last, Jolie Beckham, the outlaw bride, had her own home and family . . . just as she'd always dreamed she would.

ATRIA BOOKS
PROUDLY PRESENTS

NEVER LOOK BACK

Linda Lael Miller

Now available in paperback
from Atria Books

Turn the page for a preview of
Never Look Back. . . .

ONE

If there's a maniac or an ax murderer within a hundred-mile radius, he—or she—will come straight to me, Clare Westbrook, hapless attorney at law, like steel filings to a magnet.

Guaranteed.

Take Peter Bailey. Please—take Peter Bailey.

The very day I opened my new storefront office, in one of Phoenix's less-sought-after neighborhoods, he wandered over from the mental health clinic next door and peered at me through the glass door, hands cupped around his face. It was a childlike stance, reminiscent of a little boy yearning after puppies gamboling in a pet store window.

Of course I didn't know his name yet. Nor did I know he was under psychiatric care, though it wouldn't have taken a nuclear physicist to figure it out. He had that look: eyeballs spiraling in two directions, lean body seeming to hum with that frenetic energy peculiar to those whose brain chemistries are seriously out of whack.

I remember that I sighed philosophically and

reminded myself that I'd chosen my office because it was smack in the middle of Dysfunction Junction. I'd recently inherited twenty-odd million from the father I never knew, and after weighing my suddenly expanded options, I'd taken the high road. Since bringing in a paycheck was no longer a matter of desperate compunction, I had decided to use my law degree and my hard-ass reputation to strike a few blows for the underprivileged. The ones who needed my expertise but were unable to write a retainer check—one, at least, that would clear the bank.

The man staring through my door probably qualified.

I crossed the mostly unfurnished room, turned the lock, and let in a rush of hot desert air. October, and the temperature was still high enough to roast a lizard on a rock.

"May I help you?" I asked.

He recoiled as though I'd thrust something sharp at him, and for a moment I thought he was going to bolt.

"You're Clare Westbrook," he said, shifting from foot to foot. "I've seen you on TV. Lots of times."

Thanks to my recent involvement in some very high profile cases, just about *everybody* had seen me on TV or in the newspapers. He looked me over, and his mouth quivered a little. Drool gathered at one corner, and he wiped it away with a feverish motion of one hand.

"You're prettier in person," he added earnestly.

I'm used to comments about my looks—shoulder-length dark hair, fairly good body, brown eyes, and high cheekbones. When I look in a mirror, I don't see those things. I just see *me*, a complicated bundle of faults, foibles, and contradictions. I'm smart as hell, for instance, but common sense often eludes me.

"Thanks," I said. "Was there something you wanted?"

"My friend, Angela—I think she's in trouble. A *lot* of trouble."

Now we were getting somewhere. I stepped back so he could pass. "Come in."

He hesitated, wringing his hands a little, then ducked back to the middle of the sidewalk to look both ways and then up. That, like his eyes, should have been a clue to his mental state, but I was trying to set up a pro bono practice, and for that, I needed clients. Just then, I wasn't too picky.

"This isn't a good place, you know," he observed, edging nervously over the threshold, sweeping the room with his gaze. "The bad people know you're here. They might try to hurt you."

A spark of uneasiness flashed in the pit of my stomach.

"Tell me about Angela," I said carefully, indicating the client chair facing my newly purchased desk. I hurried to move a box of file folders so he could sit down. "What kind of trouble is she in?"

He didn't sit. He seemed too agitated for that. "I shouldn't have come here," he said. "I'm supposed to be next door. I have an appointment with Dr. Thomlinson. Do you know Dr. Thomlinson?"

Ah, I thought. Yes. The doctor had introduced himself earlier that morning, warned me that one or two of his patients might stray my way. Many of them were paranoid schizophrenics, he'd said. No need to be alarmed—they were mostly harmless. Pick up the phone, and he'd send someone to round them up.

"I know him," I affirmed pleasantly, edging a little closer to the telephone on my cluttered desk. "If you're late for your appointment, I'll certainly understand if you have to rush."

He shook a finger at me, already backing toward the door. "You need to be very careful. The dolls. You have to look out for the dolls."

"Right," I said. "I'll be careful."

With that, he was gone.

I sagged into my chair, hoping that interview wasn't going to set the tone for the rest of my career.

After a few minutes I was over it. I got back to work, and since nothing out of the ordinary happened that day, or the next, I figured I was home free. I was destined to save the downtrodden.

Three nights later, feeling industrious and—okay—avoiding some things that were going on in my personal life, I decided to paint my office.

My on-again, off-again lover, Detective Anthony Sonterra, and I were in the "off" phase again, leaving a serious gap in my social calendar. So there I was, at ten-thirty, with only my niece Emma's dog for company. Perched on the top rung of a folding ladder, I glanced with pride at the legend newly scripted on the barred window. My name, my degree.

It still did something for me, seeing them so prominently displayed. I'd earned my sheepskin the hard way, waiting tables at a Tucson bar by the ridiculous name of Nipples, hitting the books on every break, sleeping a maximum of four hours a night. After graduation, I put in five years of indentured servitude with Harvey Kredd—a.k.a. "Krudd," in police circles. Harvey specialized in setting the guilty free, and he was the shyster's shyster.

Believe me, I paid my dues.

Beneath my name, in smaller letters, was the proviso: Qualified Clients Defended at No Charge.

By "qualified," I meant innocent—as I defined the word. Much to Sonterra's annoyance, not to mention that of the prosecutor's office, I see shades of gray, and I make allowances for extenuating circumstances. In the three days since I'd signed the lease on the storefront— a former lawn-mower repair shop wedged between Dr. Thomlinson's clinic and a thrift store—I'd already turned away half a dozen prospective clients, and I wasn't even open for business yet. I'd accepted two others: Barbara Jenkins, a woman accused of conking her abusive husband over the head and rolling him into the fishpond in their backyard, where he subsequently drowned, and a slightly nerdy and very overweight young man named David Valardi. David was a computer whiz, allegedly the creator of the insidious Barabbas virus.

Now, paint-smudged, tired, and ravenously hungry, I was ready to call it a night. I stepped down a rung, and in one seemingly eternal moment, my front window splintered with a horrendous crash. A barrage of bullets slammed into the wall, inches above my head.

I dived for the floor and scrambled under the desk, where the dog, a Yorkshire terrier called Bernice, had pressed herself into a corner, whimpering and shivering. I groped for her, checked her for wounds, then gave myself a hasty once-over. Fortunately, neither of us had sprung a leak.

It's the neighborhood, I thought, with that odd detachment that comes of abject fear, remembering Sonterra's admonition. "Counselor," he'd said, just before our last big fight, "in Phoenix, nobody in their right mind sets up shop on a street named after a president."

I waited, bracing for another round of artillery fire. My heart was beating so hard that for a few moments I couldn't hear anything but the blood roaring in my ears, and I was definitely hyperventilating. Clutching the dog to my chest with one arm, I used my free hand to ferret through the bottom drawer of the desk for my purse, and the .38 and cell phone inside.

I had barely connected with the 911 operator when I heard the sound of sirens and screeching tires in the near distance.

I gave the dispatcher my location.

"Officers are en route," she told me calmly. "Are you injured? Is the assailant on the premises?"

I closed my eyes, breathing deeply and slowly, trying to regain my equilibrium. "I have no idea where the assailant is," I answered after a few more desperate slurps of oxygen. "I don't think I'm hurt, but I'm scared." *Shitless,* clarified the voice in my mind, which always wants to put in its two cents.

More squealing of tires. A hard rap on the street door, apparently still intact. A shout of "Police!"

Still holding the dog, which had just peed down the front of my T-shirt (a violation I could well identify with, given the circumstances), I crawled to the side of the desk and looked around the far edge. After all, anybody can lay rubber, knock on a door, and say they're the law.

There, where the inside and outside light met in a blurry pool, I saw two cops, guns drawn. One was scanning the street, the other squinting between the bars on the door.

"That was fast," I told the dispatcher.

"Let them in," she prompted.

Duh, I thought. "Now, there's an idea," I replied aloud, getting to my feet, dog, soggy T-shirt and all. "Thanks."

The dispatcher chuckled good-naturedly, and I imagined what she was thinking. *Shots fired? All in a night's work, and not uncommon here in Presidentsville.* "Stay on the line, please. I need to confirm a few things with the officers. By the way, what's your name?"

"Clare Westbrook," I answered shakily. I was on a cell phone rather than a landline, which meant the pertinent information wouldn't necessarily pop up on her computer screen.

My legs were like noodles. I swayed on my feet, took a firmer grip on the dog, and braced the cell between my ear and shoulder. Somehow, I got across the room, worked the deadbolts, and admitted the cops.

"Are you all right, ma'am?" asked the one on the left, who had been covering the street. His gaze dropped to the dog.

"Yes," I answered, surprised at the steadiness in my voice, and introduced myself. My internal organs had turned to jelly, but I'm resilient by nature. In a crisis, I slip into my inner phone booth and become Super-Lawyer, saving the hysteria for later. "The dispatcher wants to speak with one of you."

The other officer accepted the cell phone I thrust at him, while his partner took me lightly by the arm and squired me to the nearest chair.

"What happened?" he asked. I've heard these words so often, they could be carved on my tombstone. Crouching in front of me, with a creak of his leather service belt, he took one of my hands and simultaneously patted Bernice's furry little head.

While I explained, as coherently as I could, the other policeman finished his conversation with the 911 operator. I watched, out of the corner of one eye, as he took out his own cell phone, dialed a number, muttered a few words, then grabbed a bottle of water from the miniature refrigerator on a nearby wall and brought it to me, politely twisting off the lid first.

I narrowed my gaze, even as I accepted the water with a nod of thanks. I'd seen this guy before, I realized, in the group photo of Sonterra's softball team. I guessed, accurately, it turned out, that he'd just called his good buddy and given him an update on the adventures of Clare.

Without a trace of chagrin, Cop Number Two gave a slight, crooked grin, confirming my suspicions.

"Anybody out to get you?" the crouching cop asked. His name tag read "Atienzo," and I decided I liked him. His manner was gentle, nonconfrontational.

The dog began to squirm, and I set her down on the floor, stalling while I weighed the question. Two months before, I'd had some problems, but that was over. It didn't even occur to me to mention Peter Bailey; I'd written him off as local color.

"Not that I know of," I answered between restorative sips of ice cold water. In Arizona it's important to stay hydrated, particularly in times of stress. I get those a lot.

"It was probably a drive-by," the standing cop said with weary resignation. "This isn't the best part of town."

Shades of Sonterra. Okay, so there are a lot of pawn-shops, seedy dives offering "adult entertainment," and boarded-up businesses around my office. There are also some decent restaurants, well-stocked supermarkets, churches, and community centers. Should the good guys bail out and leave the place to the scumbags?

I held the wet part of the T-shirt away from my stomach. "No," I said carefully, "it's *not* the best neighborhood. All the more reason for me to be here. I like feeling needed."

The guy rolled his eyes, and I could guess what was going through his mind. If he and Sonterra were pals, then he'd most likely been filled in on my history, my stubbornness (to which I readily admit, by the way), and probably my inherited millions, too. I guess he couldn't be blamed for wondering why I didn't just paint my toenails, lounge by a swimming pool somewhere with champagne flute in hand, and watch the dividend checks roll in. On the other hand, it was none of his damn business if I cut each and every dollar bill into little pieces and flushed them down the john. It was, after all, *my* money.

"According to what's left of the window," Atienzo observed, rising to his feet with another symphony of leather and jingling handcuffs, "you defend people for free."

"If I think they're innocent," I specified.

"Innocent," murmured the second cop, as though nobody had ever been accused of something they hadn't done in the checkered history of American jurisprudence.

I sighed. A lot of cops take a dim view of human nature, and it isn't hard to see why. In Phoenix, or any other major city, they run across so much blood, insanity, and flat-out meanness that they come to expect it. They are out-gunned, under-funded, and mostly unappreciated. You couldn't pay me enough to do what they do, so I try to keep perspective.

"Some people, Officer"—I squinted to read his name tag—"Culver, are simply in the wrong place at the wrong time."

Culver gave a grunt. He was obviously unconvinced. Oh, *well*.

Just then, through the shattered window, I saw Sonterra's SUV whip up to the curb. He'd made good time, I thought ruefully. He must have been close by. Homicides were common in that section of the city, and even though Sonterra's official beat was Scottsdale, he often worked in conjunction with the Phoenix PD. When he wanted to get somewhere quickly, all he had to do was snap his handy-dandy cop light onto the roof of his car and put the pedal to the metal.

Atienzo busied himself checking out the arc of bullet holes in the wall, making notes for the inevitable report.

Sonterra boiled into the office like a dust devil and slammed the door so hard that the last tiny fragments of glass tinkled from the front window.

"Fancy meeting you here," I said. We'd had our most recent disagreement two weeks before, when I insisted on moving into the modest house I'd bought in Scottsdale instead of taking up permanent residence at his place, and we'd been at an impasse ever since. I operate on a need-to-know basis; if I'd cussed and moaned and even shed a few tears over the estrangement, well, Sonterra didn't need to know.

"Jesus," he said, taking in the shambles with a sweep of those chocolate-brown miss-nothing eyes, "this place looks like a backstreet in Baghdad."

"Of course I'm okay," I said pointedly.

His jawline tightened. Sonterra is a specimen of true genetic excellence, with his dark hair, smoldering eyes, and GQ body, but his personality could use a little work. The concept of winning friends and influencing people is beyond him.

"Is the dog all right?" he asked. Bernice scrabbled at his shin with her front feet; he bent to scoop her up, and even let her lick his face. She was in one piece, and there was no blood, so I didn't bother answering. I merely folded my arms and willed him to leave.

He eyed my yellow-stained T-shirt and allowed himself a shadow of a grin. No doubt it cheered him up to know I'd been peed on. "Get your purse, Counselor," he said. "I'm taking you home."

Half an hour alone with Sonterra, with him lecturing me on my poor career choices—just what I didn't need. I looked to Officer Atienzo for some sign of support, since I knew Culver would take Sonterra's side.

"You'll need to give a statement," Atienzo said.

"Tomorrow," Sonterra said flatly. I thought Atienzo looked mildly bent out of shape—detectives outrank uniforms in the cop hierarchy, and sometimes that rubs the guys and gals on the beat the wrong way—but in the end, Officer Friendly merely shrugged.

Sonterra, still holding the dog, fixed me with a glower. "Your car is in the alley, I take it, since I didn't see it out front?" The subtext was, *I've told you a million times: park in well-lighted areas. Are you trying to get mugged, raped, or murdered?*

"Right, as always," I said brightly. "Good thing I didn't follow your sage advice. If I'd left my car on the street, it would look like Swiss cheese right about now."

Sonterra lowered his eyebrows and frowned, but I wasn't intimidated, and I let him know it with a level look. That always pissed him off, and it prompted me to wonder what he saw in me, since he obviously preferred the acquiescent type. "Perhaps one of these good officers will do us the favor of driving it home for you," he intoned.

"I'll do it," Culver said, like a Boy Scout going for a badge. What a suck-up.

"I'm perfectly capable of driving," I submitted.

Sonterra opened my purse, helped himself to the keys, and tossed them to Culver. "Thanks," he told the other man without breaking his visual headlock on me. "Fifteen Twenty-two Cactus Creek Road. Just leave it in the driveway."

Culver jingled the keys. "Where should I put these?"

It was all I could do not to tell him *exactly* where to put them.

"Lock them in the vehicle," Sonterra said. "There's a duplicate set."

I took the dog back, but gently. It wasn't Bernice's fault that Sonterra suffered from an excess of testosterone.

"Done," Culver replied. He found the backdoor on his own and went out.

Atienzo paused beside me and laid a hand on my shoulder. "You're all right with this?" he asked, ignoring Sonterra's eyeball scorch. Atienzo had guts. I like that in a person. Plus, he was cute, with brown hair and green eyes and a very nice butt.

"Yes," I said. One of the things you learn while treading the hallowed halls of justice is to choose your battles. Sonterra being on authority-overload, I was sure to lose this round, so I decided to conserve my personal resources for the next one. "I'll stop by the station tomorrow to sign the reports."

"Good," Atienzo said mildly. He ruffled Bernice's floppy ears, leveled a look at Sonterra, and strolled out to the waiting squad car.

Sonterra and I just stood there for a long moment, trying to stare each other down. I swear, if the sex hadn't been so good, I wouldn't have given him the time of day, let alone a big chunk of my life.

I watched as Atienzo got behind the wheel, switched off the blue and red flashing lights, and drove away. I inclined my head toward the street. "Is he married?" I asked sweetly.

Sonterra isn't the only one who knows how to get under somebody's skin.

CPSIA information can be obtained
at www.ICGtesting.com
Printed in the USA
LVOW11s1602100418

572943LV00001B/90/P